I0841124

St. Sebastian School of Law

Tim Greaney

For Nancy, who is everything to me.

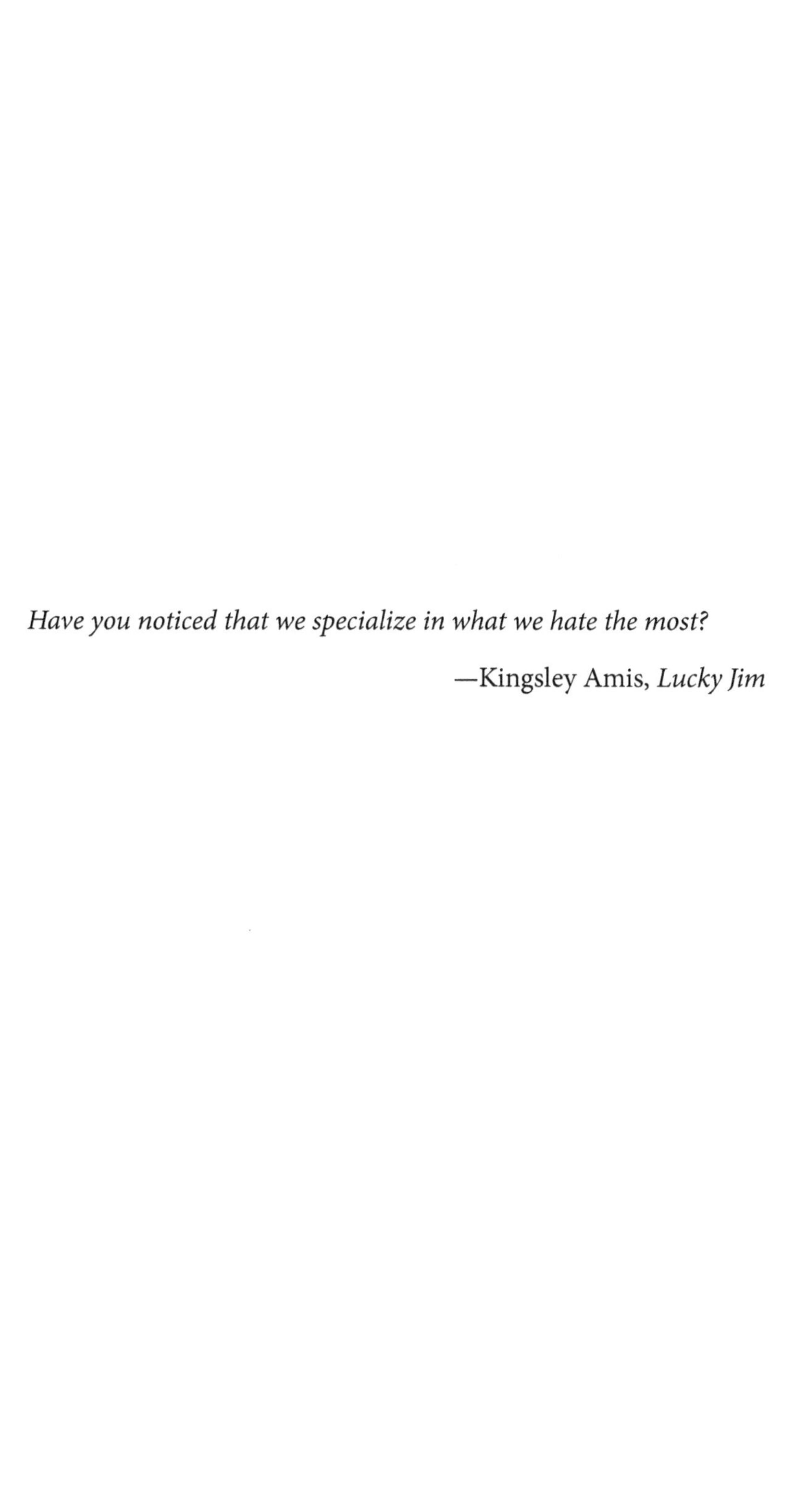

Have you noticed that we specialize in what we hate the most?

—Kingsley Amis, *Lucky Jim*

1

In poker you never play your hand. You play the man across you.

—James Bond, *Casino Royale*

He made a church steeple with his fingers, smiled ruefully, and looked over at the life-size painting of St. Sebastian on his office wall, "Did you know that Pope Paul IV found Michelangelo's Final Judgment a bit scandalous and commissioned a guy to cover some of the nudity? De Valerro was his name and Italians nicknamed him 'the breeches maker.'" Father Victorio Balducci, S.J., President of St. Sebastian University in Baytown, New Jersey, loved nothing more than to show off his love for Italian culture and contempt for the papacy in a single story.

His audience, Mitchell "Bucky" Buckner, CEO and Chair of Meadowlands Construction Enterprises, was neither Catholic nor Italian and missed most of President Balducci's sly references but knew that this was an academic he could do business with. Spicing the conversation with an occasional "fuck" and rolling his eyes when affirmative action was mentioned, Father B knew how to make his donors feel comfortable. He joined their posh athletic clubs, drank their Macallan, and attended every sporting event in the area. Just one of the guys, collar and Ph.D in philosophy notwithstanding.

"Well, you know we'd like to break ground within two years. We have a shot at getting into the Big East in the next couple of years. Got a hot-shit point guard from the Bronx all but signed."

Father Balducci's voice had the flat midwestern affect of his Indiana roots, but when agitated it took on the resonance of Bob Sheppard at Yankee Stadium. "But my fucking board won't let me think about laying a brick till I have $40 million . . . committed!"

Bucky offered a sympathetic smile and decided to share the acquired wisdom of one CEO to another, "Pantywaists! I spend half my time ignoring my board and the other half hiding the ball from them. So, Father, what do you need?"

Father B raised an inviting eyebrow and spoke slowly, "I'd like you to lead the charge on this. Obviously, an initial gift from Meadowlands Construction would be needed. But my hope is you'll take a more . . . well . . . participatory role. I want you to be my *capo* on the project."

Bucky knew that Balducci's mob references invariably preceded The Ask.

"As my *capo*, you can motivate the Civic Progress crowd to chip in, lean on the nonprofits, and take care of the law firms and accountants. If you can start the ball rolling with one or two million, it's practically a done deal. None of the big guys will come in any lower."

No eye contact during The Ask. That meant the padre expects resistance, thought Buckner. This is going to be easy.

Bucky expressionless, twirling the Macallan in his glass. "You got it."

"Really?" Father Balducci tried to recall the word immediately after it slipped out. Too late. Worse yet, the "ee" stuck in his throat, undressing him as surely as if he had unbuttoned his cassock and pulled down his boxers.

"Sure. Consider it done," Bucky said, sipping the Macallan without looking up.

"Good. Good." Shifting a little in his chair and still avoiding eye contact, Balducci adopted a casual tone, "Well St. Sebastian, the community, the students will very much appreciate . . ."

Bucky waved a silent *basta* with his hand and leaned forward, "I need to deal with my CFO and board of course, so the timing of this thing is important. I'm thinking now about the contracting for your arena's construction—which of course Meadowlands Construction will be first in line to bid on, and I hope, first in your heart—all that won't go forward for two years, so my people are going to want some up-front comfort food."

"Comfort food?"

"Yeah, you know, I think you guys call it 'anti-pasta.' Something to nibble on until the main course comes. Our building maintenance subsidiary can handle all the needs of your main campus. My people tell me your contract with Della Rosa ends in three months, so we'll be ready to step in on day one. And I can promise that the unions won't be a problem. Will be a seamless transition." Bucky flashed an ingratiating smile, killed his Macallan, and gently dropped the glass on a St. Sebastian coaster.

Balducci never played poker, but he'd seen this kind of thing happen on ESPN. One guy pretends to look nervous, fiddles with his chips, calls the other guy's bet for the first couple of cards and then, BANG, shoves in all his chips on the river after the poor fish raises the bet.

Bucky narrowing his eyes and leaning forward, "And of course, the beach house in Cape May is always available for your academic conferences. As are the Meadowlands Construction properties in Florence and Madrid."

Cape May. A vision of a stunning topless blonde dancing with Sympathy for the Devil playing in the background momentarily hit Father Balducci with the force of a double espresso. Recovering, but still avoiding eye contact, he said, "Well, St. Sebastian would be a very different place without the generosity extended by the corporate community. In any event, I will certainly have my VP for Finance look into the maintenance contract issue."

Bucky thinking, this guy is manna from heaven. His high stakes poker game had taught him a thing or two about spotting a fish and how to land it. I could probably sell him the Verrazano Bridge, he thought, but for now I'll settle for getting him on board for my Baytown Opportunity Zone. Going to be much easier than dealing with those snotty lefties at Princeton. No sense killing the golden goose before Christmas. Rising and shaking Father B's hand, he spoke cheerfully, "Great, great. This arena is going to put St. Sebastian on everyone's radar screen. Get into the Sweet 16 and you'll own this town."

Didn't Father Balducci know it. Obscure Catholic schools like Seton Hall, Gonzaga, and Loyola-Chicago became household names after making a Cinderella charge in the NCAA basketball tournament. More important, alumni came out of the woodwork, annual giving skyrocketed, student applications doubled, and SAT scores went through the ceiling. Like winning the lottery. Or landing an archbishopric.

Yossarian: That's some catch, that Catch-22.
Doc Daneeka: It's the best there is.

—Joseph Heller, *Catch-22*

"Can I declare bankruptcy?"

It wasn't the first time he was asked that question, but it left Associate Dean Tommy McNeely dumbstruck. The student he had just dismissed from the law school, dreams shattered, humiliated, and defeated, had summoned up the temerity to ask the obvious. *How the fuck do I dig out of this hole and start a new life? I'm carrying $54,000 in student loans. And while I'm sitting here, can I get some free legal advice? Seeing as how I didn't stick around long enough to take the bankruptcy course.*

For McNeely, it was far worse than "what do I tell my dad?" or "becoming a lawyer was my life's dream." The unsettling part for him as Associate Dean was the law school's complicity in the student's abject demise. Sure, she probably had screwed off or maybe just wasn't hard wired to figure out how to categorize the law's tidy little precepts and rearrange them to answer law school final exam questions. But it was St. Sebastian School of Law that cheerfully admitted at least 25 students it knew probably wouldn't make it. Indeed, the school had a strong incentive to flunk out a respectable number of students in order to maintain its second tier ranking in the *U.S. News and World Report* Ranking of American Law Schools. All so it could attract a higher caliber of applicant next year. Then, if all went well, St. Sebastian could aspire to someday flunking out an even higher caliber of students.

"Well, bankruptcy is a serious step that can jeopardize your finances for many years to come." McNeely shifted uncomfortably in his chair thinking, of course so is a $1400/month note when you're working as a bank teller. He didn't have the heart to tell her that Congress had passed a law in 1976 barring students from discharging their debts in bankruptcy. Or that the law was the product of intense lobbying by the insurance industry with a wink and a nod from the nation's institutions of higher education.

Shuffling the papers in his "Dismissed 2Ls" file and offering a sympathetic nod, McNeely tried out an upbeat tone. "The financial aid office can work with you on payment arrangements. But now is not the time to focus on all that. Let's start planning what you want to do in terms of a career."

No sense pointing out the ethical conflict of interest inherent in him giving her advice about the primacy of her obligation to repay the loan she owed to his employer. She has enough on her mind.

"I was a business major in college," her voice almost a whisper.

"Lots of opportunity in the business sector now that the economy's turning around. Good article in the Journal yesterday, saying . . ." Just keep the conversation going. Standing, edging her to the door. "Let me get Gina in financial aid to see you."

"Jewel, please call Gina to make an appointment for Ms . . . for this student. Also, see if Father Fitz is around."

He was always surprised at how meekly they took the news. Most knew it was coming of course, but there was a resignation that was worse than the very few who broke down sobbing or became belligerent. Often, they expected to get yelled at and were relieved to just get out of the building without a lecture. He liked to think that some were assuaged that the burden of expectations—their parents', their friends', their own—was lifted. Or maybe that just made the Associate Dean feel a little better.

McNeely always chose to start the day addressing the most dispiriting task confronting him. Or at least the one that seemed so at 8 a.m. Knowing he had a student dismissal on his schedule would eat at him all day. Thankfully that was behind him now. Down deep he knew there was comparable unpleasantness in store for him today, but none was calendared on his iPhone as yet.

Lifting himself out of his chair with a grunt, he walked over to his office window to gaze at the phalanx of Jersey City skyscrapers blocking his view of Manhattan. It always gave him a bracing dose of schadenfreude as he contemplated the bundle of problems, dashed hopes, and fading aspirations of the teeming masses on the other side of the Hudson. McNeely had seen a lot of white-collar crime in the New York melting pot during his six years as an Assistant US Attorney in the Southern District of New York. Crooked WASP bankers and hedge fund managers, Indian insider traders, shady Jewish consultants, shameless Irish personal injury lawyers, money-hungry Asian doctors, criminals of all ethnic backgrounds engaged in visiting theft and fraud upon their fellow man. And now he was getting an introduction to donation-hungry clergy and academics. All nibbling on the GDP like pigeons in Central Park darting around an old woman's bench—not to mention propping up demand for the legal profession. He had spent most of his years as an AUSA chasing the poster boy of Wall Street corruption, Steven Cohen. The notorious insider-trader had been the target of a closely knit team of lawyers and FBI agents who pursued their target with Javert-like passion. While the experience cemented McNeely's priors on corporate chicanery, it was Cohen's échappé around the criminal justice system that ultimately drove him into the arms of academia.

A glance at the front page of the *Star Ledger* didn't settle his stomach. An evangelical praying for Supreme Court Justice Ginsburg to die, asking Jesus to call her back so the religious right can get that fifth vote. Same kind of guy who asks viewers to put their hands on the television and receive his healing benediction for their physical and emotional ailments—once their credit cards clear. A Republican congressman branding radical Islam as a wacko religion while faith healers get an audience with a long line of American Presidents. Trump on a psychotic rant about the Deep State in the FBI and the out-of-control Department of Justice pursuing him. The Knicks looking for a point guard to replace a wife beater and drug abuser. Move on, email check. 65 unread messages. Thankfully, nothing from California or Father Balducci. The rest can wait.

His 10 a.m. corporate law class had become a glorious escape. Teaching was something he never appreciated until he took on the administrative duties of Associate Dean. For fifty minutes he could control events, free from doing others' bidding. An opportunity to talk about something interesting and plant a few seeds of doubt about the performance of the U.S. legal system. Maybe give his students a peek at the dirty underbelly of the corporate world—and the legal system's complicity in the economic injustice all around them.

The principal opinion for analysis in his corporate law class today was that old chestnut, *Dodge v. Ford Motor,* a case that bristled with lessons about corporate power. The Ford Motor Company had accumulated more than $112 million—big money in 1919. The huge profits were the product of Ford's pioneering in assembly line manufacturing and building cheap, reliable cars that suddenly the whole country wanted. Old Man Henry Ford, who owned more than 90 percent of the company and controlled its every move, had a vision for America. He saw a country in which the average guy could afford a car and he paid his workers a decent wage so they could afford to buy one. He also foresaw a country in which politicians would build an interstate road system, enabling workers to move out of the city and travel at will. He saw the future and helped usher it in.

The problem was he didn't want to charge what the market would bear for his cars. Model T Fords were selling for $260 when the company could have charged almost twice that much. Making cars affordable for the average guy was part of a grand plan. Henry Ford also felt his shareholders had made enough money already and refused to declare dividends despite the company's huge surplus. Two prominent stockholders, the Dodge brothers, were anxious to get their hands on some of that capital, for what, in hindsight was a worthy goal: starting a rival car company.

McNeely wanted his students to see the complexities of the case and appreciate its relevance to the current business environment. Crazy old anti-Semite that Ford was, axle grease in his hair, but damn it, he had a vision. One that saw the mutual, interdependent interests of capital and labor to share the rewards of capitalism. The Supreme Court of Michigan saw it differently, ruling that Ford had to pay out dividends unless he had a good business reason not to do so. Still widely cited, that ruling established the motto of our times: the *only* objective of the corporation is, in the infelicitous language of corporate law, "shareholder wealth maximization."

A perfect time capsule. The father of the modern industrial era trying to constrain the avarice of the moneyed class in order to promote domestic tranquility and make sure the market would grow. Will students see that as a quaint relic of a bygone era? Or might it encourage them to reconsider their assumptions about the role of the modern American corporation?

Striding resolutely to the podium, McNeely decided to dispense with cloying chit chat and the "how was your weekend" stuff and start right in. Sometimes best to wake them up early, he thought. "Ok, let's get started with Dodge v. Ford." Student chatter slowly diminishing with almost all staring downward, intent on not making eye contact with McNeely, lest he think they wanted to be called on. A few students flipped through the pages of their casebooks, steeling themselves for the dreaded "cold call." A student huddled in the back row was his first target.

"Ms. Arelio, what did old man Ford do that upset his shareholders?"

"Well, they wanted more . . . he wouldn't pay them."

"Pay them what?"

Hurriedly scanning her casebook, the unlucky target alighted on a key word, but phrased her answer in the form of a question: "Dividends?"

"Okay, what are dividends?"

"Well, they're the money the corporation owes the shareholder."

"Owes them? Did the corporation borrow money from the shareholders?"

Sound of silence. Some fidgeting noises. Finally, a couple of hands go up, maybe trying to rescue a friend.

"Yes, Ms. Bell."

"Dividends are the share of the company's profits that the board can elect to distribute to shareholders. Ford didn't want to pay dividends because he felt the shareholders had made enough money already. The shareholders sued and the Michigan Supreme Court made Ford hand out some dividends."

God bless the gunners like Ms. Bell, thought McNeely. Time to get them thinking. "OK, but what right do shareholders have to demand money? Ford was the entrepreneur, he revolutionized American manufacturing with the assembly line. Ford and his Board of Directors were in charge of running the company, and they felt they had other uses for that surplus, didn't they?"

Ms. Bell blinked. No eye contact even from the gunners, mostly seated in the front two rows, another seventy pairs of eyes scanning the case for an explanation.

Finally, a hand. A pink round face, wearing a bow tie that all but proclaimed Federalist Society, Law Student Division.

"Yes, Mr. Oswald?"

"It's a fundamental principle. Derived from natural law theory. The shareholders *own* the company. What belongs to the company belongs to them."

Oswald's voice rising. a bit tremulously, "They are entitled. Entitled as a matter of law *and ethics*, to the dividends."

McNeely surveyed his flock, "Everyone agree?"

No one was about to take on a Federalist Society acolyte and someone who had worked in a white shoe Manhattan law firm during the summer to whom the Secrets of The Street presumably had been revealed.

"OK, but why was Old Man Ford holding back dividends? What was he trying to do?"

Ms. Bell back in action, "He wanted to build a smelter. Invest in the company's infrastructure."

"Right, and what did the Michigan Supreme Court say about that?

Gleaming, Ms. Bell realized she was on to something. "They said he *could* use some of the money for that."

"So why was it OK for Old Man Ford to spend money on a smelter, but wrong for him to make another business decision, namely, to withhold dividends?"

"Well, investing in the smelter was for the good of the company."

McNeely pouncing with the key question, "And how did the court know the withholding of the dividends was *not* done for the good of the company?"

"Uh, I think Mr. Ford said so," Ms. Bell sounding a little less confident.

"You got it!" McNeely betraying some unexpected enthusiasm, "Henry Ford took the witness stand at trial and said in effect, 'Screw the shareholders, they've made their money.' So, he simply didn't want to pay dividends to them. But all he had to do was come up with a business reason for withholding dividends and putting the money into the company. Anyone see a business rationale that might have saved him?"

Nothing. Time to deliver the punch line. "What if I told you that Ford's genius was figuring out that if he paid his workers a *decent wage*, and *didn't exploit his monopoly* by charging high prices, the *workers* would be able to buy motorcars, *Ford* motorcars? And if other companies were forced to do the same, there'd be lots of people buying cars. The country would be teeming with motorcars. And if that happened, the government would start investing in an interstate highway system. And eventually people would be able to drive from Newark down to the Jersey shore on weekends. And, you know what? *That's exactly what happened!*"

"So Old Man Ford had a legitimate, long term business reason for withholding dividends. But because of his ego, he didn't explain it. Instead, he said, 'It's my damn company and I'll do what I want with the profits.' But the Michigan Supreme Court said, 'Not so fast. You didn't justify withholding the profits from the shareholders. They own the company, so pay out some dividends.'"

Mr. Oswald's pink face now glowing. A couple of others stirring, some looking thoughtful, some even making eye contact with McNeely.

"It all comes down to questions I posed on the first day of class. Who "owns" the corporation? What are its responsibilities to society? What are the duties of those who run corporations?"

Wait till later in the semester, McNeely told himself, to reveal to the class the disquieting news that American corporate law has devolved to giving CEOs enormous power but with one big caveat: Everything they do must be directed to increasing "shareholder wealth." With that will come the additional depressing fact that giving corporate titans untrammeled discretion has not benefited workers or the public, executive compensation has soared, environmentally conscious corporations are punished by the stock market, long term goals are sacrificed for short term profits, and so on and so on. And wait till they hear what so-called charitable, nonprofit corporations do with their profits.

Mr. Oswald will cheer up.

3

Better pass boldly into that other world, in the full glory of some passion, than fade and wither dismally with age.

—James Joyce, *The Dead*

The last ten minutes were always the worst, she thought. Professor Pompeo routinely ran out of things to talk about and filled out the hour with open-ended "thought provokers": "Should we regulate thought?" "Why do Republicans hate regulation?" "If you could regulate anything, what would it be and why?" Or his favorite, "What have we learned today?" Not much, she thought. Except that lifetime tenure for professors is something badly in need of regulation.

Laptop open, casebook balanced on her lap, mind wandering, second year law student Maggie Holloran was beginning to realize that some of her professors had put their courses on autopilot. Some quick math on her calculator app revealed that this four-hour snooze fest represented $7,333.33 of her $44,000 second-year tuition, not counting the interest that had already started accruing.

How could Administrative Law turn out to be such a bore, she wondered. Workers depend on OSHA for their health and safety; the FDA keeps big pharma from poisoning us; the EPA made it possible to sit by the Rahway River at dusk and not be repulsed by the smell or see a New Jersey whitefish (condom) float by. Instead, it was a series of mind-numbing cases involving the Administrative Procedure Act, a law apparently designed to allow Republican judges in federal courts to overrule much of what administrative agencies were designed to do. Or make them jump over so many procedural hurdles that any new regulations would not go into effect before the next President could revoke them. And now the Trump Administration is apparently only appointing judges who want to cripple administrative agencies. Maybe Professor Pompeo could mention that?

Today it was Maggie's friend Josey on the hook for "what did we learn today?"

"Well, I think the district court ignored what the Affordable Care Act was trying to do."

"Why would it do that?" Professor Pompeo feigning innocent surprise.

"The Constitution?" Josey committing the cardinal sin of answering a question with a question.

Pompeo responding with his idea of a Socratic curveball, "Isn't that reason enough?"

"Not if it ignores precedent or is the slanted view of a political hack," said an energized Josey, who evidently had had enough law school ping pong for one day.

Professor Pompeo looked stricken. She'd knocked his hanger over the Green Monster.

You go girl, Maggie thought. As the clock hit 5:00, there was a loud clamor of notebooks snapping shut, zippers zipping, water bottles sloshing, and restless students swiveling their chairs in preparation for a bolt to the exit.

Ok, for Thursday, don't forget to read . . ." Words inaudible. Students exiting en masse, voices exchanging names of saloons, gyms, friends with weed, and other destinations to put the day behind you.

Maggie thought ahead to the crucial inflection points of her next thirty minutes. Run to locker, unload sixteen pounds of casebooks, grab a sweater, dash for the 5:15 PATH Train to Newark and hope to catch the 5:30 local to Rahway. If she missed it, a $40 Uber loomed.

She caught the PATH quickly, grabbed the last aisle seat on the NJ Corridor train, opened the make-up kit in her backpack, and applied eyeliner, lipstick, and gloss, deftly overcoming the frequent lateral jolts supplied by NJ Transit's long-neglected rails. She unpacked her shoulder-length, permed blond hair from its captivity under a Mets cap. At 5 foot 10, her green eyes and sculptured eyebrows had the guys at the bar staying for one more. Appearances matter when you're bartending.

She found her father seated in a booth chatting with one of the local cops who regularly patrolled the bar. Reminding him of his solemn vow that he'd always leave by 4 p.m., she tut-tutted, and told him to go home, lie down, and watch his precious Mets score one run and waste another good outing by deGrom.

The Terminal Bar, the Holloran family's proud enterprise, was active even for happy hour. Just 25 yards from the Rahway Train Station, the Term's location gave it a predictable daily cycle. Tonight, she spotted a couple of day drinkers who had probably opened the place and were nursing their fourth Seven and Seven, but was pleased to see that a pretty good gaggle of youngsters had begun to filter in. Always present were a few suburban yuppies eager to visit an authentic dive bar and who invariably wound up discussing how quaint the wall hangings were and debating what the most authentic dive bar drink would be.

Maggie knew well the Term's biological clock. Commuters freshly released from offices in city skyscrapers would be arriving soon for a drink or two before catching the local to the suburbs. The younger, single ones and the roaming husbands would stay for an hour or two. Both were pretty good tippers if she played her cards right. Maggie slipped into the back room and put on a low-cut top. Dressing a little slutty was good for an extra $50 in tips, she had calculated. And over the years it had also sharpened her skills at reading the male cortex.

She saw two things wrong the minute she returned from the kitchen. Kelly, the waitress with the best figure was the Term's "rainmaker," responsible for flashing an inviting smile at potential customers looking in at the door and offering some cheerful chatter about the Happy Hour specials inside. Tonight however, Maggie found her leaning on the end of the bar engaged in a giggling chat with a blond guy wearing a $200 DiMaggio replica jersey—the male equivalent of Kelly's fuck-me shoes. No one at the front door to offer the intrepid commuter the illusions of sex and drink that keep bars in business.

The second matter for concern was that three young guys at the bar had double shots in their glasses and no money on the bar. Serious drinking and no money on the bar meant either they were running a tab on a credit card or, more likely, slipping the provisional bartender she had just hired a big tip in return for a free one or heavy hand on the bottle. Money disappears quickly when the bartender is working a contract.

Maggie had been a fixture at the Term since she was five. Her mother handled the cooking for lunch and dinner servings, so Maggie's day care entailed a seat in the last booth, a coloring book, and a glass of chocolate milk, all under the watchful eyes of her parents. As she grew older and came by after school with disturbingly captivating green eyes, promisingly developing breasts, and sometimes wearing what her mother called "provocative clothes," concerns mounted. Fortunately, the Term was a favorite stopover for Rahway's Finest. They hung their police caps outside the booth next to Maggie's and proved to be a good deterrent to the inquisitive male. Once when she was in junior high, a guy strolled by Maggie's booth and casually asked what she was reading. Sergeant Brodie Flanagan, unseen in the next booth, called out, "I believe it's an article on statutory rape." The suspect scurried on to the men's room and took a different path returning to the bar.

Her mother was diagnosed during Maggie's sophomore year in high school. Lung cancer. Never smoked a cigarette in her life, but twenty-five years in the Term's haze was as good as a couple of packs a day. The news of the diagnosis sent young Maggie across the river to the NY Public Library, where she discovered that, notwithstanding its denials, Big Tobacco had a pretty good idea of what was going on with its nicotine addiction scheme. She found a report by the Surgeon General of the United States that concluded "cigarette smoking is causally related to lung cancer in men; the magnitude of the effect of cigarette smoking outweighs all other factors." Published in 1964, for fuck's sake, she fumed.

Next, she learned that there were thousands of pages of incriminating internal documents from the largest tobacco companies that had been made public as part of the settlement of a lawsuit in Minnesota. They provided compelling evidence that a dozen of America's leading corporations had knowingly unleashed a plague of addiction, cancer, and death across the nation. She read with wide-eyed astonishment the details of a pitched battle waged on all fronts— academia, courts, and state legislatures. The battle lines had shifted over time, but they told a tale of corporate greed and misinformation. Over a fifty-year span, the industry had conducted a methodical public relations retreat from "tobacco doesn't cause cancer" to "tobacco is not addictive" to "secondhand smoke doesn't cause cancer" to "tobacco generates needed jobs and taxes."

Maggie was both infuriated and puzzled. How did it take so long for this highly educated, democratic republic to come to grips with what scientists had conclusively proved was a matter of life and death? The answer came in an article on the history of the war against Big Tobacco. Lawyers had helped engineer and implement the strategy. An investigative reporter in *The Atlantic* described the industry's success in "creating false doubts about the health dangers and addictiveness of smoking, scripting deceptive quarter-truths to deflect inquiries, invoking the attorney-client privilege to hide evidence, keep suppressing inconvenient research, keep manipulating science, people, and language to hide the truth. And the body count mounted."

That was it: the political and legal systems serving as handmaidens to Big Tobacco's cancer delivery device.

Permanently embedded in her mind was the image of her mother lying in the ICU of that God awful, decrepit Holy Mother of Hoboken Hospital. Down to seventy-five pounds, tubes running in and out of her, and a fog clouding her eyes,

Norma Holloran knew her time had come. In one of Maggie's last visits, her mother laid down the law with a raspy insistence:

"You're going to do three things for me. One, make sure your father doesn't become a mope. Get him out of that bloody bar and make him start living his life.

Two, do something with yourself. Help make this goddamn world a better place.

Go to Mass on Sundays. I don't care if you don't believe in all that crap but go because it's who we are and it matters to your father.

Ok, one more. Don't marry an asshole."

Tarted up for her five-hour stint, Maggie flipped up the hinged entry hatch and assumed her station behind the bar, hoping the shift would divert her thoughts away from her mother's final days. Easier said than done. That day in the NY Public Library and her deathbed pledge to her mother to do something worthwhile was her epiphany and the reason she was working her butt off behind the bar. Law school, she had decided, was the only road to settling the score.

Then, with a hot rush of anger that lit up her forehead, she remembered that tomorrow it was *she* who would be on trial.

4

I'm too old to know everything.

—Oscar Wilde

Quiet time. Ten minutes for what his grandfather called a sit down. "Elvis died on the crapper," he had warned him. Nevertheless, McNeely thought, not a bad way to go, squatting and languidly reading the sports page.

For God's sake. The German youth camps had nothing on these guys, McNeely mused to himself as he entered the faculty john. They are so programmed to do what's expected of them, they'll follow any command. He had just walked into the men's room to discover one of the junior faculty engaged in an activity he never dreamed he'd see in a public men's room. Ridgeway was brushing his teeth. With toothpaste which he apparently stored in a trim leather pouch that also accommodated his brush and a roll of floss, all now neatly arrayed on the sink awaiting his summons. Unembarrassed, he waived the wand at McNeely and went about his business.

And this wasn't the first time. He had walked in on another young professor a couple of months earlier engaged in the same intimate activity, but thought, well, maybe the guy's got a gum disease. Judge not. Now two of his most dedicated young scholars shamelessly tending to their teeth, gums, and God knows what else. If their doctor told them that massaging their prostrate every hour prevents cancer, they'd be at it. In the library if necessary. I've lived too long, he thought.

Not that the old timers didn't have their quirks. Last year, Professor Emeritus Nicholas Albertson pursued him into the john to complete his recounting of the day Judge Masterson had quoted his law review article (in a dissent). "Old Man Masterson got it right, but the Marxists on the panel prevailed." Not only had Albertson continued his reminiscence as they walked in, but the old codger continued his improbable tale without missing a beat after entering a stall and bolting the door. McNeely grunted a few times from the urinal, washed up, dried his hands as quietly as possible, and slipped out as Albertson droned on. A few months later, at Albertson's memorial service McNeely found himself snickering, wondering whether the old guy managed to finish his story for another visitor.

As Associate Dean of St. Sebastian Law School McNeely's role was to be the eyes, ears, and flack-catcher on "internal" law school matters. This entailed overseeing the day-to-day administration of the school, addressing curricular and student issues, and most importantly, keeping an eye on what the faculty was up to. Under their shared responsibility model, the Dean of the law school, Deborah Eckstein, was an "external dean," who coordinated with the University President and raised money and promoted the law school through public appearances and serving on local and national boards. She had recruited McNeely to shoulder the part-time administrative duties of Associate Dean shortly after the faculty had awarded him "early tenure" a full two years before the six-year norm. Grateful for the vote of confidence and thinking it a good way to learn the intricacies of the law school enterprise, he had happily—and it turned out quite naively—agreed to step in.

Noon in the faculty lounge offered McNeely a chance to take the temperature of his colleagues. It was not his favorite part of the job. Schmoozing during these weekly faculty lunches, his role was to play the part of hale colleague, trading disparaging comments about the Yale Law faculty, bemoaning the incompetent judges Trump was appointing, commiserating about the stupidity of student law journal editors who couldn't apprehend the relevance of Wittgenstein to textual analysis. Just one of the guys. But as every faculty member well knew, he shared responsibility with the dean for making the decisions about matters they cared most about: their teaching loads, class schedules, committee assignments, annual merit pay increases, and sabbaticals. *This is the business we have chosen,* he would remind himself and the Dean as they performed the delicate balancing act of running the law school while also herding cats. Once he had accepted the appointment as St. Sebastian Law School's Associate Dean, relationships with his colleagues had changed significantly. Now serving an admixture of roles—supervisor, mole, ward healer, and confidant—his principal job was to *be available* to his colleagues. Available to entertain their entreaties, complaints, and braggadocio. And then process the accumulated intelligence to help the dean avoid insurrections.

The lunchtime seating patterns were revealing. Youth sat with youth, usually in political or subject matter clusters. The junior constitutional law and human rights contingent seldom lunched with anyone except themselves, though occasionally one of the several senior leftists would invite him or herself to crash their party. The older faculty tended to lunch in long-established cliques that bespoke longstanding friendships. In some cases, the separations signaled rivalries and ancient slights the origins of which were forgotten even by the aggrieved.

One group that invariably clustered together were colleagues McNeely had secretly nicknamed the "Young and the Restless." The group consisted of four or five recently hired professors who, although not yet tenured, were better credentialed than most of the older faculty. All were certain that St. Sebastian was just a stopover before ascending to their rightful spot at a top-10 law school. They knew all too well the prevailing snark about St. Sebastian University: SSU, short for "Safety School U"; sixth-ranked *Catholic* law school in the Metropolitan area (out of seven); "a good place to retire"; and so on. But to a man (yes, they were all men), each of the Y&R firmly believed SSU was for them just a stop-over, like landing in Frankfurt en route to Casablanca.

To his discomfort, McNeely noticed that one senior faculty member seemed to appear more and more frequently among the Y&R: Julian Cathcart, McNeely's predecessor as Associate Dean, whose brief and spectacularly unsuccessful candidacy for the law school deanship had left him a man in search of a constituency. All of which made him the colleague most likely to find fault with whatever the Eckstein/McNeely administration wanted to do. Most men of Cathcart's unprepossessing stature and limited charm wound up selling life insurance or managing an Applebee's at the Hudson Mall, thought McNeely. But he was a member of what Colly McNeely called "The Lucky Sperm Club." Cathcart's father, who graduated from NYU Law School and practiced for 30 years at the whitest of the white shoe law firms, Debevoise & Plimpton, got Julian admitted to his alma mater as a "legacy with benefits." Timely financial contributions had sealed the deal for his son.

Most recently, Cathcart had begun to devote his energies to engaging the legal academic community and his students via social media. His Facebook and Twitter postings displayed frequent mentions of his own work, cloying praise for leading scholars who he hoped would return the favor, and insights into his mastery in the kitchen, last week sharing a breakthrough raspberry vinaigrette recipe with his waiting public. Internet self-promotion among legal scholars was no longer confined to shameless prating about one's academic work, McNeely concluded. It had come to resemble a dating site.

McNeely had expected to encounter the quirky, the solipsistic, the odd duck, when he entered academia but never dreamed he'd be exposed to the full panoply of diagnosable personality disorders. His complex taxonomy of the faculty had many species, orders, and phyla. Another prominent category consisted of colleagues he called the Lotus Eaters—a group that had gorged themselves on the sweet leaf of tenure and had drifted into a restful, passive academic life. Most produced little or no scholarship and taught from the same syllabi and lecture notes they had created decades earlier. Today was one of the rare occasions when so many of the faculty had gathered for lunch that the orbits of several groups collided. Finding themselves crowded together at the same table as the Senior Doctrinal Catholics (a subspecies of the Lotus Eaters), the Young and the Restless found themselves forced to engage in banter with colleagues they suspected of being sympathetic to war criminals.

Raymond Williams, a sallow marathon runner, led the Y&R hunting pack, "So, Joe, before you sat down, Dan was saying that he agreed with Christopher Hitchens that Kissinger should be tried for war crimes for his complicity in the Pinochet killings. My position is that the man hit the triple crown, with war crimes in Vietnam, Argentina, and Pakistan, so why focus on only one part of the man's illustrious career?"

Directing the riposte at Joseph F.X. Mulligan served several purposes. Not only had he written editorials supporting the economic policies of Reagan, Thatcher, Bush 2, and Trump, but he was also rumored to be a member of Opus Dei. No one had ever pinned him down on his affiliation with the society, though he was not reticent about defending the Church's most extreme followers. Opus Dei, the secretive Catholic organization founded by Spanish Bishop (now Saint) Josemaria Escriva, espouses an extreme, conservative flavor of the church's doctrine and members' role in society. Among the world leaders its adherents vehemently deny having supported were Augusto Pinochet, Francisco Franco, and an assortment of other dictators. Although some members are celibate, most are "supernumeraries" —married men with children. Supporters say they are no different than the Elks or Chamber of Commerce except that they say a lot of Hail Mary's and enjoy corporal mortifications such as sleeping on the floor and wearing a self-penitential band of metal thorns called a cilice on their thighs.

Mulligan was not about to rise to the bait. Flashing a broad ecumenical smile at his young tormentor, he stood up with his plate in hand, "Raymond, I think your blood sugar is dropping. Can I get you a slice of that lemon meringue pie while I'm up?"

Score one for the dinosaurs, thought McNeely as he edged over toward the food tables. He was immediately cornered at the salad bar where he was forced to entertain several colleagues' tales of crises that their committees faced or pleas for teaching release in order to finish some long-promised writing project. Looking for an escape route, he scanned the room and spotted Father Francis Fitzgibbon, S.J. seated alone at a corner table. Father Fitz, a 73-year-old Jesuit, had been assigned by the Order to serve as the law school's Spiritual Director. An amiable fellow with a ready smile, a cheerful word for everyone, and a close rapport with many students, he was generally ignored except when the subject of snarky comments by the faculty. He conducted a sparsely attended daily Mass in a small chapel in the law school basement, but also maintained a steady stream of students who seemed to enjoy his company. McNeely once overheard one of the Y&R refer to his gatherings as "Father Flanagan's Boys' Town" and was sure there were pedophilia insinuations he hadn't overheard.

McNeely hovering by his table, "Father, may I join you? Or are you deep into Aquinas?"

"By all means, Dean. No, no, in fact it's Orwell." Holding up the 'Collected Essays' of George Orwell.

"Orwell? The Atheist?" McNeely offered with a conspiratorial smirk, "Don't let the archbishop hear about that."

"Oh, I love the atheists. So sincere, so committed. True believers one and all," Father Fitz beamed.

In contrast to his flock on the law school faculty, McNeely thought. "So, are the 'worried well' keeping you busy?"

Father Fitz was not about to ignore the not-so-subtle suggestion that only the neurotic sought his help. "Oh, I've seen a few of the law school's forgotten souls."

Ever the lawyer-turned-bureaucrat, McNeely triaged the worst possibilities for the law school from losing some souls: lost tuition, complaints to the attorney general, postings on the *Inside the Law* blog, suicide. "Well, anything I can help with?"

"I'll let you know . . . if all else fails," Father Fitz responded with a twinkle in his eye.

God, the Jesuits are sly, McNeely thought. No need to say "Fuck you" when you can slide the dagger in quietly.

Rather than witness more intellectual carnage of the Young and the Restless feasting on their prey, McNeely retreated to his office after lunch. Less temptation to verbally assault someone there, he thought. The ninety minutes he carved out between committee meetings, office hours and other mind-numbing tasks were what kept him alive. Sometimes he just stared out the window at the Hackensack River. Hoping to see something—or someone—interesting float by.

His meditation was broken by a shout from his assistant, Jewel Henderson, calling out from her desk, "Ms. Battaglini here to see you."

Every professor was assigned a student research assistant, usually someone uncommonly bright, ambitious, and hard working. RAs were sometimes ignored after their first meeting with a professor. Unrestrained earnestness proved too much for some faculty, especially those not producing any serious scholarship. Others were dismissed for errors in judgment, such as finding a fatal flaw in their professor's article. For his part, McNeely wanted to make the experience useful—for the student if not for himself. He made it a point to come up with abstruse research assignments that he probably would never use but would pose a big challenge. Whether they wound up in Big Law or solo practice, he knew that sooner or later every student would find him or herself in that dark night of the soul, computer aglow at 3 a.m. trying to solve an intractable legal problem on a totally unfamiliar corner of the law with no one there to help. Maybe working for an overbearing partner who gave them zero guidance and insisted on perfectly manicured memos that relentlessly ran down every possible doctrinal rat hole. Or, out on their own, representing an immigrant family about to face eviction the next morning. Fulfilling his part of the bargain, McNeely usually explained that this was the business they had chosen, that everyone feels inadequate, and anyway, there were no right answers to most complex legal questions. He showered his RAs with praise and wrote glowing recommendations to law firms and judges, a handful of whom thought it important that a law professor would praise a student's work. Jennifer Battaglini was one of his greatest success stories. She had come to him as a laid back, somewhat insecure liberal arts major, and now was loaded for bear, ready to tackle the beasts in the land of Big Law.

"So, Jenny, how's it going? Exams treat you well?"

"Not too bad. I had two courses with papers, so only two exams last semester. Aced them both. The job at Worsted and Pflum will pay off my loans in four years, then I'm free."

"To . . . ?"

"Bowl in the Women's PBA, maybe try roller derby . . . who knows?" Battaglini said with a cheerful smile signaling she didn't need any avuncular advice today. But she immediately switched gears with a frown, "However, some of my friends are in total crisis mode. No job, no interviews, and $150,000 in student loans."

"Well, don't despair. Everyone winds up somewhere." McNeely recoiled immediately at his own insensitivity. If he had made this asinine a remark in an email, he could recall it. Somewhat flummoxed, he ventured into uncharted waters. "Well, on balance, all things considered . . . that is besides the student debt issue, which I totally agree is an outrage . . ."

A revealing ten-second pause, while his cortex flashed an IM reminding him that the huge debt load weighing on almost every student was St. Sebastian's doing.

A reply IM offered a defense strategy: *Only in part. It's the whole fucked-up system.*

Ms. Battaglini leaned forward and looked directly into McNeely's eyes. "But since you asked, you should know one of my best friends is getting screwed by a faculty member."

McNeely blinked three times and his eyes opened wide. Instantly he knew his first reaction was humiliatingly old school. At 37 years old, he was borderline Gen X.

Suppressing a smirk, she waved him off. "No, no, not that, professor. She's being treated unfairly by a faculty member who's made a complaint to the ethics committee."

"Well, she'll get due process, representation by a faculty member, and I'm sure the ethics committee will give her a fair . . ."

"Not likely. Sorry professor, but it's not in the cards for her. The deck is stacked against her."

"Why?"

Battaglini issuing a world-weary sigh, "Long story that involves girl-girl confidential privilege. But, believe me, it's a travesty."

McNeely stuttering, "Well I can't talk about it since I'm the *ex officio* member of the committee and I have plenary jurisdiction on appeal. You know what plenary jurisdiction means? I'm sure it's taught in . . . Oh, I guess it comes up in . . . many courses. At Saint Sebastian, we . . . we take very seriously . . . very seriously, all sides in . . . uh, these cases. Due process, as I'm sure you've studied over and over again assures . . . well . . . fairness. Fairness is really the essence of . . . of the law. So, I can assure you she'll get a fair hearing. A *very* fair hearing."

McNeely realized he was both sweating and his cheeks were turning a bright crimson. He remembered cross-examining witnesses who reacted like this. They'd start stammering, then color up, and finally something in their eyes yelled out "OK, I'm full of shit. I know it."

He glanced up at Battaglini. Not hard to detect a tell on her side either. Another sigh, pursing of the lips, and snapping open a notebook, signaling *let's move on*. To McNeely's latest convoluted research assignment. Not buying that fair hearing/due process bullshit for a second.

Ten minutes in, they were interrupted by a knock on the door. McNeely's assistant Jewel Henderson's head curling around the door with a raised eyebrow that bespoke concern, "Sorry professor, it's Father Balducci's office on line one."

The call was brief, from Rodney Leporello, the University President's chief of staff—a new title designed to remind everyone that St. Sebastian was a $55 million enterprise—delivering crisp instructions: Come by Bishop Sheehan Hall at 2:30 to meet with Father Balducci. Don't mention this meeting to your dean. Bring a copy of the last two years of your faculty meeting minutes.

As summonses go, this one had felony indictment written all over it, McNeely mused. Better call Griff.

5

By 2005, the Olin Foundation had supported eleven separate programs at Harvard, burnishing the foundation's name and ideas and proving that even the best-endowed American university would allow an outside, ideological group to build "beachheads," so long as the project was properly packaged and funded.

—Jane Mayer, *Dark Money:*
The Hidden History of the Billionaires
Behind the Rise of the Radical Right

Big law in DC knows how to do things right, Frederick Douglas ruminated as he gazed from the Wolfson, Grey conference room window at a spectacular view of Pennsylvania Avenue with the top of the Washington Monument peeking out over the Justice Department building. Three prominent law firms had mustered their pharmaceutical clients to initiate the ambitious project now known as Sanus. The drug companies had come up with ample funding—the press would call it dark money, if, God forbid, they ever started asking questions—had put a professional staff together, and to top it off, subleased spectacular office space that one of the law firms was holding vacant in anticipation of the coming gold rush of billable hours under the business-friendly Trump Administration. The law firms, Ableson Pollack, Winthrop Salem, and Wolfson, Grey & Fugasi, all had large "government affairs" units that served their clients' legal, lobbying, and public relations needs, and therefore had plenty of bandwidth to conceive, deliver, and wetnurse a new trade association. Now it was up to him to put $125 million to work in service of Sanus' anonymous donors and their mission. Which was selling drugs.

Not that the pharmaceutical industry was struggling. By some measures it enjoyed the highest returns of any sector in the American economy and its products had become staples in most American households. $500 billion in annual sales delivering lifesaving and life-extending drugs and lots more: elixirs for mood, concentration and sexual performance; weight reducers and hair restorers; relief from pain, anxiety, and acne; and other remedies for myriad neuroses of 21st-century life.

But there were clouds appearing on Big Pharma's MRI scans. For one thing, the public hated them. Worse yet, Americans blamed the drug industry for the high cost of health care and many would be perfectly comfortable having the government take over their business. Even President Trump, whom the industry helped elect and who seemed willing to abandon the federal government's responsibility for virtually everything, had said during the campaign that the pharmaceutical industry "is getting away with murder" and pledged to "bring drug prices way down." Meanwhile, Democrats were falling over each other to come up with more and more draconian remedies: importing drugs from Canada, reducing patent protections for new drugs, empowering Medicare to negotiate prices on behalf of its sixty-one million beneficiaries, and even allowing the government to manufacture generic and off-patent drugs.

Frederic Douglas was the man for the job at Sanus. A former CEO of Questmat Pharmaceuticals, COO of Nexilabs, and during the Reagan years, Deputy Commissioner for Policy, Legislation, and International Affairs at the Food and Drug Administration, he knew his way around town. Probably more important, he was a golfing buddy of the Chair of the Senate Finance Committee and of the Ranking Member of the House Ways and Means Committee. He had recruited a half dozen prominent and well-connected Washington insiders to serve on Sanus' Board of Directors while also orchestrating a healthy flow of donations from anonymous and untraceable LLCs to fund Sanus' operating budget. They had assembled today to hear, and presumably approve, part of his master plan.

"Gentlemen, let's begin with a little history lesson." Displaying a PowerPoint slide with a portrait of John Olin juxtaposed with the façade of the US Supreme Court, Douglas began his seminar. "This man, John Olin, heir to the Olin gunpowder and chemical business started by his father, began a foundation that reshaped America. Indeed, one might say it restored the country to its original purpose. At first the Olin Foundation gave money to the usual causes: universities, hospitals and so on. But in 1968 Mr. Olin became appalled—as did many of my generation—by the campus unrest protesting the war in Vietnam. So, Mr. Olin decided to put his money to better use."

Douglas advanced to a slide displaying Big Olin's face and a quotation in bold Sans-serif font: **I would like to use this fortune to help preserve the system which made its accumulation possible in only two lifetimes, my father's and mine. —John Olin**

Lowering his tone to that of Carl Sagan explaining the origin of the cosmos, Douglas went on, "What ensued changed the world. The genius of his administrator, former Secretary of the Treasury William Simon, was the idea of deploying charitable funds precisely where they'd have the most impact. They funded some names you've heard of . . ."

A slide with a dozen faces and logos appeared: Allan Bloom, Milton Friedman, Ronald Reagan, the American Enterprise Institute, the Heritage Foundation, the Hoover Institution, the Manhattan Institute, and academic centers at Harvard and Stanford. "Pretty impressive, no? Note in particular one institution nestled among the academic recipients: the People's Republic of Columbia University!" Douglas let out a sly snicker to encourage audience participation. He got a few chuckles and knowing nods. "Lots of left-wing colleges have not been shy about feeding at the trough."

Advancing next to a slide showing the entrance to the newly renamed "Antonin Scalia School of Law" at George Mason University, he continued, "It also funded the Federalist Society which has established a base in every law school in the country, and, most relevant to our mission, a center for conservative thinking and law and economics at a little-known institution, the George Mason School of Law. GMU went on to treat federal judges to weeklong seminars in New Hampshire to teach them basic economic principles. And over the past two decades, many of these same judges have applied their Economics 101 training to radically reshape the law. At long last!!"

Following a brief pause to allow the brilliance of the think tanks' strategy to sink in, Douglas advanced the next slide which displayed an array of photos of pharmaceutical labs, doctors, shiny office buildings, and grateful patients. "Our job now is to advance the concept to the next stage. One of the great advances in recent years for those of us in government relations has been to focus our attention to where law is made: the courts, the regulatory agencies, and the academic institutions that feed them their ideas. You all know about Heritage, the Manhattan Institute, Cato, etc., etc. Well, our vision is to *improve* on that model. Our new project will direct a laser-like focus on courts and academia for a very specific purpose: Advancing understanding of the critical role of the pharmaceutical industry."

Pausing to survey his board, Douglas noticed several checking their cell phones. Enough corporate bonhomie, time to wake them up. Raising his voice and gesticulating vigorously, he went on, " I won't try to pretend it's a slam dunk. We've got to overcome the damage done by—pardon the expression—assholes like Martin Shkreli, raising prices 5000% to treat a rare disease, and Mylan with its damn EpiPen fiasco. Things that set the pharma industry back thirty years in terms of public opinion and government relations. Meanwhile, doctors and hospitals who are responsible for 80% of the cost of health care get way scot free. And claim that *we* are the robber barons, and they only care about their patients! Bullshit on toast! Ascension Healthcare, a *"nonprofit" "charitable" "Catholic"* hospital system, has $19 billion lying around in cash, and is now operating its own *venture capital* operation! And their CEO made $14 million last year! Nonprofit??? Give me a fucking break."

Pausing, exhaling a deep breath and offering an apologetic smile, Douglas went on, "Sorry, sorry. I get a little worked up at their hypocrisy." He advanced a slide showing a glowing orb displaying a round "Sanus" emblem encircled by spokes leading to photos of leafy academic buildings, the Capitol building in Washington, stacks of academic journals, and a courtroom. "So, our plan is to generously fund one law school to be the hub of our academic outreach. We'll give them a boatload of money . . ."

Offering a conspiratorial wink to his audience, Douglas's voice dropped to a hoarse whisper—"subject to our close oversight of course—I promise you we'll make sure the funds are used for advancing our cause and *not* for enabling academic slackers."

Aware that the gritty details and necessary financial commitments would be less well received, he spoke faster, "The initial outlay is $30 million over a five-year period. But don't worry, we've loaded a lot of deliverables that our little law school subsidiary will never be able to deliver. In any event, we anticipate that the school can be the training ground for future advocates, judges, and regulatory officials. It will become the epicenter of academic literature explaining the damage that wrongheaded regulation can do to the pharmaceutical industry—and of course to the nation's health. And very important, it will be ground zero for legislative lobbying and litigation. Performed by a respected *and ostensibly unbiased* academic institution."

"Finally, I think we've identified a suitable site to serve as our law school base. Like George Mason, it's not a household name, but it seems to have an ambitious President who's plenty eager to make new friends and, I think, will talk turkey."

An artist's impressionistic drawing—not a photograph—of St. Sebastian School of Law appeared on the screen.

I regret profoundly that I was not an American and not born in Greenwich Village. It might be dying, and there might be a lot of dirt in the air you breathe, but this is where it's happening.
—John Lennon

Long day. Getting off the PATH at Christopher Street, McNeely shouldered his way through a gaggle of oncoming tourists in search of uptown trains to take them to their musicals, tchotchke shops, and chain restaurants in the Disneyfied Time Square he had come to abhor. Zagging around a blue-haired senior elbow deep in a tote bag fishing for her MetroCard, he jogged to the escalator. The welcoming evening glow of the West Village and the cacophony of cars, music, and scurrying pedestrians never failed to excite him. Exiting the station, he quickened his pace to match the up-tempo stride of Manhattan pedestrians. Not in Jersey anymore.

Friends often hinted their concern that he must be depressed and isolated living alone in a tiny studio apartment in the big city. How, he would parry, could anyone be anything but energized and alive living at the center of the civilized world? He had spent his youth trying to find an exit ramp out of New Jersey, and this was working out just fine, thank you very much. Moreover, he was used to being alone. An only child, father killed when he was five, and an absentee mother, he'd learned to entertain himself and enjoyed his own company as much as anyone else's. His three-year marriage to his high school sweetheart had ended abruptly. Her departure to California with their severely disabled daughter had cemented his preference for a solitary, unencumbered life.

Tipping the scales at 243 pounds with a BMI of 35, McNeely had promised himself he would always "two-time" stairways—take two stairs at a time. He had been the fattest kid in every grade from kindergarten to his last year of law school, which took a toll on his social life. On the other hand, his bulk had helped make him the starting left guard on the Roselle Catholic High football team and turn him into a pretty good power hitting catcher . . . whenever he happened to make contact. As he sprinted up on his two-time stairway routine, he took some satisfaction in knowing he was not paying $250 a month for an Equinox Club membership. *Burning as many calories as I would there, and don't have to watch ripped investment bankers showing off their abs*, he rationalized.

The ascent to his fourth-floor studio offered a microcosm of the sounds and smells of dinnertime in the city. Kimchi odors wafted out from 1A accompanied by the familiar whirr of the spinning Wheel of Fortune on Channel 4. 2B offered the garlicky scent of mofongo and a lively Spanish language talk show emanating from somewhere in cable's netherworld. 3A reliably gave off a pungent dosage of weed with Metallica providing the soundtrack. His 525-square-foot studio apartment at 4A—fraudulently listed as a one-bedroom premised on a thin bamboo room separator angled between the bedroom and kitchen/bathroom/washer-dryer stack—suited him just fine. "Small but cramped," he liked to say.

Flipping on the overhead light, he had a flashback to the first time he had brought a date back to this apartment. She was a fourth-year associate in the tax department of a law firm at the top of the legal food chain, Cravath, Swaine and Moore. McNeely estimated that she was probably pulling down over $350,000 plus bonuses—at least three times his salary—and living in rather more elegant surroundings on Park Avenue. The astonished look on her face told him everything. Visualizing it through her eyes, he saw his dingy apartment anew: a small bed thinly disguised as a couch by two fluffy throw pillows, a blonde desk that screamed out IKEA, a worn leather office chair he snagged at a Canal Street thrift store, a huge fully-stacked bookcase, a tiny Persian rug, just to tie the room together, and a giant TV monitor. McNeely read her thoughts: *How can this be?* She had worshipped her worldly, urbane mentors at Yale Law School, men and women who were not just erudite, but who had the cosmopolitan bearing of academic royalty. Their homes bespoke elegance and taste. This place bespoke City College undergrad. Last time he brought anyone back.

But the judgments and fretting of others never really bothered him. He knew he had made the right decision shifting to academia, even though it meant abandoning a job—perhaps a calling—that he loved. The work as a federal prosecutor was engrossing and demanding and it gave him no small satisfaction to put away well-heeled executives who knew exactly what they were doing and deserved their fate. Even the monastic life of 13-hour workdays with little time for what his friends euphemistically called a "social life" suited him just fine, perhaps as a kind of penance for the mess he'd made of his marriage. What was missing was a sense that all those hours he put in as an Assistant U.S. Attorney had actually helped anyone. There was no identifiable human being whose life he had impacted. No one had ever pulled him aside on the subway to thank him for putting away those nasty insider traders.

St. Sebastian promised to fill that void. A school located in a gritty neighborhood near where he grew up and populated with a fair number of working-class kids—some just like him—all aspiring to do well, and most to do good. A student body far removed from his classmates at Harvard Law—privileged one-percenters who viewed a law degree as a matter of birthright. Most of them had eventually migrated upstream to the Wall Street law firms—ironically located, he thought, just a quarter mile away from his seedy West Village apartment.

Academia had its upsides. Unlike many of his colleagues, McNeely devoted extensive "office hours" to meeting with students, and took special satisfaction in nurturing "first gen" students—those whose parents had not gone to college and who often were plagued by self-doubt when they realized they were surrounded by others who had the benefit of a much more sophisticated undergrad education. And perhaps equally important, the priviledged class knew how to effortlessly chat up law firm partners. Many of the first gens, he realized, were taking pains to hide their humble roots. Their résumés never listed their jobs in construction or having begun at junior colleges. Evidence of working-class origins such as a few years taking care of their parents or siblings needed to be whitewashed. All to fit the Big Law mold.

Unfortunately, McNeely knew there is no easy escape from one's past. The uncomfortable, incontrovertible fact was that humble roots *did* matter to the Big Law interviewers. Can't have someone with rough edges dealing with investment bankers, hedge fund managers, and other upmarket clients. They might order a rum and coke at lunch with clients for God's sake. He gave the best advice he could offer: *persuade the law firm that your background makes you hungrier than the average bear. You'd happily install a Murphy bed in your office to help you get to 2500 billable hours per year.* His other mission was to acquaint students with opportunities that didn't require taking golf lessons or memorizing names of vineyards turning out respectable pinots. Public defenders, prosecutors, city, county and state government jobs, all offered the opportunity to develop real lawyering skills while fighting for something you could believe in. Unfortunately, a tough sell to kids about to graduate six figures in the hole.

At least he could try to help a few find their way. And in the meantime, maybe he could find time to write something to move the needle a little on the crooked legal compass.

7

Someday the capitalist system will disappear in the United States because no social class system is eternal. One day, class societies will disappear.

—Fidel Castro

In retrospect, Maggie credited her academic advisor at her junior college for helping put her on the path to law school. Just a month into her first semester at Union County Junior College, colloquially nicknamed "UC Juicy," she sat down with Mrs. Jaworski to discuss her academic choices and career aspirations. When asked about the latter, Maggie was clear. She wanted to go to law school. After that, she would work at a legal services clinic and help clients who couldn't afford a lawyer but needed help navigating their problems, whether it be housing, discrimination, or family matters. Mrs. Jaworski's response was a seminal moment in Maggie's life.

"Well, you know, law schools have very high admissions standards. And the costs are enormous. Hard to tackle all that in the first place, let alone begin a family. It's always good to take one step at a time. Paralegal school is a good place to start if you're interested in the law."

That was all Maggie needed to hear. She reviewed the subtexts. *Law school? You don't have the chops. Shoot for something more realistic. And because you're here in a junior college you probably don't have parents who can foot the costs. So why don't you become a helper to real lawyers? It's an important job. And you do want to have kids, don't you?*

Counselors at junior colleges knew the hard truth and so did Maggie. Only one in seven students went on to receive a B.A. at a four-year college The percentage going further to get a J.D. or other advanced degree was vanishingly small. Mrs. Jaworski felt she had two jobs: give students a healthy dose of reality while also encouraging them to strive to overcome the odds. But when counselling 135 students per semester, one didn't get to know one's students. For Maggie though, the session was invigorating. *Sister, sister, you telling me I can't make it?* She didn't need

"

much more motivation than her mother had already provided, but that advising session provided a booster shot. Looking back, Maggie wondered how many students had followed Mrs. Jaworski's guidance and gave in. She certainly wasn't about to.

Most of what she knew about the law came from the cops who hung out at the Term. There was no end of stories of psychotics who needed to be disarmed, random shootings in the projects, and physical violence visited on spouses and kids. But in the cops' quieter moments, their voices softened by a few brews, she heard a more nuanced story. The police were patrolling a society gripped with all manner of afflictions, ranging from narcotics to toxic frustrations owing to poverty and injustice. The law, if it was to do its job, needed to provide an infrastructure that helped people deal with pain, poverty, and addiction.

Maggie had doubled down at UC Juicy, racked up perfect grades, and had three professors singing her praises. All of which was enough to get a transfer to Rutgers in Newark for her junior and senior undergraduate years. With her mind set on law school, she wasted no time. On her first day on the Newark campus she visited the professor in charge of pre-law advising, took careful notes on what courses to take, and learned how to pad one's résumé to look law-school-ready. All of which led her to overload on courses in political science, history, and economics, join the pre-law student association, and start cramming for the LSAT, the law school admission test.

For Maggie, however, undergrad life at Rutgers turned out to be a far cry from the endless parties and hijinks she'd seen in the movies. She found her randomly assigned suitemates to be remarkably shallow and immature, interested primarily in getting drunk on Fridays and Saturdays and talking about it the rest of the week. Having been exposed to drunken college students at the Term for much of her youth, dorm life was not for her. She also felt obliged to spend every other weekend in Rahway checking on her dad's emotional and physical well-being, and trying to keep her promise to her mother that she wouldn't let him become a mope or a drunk.

Her relatively solitary life and single-minded focus on school paid off. She graduated with honors and thought she had scored well enough on the LSATs to have several law schools to choose from. Not so. Her law school advisor had been frank with her about the admission process. Highly ranked law schools would look askance at her because she had begun at a junior college, which to them was a red flag signaling that she lacked the polish and social *je ne sais quoi* that comes from the conventional BA path. Middle-tier schools would be fearful that her undergrad performance might reflect grade inflation and that she would eventually fail the bar exam and hurt their *US News* ranking. She ultimately chose St. Sebastian because it was close to home, cheaper, and seemed to have a less high-pressure vibe than Rutgers.

Once she settled in at St. Sebastian Maggie discovered that she had a talent that set her apart from many of her fellow students. She could write. Fluently and clearly—a product of the many hours spent cloistered in her back booth at the Term keeping a diary of what she observed in the bar. She came by skills to dissect facts crisply, analyze situations incisively, and most important, remember stuff. All of which served her well on law school's four-hour essay exams and cranking out memos and briefs for moot court. To her surprise and immense satisfaction, she found herself in the top ten percent of her first-year class.

But Maggie attributed her success to an even more important factor. Listening to a professor drone on for an hour about the origins of American property law in medieval England on her first day of law school at St. Sebastian, the girl sitting next to her passed a note. "Hi, my name is Jen. If this is what it's going to be like, I'm going to dental school. How 'bout you?" Maggie's involuntary snort/laugh made several heads turn and caused the professor to pause for ten seconds and stare in their direction. The two friends would retell the story, with embellishments, for years to come. Having someone, for the first time since her mother's death, to share the ups, downs, and absurdities of life, especially in law school's anxiety-ridden cocoon, made all the difference.

Fate's arrow, when expected, travels slow.

—Dante Alighieri, *Paradiso*

"Your friend has got her decanal tit caught in a wringer." The raspy voice on the phone was unmistakably Annie Griffin, St. Sebastian's University Provost.

"Say what?" McNeely sputtered. Griff, he knew, was not one to beat around the bush.

"Jesus am I dating myself? I need a new set of colorful expressions. Put her ass in the microwave? Anyway, it's serious and you better let her know it. Balducci is calling in the guardia."

"Griff, what did she do?"

"You teach corporate law. Remember Martha Stewart? What did she do? Saved herself $60K? And who was hurt? Nobody. And she did six months."

"You mean the Dean's involved in insider trading?"

Griff raised her voice an octave to signal coming upon a noteworthy insight. "I used to wonder why law students turn out to be such literal-minded dweebs when they become lawyers. You must teach a course in it. You know better than anyone what the fuck Martha did! *She lied!* Worst crime of all: she lied to federal prosecutors. And she did jail time. Same deal with lying to your University President and your board of directors." The provost paused, and McNeely was pretty sure the sound he heard was Griff taking a hit on her cigar.

"And in Father Balducci's cosmology, lying about money triples the offense. Your Dean is on her way to the Fifth Circle. Right next to Pope Nicolas III." Griff had taught Dante for fifteen years before she became provost.

Round, loud, and exuberant, Griff wore large mumus reminiscent of Mama Cass and wielded vast authority over university academic affairs as provost. She was careful however to remain circumspect regarding the three items that mattered most to President Balducci: fund raising, real estate, and basketball. She drove a

2009 Ford pickup to Baytown from her co-op in Brooklyn, arriving on campus at 6 a.m. every morning. Never seen accompanied by a male and rumored to having been in a convent before getting her Ph.D. from Yale, most assumed she was a lesbian. In reality, her only partners were the 12,000 St. Sebastian University students hoping to improve their lives.

The news that his Dean had misled the University President didn't entirely shock McNeely. Deborah Eckstein had not become the second youngest woman law school dean in the country, not to mention the first Jewish woman dean of a Jesuit law school, by being timid. When the faculty first interviewed her for the deanship, she announced that she firmly believed what they needed was a real advocate, a fighter. To get the recognition, funding, travel money, that a gifted faculty like SSLAW's so richly deserved. "Someone willing to take on the cocksuckers and bloodsuckers in the University hierarchy." She had them at cocksuckers.

McNeely guessed the President's current gripe concerned the size of the entering class, which constituted the sum of his interest in the law school. Add an extra thirty students at $44,000 tuition per year, plus fees, times three (years—if they last that long), and you're talking real money. Some big money was left on the table when enrollment lagged. All at a time when Father Balducci was dealing with some highly problematic issues: investigations by the Federal government into the Medical School's billing practices, forced expansion of the women's sports program under Title X, an alumni base demanding a top 25 basketball ranking, to name a few.

On the other side of the ledger was the effect of admission decisions on the law school. Those extra thirty law students carried a poison pill: low LSATs and GPAs and the statistical certainty that many of them will flunk the bar exam. Which would be an anchor that will drag St. Sebastian School of Law down ten slots in the *U.S. News and World Report* Ranking of Law Schools. Followed in two years' time, as night follows day, by a worsening pool of applicants and St. Sebastian entering the inescapable vortex that traps declining law schools.

Responding to Griff's warning, McNeely fished for a lifeline. "OK, I'll look into it. It's pretty serious though, I take it? Any escape route?"

"Well, in fact she may be able to buy herself a plenary indulgence," she offered.

McNeely looking at the ceiling, as if willing a spiritual intercession. "How?"

"Father B has been talking to a prospective donor who wants to . . . and these are his words . . . invest in something that will *maximize consumer welfare*. Some kind of institute to be housed at the law school. Endowed professorships, annual operating funds, scholarships for students, faculty research money."

McNeely knew better than to see the glass as half full. "I'm guessing there's something distasteful floating in the punchbowl?"

"I'll let Father explain it to you. He also said no need to get the Dean involved at this early stage. He wants to talk to you because it's something that *you corporate guys* will understand. His words again, not mine."

Griff paused and seemed to be choosing her words carefully. "You know, as some men grow older, they become obsessed . . . let me rephrase that . . . they become more and more concerned . . . about leaving a mark. Erecting a monument with their name on it. Starting a new something or other that they'll be remembered for. That often leads them to wind up with some inappropriate bedfellows. I think of that line at the beginning of *The Inferno*, 'the straight road has been lost sight of.' You know, sometimes I think that miserable creature in the White House was sent here to display all the human foibles we need to watch out for. Anyway, should be an interesting meeting for you with *our* President. *Buono fortuna.*"

McNeely hung up, puzzled by Griff's parting words. Some of these career academics, he had learned, spoke obliquely, as if their words contained a parable to be unraveled. Maybe she thinks she's like the guide who showed Dante around the underworld. Whoever that was.

He stared glumly at the row of files neatly arranged by his assistant on his dark mahogany conference table. Each manila folder overlay another one and he drifted back twenty years. The triangular pattern of the files reminded him of his first fall months in Cambridge sitting on the banks of the Charles River with his law books watching the sunfish sailboats on the Charles which amazingly were available for free to Harvard students. Contracts cases with words like estoppel and demurrer he would have to look up when he got back to the dorm. He recalled the thrill that made him shudder in those days. How unbelievable, he thought to himself, looking out on the boats, single shells and eight-man crews working their way up and down the river, a place in the Harvard Law class, a ticket to whatever he wanted to do. There just for the asking: show your student ID and they gave you a boat. Never been in a sailboat, but he now had a ticket to just go down and claim one. No one over twenty-five on the shore, an idyll that he never dreamed he'd live to see. Girls he secretly assumed would swoon when they found out who he was, hear his carefully constructed but modestly presented plan to go to Washington and maybe someday run for Congress. Just claim one, like the sailboats. It was a comfort even then to know that he would never look back and say he didn't appreciate what he had then. He couldn't wait to describe it to his grandfather on the phone, and that he was living both their dreams. Maybe take you out sailing when you come up. "Me, shanty Irish on a Harvard sailboat?" his grandfather would say. "That'd be a piece of heaven, laddie boy."

La dolce far niete—the pleasure of doing nothing. On the banks of the Charles.

He can compress the most words into the smallest idea of any man I know.

—Abraham Lincoln, describing a fellow lawyer

McNeely knew a hanging jury when he saw one. Surveying those seated around the wide mahogany conference table in the moot court hearing room where the Ethics Committee conducted proceedings, he saw little hope for the defendant. The three faculty members were carefully chosen, not for their expertise in ethics or adroitness with matters of procedure, but as a last resort. They were a group whose administrative talents and interpersonal gifts—even among the shallow gene pool of law school faculty—disqualified them from any other role in the self-governance of the school. Important, substantive committees like Finance and Resources; Faculty Recruitment; Admissions; and Development (fund-raising) were obviously out of the question. There were only a few alternatives, such as the Library Liaison and the Student Activities committees, where little damage could be inflicted. Most of the three placed on Ethics however, had floundered even in those settings because of their intolerance of staff, students, and anyone without a law degree. The consensus was that Ethics suited this group well. It was a spot where disdain for students was generally considered a plus and an unfamiliarity with the niceties of procedure helped move things along. Two student representatives also sat on the committee. Both had clawed their way up the ladder to the top of their class and were not about to allow anyone to take the elevator. The Ethics Committee heard all charges of cheating and plagiarism and had suspended or dismissed every student appearing before it for six years running.

Waiting for the defendant to arrive, McNeely chanced some small talk with one of the faculty members of the committee. "I hear that Siggy Rosenthal may come and give a talk. Quite a coup."

Ezekiel Adams, leader of the faculty working paper discussion group looked annoyed. This group did little actual work, primarily arranging lunches at which well-known faculty from more prestigious law schools delivered scholarly papers while the St. Sebastian faculty ventured fawning questions while trying to sound erudite.

"Oh, as usual he wants to prattle on about Thing Theory and Property Law. But as to his coming here, it's a bit complicated," an unsmiling Adams answered.

"Oh?"

"Well, Friedlander sat next to him at some Crits conference in Boston and told him about our workshop series and Siggy was interested. But Friedlander, ever the glad hander, tells him, 'Our chair will call you.' Can you fathom that? The guy has no sense of tactics. He doesn't understand what a workshop is all about."

"What do you mean? We want Rosenthal don't we? His piece in the *Harvard Law Review* got more hits on Lexis' webpage than any other article last year . . . except for that cyberporn piece with the pictures."

Adams narrowed his beady eyes and let out an exasperated sigh. "It's one thing to want him to come here. It's another to go crawling to him. I made it clear that Rosenthal has to email me, the chair, and ask to be invited. I can hardly call him. We'd look ridiculous. Workshops are like litigation, Neels. You have to establish up front who's doing whom a favor."

Reasonably confident that Rosenthal hardly knew of St. Sebastian Law School, and absolutely certain that Adams had never set foot in a courtroom, McNeely registered a shot of adrenaline, but resisted the temptation to respond. He surmised that putting the committee chair in an even fouler mood would surely doom the student-defendant.

McNeely had risen to the Associate Deanship based on the simple fact that nobody actively despised him and he seemed capable of handling soul-crushing administrative responsibilities without sending the law school into disarray. He had developed a reputation as a good colleague by smiling and nodding when others spoke and rarely disagreeing with what they said. Most credited him as being bright for apprehending their insights while simultaneously downgrading him for not challenging their bullshit.

Another factor in McNeely's favor was that he was an actual practicing Catholic. Behind his back, some colleagues' chosen nickname for him, "Neels," in their minds was spelled "Kneels." However, it came in handy when they needed someone to show up at the President's Annual Red Mass, meet and greet visiting bishops, or allay concerns of some members of the University Board of Directors that the law school was not dancing to the Vatican Rag, as Tom Lehrer once sang it.

This also meant that McNeely had to serve as the designated flak-catcher on all matters religious. One of his first and most challenging episodes occurred when Father Balducci announced that all University classrooms had to display a crucifix—an edict that sent several of the law school's Jewish faculty into a tizzy. Following a month-long exchange of emails on lessons from visual neuroscience about student learning in the classroom and reminders of the role of Pope Pius during the Nazi regime, McNeely engineered a compromise. The objecting faculty agreed to a four-inch monochrome crucifix containing no disturbing blemishes on the Christ figure while the law school would create a new $5000 fund to establish a Jewish Law collection in the library. McNeely prided himself about knowing a thing or two about the art of the deal.

As is the case for every academic administrative position, a principal qualification for the St. Sebastian Associate Deanship was a thick skin. At first, McNeely felt he was too sensitive, like Billy Martin, the former manager of the Yankees, who it was said could hear someone giving him the finger across the room. "Rabbit ears" was the baseball expression for the overly sensitive. Legend had it that Martin would occasionally take a swing at one of his own players and then duck behind another player before an actual fight could start. Over the years however McNeely had grown the carapace of an armadillo. Carping, whining, and complaining from spoiled faculty colleagues had become just background noise to him. He liked to think he possessed a special strand of Celtic grit passed along in the McNeely DNA for generations.

Fighting as the Boston Bad Boy after World War II, Colin "Colly" McNeely's brief, unsuccessful boxing career spanned four fights and included three knockouts, two of which were not of his doing. His love of the sweet science undiminished, he worked in the ring as a cut man for a variety of fighters in Boston, Brooklyn and Newark—even when he was sweating out ten-hour days in the bowels of the soon-to-be-condemned shipyards of those cities. McNeely ate up his grandfather's stories. Ears flapping loose from their moorings, cuts so deep you could see bone, hurried stitching done in thirty seconds that held the fighter together long enough to deliver a stunning left hook to TKO an arrogant German—to the delight of an Irish crowd on St. Patrick's day, 1938. The old man reveled in telling his grandson the stories, "His trainer cut off his gloves and the crowd carried him out of the ring, straight down to O'Reilly's Taproom. It was something to see. Him drinking a beer with a left eye closed that I stitched up with thread."

The cut man, younger McNeely came to understand, played a pivotal role in a fighter's entourage. Not only did he mend cuts, salve bruises and open the closed eyelids for his fighters, he gave them advice, comfort, and fortitude. Boxers faced unfathomable psychological hurdles. Walk into a 10x10 platform surrounded by drunken yahoos yelling curses at you . . . and seeing across the way a monster with a Cro-Magnon forehead and the biceps of a gorilla. Colly often laughed and yelled back at the TV set when a prissy golf or basketball announcer would talk about the "pressure" those athletes faced. "A guy you've never met before, built like a brick shithouse, meets you in the middle of the ring, taps your gloves and in the first ten seconds hits you in the teeth harder than you've ever been hit. Three times. 'Good morning, chappie,' he says and he smiles. Now *that's* pressure."

Corner men had sixty seconds between each three-minute round to cut through the fog in their fighter's skull and persuade him that, evidence of the last three minutes notwithstanding, his opponent was clearly wearing down or perhaps that the opponent had revealed a vulnerability the corner had just discovered.

As his grandfather told it, fighters would come back to the corner crying, begging to quit. Some would even crap their pants, he claimed—an item swept St. Brigid's schoolyard the day after he first revealed it to his grandson in a bedside chat. Sometimes tough love was in order. "What's your dad gonna to tell his friends at the dock tomorrow?" the cut man would ask his fighter. "You're gonna make a lot of guinea punks on Vesca street who bet against you very happy."

Colly McNeely's bedtime fight tales to his grandson all had happy endings. Kids found courage, will, and stamina and fought with a fury they didn't know they had. And the crowd went crazy. Colly's end was less happy. Three shipyards closed on him, all departing the scene without leaving a trace of his pension payments. He did retain a spot of asbestosis on his lung, which made his last two years a tough go. With McNeely's father dying when he was five and his mother busy working and bringing home a large assortment of assholes, Colly McNeely had supplied the parenting, humor, and discipline with a touch of County Kerry Ireland charm that ultimately helped land his grandson a seat at Harvard Law School. And also prepared him to take on duties not unlike those of a cut man as a law school dean.

The Ethics Committee hearing finally got under way, thirty minutes behind schedule owing to the unapologetic late arrival of one of the faculty judges. Although not a member of the committee, McNeely had final say on all Student

Ethics Committee matters by virtue of his position as Associate Dean. While not required to attend, he usually back benched portions of hearings in order to get a sense of the charges and use his experience as a prosecutor to size up the accused. And the accuser.

The student/defendant arrived accompanied by Professor Wagner, whom McNeely surmised was serving as her appointed counsel. Attired in the standard navy blue, female law student interview suit, white blouse, and sensible shoes—apparel only seen when law firms are conducting interviews—the young woman seemed calm and even threw a wave to Father Fitzgibbon who was seated in the back of the room. Calling the meeting to order was the committee chair, Professor Leland Boylan, whose academic specialty was admiralty law, although his last article on that— or any other subject—was written during the Clinton Administration.

Fumbling with his notes, Boylan began, "OK, let's get started. The committee has before it the matter of . . . Is the audio tape running?"

Student judge Frederick Klein leapt to his feet, quickly circled the make-shift dais of tables set up to give a semblance of a courtroom, and flipped on the recording device.

"Ok, once again, the committee will hear the matter raised by Professor Gleason regarding violations . . . excuse me, *alleged* violations . . . of the Student Honor Code, Section . . ." Several minutes of silence ensued, broken only by the sounds of Reynolds shuffling through a yellow pad, feeling through both breast pockets of his sports jacket, opening his laptop, and signing in twice due to confusion about his passcode.

Student judge Klein again to the rescue, obsequiously handing Reynolds his copy of the Honor Code which was festooned with multi-colored stick-ems. "It's section 103, Professor." Leaning over Reynolds, he flipped open the document and jabbed at a page marked with a crimson tab. "See? Right here."

Reynolds silently read the passage for several seconds and then nodded vigorously, "Ah! Yes, yes. Section 103 provides, *No written work shall . . .* Well, it's a long passage, and I'm sure we've all read it. So, in the interest of getting us all out of here by 4:30, I'll let the complaining witness explain the charge and so forth. OK, OK. Professor Gleason, I believe you have the floor."

Professor Francis X. Gleason had begun teaching at St. Sebastian 20 years before McNeely took his LSATs and was the leader of the senior Catholic contingent of the faculty. His area of expertise was "Legislation and Statutory Interpretation," which focused on questions at the heart of legal analysis that had kept legal scholars busy for two hundred years. What do those damn words mean? Does it matter whether the defendant understood the statute? What did the drafters intend? Does it matter what the words meant 100 years ago? Are judges, mere mortals, able to read the minds of the legislature? Can't we just look at the words of the statute? And where it helps, why not just consult the OED? For Gleason, it boiled down to a simple proposition. The law, as written, is the law.

Gleason had the looks of a 1940's movie star. Six foot two, broad shoulders, sporting an immaculately groomed head of silver hair, and dressed in a dark pin striped suit complete with a white pocket square, he cast an imposing image. His voice was deep and when speaking in class or faculty meetings often had a reso-nance just short of a shout. He rose slowly, proceeded deliberately to the lectern, and looked in the eyes of each judge before beginning:

"Ladies and gentlemen, it's my unfortunate duty to call to your attention what I believe is a serious violation of our honor code. A violation of one of the fundamen-tal rules of our beloved institution. A violation that bespeaks unfitness to enter into the practice of law—a profession that we all know requires complete, constant, and enduring honesty. A 'punctilio of honor the most sensitive,' as Judge Cardozo once put it. A profession that requires the highest standards of conduct. Moreover, as a Jesuit institution, we at Saint Sebastian have long held ourselves to an even higher standard. One that our Lord and Savior made clear when he told us to 'put away falsehood.' The word 'truth' appears hundreds of times in the New Testament. Or for those who prefer to consult the Old Testament, *whoever walks in integrity walks securely but whoever takes a crooked path will be found out.* Proverbs 10:9."

McNeely stole a glance at Father Fitzgibbon who was sitting at the back of the room. He had a look that McNeely hadn't seen before. In place of his customary avuncular smile was a steely stare, pursed lips, and reddening cheeks.

Gleason paused for a full thirty seconds, scanning the judges' faces again. Then with a flourish he held up the remote device and activated PowerPoint slides on two large screens. "Alright, let's get down to the facts and examine the conduct at issue before this tribunal."

Displayed side by side were two documents. The left screen bore the title *Abortion Conundrums: Will Roe Survive the Trump Administration?* by Professor Hilda Sessions, 43 Hofstra Law Rev. 125. The right side screen also displayed a title: *Anti-abortion Legislation: Does Science Support the Remedy?* Student Seminar Paper First Draft, Margaret Holloran.

Under each title was some text, mostly case citations, with portions high-lighted, blue on the left side, red on the right side. Both highlighted segments had five footnotes cited in traditional law school blue book fashion. The highlighted passages were identical.

For the next several minutes, Gleason proceeded to read each case name, its citation, from the left panel and then slowly recited the identical passage high-lighted in red. As he reached the end of each citation, he announced in a loud sten-torian voice, "*Identical! Res Ipsa Loquitor.*"

Not content to allow the thing to speak for itself, Gleason went on to offer some color commentary. "Let me point out a few of the telltale aspects of these two documents. Notice that in the *Hofstra Law Review*, the author, Professor Sessions, deviated slightly from what I'm sure you students all remember to be standard *Harvard Blue Book* citation form . . ."

Pausing with a chuckle to look at the student judges, "Didn't think you'd ever see the Bluebook form pop up as probative evidence in a trial when you were grinding through Legal Research and Writing as a 1L did you?" Pivoting his head in search of a smile, he was obliged by Mr. Klein who added a conspiratorial nod of his head. "Well, when I looked at the two documents, I said to myself, 'there's some-thing else peculiar here in the state of Denmark.'"

Grabbing a laser pointer, he aimed it at the screen. "Notice if you will, that both documents cite a case, American Medical Association versus Federal Trade Commission. *Note bene*—that's Latin for 'note well'—*BOTH* abbreviate the word 'Association' to A-S-S-O-C. Well, now let's see what the Blue Book has to say about that abbreviation." Gleeson advanced to a new slide displaying a page from the Harvard Blue Book, the definitive manual governing citation form in legal writing.

"As you can see, the correct Harvard Blue Book abbreviation for the word 'Asso-ciation' is A-S-S-Apostrophe-N." Gleason's voice rising, "*AND NOT* A-S-S-O-C!"

Pausing for a beat, Gleason gave a rueful smile. "SO, it appears that Professor Sessions, in the Hofstra Law Review got it wrong, and her editors failed to spot it." Lifting his voice to a shout, he went on, "*AND SO DID MS. HOLLORAN* when she *LIFTED THIS CITATION* and inserted it in her draft seminar paper!"

Another twenty-second pause ensued with Gleason's head rotating as he sur-veyed the judges and student judge Klein scribbling furiously in his notepad.

All of which proved too much for McNeely. Guessing that another ninety min-utes of faux courtroom drama lay ahead that might push his blood pressure past the threshold his doctor had cautioned about, he decided to slip out through the back exit. He knew he would get a transcript and recording of the hearing when the student appealed the committee's inevitable verdict.

10

Sure the fight was fixed. I fixed it with a right hand.

—George Foreman, Heavyweight Champion

McNeely knew the meeting with Father B was not going to be pleasant. Griff had made it clear that Balducci's longstanding distain for the Dean had metastasized. Under the President's oncology, that required one remedy: full resection—of Dean Eckstein. Which would mean McNeely would become "Interim Dean" until a suitably compliant replacement could be found. From what he had seen in his three years as associate dean, assuming the role of . . . *interim, acting, pretend, fugazi, Dean sans portfolio?* . . . would be hell on earth. Not to mention that it would empower Father B to shape the law school to meet his vision of what legal education should be. Which, in turn, meant advancing the good Father's personal agendas. Of which there were several.

Sitting in the outer office of the President's executive suite, McNeely felt the familiar rush of adrenaline that he had often experienced as a federal prosecutor. He reminded himself that this was not his first inquisition. His initiation as a federal prosecutor in the SAC Capital case had indelibly shaped his outlook on the world. Working thirteen-hour days on the investigation as an Assistant US Attorney in the Southern District of New York, McNeely felt something akin to a religious calling. Here he was, two and a half years out of law school, going after the largest, and surely most corrupt, hedge fund on Wall Street. SAC Capital bought and sold stock using a rapid-fire buy and sell strategy that accounted for trading 100 million shares daily, nearly two percent of the nation's overall stock activity on a given day. Its owner, Steven Cohen, was legendary for his stock picking acumen. And for much else, it turned out.

The fact that Cohen was able to post returns of over 30% per year for more than decade should have raised some eyebrows. But in the heady days of worshipping the superheroes of finance in the 1990s, anything seemed possible. Of course, most of the Wall Street cognoscenti knew one true thing: the only fuel capable of powering such success was information. Information about pending mergers, pharmaceutical breakthroughs, government contracts, and, best of all, pending corporate disasters. And, most important, it needed to be information that no one else had which gave traders an advantage, sometimes called a "black edge." If you picked up financially significant information—good or bad—about a publicly traded corporation before anyone else you were going to make some money. If you got that information improperly, your edge was "black" not just because it put you in the black, but because, as everyone knew, trading on material inside information is a federal crime and could subject you to huge fines and imprisonment. Prominent lions of Wall Street like Raj Gupta, Michal Milken, Raj Rajaratnam, wound up doing serious jail time for violating the infamous commands of SEC Rule 10b-5: "It shall be unlawful to employ any device, scheme or artifice to defraud."

Despite a near consensus that something fishy was going on, Cohen's investment winning streak went unchallenged for at least a dozen years. SAC had something on the traders of Wall Street that bought their silence. SAC Capital's trading—100 million shares per day—produced huge brokerage revenues for the old guard, like Morgan Stanley and Goldman Sachs, who executed those transactions. SAC's specialty, short-selling ("shorting") stocks—placing bets that a stock will fall—was especially profitable because before the explosion of hedge funds shorting it was both risky, and in the view of the old lions on the Street, it was more than a tad unseemly to profit on failure. Stevie (a nickname he hated) Cohen had no such compunctions. Nor it turned out did he blanche at violating federal and state insider trading laws—or so it appeared to McNeely's boss, the US Attorney for the Southern District of New York, Preet Bharara. Bharara had secured more than 70 insider trading convictions or guilty pleas without losing a single case. And going after the big guys on Wall Street was a politically popular cause in the aftermath of the 2008 financial crisis, which many perceived as an episode in which the real culprits—banks and investment firms—got bailouts rather than jail terms.

McNeely was assigned as a junior member of the "Martoma team" on Bharara's investigation of SAC Capital. Mathew Martoma was viewed as the one person who could link the bad acts going on at SAC to Cohen personally. Without some evidence of what the law calls "scienter"—knowing involvement in illegal activity—individuals cannot be criminally prosecuted. Implausible as it may seem that a bottom-line-focused control freak would not know the details of the trading on insider information that was making his fortune, McNeely's supervisors feared a jury just might buy it as a defense. In fact, Cohen's relentless and often cruel handling of SAC personnel could work to his advantage. Skillful defense trial lawyers might persuade a jury that his *in terrorem* management drove his terrorized crew to flout the law in order to satisfy a hard-driving boss, but that they did it on their own. Cohen could claim ignorance of the wrongdoing of his rabid subordinates. Perhaps most exasperating to prosecutors was how blatant Cohen's naked ambition was. He made no secret of his contempt for those playing by the rules, and proudly displayed in his offices Damien Hirst's *The Physical Impossibility of Death in the Mind of Someone Living*—a giant shark floating in formaldehyde.

McNeely came on some four years into what would be an 11-year investigation. Cohen had hired Martoma because he knew people—useful people to know such as academic physicians involved in pharmaceutical research who could provide advance notice of the results of clinical trials and the likelihood of government approvals of new drugs. As every securities trader can attest, modern medicine has yet to discover a pharmaceutical stimulant as fast-acting or potent as the effect on the stock market of a tip about a new drug clearing an FDA hurdle has on the stock market.

The Martoma team knew they had their man dead to rights and were confident he would "flip"—i.e., supply the testimony they needed to nail Cohen. Wiretaps had revealed that he had befriended Dr. Sidney Gilman, an elderly professor at the University of Michigan Medical School who served as chair of a committee overseeing the clinical trial of a potential breakthrough drug for treating patients with Alzheimer's. Martoma hired Gilman for SAC as an industry expert to provide scientific consultations for SAC. According to documents signed by Gilman, he was to "hold in strict confidence all information he learned in connection with his participation in the Alzheimer clinical trial." Which he did not.

Initially, Gilman's secret information seemed to point to a major pharmaceutical breakthrough. The two drug companies sponsoring the trial, Elan and Wyeth, looked to be on the verge of getting FDA approval for a drug that could generate revenues exceeding $30 billion. Unaware of the purloined information, no one at SAC understood how Martoma had persuaded Cohen to approve investing an unprecedented amount of money in Elan and Wyeth. Senior health care experts at SAC repeatedly questioned these "long positions" arguing there was no public evidence to support taking on enormous risks. It proved the skeptics were right. The results of the FDA's Phase II clinical trials were not favorable, and Dr. Gilman prepared a PowerPoint slide presentation to make public the negative results. At which he gave Martoma an advance peek. Whereupon SAC responded not only by selling all of its positions in Elan and Wyeth, but also by taking enormous short positions so as to profit on the impending crash in those stocks. Which of course it did.

The SAC/Cohen case did not end well, at least from McNeely's perspective. True, SAC paid a record $1.8 billion fine, Cohen was banned from trading on behalf of outside investors for two years, and Martoma got a 9-year prison sentence. US Attorney Preet Bharara claimed an historic victory. But to McNeely's bitter disappointment, little Stevie Cohen himself was never charged. He was allowed to trade on his family fortune's account which had some $10 billion left over after all was said and done. Martoma stubbornly refused to flip, despite overwhelming evidence that there was no way SAC's huge initial investment and sudden reversal to short the stock and to make hundreds of millions could have occurred without micro-manager Cohen knowing exactly why such huge trades were being made. For McNeely and most other prosecutors, taking gargantuan positions that could jeopardize SAC's very existence was inconceivable without the elixir of inside information. Or without Cohen's approval. But under the civil settlement, Cohen escaped criminal prosecution and was allowed to continue to trade his own fund. And now he was rumored to be in the market to add the New York Mets to his other collectibles.

McNeely emerged with several hard-earned lessons from his time on the SAC case. Much of what went on in Wall Street involved fraud, deceit, and dirty money. Law is mostly ineffectual in deterring financial crime. The hierarchy of the Department of Justice was more concerned with their won/loss record than sending a message to the bad guys on the Street. Landing one or two big fish seemed to have no effect on the feeding patterns of the rest of the school. The giant sharks knew how to protect themselves. Proving scienter—that the guys at the top knew what was going on—required concrete evidence that wasn't often going to be available. At bottom, systemic reform was needed. As for him personally: Better to be a law professor who could shout from the rooftops than remaining a prosecutor chasing his own tail.

A young assistant interrupted his reminiscences. "Father Balducci will see you now." McNeely rose and walked briskly into a surprisingly darkened office.

An unsmiling President Balducci did not move from his seat behind a massive rosewood desk. A warm glow reflecting off his well-tanned olive pate, he silently pointed a manicured index finger to a leather wing chair and followed his visitor with a steely stare as he crossed the room.

11

Women must learn to play the game as men do.

—Eleanor Roosevelt

The hearing went even worse than she'd dreamed. Not since her abortion had Maggie felt so down. And alone. And abused. She had spent three hours listening to that pontificating ass, reading the "smoking gun" again and again. Restating the obvious. It was lifted. Five footnotes. 323 words. A cut-and-paste job.

To prepare for her upcoming appeal before the Associate Dean, she decided to do what any good lawyer would do: draw up a legal outline of the facts and law. Sitting down with her laptop, she set out the salient elements of the case as a disinterested lawyer would. First, she bullet-pointed the components of her alleged crime and their legal implications.

- Exact match of her footnotes and those in the law review article. *Actus reus.*
- Testimony from her first-year legal research and writing teacher: "Yes, we do teach again and again that it is a violation of the honor code, and indeed is against professional standards, to plagiarize." *Mens rea.*
- Professor Gleason's account: "She flatly denied it when I confronted her." *Concealment.*
- Her angry exit from the professor's office, obscenities shouted at Professor Gleason. *Lack of remorse.*

Turning to her defense, she recalled from her Civil Procedure class that the law allows "pleading in the alternative," i.e., arguing inconsistent defenses. She bullet pointed three plausible justifications.

- Didn't understand that plagiarism applied to footnotes.
- Total accident, had cut and pasted text for her research notes, and it got transferred accidentally to her paper.
- Meant to go back and fix the downloaded notes but ran out of time.

All good arguments. Might get her off with a one-semester suspension, her counsel had advised. Unfortunately, all three were untrue. Nicki Minaj, *Bed of Lies* now playing in her mind.

Maggie had resolved that in her meeting with the Associate Dean, who would decide what penalty to impose, she would present a full and truthful account of what she was thinking when she wrote her paper. But as she mulled over her alternatives, things seemed hopeless. Truth? Which was what? I was in a rush, didn't give it much thought, but felt I had to rush because, well, there was this . . . family crisis? Personal issues? Long standing responsibility for someone? But I will not mention the condition of my father that day, or of the memorial service for my brother. Not gonna put on a pity-the-poor-working-girl plea for mercy. Taylor Swift now supplying the background music, *I'm gonna shake, shake, shake, shake it off.* Father Fitz was a good character witness. Sweet old guy. Guess it can't hurt to have him on my side. Maybe his word will play well with the Associate Dean when he decides my fate.

Maggie knew better than to let herself spiral down a rabbit hole of remorse. Taylor reappearing, *No one notices till it's too late to do anything.* She had some immediate problems she had to address in the next few hours that would serve as a welcome distraction: extracting her father from the bar, checking the cash and credit card receipts for the day, and supervising a rookie waitress trying to handle a loud, drunk, and horny NCAA Playoff crowd.

Although it took several years after the downturn following her mother's death, the Terminal Bar had righted itself. Maggie soon learned the hard way that she needed to take over the bookkeeping and perhaps much more. Her mother had always kept careful track of inventory, cash flow, bills, credit card accounts, and taxes. As the first Tax Day since Norma's death approached Maggie asked her father whether he'd sent the paperwork to their accountant yet. His evasive reply sent her scrambling to what passed for an office in the back of the bar, where she found a file folder with a hand scribbled word "tax" on the tab. It consisted of an unorganized stash of hundreds of receipts, pay stubs, credit card reports, and indecipherable handwritten notes.

Channeling latent CPA skills she never knew she had, Maggie spent two weeks sorting through the chaos and walking the Term's accountant through a maze of crumpled, soiled paper records and receipts. She also instituted a rigorous regime of protocols and back-ups governing all financial matters at the Term going forward and took command of operations, supervising the bar staff, hiring a reliable cook to handle the food and manage the kitchen, and watching every cash-out at the end of the day. Maggie added "Terminal Bar COO" to the CFO on her imaginary corporate titles, both of which she hoped would only be temporary. But she did have the satisfaction of seeing her efforts pay off. A steady flow of commuters during the week, big money on major game nights, especially the big three: Halloween, St. Paddy's Day, and New Year's Eve, and a growing crowd of hipsters and joe-colleges for whom The Term was actually becoming a destination on weekends.

What wasn't going so well was her father's mental state. He wanted to hang around the bar in the evenings, and after ten years on the wagon had begun drinking again. He had promised that his last drink would be at Norma's wake. An Irish wake is an iconically festive, celebratory event, and Maggie felt her dad throwing down a few Jamies couldn't hurt. She fondly recalled how alive he seemed hosting the event at The Term that night, as he recounted for the crowd how he and Norma first met at a pool hall in Hackensack.

Rising to the occasion, Michael ("Holler'n Mickey") Holloran stood on a bar stool and painted the scene of their romance for the smiling, teary-eyed audience, "She comes in to Hack's Racks, yelling her head off looking for her kid brother. Finds him and threatens to beat the shit out of him when he got home. So she grabs the six-foot-two, 240-pound lummox by the collar and marches him out like a first grader. The pool hall breaks out in applause and she's out the door with him, still holding his collar. So, let me tell you something. You all know I'm not one to believe in omens or signs, or that kind of crap, but it was kind of like what the kids call karma."

Pausing for a sip of his Irish, Mickey went on, "She's gone, I'm going back to my game, and what do I see? She's left her sweater on the pool table. So I grab it and I'm moving like I'm Ricky Henderson on greenies. She's already in her car, pulling away. So I jumps in front of the car waving her sweater like a banshee. She slams on the brakes, rolls down the window, sticks her head out, and looks at me with her big brown eyes and says, 'You're precisely why I don't need him hanging around this dive.' But she's smiling. And that was it. I knew right then and there. Me falling for an Eye-talian!"

But at home Maggie had begun to notice some disturbing things. She had seen him repeat the exact same story twice within ten minutes, forget to zip up a dozen times, and call her Norma. She knew going home alone to that three-bedroom split level spelled trouble. Her empty bedroom, still decorated with the New Yorker cover pages on the walls and the life-size poster of Prince. And Jimmy's shrine, his football shirt, track medals and the army commendations. He was nine years older, and her idol and protector growing up. She didn't know until long after he died about his drug busts and escape by enlisting in the army, his volunteering for assignment to the Third Infantry Division in Iraq, or his convoy tripping a roadside IED in Afghanistan. Maggie had disciplined herself never again to go into his room, but on several occasions found her father there, sitting on the bed and staring at Jimmy's memorabilia. For her it elicited a second dose of fury about fucking George Bush and the limp-dick males who sent her brother out to die in the desert.

As it turned out, The Term proved to be her dad's refuge, a place where he could hang out with his pals and his verbal slip ups would go unnoticed. There were regulars from all parts of town who were like family. Pillars of the community, aldermen, and state reps. Cops, gamblers and hookers that balanced each other out at the bar—and sometimes did some business with each other. Someone for her dad to talk to when there's no one back at home. The place now seemed to her like a living diorama, with the bar, the kitchen, the Formica tables, and her private booth in the back bringing back warm memories of her family history.

Maggie's mother, Norma, had engineered the Term's transition from hole-in-the-wall train station bar to a somewhat more upscale spot. The biggest move was food service. When the video rental store next door closed, she negotiated a five-year lease, installed a full kitchen got some discount tables, chairs and equipment from an alleged fire sale, and voila, the Term served lunch and dinner. Norma was second generation *Napolitana* who not only knew her way around the kitchen, but could navigate expertly the produce and meat markets of greater Rahway. What her father called, "mom's hobby" soon started bringing in customers who were not there just to nurse a Jack for two hours and watch a game. They ate, they drank, and price didn't seem to matter.

With those upgrades came added bookkeeping, purchasing, hiring, firing, and most of all, watching everything and everybody like a hawk. Norma had carried that load for 20 years, even showing up after chemo treatments, accompanied by hysterical shouts and curses from Mickey. After her mother's death, Maggie's elevation to CEO, CFO, maître d', and fill-in bartender at the Term took a toll on her social life. She moved out of the dorm late in her senior year at Rutgers and reclaimed her small bedroom in her father's house. Rather than rue her changed circumstances, she proudly announced her career path on Snapchat and Instagram. *Future public interest lawyer now running Yelp's third-ranked dive bar in North Jersey.*

Now if only she could somehow avoid having it all snatched away.

12

People should either be caressed or crushed. If you do them minor damage they will get their revenge; but if you cripple them there is nothing they can do.

—Niccolò Machiavelli

Father Balducci's office was sumptuous: deep crimson walls, mahogany cases filled with books with gleaming golden binders, thick cut pile carpeting, and indirect lighting casting a warm glow around the room. But the eye-catching feature that stunned every visitor was a life-sized six foot painting of Saint Sebastian. Arms bound behind him and pierced by a half dozen arrows, the young man was gazing upwards with a look of quiet expectation—though some suggested it was curiosity about whether and when the Big Guy was going to intervene. Father B always dodged inquiries about the painter and was quick to brush aside suggestions that it made an expensive hit on the University endowment. "Just a local *pittore* I came across in Genoa. Not quite the Saint Sebastian of Rubens or Botticelli," he would say, "but that face does show the *carragio* that we like to think inspires our little community here in New Jersey."

There was no such exchange of pleasantries with McNeely. After a long pause, Father B said icily, "You're looking at one unhappy Jesuit."

McNeely summoned up a concerned, furrowed brow, "Very sorry to hear that, Father. What can I do to help?"

"First of all you can make sure your dean is reporting accurate data to me when she submits her budget. The law school has come in way, way under the enrollment numbers I was promised."

"Well, Father, as you know, we're in an awfully competitive market for law schools. The New York/ New Jersey area has at least six other . . ."

"Yeah. Yeah. We know all that. And the reason you're losing students to Fordham and Rutgers reveals another broken promise."

"I'm sure the dean didn't mean to say that we'd get . . ."

"She told me she'd have the law school in the top 50 in three years. And what do I see in *US News and World Report*? *97th place!*"

"Well, as I'm sure the dean has told you, the methodology *US News* uses to rank law schools is a completely inaccurate gauge of . . ."

"We're behind Cardozo, Saint Johns and Seton Hall for God's sake! You're behind the University of fucking Arkansas! *Arkansas!*" Father Balducci looking over to the portrait of St. Sebastian for solace.

"We've hired a new director of admissions and right now Dean Eckstein is on a five-state trip . . ."

Father B threw up both palms as a stop sign. "Having pricey dinners with alums who don't give enough annually to cover the fucking dinners, let alone bear some part of our financial burdens. Look, I've been very patient, but my message is this: there's no shortage of capable lawyers around here who'd be happy to take on the deanship. And these are the kind of guys who would be able to crack a whip. Herd your fucking cats. *Capisce?*"

McNeely eager to catalogue the law school's long-term planning, "Yes, Father. We're committed to raising the profile of the law school, and to that end, we're undertaking . . ."

Father B's jowls sagged, giving him a look that reminded McNeely of Paul Sorvino in *Goodfellas*. "Well, it turns out, I've got an *undertaking* for you. I've been in negotiations with some very connected finance guys from the city. They're on the board of the Sanus Society. Heard of it?"

"Yes Father, I understand it's an institute funding conservative causes around the country."

"Well, as they've explained to me, they're interested in promoting business opportunities where it's most needed. That is, in places like ours. To do that, they want to fund a "Law, Health and Business Institute" at Saint Sebastian. We're talking about a very big chunk of money, probably a building down the road, student schol- arships."

Father B paused and his face pushed out a tight smile, "and maybe an endowed professorship."

McNeely knew a return smile was expected. Fighting off a rush of hot bile, he obliged.

"Thought that'd get your attention," Father B continued with a self-satisfied nod. Reaching to a shelf behind him, he pulled out a three-inch thick binder and handed it to McNeely. The cover displayed an artist's colorful rendering of a chic office building bearing the name "The Sanus Institute for Law, Health and Business."

"You'll notice they have provided a curriculum outline and possible student internship programs with some of the sponsors' corporate counsel. And they've promised to bring in foreign lawyers to get LL.M degrees. Not to mention an annual symposium. In Florence."

McNeely was genuinely puzzled. "How did it happen that they came to us?"

"I play squash now and then with one of them at the Metropolitan Club. He made the point that St. Sebastian is located at the epicenter of the biggest growth industry in the nation. Pharmaceuticals. We've got more Big Pharma in North Jersey than the rest of the planet. And, our benefactors say, it's an industry under attack. Needs good lawyers. And smarter judges. And less interference from Washington."

McNeely nervously cleared his throat and said, "Well, we will have to look carefully at it. Assess the financial implications. Get faculty buy-in if there are new teaching needs. Lot to consider, but I'm sure it will get our full attention."

Father Balducci casting a malevolent look, his voice quavering, "They're talking a $30 million endowment! That should garner your *full attention*. Plus, that feature of bringing in foreign students is nice. The Chinese government pays full tuition, God bless them. Welcome change from you guys giving away scholarships to anyone with a pulse."

McNeely now figuratively prostrate. "Well, again, Father, the highly competitive law school environment requires us to match or beat other scholarship offers . . ."

"Sure, sure. But this is a way to put St. Sebastian *into the game.* The sponsors told me they don't want to waste their money and commitment on the Columbias and NYUs of the world. They feel they'll just piss their money away trashing the American free enterprise system."

He's Don Fanucci, thought McNeely. Always wants to wet his beak.

Father B saw McNeely's jaw tighten and decided to pump the brakes. Lowering his voice to the soft tones of a sommelier offering a good Barolo, "Look, I know you're in a tough spot, and I really think this is a life raft. I don't want to be one of those interventionist presidents, meddling in the law school's affairs."

McNeely fought to retain his composure as the memory of the President's long history of meddling flashed by. Like the time during graduation week when he angrily emailed Dean Eckstein because the balloons decorating the law school lobby were not the correct shade of magenta to match the University's school colors.

Suddenly breaking out a bright toothy smile, Father B opened his gift bag. "But when I can facilitate a deal that serves everyone's interest, well, that's what they pay me the big bucks for, ha ha."

While the priestly vow of poverty meant a modest salary, most of which the President had to turn over to the Jesuit order, McNeely knew there was other compensation for a worldly President. Squash at the Metropolitan Club. Dinners in Manhattan. Summers in Rome. Not exactly what Pope Francis, himself a frugal, modest Jesuit, was looking for in a Bishop.

But McNeely knew now was the time he had to do what every dean must do: *Eat shit and smile.* "OK, Father. Going to get right on it. Will clear away my agenda immediately."

"Great. You've got a lot on your plate. Unruly faculties. And I know the old joke: 'Deans eventually lose their faculties.' And the students these days! Most need a dose of tough love. Teach them some discipline. And I trust you will clean up this cheating stuff. Not something we tolerate at a Jesuit law school."

McNeely was stunned. How in the world, he wondered, did the President get wind of a law school plagiarism case? A minor event in the larger scheme of things for the university, and not over yet, the hearing having just been completed. Not the stuff a University President gets into. Important not to rise to the bait, he reminded himself. His many hours at Atlantic City's poker tables had taught him how to take a bad flop: Equanimity wins. "Well, we've got a lot going on, that's for sure. Thank you, Father. I'll get back to you next week."

Walking back to the law school, McNeely reviewed the steaming pile of problems on his plate. And tried to erase from his memory the spectacle of his own fawning, gutless performance.

13

This game is rigged man. We like the little bitches on the chess board.

—Bodie, *The Wire*

How'd it go? J
Shit show. I be gone. M
TSIF!!!!! U round tnite? J
Tending at the Term. Come. M
K. I have a plan. J
Me too. Brazil. M
Come on girl! We can take down Geekson. J
I wish! CU. M

Jenna Battaglini arrived at the Term and was surprised to see Maggie hunched over the bar reading a law school casebook. "Thought you were through with law school?"

"Oh, I'm done for, no doubt. But not going to get called on in my last couple of classes looking like someone who had to cheat. Going out in style."

"Styl'n! For sure. But let's talk about finding you an escape route."

Grabbing a bottle of Patron and two shot glasses, Maggie pointed to her customary booth at the back of the bar. "Let's adjourn to my office."

Jen slid into the booth, frowning and worried, "So what the fuck happened?"

"I'm pissed beyond words. Gleason recites the footnotes I copied about five times, starts pontificating about honor, duty, and the St. Sebastian Way. And that little prick, Freddy Klein! Wearing a bow tie for fuck's sake! Playing courtroom lawyer. *'Ms. Holloran, isn't it true that you knew exactly what you were doing? Are you going to have us believe that this kind of conduct won't repeat itself if— somehow — you do become a member of the bar? Do you have any remorse about what you did?'"*

"So what did you tell them?"

"The truth. That I'd spent five weeks tracking down the legislative history of every major state anti-abortion statute. Read all the bogus science they were spreading. Then researched their alleged "science." Almost all total, unequivocal, steaming bullshit. Like laws saying stuff like '*doctors who perform abortions in their own clinics must have staff privileges to admit patients to hospitals. If something goes wrong, the doctor must be sure the woman can get access to a hospital.*' Total crap! Hasn't been a hospitalization for an abortion patient in most states for years. In any event, hospitals are required by law to take patients in emergency conditions."

Maggie paused and downed her second Patron. Pointing the bottle at Jenna, she went on, "And doctors can't get admitting privileges on hospital staffs anyway. You know why?"

"Give up. Why?"

"Because they perform abortions!! Hospitals justify this by saying they have to deny admitting privileges to doctors who don't have a history of *good standing on hospital staff*s. Know why these doctors don't have that history of *good standing?*"

"I think I know the answer to this one, Professor."

Maggie too wound up to let Jenny answer: "Because no hospital will give them staff privileges!"

"After all you went through, living it firsthand, why did you write a paper on abortion in the first place?"

"Just had to. Too many teenagers who couldn't navigate the system like I did. *Babies having babies* as Jesse Jackson used to say. Is he still alive? Anyway, it's more satisfying to write about something you believe in."

Maggie now rising half out of the booth and pointing at an imaginary Supreme Court justice at the Term's bar. "And the cases!! You need to read what these pious hypocrites say and do in the abortion cases. There's this Supreme Court case, Gonzales v. Carhart, and that blowhard Justice Kennedy says, out of nowhere, 'you know, many women will come to regret having abortions.' No evidence, no footnotes, no citations for that piece of wisdom. It's just what this decrepit 80-year-old white guy thinks. What *he thinks he knows* about women. Justice Ginsburg tried to set the record straight. So now, the US Supreme Court is on its way to doing exactly what it did during the Jim Crow era. And they're putting that lame-ass frat boy and wannabe rapist Kavanagh on the Supreme Court! _He_'s going to tell women how they should comport themselves? It's gotten so crazy I'm about to . . ."

Jenny offering the "relax" signal with a gentle wave of her hand, "OK, OK, but let's look ahead. I've got some ideas about your problem."

Trying to disguise her skepticism, Maggie poured another round of Patron, and hoisted the shot glass for a toast, "Ok, who are you? Emma Chamberlain? Have at it."

"OK, I know this is the oldest one in the books, right out of one of those old black and white movies. Seduce the old bastard!"

"Say what? You're cut off." Maggie sliding the bottle out of reach to the far corner of the table. "No mas, hermana!"

"No, no. You don't fuck him. You just trap him into hitting on you. Then, the itsy-bitsy spider . . ."

"I just had dinner, and this may just get me throwing up in my mouth."

"Look, just ask for a meeting, dress provocatively. You know how. You told me you do it on Friday nights to boost your tips. And get him talking. About how it was when he was in law school. How he must have been the hottest of the hot shits at Yale. Top of his class. Stroke that boy's undernourished id."

"OK, best case. He falls for it. What do I do then?"

"First, get your sweet ass out of his office quickly. Then go see Professor McNeely."

"Why him?"

"Well as Associate Dean, he makes the final call on your punishment, and working as his research assistant, I got to know him pretty well. He wishes he was still prosecuting white collar criminals. He'll castrate the bastard."

Maggie shaking her head, "No way. It's just my word against Gleason's. He'll deny it. Slutty girl who works in a dive bar, came on to me to get out of trouble, Yada yada . . ."

"OK, we're going to practice. This course is called Cell Phone 101. I think you have one of these?" With that, Jenna pulled her iPhone out from her backpack, pressed the screen, and their entire tequila comfort session played back, clear as a bell.

14

Money won is twice as sweet as money earned.

—Paul Newman, *The Color of Money*

Bucky was not one to spend extravagantly on his employees' creature comforts. The Meadowlands Construction conference room was cramped, its office building second tier, and the view of the Hackensack River uninviting. An open box of Dunkin' Donuts sat in the middle of the small circular conference table. He had called his team leaders together for an 8 a.m. meeting to map out Meadowlands Construction's strategy for advancing his Opportunity Zone project for West Baytown. Judging from their demeanor and alcohol scents drifting across the table, he was glad to see that his trusted advisors all had had rough nights. Bucky liked to have them on edge when he conducted a roll call on their progress regarding his pet project.

"OK, listen up. Here's where we are. The Opportunity Zone plan is fully approved and we're in a position to guide its future. Gentlemen, this is a high stakes poker game for Meadowlands Construction. And, I might add, for your annual bonuses. We need to know who we're dealing with and how many chips we can get him to push into the middle of the table. So, there are two next steps for Meadowlands Construction. First, we've got to come up with some capital. That is, *someone else's* capital. I'm not about to bet the ranch on this, even though it looks like a pretty sure thing. But I think we've found our mark. Second, we need to get a firm handle on the properties in the Zone. Who owns them and how can we squeeze the owners. So, let's hear what you guys have come up with. Charlie, you've been scouting the real estate market, what's your read?"

Charlie McCandless, a retired real estate broker and former Baytown City Councilman, trained his bleary eyes on a small notebook he pulled from his hip pocket. "Well, it's all good news. Shit-hole split levels, ancient Bayonne Boxes, dilapidated apartments full of impoverished students and seniors waiting for the call. Even a couple of SROs . . ."

Bucky interrupting with a self-satisfied smile, "Wonderful, just what we thought. How about retail?"

Charlie suppressed a laugh and channeled Allen Iverson, "Retail? Retail? We got rows of empty storefronts, abandoned Blockbuster Videos, barber shops, Dollar Stores, and the like. Only the payday loan and pawn shops are prospering. No one's going to miss their local Korean food market."

"And you've chatted up some of the residents?" asked Bucky.

"Sent out my niece and her boyfriend to talk to some homeowners. Pretended they were a young couple interested in buying. They found that half of the dinosaurs were ready to sell on the spot. Lots of concern about a *changing neighborhood*. We can make a lot of headway pushing that story line."

Bucky turned to the youngest member of the team, Bill Freehan. Besides being Bucky's nephew, Freehan had some other qualifications for his position as COO of Meadowlands Construction. He had graduated from Fordham with a major in urban planning, picked up an MBA online, and knew a thing or two about gentrification in the 21st Century. "Billy, have you prepared the sales pitch for our Jesuit friend in Baytown?"

Attired in his Filene's Basement investment banker suit, Freehan rose and triggered a slide show on the conference room screen. The first five slides revealed a series of glittering photographs of major sports arenas. The pictures highlighted urban exteriors of athletic palaces with well-dressed fans and their gleaming late-model SUVs in the foreground. "We're putting together a briefing book you can bring when you have your next sit down with the priest. We'll put in these photos of big-time university venues: Purdue's Mackey Arena; Syracuse's Carrier Dome; UNC's Dean Smith Arena. And it's not just the big boys: DePaul and Marquette —both mid-size Catholic schools like St. Sebastian, by the way—have just put up a couple of sweet basketball stadiums. Not only good for attendance, but essential for recruiting those 17-year-old point guards from the city."

Bucky nodding vigorously, "Good, good. I think we can show that without a first-class stadium, you're going nowhere. Now what about our University President? Brent, have you put together the profile?"

Brent Ashford, Meadowlands Construction's Director of Human Resources, was loaded for bear. "You bet. Long story short: He's there for the taking. Father Victorio Balducci has been President of Saint Sebastian for 21 years. He likes his Barolo, travels to Rome and Atlantic City whenever he can, and above all, wants to get noticed. Basketball, specifically getting into the Big East Conference, is front and center on his radar screen. And here's the good news: He calls the shots at St. Sebastian. Has a discretionary fund that he personally controls, and his board rolls over with their paws in the air whenever he needs something. We're looking into St. Sebastian's endowment, which isn't huge, but they've got a couple of million to spare that wouldn't be noticed. More important, it's not going to be hard for them to float a bond."

"And, by the way, he loves real estate. He's bought up a dozen parcels in the last couple of years. So, I'm putting together some data showing that Columbia and NYU hold close to a billion dollars of property. EACH! I'm sure you can charm him into a partnership for a sizable investment in the Zone. The pitch is a perfect trifecta for him: revitalizing Baytown, new dorms with swimming pools and hot tubs for the students, and valuable parcels in the Zone he can lease or sell. All in all, he's there for the taking. Especially for you, Bucky. You could sell ice cubes to Eskimos."

Bucky was not one to balk at shameless flattery from his subordinates, "Great work, Brent. You guys have nailed it. I think it's a go. I had a sit down with the priest a couple of weeks ago and he almost wet his tunic when I promised to kick in on his basketball stadium fund. I'm pretty sure when I unveil the Opportunity Zone numbers, he'll have his legs in the air. Let's get this party started." Bucky reached to the middle of the table, grabbed the box of donuts, and jogged back to his office.

15

Education is not the filling of a pail but rather the lighting of a fire.

—W.B. Yeats

McNeely had a rough morning. Waking with a thin wire of spittle linking him to his pillow after a late-night listening to a Sonny Rollins tribute at the Vanguard, he was greeted by NPR accounts of the President of the United States kissing up to Vladimir Putin, praising Tayyip Erdogan, and disparaging "shithole countries." A 40-minute stoppage on the PATH train had him sprinting to make it to his 10 a.m. class. All of which left him spoiling for a fight, if only with an imaginary concept. He decided to roll out that old legal chestnut, "The Rule of Law." And add a little hot sauce. A principle, dogma, aspiration, whatever, the core idea being that all members of society including those in government are equally subject to legal codes, regulations, and processes. Standing for the principle that law must take precedence over the will or whims of individuals, it is a concept deeply held, revered, and preached by all law professors, left and right and McNeely was no exception. For him, jailing corporate criminals was the ultimate expression of the Rule of Law. The same law applies to all, and nobody, including Presidents and Justices of the Supreme Court, should be held to a lesser standard.

"OK, ladies and gentlemen, before we get started on today's cases, I have an announcement. I'm sure you all are following with great interest the Senate Judiciary Committee hearings on the nomination of Mr. Kavanaugh to the Supreme Court. Needless to say, this is a momentous time in our country's history. And you know what? It's a decision that will affect all of you for most of your professional careers. Mr. Kavanaugh is relatively young and could serve on the Court for forty years. Some of you may retire before he does. And it's no secret that his nomination was heavily influenced by his judicial philosophy. I'm sure your Con law professors have run you through the debates over originalism, textualism, the living Constitution, and so on. We will see all those issues debated in the hearings underway on his nomination. So, what is this principle called the Rule of Law? Have any of your other professors mentioned it?"

No one moving a muscle. As McNeely knew well, students wouldn't say anything even if their Constitutional Law professor had spent a week on it, because then they'd be on the spot to explain it to the whole class. Everyone knew it was a rhetorical question anyway.

"Well, it's a core principle that underlies our entire legal system. It's something that every country in the world with a legitimate legal system strives for. Goes all the way back to Aristotle. As he put it, 'It is more proper that law should govern than any one of the citizens.' It means that we want legislators, presidents, and yes, Supreme Court Justices to be bound by the exact same rules that apply to the humblest citizen. So, as I'm sure you've heard, there are some serious accusations about Mr. Kavanaugh's conduct when he was younger. And tomorrow, the members of the Senate Judiciary Committee, the committee responsible for approving or disapproving the nomination, will question him. Doesn't get much more reality TV than this."

Two heads popping up at the mention of reality TV.

"Now Professor Roth-Himmelfarb has offered to hold a Confirmation Watch session tomorrow morning, beginning at 9 a.m. We'll have a couple of big monitors set up in the courtroom to air the rest of the confirmation hearing. You may come and go as your schedule permits. And, as if that wasn't enough, we will have some expert commentary during the breaks and at the end of the hearing from Professors Joseph, Stewart, and Roth-Himmelfarb. I don't want you to cut any classes, but please try to stop in during your free hours. This is an event you may be telling your grandchildren about."

McNeely second-guessed himself about whether he should have promised donuts but judging by the fact that a number of students pulled out their cell phones, presumably to mark the event, he was confident the session would draw a good crowd, especially because of the lurid accusations involving Mr. Kavanaugh. He thought about the historical context he really wanted to share with his students, like the fact that Russia wasted billions on spies, coups, and nuclear weapons, when all it took to cripple the U.S. was getting a moron elected President. But that's not my job, he reluctantly concluded.

Heading back from class, he decided to drop by Professor Elaine Roth-Himmelfarb's office. ERH, as she was known, was the Distinguished William Brennan Professor of Constitutional Law and undoubtedly St. Sebastian's most well-known faculty member. She had achieved celebrity status owing to her national reputation as an expert on the Supreme Court and frequent appearances in national media. While highly regarded as a scholar, her cachet came from her standing as a certified "public intellectual"—a commenter in the national press, TV, and countless legal blogs and whom Rachel Maddow once called "my go-to authority on the Constitution." Her salty comments about the Kavanaugh nomination, which had drawn loud laughter from Senator Booker who was seated next to her on one cable broadcast, had gone viral, and made her a cable TV folk hero, at least among MSNBC viewers. It had even earned a personal note from Father Balducci, for whom any mention of St. Sebastian on national media was a personal triumph.

ERH had another feature that distinguished her from her St. Sebastian colleagues even more than her media appearances: It was her personal appearance. Without fail, she dressed elegantly—Tagliatore suits and Louboutin heels—and was never seen without eye make-up, cheek blush, and other facial accoutrements. To put it mildly, she stood out. She had begun her legal career at a big time Manhattan law firm, Paul Weiss, where she learned how to think—and dress—like a lawyer. Her marriage to the Paul Weiss' managing partner ended her career in private practice but led her to an academic career that turned out better suited to her talents and passions.

Her door was open as she was ending a Zoom call. "OK, I'm available whenever. If you want me to pop over to the studio in the city I will, but if you can send a camera crew out here to swampland it would be better for me. In any event, see you soon." Tapping her screen to end the call, she spotted McNeely. "Hey Neels, come on in. Just got off the phone with Rachel. She's really pumped. I'll get a couple of minutes on air."

McNeely was even more excited than she appeared to be. "Wow, how terrific! Mom and Dad are very proud of you. Make sure Rachel utters the words *St. Sebastian* at least five times. Ha ha."

ERH offered a polite chuckle. "Now, Neels, we've been over this before, and believe me I really appreciate the support you've given me on this but . . ."

McNeely interrupting with a grandiose wave of his hand, "Abortion. I know. I know. You're going to talk about it and you're going to make your views clear to a few million people tuning in, many of them Catholic. Not to mention a University President and an Archbishop."

McNeely paused for dramatic effect. "No problem!!" he exclaimed offering a big ingratiating smile. He didn't expect an outpouring of emotion, but the smile, nod, and direct look in the eye ERH gave him was good enough. He'd done something worthwhile but knew the repercussions would start hitting his fan by 11 p.m. tonight.

Walking back to his office and taking refuge in his own thoughts: Abortion, again and again. Every judge nominated by a Republican President performs the same Kabuki dance. They solemnly promised their fealty to the principle of *stare decisis*. You don't overturn precedent without a really compelling reason. Like the world has changed dramatically. "Moderate" Republican senators like Susan Collins who claim they support a woman's right to choose, vote to affirm each nomination, explaining that *this* nominee had explained to them in their one-on-one interview that he really and truly believes in *stare decisis*. Meanwhile, the other 50-plus Republicans vote to uphold the nomination *precisely because* they believe *he will* eventually vote to overturn Roe v. Wade. If Vegas offered Supreme Court futures betting, Brett Michael Kavanaugh, as Catholic as the Pope's mother, would be a pretty safe bet to overturn Roe, *stare decisis* be damned. And not only did the future of abortion rights hang in the balance, but so did a host of regulatory, corporate, and civil rights protections that Americans had come to take for granted. All summoning up for McNeely the haunting memory of his cowardly failure to discuss the possibility of an abortion nine years ago.

McNeely had known guys like Kavanaugh at Harvard Law School. He called them the "Scarsdale Irish": Khaki pants, penny loafers without socks, pink button-down Brooks Brothers shirts. High school summers abroad in enrichment programs, Princeton, or Dartmouth undergrad, and maybe a gap year backpacking in Italy before law school. Parents were lawyers or doctors who paid full tuition. Until law school, McNeely never knew this subspecies of his breed existed. He always saw his Irish Catholic peers as gritty fat guys like him with parents hard-pressed to make their mortgage payments.

What amused him most about Kavanaugh was how often the latent Irish roughneck came creeping out. He drank beer with great enthusiasm and pride, got wasted regularly, and probably assaulted a girl when he was in high school. On top of that, he showed flashes of out-of-control anger when he needed it least. Astonishingly, in his confirmation hearing he tried to bully a U.S. Senator who asked him whether he had blackouts: "I don't know. Have you?" Apparently, he hadn't done his research, so he didn't know Senator Klobachar's father was an alcoholic, something she had written about. She nailed Kavanaugh with the memorable comment "when you have a parent that is an alcoholic, you're pretty careful about drinking." This guy may self-destruct, McNeely thought at first. But remembering how Clarence Thomas overcame his sexist misadventures by exploding with anger and intimidating the Democratic committee members, he wasn't so sure any longer.

McNeely's aversion to bullying was long standing. As the fattest kid by 20 pounds at St. Bridget Primary School, he'd been ridiculed, pushed around, and taunted by other fifth graders. Nicknamed "Tommy the blimp," last in the relay races, unable to do a single sit up, he had to squeeze into the picnic table bench at lunchtime. Coming home sobbing one day, his grandfather, the cut man, sized up the problem and took him down to the basement for a tutorial in the sweet science. The basic lesson was simple. *You're big enough to defend yourself. Punching power comes more from your legs and hips than your arms. Move forward twist your hips as you throw your right hook. Using all that lower body muscle and twist. The torque doubles your power. Follow with a straight right or left straight to his nose. If he's a lot taller, then you hit him in the Adams apple.*

His grandad hung an old laundry bag from the ceiling in the basement for practice. There was one important caveat. "You never start a fight. You only throw your weight around when you or someone else has been attacked." A couple of fights later, including a TKO of a sixth grader, the rough guys took him off their target list.

Colly had told his young grandson that he looked like a TV star, which he did. He had Jackie Gleason's jet-black hair, a curl dropping over his forehead, blue eyes, bugling cheeks, and ample girth. At first, McNeely loved it when Colly called him "Jackie" until he caught an episode of "The Honeymooners." Jackie Gleason, a huge bus driver living in a squalid, bare tenement, threatening his wife with a punch. *You're going to the moon, Alice.* Not the self-image he needed at twelve. Reminded at school every day that being the fattest kid meant you had only a couple of choices: Be funny or be smart. But girls, he discovered, were not looking for either one.

Colly McNeely knew he had a mission: Teach his fatherless, fat grandson self-confidence, give him skills and the opportunities he never gave his own son, and let him know he had a family heritage to uphold.

16

I have never killed a man, but I have read many obituaries with great pleasure.

—Clarence Darrow

Living in the West Village had some downsides. Exorbitant rent, 525 square feet of living space, a three-floor walk-up, incessant noise from the street and the family with four kids on the second floor. But like every kid from North Jersey who spent his teenage years wandering around Manhattan, McNeely thought it was paradise. Food, music, bars, museums, parks, ballparks, all within reach. For a jazz buff, mecca—the Village Vanguard—was four minutes away. And he could get to St. Sebastian in 22 minutes, door to door, at least when the PATH train was in a good mood.

His usual routine after work was to decompress with a drink, throw together some sorry bachelor concoction in the wok or microwave, and do an hour sorting through paperwork or preparing for the next day's classes. If all went well, he'd treat himself tonight to a late-night visit to the Vanguard and maybe an ice cream venue. McNeely realized that his friends who relentlessly and unsuccessfully tried to fix him up assumed he was lonely and depressed. In fact, quite the opposite was true. An only child, fatherless and essentially motherless, he knew how to entertain himself and usually felt he provided pretty good company. For himself. Above all, McNeely prized his autonomy and freedom to do exactly what he wanted every evening—the antithesis of his daytime regimen at St. Sebastian and a partial antidote to memories of the mess of his marriage and the ever-present, haunting thoughts of his disabled daughter.

Tonight, he had grabbed a garlic Szechuan noodle carry-out as soon as he got off the PATH train, and once back in his apartment faced the decision of which pile of documents was less likely to ruin his dinner. Picking up the Sanus Institute binder, he scanned the table of contents: *Our Mission, Legal Curriculum, Student Engagement Opportunities, Outreach to Business, Global Footprint.* Flipping through, there were high-end glossy photos on almost every page. The Global Footprint chapter had photos of Rome at night and what looked like a beach on Maui. The same approach corporate shills deploy in their annual reports to shareholders, McNeely thought: glamor, excitement, and empty promises. Better to tackle the Ethics Committee file first.

The Committee's binder contained 300 pages of transcript, briefs, PowerPoint slides, and supporting documents. The first document gave the Committee's verdict in a succinct paragraph:

The Saint Sebastian Law School Committee on Student Ethics and Responsibility has unanimously concluded that Margaret Holloran did knowingly and willfully plagiarize portions of a seminar paper for Professor Francis Gleason's seminar class, Legislation: Theory and Practice. The committee recommends by a 4 to 1 vote immediate and permanent expulsion from the law school.

Having heard the opening salvos at the beginning of the hearing, McNeely scoured the transcript to get to the facts supporting the allegation. Certain that he was missing something, he found it necessary to flip back and forth through the testimony and numerous documents. After a frustrating hour of searching and rereading the docket, he realized that this was not a simple plagiarism case. It was a lynching.

The gist of the complaint was that the student had submitted a first draft of her seminar paper that contained five footnotes that had been lifted from a published law review article. The first remarkable aspect of the case was that this was a first draft, not the final version of the paper. While plagiarism rules applied to all submissions, it was extraordinarily unusual to go after a student who may have been sloppy or careless in a rush to get a rough draft in. But what set McNeely's heartbeat racing was the realization that all the student had "lifted" was a handful of footnotes. There was no claim that any of the actual text of her paper was plagiarized or written without attribution to an author.

As he thought about it, McNeely wondered how Professor Gleason would have even noticed the alleged plagiarism. After all, Professors are hardly going to scrutinize footnotes, except maybe to see how thorough the student's research was, and maybe catch improper technical mistakes in legal citation. The infamous Harvard Blue Book sets forth precise rules for citing cases and books, but the challenged citations were done correctly. So how, and why, he wondered, did the lifting of footnotes from an obscure law review article catch Professor Gleason's eye?

Belching meditatively, he decided to tackle the paper itself. "Anti-abortion

Legislation: Science or Fiction?" Slick title, he thought. The paper analyzed a number of state laws designed to curb the practice of abortion. Red states had become laboratories for schemes to make women's right to abortion as difficult or unpleasant as possible. An endless series of regulatory hurdles, parental consent, waiting periods, medically unnecessary tests, mandatory counselling, paperwork, and even liability for physicians. The student's thesis was that each of the statutory roadblocks lacked any scientific basis in either preventing harm to the mother or promoting an informed choice. But again and again, state legislators and governors couched their decisions on purported empirical evidence. The first paragraph summarized the student's thesis: "The fundamental problem is that proposed laws are driving the alleged science rather than vice-versa. State legislators have been content to rely on highly dubious versions of "science" that purport to protect the health of the mother or enable an informed decision. The plain truth is that faux science is being deployed as window dressing."

McNeely finished reading the paper and threw his chopsticks across the room. This student paper—and it was a first draft for God's sake—could probably get a professor tenure at half the law schools in the country, including St. Sebastian. If it wasn't about abortion of course. Sure, there was some hyperbole, and occasional awkward writing, but the thesis was compelling, the discussion of the scientific literature thorough, and her argument well-structured.

Just one problem, a catastrophic lapse in judgment: Writing a paper on abortion law for a card-carrying, cilice-wearing, Opus Dei supernumerary.

17

There is nothing that keeps wicked men at any one moment out of hell,
but the mere pleasure of God.

—Jonathan Edwards,
Sinners in the Hand of an Angry God Sermon, July 6, 1741

McNeely was pretty sure most of the class had heard of Enron. Maybe some of their parents were victims of the collapse of the stock market in 2008, but he feared that most of the country had pretty much forgotten about it. Wall Street had been totally buffaloed by a large corporation that engaged in unmatched fraud, yet the event had quickly been pushed into the dustbin of history, as Trotsky liked to say. Just a few years later, the misdeeds and greed of Lehman, Countrywide, and every major bank in the U.S. and E.U. nearly precipitated the collapse of the world's financial markets. Again, all but completely forgotten. Facebook now jeopardizing privacy, Amazon abusing its workforce, Google driving small businesses under, all with hardly a peep. So McNeely decided to take it upon himself to light a fire and spread his gospel that corporate crime is not to be tolerated.

Ditching the customary Socratic dialogue, he decided to unleash a full-throated, hellfire lecture worthy of Jonathan Edwards. Opening his notebook, he began, "Just a few years ago, the American economy almost collapsed. A perfect storm of greed, regulatory failure, and blind faith in the market led investors to walk off a cliff. A cliff of debt and billions invested in chimera. Banks, retirees, and unions buying financial securities that most admitted they didn't understand. Lenders inveigling homebuyers to overextend on home mortgages and consumers to stack up credit card debt beyond their ability to pay, while banks and pension funds placed their investors' money in Ponzi schemes."

He went on for 30 minutes. Every now and then, his voice grew loud, almost a shout. "That's why some of your grandparents lost their retirement savings, why many homeowners faced foreclosure, why . . ." A few students in the back benches looked startled, paused their online shopping, and a few pulled off their head-phones to see what was going on. They hadn't expected an outpouring of raw emotion. Especially in a Corporate Law class.

He decided to wrap up with an appeal across the political divide. "This critique of corporate and financial failure isn't just me, or a bunch of liberal pundits. No less an authority than Richard Posner—you've all encountered Posner in your classes, right?"

No response, one or two heads nodding.

"Well, even Judge Richard Posner, doyen of the Chicago School, free market advocate, and leading judge and scholar, said it best. Enron was a *government* failure. A failure to *regulate* banks and investors!"

Scanning the room for signs of uptake, agreement, or consciousness, McNeely happy to settle for thoughtful silence. A pudgy pink hand went up.

"Yes, Mr. Oswald?"

"Professor, isn't there some rethinking of all that today? President Trump has said job killing regulation is the biggest drag on our economy. He's cut regulations in half and wants to free up the marketplace. And the stock market is booming. So doesn't that show that less regulation of business is better than crushing regulation?"

Those free student lunches sponsored by the Federalist Society are paying off, McNeely thought. The kid has given a capsule summary of the morning line of the *Wall Street Journal*, Sean Hannity, and those omnipresent Koch Bros. And a pretty capable one, at that.

"Good points, Mr. Oswald. One must question however whether the stock market actually reflects the real performance of the economy or whether it, too, is subject to manipulation. We're going to spend a couple of weeks dealing with a famous regulation promulgated by the SEC, called Rule 10b-5, the insider trading prohibition. It says you can't take advantage of private information, like some CEOs do, and buy or sell stock when the public doesn't have access to the same information. We'll see, among many other crimes involved, Enron executives and board members were involved in insider trading."

Mr. Oswald was not about to surrender. "So, the SEC is in charge of controlling information? Isn't that a violation of the First Amendment?"

"Well, I think today's cases will shed some light on that. For now, let's just say that where there is out and out fraud—like Enron deceiving its own shareholders by cooking its books—there isn't a First Amendment defense." McNeely wanted to add "at least not yet," but held his tongue.

Heading back to his office, he reflected on the class. Got that off my chest. Come the next financial crisis, they won't remember who told them, but maybe they'll recall where it all began and how many times the legal system has dropped the ball. Anyway, that Oswald's got gumption. Give him that. Headed in the wrong direction, but at least he gives a shit.

Entering the Deanplex—the office suite he shared with Dean Eckstein—McNeely immediately knew she had returned from her scavenger hunt. Her two assistants, heads buried in their word processors, were ostensibly hard at work. Some loud exclamations were emanating from the Dean's office.

Venturing in, McNeely offered his welcome. "Deb, great to have you back. Happy hunting?"

"Got a few nibbles. We'll see. But more important," holding up the Sanus Institute binder, "What, for Christ's sake, is this?"

"Well, Father B summoned me to come over and handed it to me. Seems like . . ."

"Seems like a corporate fucking takeover of the law school. They want to turn us into a shill for every lunatic right-wing idea that the Business Roundtable can dream up."

"No doubt. I'm not sure how far down the garden path they've walked Father B, but he's throwing around a big number . . ."

Eckstein interrupted, "Let me guess. $10 million?"

"30."

"Such generosity! Renews my faith in Wall Street. OK, top priority. Drop whatever you're doing and put a dagger in this sucker. Father B likes you."

"Well, he knows I attend Mass and teach corporate law, so I think he thinks I'm persuadable. Even mentioned an endowed chair."

Eckstein now adamant, "Machiavelli!! That's who his hero is! Patron saint of Italian crooks. Should have his portrait glowing in his office instead of St. Sebastian's."

McNeely backtracking, figuratively and literally. "I'll get right on it. Top priority."

Eckstein, eyes glaring, shot back, "And whatever you do, do not, I repeat, DO NOT, utter a word to the faculty. They'll issue a fatwah on my ass for even talking about it. Can you imagine what Elaine and her band would do if they hear about it? It will be in the New York *Times*, the *Chronicle of Legal Education*, and every left-wing blog within twenty-four hours. And she'll book herself on her pal Rachel Maddow's show and make us look like the second coming of the Heritage Foundation." Elaine Roth Himmelfarb, leader of the progressive, left-leaning faculty at the law school, was not someone the Dean wanted to get riled up.

"I'll sure see what I can do," McNeely said half-heartedly, feeling a bit like St. Sebastian must have felt when Emperor Diocletian took out after him. He thought he needed his own Saint Irene—the young maiden who had saved St. Sebastian's life, untying him from the tree he was bound to, pulling out each of the arrows that had pierced him, and nursing his wounds.

While not exactly a blonde maiden, Jinx will do the trick, he comforted himself.

18

Alonzo Jenks was one of those all-around, five-tool agents the FBI prized. When he was first recruited his superiors followed their unwritten racial profile by giving him assignments in the Violent Crime and Major Offender Program—one that required "street smarts"—interviewing uptown (read Black) witnesses, working with cops, handling violent crime cases. But he soon took advantage of the technical skills he developed in the years he spent working in the back room of his father's RadioShack store in the South Bronx. When the agency offered training in wiretapping, electronic surveillance, and data recovery, he was first in line, mastering all manner of sophisticated investigative technology. Personally, he was both street smart—he could talk the talk of doormen, cabbies, waiters, and hookers—but, owing to three semesters of night school at Fordham, he also had all the business savvy needed to work the financial side of the street.

Looking up from his stool at the Ginger Man as McNeely walked in, Jenks greeted him with the item he knew they both were stewing over. "You see what that fat orange cracker said the other day? Called us scum. Says the agency is broken. And claimed that the FBI investigating his appointees—several of whom incidentally happen to be sucking Russian cock—is the work of the 'Deep State.' Man, I'm glad I got out when I did."

"Me too. Just in time to avoid the reign of terror. How you doin' Jinx?" McNeely slid into the adjacent stool and ordered a Smithwicks.

"Tommy boy, there's a lot of money floating around this city looking for security. I'm turning away business. And the travel! Easy grab, man! Been to Kenya, China and Mexico in the last couple of months."

"Whoa! Who's buying?"

"Every corporate stiff trying to break into 'emerging markets.' They know there's gold in them hills but are scared shitless of traveling there. So, here I am. AJ Security Consultants. Man with a plan. And some friends. And a gun, as needed."

"What do you do?"

"I scope out safe hotels, reliable transport, and follow them around like when you take your kids to Disneyland. If they're going out to dinner, I make sure it's safe. If they need to get to a meeting, I check the route, hire a trustworthy driver, and ride shotgun in the front seat."

"And if they want to get laid?"

"I draw the line at being a food taster, but I check out where they can find a clean, safe, and obliging companion."

McNeely patting his mentor on the shoulder, "Man, the FBI would be proud."

As a rookie Assistant U.S. Attorney, McNeely had been thrown into the deep end of the pool. He was assigned to work with the FBI agents digging into SAC Capital, the biggest and most notorious hedge fund on Wall Street. Wiretaps, boxcars of documents, surveillance, interviews with strippers—the meat and potatoes of criminal investigations into the superrich of the 2000s. He discovered that this part of the job—snooping into the private lives of corporate criminals and their friends, business associates, mistresses—was way more interesting than writing appellate briefs. Also, working with the agents was a good fit. They were in many ways McNeely's kind of people. Most were from middle- or working-class families, lived in Queens and the Bronx, and, among the younger cohort, were a pretty diverse group, in race, ethnicity, gender and politics.

Assigned to work with the wiretap and investigative team on the SAC case, McNeely had the good fortune of working side by side with Special Agent Jenks. Jenks himself had only six years with the Bureau, but to rookie AUSA McNeely he seemed like a grizzled veteran. He also was a highly simpatico comrade; they bonded, drank, and commiserated together regularly. Jenks was at the center of the wiretap team, and in their weekly drinking sessions he shared not only his methods, but also some illuminating insights into the rich and powerful gleaned from his hours of listening to audio tapes.

To this day they shared a common bond: their White Whale, the big one that got away. They had assembled what by any reasonable assessment was clear and convincing evidence that Stevie Cohen was butt-deep in securities fraud. His company, SAC Capital, eventually forked over a couple of billion in criminal fines, but he walked. In their weekly reunions since leaving the government, they vented about the goings-on at their respective alma maters, the FBI and the Department of Justice: Trump and Barr were undermining the work of career attorneys and agents, hamstringing the Special Prosecutor, and denigrating the people trying to stem the tidal wave of corporate corruption that they themselves had unleashed. More than enough to sustain a night's drinking, reminiscencing, and bitching.

"So, how 'bout you?" Jenks asked, downing his scotch and waving two fingers at the bartender.

After listening politely to McNeely's five-minute description of the prosaic day-to-day life of a law professor, Jenks could not resist a dig, "Man, you must be mainlining espresso to keep from lapsing into a coma. Do the Jesuits frown on amphetamines?"

"Well, turns out, I have need of some expert intel-gathering regarding some of the rich and infamous of this fine island," McNeely said smiling. "Might afford you a chance to take a break from being a corporate sherpa and get back to playing for the home team."

McNeely proceeded to describe the Sanus Institute proposal and explain his reasons for needing Jenks' assistance. "Bottom line, I'm looking for dirt. A way to convince the good Father that he's signing a pact with the devil. Failing that, I need some leverage. Some way of persuading these corporate douchebags that linking up with St. Sebastian will be like marrying into the Gambino family."

McNeely chose a crime family that Jenks knew well from having cut his teeth at the agency working on a takedown of the racketeering, narcotics, and loan sharking business of the Gambinos. Jenks' undercover work on the team investigating the La Cosa Nostra's recruitment of illegals to work in their strip clubs around the greater New York area had earned him a special commendation from the agency and, the nickname "Special Agent Lap Dance" from his colleagues. But the nickname that stuck—Jinx—was a tribute to his effect on the targets of his investigations. Over a two-year period, five had fallen victim to serious accidents or career-ending dust ups with their organized crime colleagues.

"I've kept up my contacts with friends in what I'll call the service sector here in the city," Jenks said. "Seems like the bull market has been pretty good to those who live off the care and feeding of the one percenters. There's a reason why Scores and Per Se are booming. And man, the technology today! You can listen, follow, and watch your targets round the clock if you need to. It's not just the Russians who know how to peek inside everyone's electronics."

McNeely nervously sloshing his pint, "OK, but . . ."

"Yeah, yeah, I know, Professor." Jinx raised his right hand, "I hereby solemnly pledge not to venture outside the boundaries drawn by your fine American legal system. Though, truth be told, those boundaries are not so clearly marked. You know how it is. Like, sometimes you're out for a drive, take a random exit, and bang! You suddenly find out you're knee deep in the Secaucus Meadowlands. Didn't mean to go there, but there you are."

McNeely knew he had to get to the delicate subject of remuneration. "Now I'm going to have to fund this little excursion out of my own pocket, so please . . ."

Jenks wrapped a huge arm around McNeely's shoulder. "Don't sweat it, Tommy. You lawyers do pro bono work all the time, right? Well for me, this is like you helping some poor kid who's been run up by the cops in Queens for walking while Black. Consider it my contribution to making America great."

Everybody needs his memories.
They keep the wolf of insignificance from the door.

—Saul Bellow

The Rahway police force patrolled the bar at the Term with some regularity. Some stationed themselves there for hours on end. Maggie had a couple of favorites, but at the top of the list was Ernie, Ernesto Julio Burgos on his Puerto Rican birth certificate, but long ago he had found it easier to blend in on the Rahway PD as Ernie. Ernie had risen from being the first Hispanic on the force to Sergeant, and eventually Lieutenant. He now had access to all the levers of power in the county and state and knew how to use his position to discreetly come to the aid of those who needed help. As Maggie only recently learned, Ernie had helped smooth over a possession arrest for her brother and guide him into rehab without her father finding out about it. Back when the crowd at the Term was pretty much all white, Ernie came in with some Black colleagues and sat at the bar, surrounded by some of Rahway's less-than-enlightened regulars. Her dad had made it appear to everyone that Ernie and his pals were long lost friends, maybe buddies from the war in Nam that he never fought in and poured everyone a couple on the house—a rare event, which made it all the more symbolic. Kind of like the famous photo her dad had showed her of Pee Wee Reese throwing an arm around Jackie Robinson. She thought of it as her dad bestowing the Irish equivalent of a bar mitzvah.

In her self-appointed position as COO, Maggie Holloran took control over the day-to-day operation of the Terminal Bar, LLC. She soon came to appreciate some of the stories she heard at the dinner table over the years, especially grumblings from her mother about keeping a close eye on their bartenders and the need to install checks on their pouring techniques when neither she nor her father were around. Her kind-hearted dad was not one to crack the whip, and the bartenders knew it. Norma, on the other hand, trusted no one. "If your father had heard the stories I heard from my grandfather about running a restaurant in Napoli, he'd not be so *morbido,*" she once told Maggie.

The legendary story in the Holloran household that Norma reminded her husband about several times a year concerned a bartender named Pauly. She had noticed a dip in sales on the weeknights when he was tending bar without the Hollorans' supervision as neither Norma nor Mickey came in on Tuesdays and both left early on Wednesday evenings. Norma calculated that those time slots coincided with a noticeable drop in the Term's take. Professional help clearly needed, she called Ernie.

Dressed in civilian clothes, Rahway PD Lieutenant Ernesto Burgos arrived on a Tuesday evening at 8:30 p.m. He positioned himself at the bar, and greeted the young, heavily tatted bartender. Extending a hand for a shake across the bar, "Good evening, I'm Ernie. What's your name?"

"Pauly. What can I do for you? Menu? Drink?"

"Just a bourbon, neat. And can you put the Mets on? I like to watch car crashes." Noticing that Pauly reached under the bar for a bottle, Ernie asked, "Special label?"

"Yeah, I like this Old Forester. Want to try a taste first?"

"No, no. I'll trust your judgment." Ernie smiling, tasting, and nodding, "You're on it. Smooth."

Ernie stayed for an hour, carefully counting Pauly's reaches under the bar for customers not specifying a label and noting that a few who asked for a preferred brand were given his personal recommendation along with an offer of a preliminary taste. Ernie called Norma on his cell as soon as he got to his car.

"Your boy Pauly is running *his own* bar. A bar *inside* a bar. *Yours!* Has a stash of his own bottles under the front. Even runs his own credit card swiper. The guy has big brass ones. Could go bowling with one of them. Talks people into trying his own recommended brands, then gives them a taste. Even charges more than you do. Want me to roust him?"

Norma feeling both vindicated and vindictive. "Let me take care of him. I promise not to commit any crimes, just want to teach him a life lesson."

Ernie laughed, knowing Norma's Neapolitan roots. He remembered having to carry a patron out of the Term whom she had "accidentally" hit on the head with a beer mug after he had grabbed the ass of a waitress. "Ok, just let me know if an air ambulance is needed."

After consulting some websites and visiting a few upscale competitors, Maggie realized that the Term was the Jurassic Park of small bar/restaurants. An old-time cash register, a staff-administered credit card station, and food orders written on paper and walked back to the kitchen. The only features missing were spittoons and sawdust on the floor. She researched vendors of point-of-service registers and ordering electronics and found one that was not too pricey and met the Term's need, with features such as the ability to customize prices for happy hour, inventory management to keep track of the pouring, and quick, accurate food ordering all of which revolutionized operations. Maggie personally trained the bartenders and servers. But one student flunked her course: her dad. She was never sure whether it was his stubborn insistence that they didn't need to "go all internet to run a bar" or his dementia that was the problem. Eventually he mastered the fundamentals and limited himself to occasionally muttering "cash is king" to customers as they pulled out their wallets.

Despite the technological advances, the Term presented an endless series of challenges that Maggie had to tackle while also trying to master the nuances of multi-state class action litigation, advanced civil procedure, and estate planning law in her law school classes. Things that should be routine turned out to be totally random. Guys delivering kegs would fail to pick up the used ones, or her Thursday bartender would neglect to put them in the back alley. The cook would forget to order hamburger meat or would order enough to serve half of Yankee Stadium. Pestering salesmen would show up at 11:30 in the morning pushing their new line of vodkas in designer bottles and insist on pouring some for the staff. Her father would forget to fill the cash drawer and the first shift bartenders and waitresses would have to make their own change. Maggie often wondered whether Alzheimer's was contagious.

And then there were the toilets. Every imaginable form of garbage and human waste found its way to the men's room floor at one time or another. Bartenders had to know that part of their job was cleaning up the detritus and doing so promptly. Not that the women's room was a picnic. Despite posted signs, both humorous and threatening, toilets were regularly clogged with feminine hygiene products and the occasional helping of underwear. Probably most annoying to Maggie was the hipsters' new sport, The Mile Down Club. Getting laid in the bathroom of a dive bar had apparently become something to put on your résumé.

Most critically, someone had to watch the kids. Not only did bartenders and waitresses feel obliged to accommodate their friends, but the more enterprising ones also liked to "work a contract." A longstanding practice among the less scrupulous, it involved offering customers a refill "on the house" in return for which the patron would slide half the price of the drink into the tip well. Offer, acceptance, consideration: the textbook fundamentals of contract law, as Maggie's law training had taught her. She finally hit on the solution that most bars had begun to adopt: video surveillance, with three small cameras positioned around the bar and seating areas capturing the entire premises and available to Maggie on her cell phone and laptop, both live and archived. She had expected that once everyone knew they were on Candid Camera, she would be relieved of some of her anxiety.

Not so much. Given Maggie's compulsive personality, she found herself scanning the video archives of the Term regularly on her cell phone. She did catch the occasional freebie or over-pour and was able to monitor the cash flow more accurately, but the technology created its own stresses. One night, hard at work at 9 p.m. researching cases for her moot court class in the St. Sebastian law library, she stole a look on her cell phone to see the live action at the Term. With a loud "What the fuck?" she sprang from her seat, called an Uber, and raced out the door. She had witnessed a tall pony-tailed dude behind the bar pouring four shots of something. The dude was not an employee of the Term.

Maggie handled that and other crises with aplomb. She felt that if nothing else, her course in Dive Bar Management was teaching her how to handle pressure and prioritize things. But the pressure point that was most discomfiting was the one that mattered most to her: her dad.

"Holler'n Mickey" Holloran had surrendered none of his wit or passions to dementia. He still yelled at the TV when Trump was spewing venom and cursed his Mets at every opportunity. But he did it with a charm and humor that disguised his pain.

"I've been diagnosed," he would announce at the bar whenever he got confused or forgot a name. "Yes sir, I went to a specialist in Hoboken. He x-rayed my head, tested my blood, even grabbed my balls. Gave it to me straight. 'Mr. Holloran,' he says, 'you've got CRS.'"

Holler'n Mickey adopted a serious look, scanning the bar, "Oh my God, doctor, what is CRS? I says."

"'Can't remember shit' he tells me!" the old man letting out the loudest guffaw at his own joke and leaving his audience comforted.

Maggie was not so easily distracted by her father's bluffing. She undertook a review of every website on Alzheimer's, read medical journals, and peppered her father's doctors with questions. Among the disheartening things she learned was that the downhill spiral could come quickly and that at some point, maybe soon, her father would need someone to look after him. Now accustomed to tackling problems quickly, Maggie arranged for friends and community care clinicians to stop in to see him when she was at school.

When they were together Maggie tried to use the research she had gathered from the internet to slow his decline. Some studies had shown that Alzheimer patients benefited from having games or tasks that called for arranging items in a logical order. Using information gleaned from several peer-reviewed medical journals, she designed a hobby for her father calculated to keep him interested while stimulating the blood flow in his brain. She bought him a complete set of baseball cards for the 1969 season, and challenged him to sort out the Mets, and maybe a few other teams. He laughed at first but acknowledged that he always loved baseball cards as a kid and would take a look at her present when he had some time.

Maggie came home a day later and found her father sitting at the kitchen table with a proud smile on his face. Arrayed in front of him were nine baseball cards, each one placed in the position the player would occupy on the field. His Miracle Mets and their 1969 World Series starting line-up.

Maggie ran to her room so he wouldn't see her crying.

I'd rather be governed by the first 2000 names in the Boston telephone directory than by the Harvard faculty.

—William F. Buckley

"OK let's get started." Dean Eckstein now yelling, "OK LETS GET STARTED," next accompanied by a banging notebook on the table, "LETS START PLEASE!"

When slightly over half of the faculty had stopped chattering, Dean Eckstein started in. "OK, let the record show this is the faculty meeting of October 2, 2018. Can I have a motion to accept the minutes of the last meeting?"

Chatter renewing. "Can I have a motion to accept the minutes of the last meeting?" After a 20-second wait, a cough and a "so moved," followed after another 15 seconds of glowering from the Dean, a timid "Second."

McNeely organized the monthly faculty meetings to burn as much of the hour as possible with extended reports containing streams of PowerPoint slides displaying data on a large screen in the faculty meeting room. His job was to plan and orchestrate the sessions to give the Dean the opportunity to fulfill her obligation to keep the faculty informed about her policies and the state of the law school but without providing details that might lead to probing questions that could stoke discontent. The goal was simple: leave as little time as possible for open-ended faculty discussions. "One true thing that every dean can confirm," Eckstein once told him, "give them five minutes to discuss the state of the law school and you will have some whining and complaining; give them ten minutes, you get anger and hostility; half an hour, outright rebellion and calls for replacing the dean."

The two deans had spent hours massaging the data for the faculty presentation. In McNeely's favorite TV show, *The Wire*, they called it "jukin' the stats." Good arrest numbers had a payoff for the po'lice. As one office explained, "That's how majors become colonels in the Baltimore PD." Presenting the law school's admission statistics on an enormous screen in the faculty meeting room, Dean Eckstein recited aloud the most favorable numbers regarding St. Sebastian's entering class, while rushing past the less positive ones. A dozen Excel spreadsheets displayed data dissecting the entering class by every imaginable metric: LSAT Scores, GPAs (average, median, 75 percentile), race/ethnicity (Black, Caucasian, Latino, Asian, other), college attended, geographic home by state, alumni connection, religion, undergraduate major, area of interest in law studies, and a couple of quixotic categories like "notable names" identifying law firms, corporations, and political figures who had recommended admitted students.

Of primary interest to the faculty was additional data revealing overlap of applications with rival law schools, financial aid awarded, and perhaps most important, a category entitled "yield." Put bluntly, "yield" statistics revealed how many students had to be offered admittance to St. Sebastian in order to "yield" an entering class of 190. The result—which appeared only momentarily on the screen—was a depressing 855 admits, resulting in a yield of 22%, well below the national law school average of 34%. While the low yield percentage was due in large part to the number of alternatives in the New York/North Jersey area, it still exposed the uncomfortable truth the Dean hoped not to discuss: for many, if not most, of its students, St. Sebastian Law School was a second, third, or lower choice.

All of which made St. Sebastian's *US News* ranking of 97 (out of 207 accredited law schools) look just about right, McNeely admitted to himself. But under the Panglossian interpretation which he also firmly embraced, rejection by other schools would motivate these kids to work harder than their peers in the higher-ranked schools.

Despite the Dean's efforts to flash through the slides containing discouraging numbers, the data prompted a series of questions, grumbles, and gripes from the speed readers on the faculty.

"What are we doing to recruit Hispanic students? The percentage seems to have dropped this year."

"I note that the bottom quintile of our LSAT scores is 129. Aren't these the very students dragging down our bar passage rate?"

"Looks like we got more Jews and Muslims than Catholics."

"We've talked in the past of increasing enrollment in tax and business courses. Why haven't we targeted students who majored in business? Looks to me like a lot of English and Gender Studies majors."

"The LGBTQ number is disappointing. I thought that was a priority. Should we appoint an assistant dean for diversity?"

"Why are we recruiting, let alone bragging about, admission of gay students? The Compendium of the Catechism makes it clear that homosexuality is a mortal sin.

"How in the world do we lose our common admits to Seton Hall?"

Then, as expected, Professor Cathcart, elder spokesman for the Young and the Restless took the floor. "Deborah, I think we all agree, and . . ." surveying the room with an anguished look, "have for some years now—felt priority number one for us should be putting St. Sebastian on the map."

"We have some fine young scholars here . . ." Directing a supportive palm in the direction of the table where the Y&R had congregated, he went on in an adenoidal whine, "who are second to none of their over-hyped peers at NYU and Columbia. Bill just placed an article in the *Yale Journal of Existential Threats*. Professor Howard got a nod in the *Lawprof Blog*—though it didn't explicitly mention him by name, everyone knew who they were talking about when they mentioned emerging scholarship on video gaming. Indeed, I think our failure is one of messaging, not performance. College students simply need to get the word, indeed the message, that we are as good as anyone in the Northeast."

His small dolphin-like face emitting a smile, "I'd humbly propose that we devise a clear strategy to—if I may borrow a phrase—Make St. Sebastian Great Again."

McNeely marveled at how unabashedly and transparently self-promoting all this was. Years earlier Cathcart had campaigned for the deanship with phrases like "put us on the map" and "get us recognized." His memes were targeted not only at the Y&R, but also those of the senior faculty who believed the only reason they hadn't moved on was their anchor of years teaching at a 97th ranked law school. In the end, Cathcart's candidacy for the deanship drew no support so he redirected his energies to making life uncomfortable for the outsider who had beaten him out.

McNeely dated his deep-seated contempt for Cathcart to his first days on campus. He'd been invited out to lunch for what turned out to be a clumsy effort to bond over what his senior colleague assumed would be their shared cynicism about the humble backwater that is St. Sebastian University. After all, they had both attended top-ranked law schools and had published articles in leading law journals. Cathcart peppered the conversation with observations about the myriad shortcomings of his colleagues, the lack of intellectual life on campus, and especially the frustrations of teaching dimwitted, ill-equipped students. "Believe me, you'll earn your salary teaching here. As the old saying goes, we're all 'casting artificial pearls before real swine.'" The ensuing years had not dislodged the Buick that Cathcart's comment had parked in McNeely's craw. As grievances accumulated, McNeely found himself contemplating his own veterinary procedure: Castrate Cathcart before he can infect the sounder.

Armed with a sheaf of data from her pre-meeting briefing with the Admissions Director and McNeely, Dean Eckstein came to the faculty meeting ready to deflect implications that St. Sebastian was not holding its own or was sinking into the swamp of third-tier law schools. One important arrow in her quiver was her handling of the problem of "1L stealing." It had become the custom of some rival law schools to make eleventh-hour pitches to students admitted to St. Sebastian urging them to change their decision and jump to their school. For higher-ranked schools, the message was clear: Why attend a school ranked #97 when you can come to a school ranked 43rd? Even lower-ranked rivals posed a threat. Taking an extra couple thousand off tuition would often turn the tide. First-year student poaching sometimes even went on a week or two into the students' first semester: some who had attended their first week of classes at St. Sebastian would simply vanish, popping up in the welcome arms of a rival school across the Hudson.

However, poachers had to be careful. They needed to calculate the precise effect the new admits would have on their *US News* reporting data, especially median LSAT scores and GPAs. A drop of a single point in those scores could cost the school 5 or 10 positions in the annual rankings. McNeely had heard tales of even Big 5 schools deploying a team of number crunchers to make sure they maintained or improved on their *US News* metrics when making their poaching moves. Of course, he acknowledged, the academic law and economics crowd would say the poaching market was a mechanism to efficiently allocate resources: higher ranked law schools should be able to attract the best students.

Dean Eckstein came prepared to let her faculty know their game warden was taking care of the poaching problem. "I've called the Deans at Columbia, Cardozo, Rutgers, and NYU, and let them know what I think of this bullshit. They all deny it of course, but I've told them it's not going to look good if I have to go to the *Daily News* with this. Especially because I've assembled data showing they focus on stealing minority students, just so they can improve their diversity student numbers in the *US News* ratings. That scared the holy shit out of them, and they've promised to make sure that this practice," pausing with a sly smile and adding "which of course they maintain has never occurred, will not happen again."

Reading the faces of his colleagues, McNeely saw that the Dean's tough talk resonated with them. Most had never stared down an opponent in court—or anywhere else for that matter—so a show of toughness, much like a 450-foot home run by Aaron Judge, was something both unfathomable and miraculous to behold. It also reminded McNeely that Deborah Eckstein was someone the law school could not afford to lose.

21

Justice has nothing to do with what goes on in a courtroom.
Justice is what comes out of a courtroom.

—Clarence Darrow

Returning to his office, McNeely received the customary sartorial review from his assistant, Jewel Henderson, "Well aren't we steezy today? But that thing in your pocket, who's that for? You workin' on some new young thing up there in the Village?"

McNeely had debated for several minutes that morning whether to put a taupe pocket square in his suit jacket, and now was getting confirmation that it was definitely the wrong move.

He always dressed up for faculty meetings as a subtle reminder that he had management/business responsibilities that his ill-dressed faculty colleagues did not. But one of the main reasons he had promoted Jewel Henderson to be the first African American "secretary" (as they used to be called) to become the law school's Chief Administrative Assistant, CAA, was her pluck. She wasn't going to be bullied by the assistants and staff whom she supervised or by faculty who regularly marched into the office demanding to see the Dean claiming some purported emergency.

"OK, OK. Just trying to liven up the image," said McNeely, smiling and stuffing the square into his hip pocket.

Five foot ten, but about seven feet tall in her elevator "taking care of business" heels and muscular, Jewel Henderson was a presence in the Deanplex. McNeely once had told her she had arms like Michelle Obama which she pretended to take as a sexist affront ("I can have you suspended for talking shit like that"), only to immediately start laughing and inform him that she was now benching 140 pounds and didn't mind if men noticed. She had two adult children, one a Marine in North Carolina and the other selling Audis in Brooklyn. No men that she talked about but she had a steady stream of guys stopping by to chat her up. She regularly complained to McNeely that law was the most boring topic in the world, yet regularly attended every campus event during Black History Month.

He chuckled remembering Henderson's first challenge as an administrator. As the newly-appointed CAA, she supervised and evaluated all the faculty assistants. A recently-hired assistant whom she had upbraided for taking an extra 15 minutes on her lunch hour had responded with a loud "screw you" which prompted a five-minute shouting match that could be heard throughout the building. When Henderson returned to the Deanplex McNeely took his new assistant aside and explained that the proper course of action in dealing with an insubordinate employee was to "write her up"—put a memo in the assistant's personnel file to memorialize her behavior, so they would have documentation to justify termination, if necessary someday. Henderson took the advice to heart and produced a three-page, single-spaced memo setting forth the history and purposes of the school's lunch break rules and describing in detail her clash with the assistant. McNeely's favorite part was the concluding sentence of her report of the confrontation: "Whereupon I told her to get out of my face."

Jewel Henderson's value went well beyond cracking the whip. She was gregarious and befriended everyone in the building. She kept McNeely informed on family illnesses of the staff including the customarily ignored janitorial crew. She also was his eyes and ears concerning problems in IT services and the library. And she was not shy about passing along troves of gossip about staff, faculty, and every now and then, the President.

"Hey, got a good one for you today," she said smiling as she handed McNeely his agenda for the afternoon.

"Keep it clean."

"Always. Someone on our maintenance staff was filling in at the President's mansion. Says there's a private room in the basement with, guess what?"

"Uh-oh," said McNeely wide-eyed.

"No, no, not that. There's a tanning machine down there. Just like everyone's been saying."

"Whew, was afraid it was something that would bring the *Drudge Report* to campus. But that explains his ruddy complexion. It's not like he's out mowing the lawns. So, what do I have on tap to round out another delightful day?"

"Professor Boylan in three minutes, Jenna at 4:30, the Black Law Student Association get together at six—watch yo' mouth, whitey—and breakfast tomorrow morning with the Filmore law firm at 8:30."

Skulking back to his office, he checked his emails. 47 since noon. Bumper crop that could largely be ignored. However, a message line entitled "Recompense Demanded" caught his eye.

We are aware of the fraud and deceptions St. Sebastian University has deployed for many years. Charitable giving is meant for charitable ends. You will be contacted soon with an opportunity to disgorge funds improperly obtained and to correct all dishonest and immoral practices.

Yours in Christ
Luther Martin

The spam catcher misses some now and then, he thought. But the mention of charitable giving gave McNeely a moment's pause. What transpires inside of the black box of the University Development Office was something he'd often wondered about, but was grateful for not being involved. He suspected, however, that navigating the Sanus initiative might require a crash course in university finances.

Jewel knocked on the open door, "Professor Boylan is here." She pulled her earlobe and McNeely nodded back. The signal for her to interrupt the meeting in exactly 30 minutes was activated.

Professor Boylan's pear-shaped figure appeared in the doorway. His shabby sports jacket, ill-fitting pants and unkempt grey curls circling a hairline in full retreat epitomized the contemporary law professor gone to seed.

"Leland, how are you doing? Have a chair." Offering a hearty handshake and pointing to the worktable next to the window, McNeely pulled out a manila folder and yellow pad and joined him.

Emitting the sigh of a benighted servant, Boylan moaned, "Busy, busy. Have 95 students in Property and another 30 in Land Use Planning."

McNeely estimated the "Busy, busy" response from Lotus Eater colleagues at 95%. All wanted the Associate Dean to know they were not idlers and in fact were probably undercompensated for their tireless efforts. He fantasized that someday one would say, "Living the restful life of tenure and six hours of teaching from the same notes I created during the Carter Administration." He vowed to kiss that colleague, male or female, on the lips.

"Well I know you have the unenviable job of chairing the Ethics Committee, and I've been reviewing the Margaret Holloran file," said McNeely. "As you know I've got the even less enviable job of imposing a penalty." Confident a little flattery would loosen Jordan up, he went on, "Lee, You've been down this road many more times than I have and you've steered the committee through some rough waters. What was your read on this young lady?"

"Well, she seemed like a nice girl. But didn't put up much of a defense. Said she meant no harm, didn't think footnotes mattered. Never really denied it though."

"Was there anything you saw in her favor? Permanent expulsion is the death penalty, as you know."

"Father Fitz testified as a character witness. He's a kindly old guy. And let me tell you, I've never seen him like that. Kind of emotional. Said he knew for a fact there was no cheating in her mind, she never felt she was doing anything wrong. You know the Father. He's got a big heart. But he's not a lawyer."

Taking note of Boylan's mottled skin and what his grandfather called a drinker's nose, McNeely probed for concessions, "Still, a pretty tough sentencing recommendation from the committee. No room for mercy in your mind?"

"Well, Professor Gleason was pretty exercised himself. Told us this was a test of the law school's commitment to first principles. Even threw around some Catholic theology. I'm a Methodist myself, but he seemed to see it as a crusade, to tell you the truth."

"When did all this come out? I didn't see it in the transcript."

"He stopped in while the committee was meeting. Said he just wanted to mention a few things he forgot to testify about."

McNeely feigning surprise, "Of course that's *ex parte,* going outside the hearing to talk to you."

"True, but you know our rules allow the committee discretion to gather evidence as we see fit. No formal limitations on how we go about our fact finding. Just like you can talk to whoever you want to before imposing a penalty."

"You're right 'bout that. But what was the new information Professor Gleason offered?"

"Not much really. He repeated a lot of what he'd already said. He did mention though that the President was concerned about the case."

Both of McNeely's eyebrows shooting up as his unpleasant sit down with the President flashed in his brain, "President Balducci?"

"Yeah, said he thought the law school had to be careful with this kind of case."

Summoning up his poker face, McNeely asking as casually as if inquiring about the weather, "Any idea how the President got wind of the case?"

"Don't know. But Francis made it sound like he'd talked to him."

"Well, it's a tough one. I'll do some digging," McNeely said, trailing off with a world-weary sigh.

Jewel at the door, "Dean McNeely, you have that conference call . . ."

"Christ almighty," McNeely muttered to himself after Boylan had left. This modest plagiarism case was turning into *Godfather III*, Vatican II, and Roe v. Wade combined.

I demanded more rights for women because I know
what women had to put up with.

—Evita Peron

As a few couples and prowling singles began to populate the bar, Maggie thought back to that fateful summer before law school. There was obviously no good time for an unplanned pregnancy, she thought, but two months before her first day of law school was pretty awful. She was frantically stitching together loans, scholarships, and logging 12-hour days at the Term to get her financing in order when she realized that she was indeed pregnant. There wasn't any question in her mind when it happened, as she had had only two encounters in the last six months, the latest being a one night in and out with a college classmate she'd run into while shopping at the Farmers Market in Hoboken. A quick visit to his penthouse apartment, home by 3 a.m. Had not seen him since and had no interest in doing so.

She made a series of resolutions. *Tell absolutely no one about it. Get an abortion stat. Check the expiration date on her Natazia prescription. Stay away from anyone with a functioning penis. Work your ass off in law school.*

There was one person whom she could have talked to, but she was gone. Her mother was deeply religious, but at the same time intensely compassionate. And they had that mother-daughter thing that she'd read neuroscientists were now mapping. As Maggie pictured it, her mom would have bitten her lower lip, let out a moan, and hugged her for half an hour. Norma had hinted at hardships inflicted on her by men before she was married, but never supplied any details. Maggie imagined she'd probably been groped—or worse—a number of times, propositioned by superiors, and subjected to the catcalls and sexual banter that assholes still toss at young women passing by on Central Avenue. On the other hand, the truth would have killed her father. He'd have responded with unremitting silence and gone back to drinking. She'd had only a couple of close friends in college but felt that even they would only remember her as the first one to get an abortion.

Her experience involved a relatively straightforward process: two drugs, mifepristone and misoprostol, taken orally, aborted her fetus. Because she was only four weeks pregnant, it was about as routine as dealing with a sore throat. Medically, that is. In reality, it had left Maggie sobered and isolated. It wasn't so much the Catholic teachings—she had abandoned some of the hard-core doctrine years earlier—but it was the sense that she was that close to taking on everything entailed in being a mother that shook her. Looking back, she felt the enormous physical and emotional event she had undergone had opened her eyes to the gut-wrenching choices facing women around the country, most of whom she came to understand did not have the supposedly "quick and easy" option of a non-surgical procedure. And most had to negotiate family, financial, and social issues that she did not. But Maggie's experience was no less distressing. Isolated by the demands of managing both the bar and her father's Alzheimer's, she went through it alone.

She finally broke her silence, confiding her experience to her pal and study partner while they were winding down from their first-year law school exams. Jenna, who had spent her undergraduate years in the hipster universe of Wesleyan University, gave her a new perspective. "Oh, I knew a dozen girls who had abortions. Things really changed over the years though. At first it was a big secret, not something anyone talked about. But by senior year, everyone came out. I think the creepy politics of Ted Cruz and that Huckabee clown and the rest opened our eyes to what was going on."

Maggie was heartened to hear a perspective she never had been exposed to as an undergraduate. "You mean all that religious-right, born again shit?"

"Yeah, but for me it was about more than the mission of a bunch of religious zealots. It really was about suppression. Keeping women down. Making them stay home and . . ." Jen pausing to demonstrate snipping scissors with two fingers, "stop threatening their tiny little members."

"I came from Long Island, hedge fund money, a suburban bubble, the whole package, as you know. So, it really wasn't 'til college that I met women who'd lived in the real world. Had a friend at Wesleyan, African American, from Louisiana. She had three sisters. Every one of them had a baby in their teens. She was smart, a track star, and dodged the bullet. But every year she came back from Christmas break in Baton Rouge, and it was like she'd seen a ghost. In med school now at Tulane. The American Dream."

"For her at least." Maggie added to seal the point. They shared a sarcastic half-laugh and stayed quiet for a few minutes. Raising her glass in a toast: "So here's to Making American Great. For the first time. For everyone."

23

They carried the sky. The whole atmosphere, they carried it, the humidity, the monsoons, the stink of fungus and decay, all of it, they carried gravity.

—Tim O'Brien on soldiers in Vietnam, *The Things They Carried*

Wednesday was his day to tackle the god-awful tasks of wrangling the bureaucrats and herding his cats. Having scored a window seat on the 7:10 a.m. PATH train, McNeely opened his laptop and surveyed his morning agenda. In keeping with his practice of scheduling the worst first, he was set to meet with the Faculty Accreditation Committee at 8:30. Every seven years, law schools are "inspected" by a team appointed by the American Bar Association to evaluate the school's performance and suitability to be listed as an "ABA accredited" law school. This was an immensely important event, because accreditation carried with it the right for every graduate of the school to take the bar exam in any state. The downside was that the accreditation team often would find deficits in the school's performance—too high a student/faculty ratio, inadequate technical support for internet access, high failure rates on bar exams, dilapidated classroom facilities, you name it. Except in the rare case where it denied accreditation, the ABA committee would issue a "provisional approval" which meant the school would have to correct its shortcomings. Which in turn meant the law school dean had to go hat in hand to the University President and ask for a plenary indulgence. And sometimes a boatload of money.

For many years the process was nicknamed the "ice cream truck." In those halcyon days the accreditation process was run by the law schools themselves. Their professional association, the Association of American Law Schools, or AALS, set the standards for approval and published the evaluations of each school. Deans and professors from other law schools would conduct a site visit, attend random classes, interview students and faculty, and issue a report. Often the report would find an otherwise well-performing law school had one serious shortcoming: It didn't pay its faculty enough. Or the faculty needed up-to-date laptops. Or they were being asked to teach too many hours per week. The AALS ice cream truck pulled up, and the law faculty ordered the treats it "needed" to fulfill its academic responsibilities. The evaluation team, comprised of academics from other schools who themselves would someday be facing a site visit, almost always obliged.

All this ended abruptly when the U.S. Department of Justice sued the AALS for price fixing. The law schools were efffectively a cartel, using the acceditation system to increase their professors' salaries. The academic community was of course shocked, shocked. Not that accreditation process had become a vending machine, but that the antitrust laws should apply to them at all. The result however was no surprise. The Justice Department required that the process be reformed, put the American Bar Association in charge, and required a more rigorous—and independent—review of each law school's performance. The ice cream truck was gone, and evaluators now demanded evidence that law schools were providing a meaningful legal education and preparing their students for practice—all depositing a shitload of paperwork, meetings, and anxiety on beleaguered deans every seven years.

This morning he would meet with the faculty committee and administrative team to plan for the ABA site visit and strategize about shortcomings the inspection team might uncover. Coming in from Penn Station after a meeting in Midtown, he surveyed the landscape as the Jersey Central train emerged into the bright daylight on the Jersey side of the Hudson: a dystopian stream of abandoned factories and warehouses, mountains of automobile wrecks, and miles of graffiti-covered boxcars—a landscape that struck McNeely as an apt metaphor for his own salvage operation that day.

Walking into the Deanplex, he was greeted with an up-and-down inspection from Jewel. "Back to the grunge law prof look I see," she said, side-eyeing his faded jeans, herringbone sports jacket, and hiking boot ensemble. The days he didn't teach or have faculty meetings were his personal casual Friday.

"By the way, got an interesting video to show you later," Jewel offered with a conspiratorial smile.

McNeely gulped, knowing she was referring to the hidden video camera in the faculty lounge that only he, Jewel, and an outside contractor knew about. "Nothing X-rated this time, I hope."

"Depends on what cable channels you got. One of your favorites in action. And I mean action," she said chuckling.

At least he had something to look forward to now.

Jewel threw him a conspiratorial smile. "By the way, I did that undercover work about Professor Gangloff for you."

McNeely knew what she meant. The Dean had recently issued a "Best Practices" memo that included a variety of items that she "suggested" the faculty should follow. The anodyne word "suggested" was wiped away like the shorefront houses facing Hurricane Sandy by what followed: "These best practices will of course be part of the overall evaluative criteria under consideration for performance reviews and annual salary adjustments." One best practice addressed faculty office hours: "All teaching faculty should maintain open-door office hours of at least 6 hours per week for each course taught. Appointments with students at other times do not offset this responsibility."

Acting on her own initiative, Jewel decided to deploy what she called her "squad"—the faculty assistants who report to her—to monitor compliance with the new policy. "Just curious," she had explained to McNeely. "These guys teach law, so maybe they should follow the rules. After all, the secretaries get dinged if they're five minutes late from lunch." Not surprisingly, some faculty assistants were more than happy to squeal on the professors to whom they were assigned. The mysterious case of Professor Gangloff was a particularly intriguing one. A tall, slender charter member of the Y&R and marathon runner, his office door was always open, computer connected, and sport jacket slung over a chair or couch. Yet he never seemed to be in his office. His assistant was Natale Hammer, a 63-year-old woman who had worked at the law school for 23 years, and not one to suffer arrogance lightly. With only minimal coaxing from Jewel, she gave him up.

Smiling broadly, Jewel morphed into Inspector Clouseau. "He's had Natale move his reading glasses around on his desk, rearrange the books on his sideboard, turn out the lights and lock his office at 5 p.m. when she leaves. He even instructed her to tell students he was doing research in the library if they couldn't find him in the office."

McNeely shook his head. "I promise, word of honor, this will not be ignored. And, Jewel, if you want to apply for a job with the FBI, let me know. You're better than that Mueller guy."

Later in the day, with three morning meetings and two double espressos under his belt, McNeely walked briskly into the faculty dining room. On Wednesdays, the law school hosted what he privately called "The School Lunch Program"—a free buffet for faculty designed to encourage his colleagues to mingle and exchange ideas, all in service of promoting faculty harmony. But what seemed to him an almost genetic predisposition to one-upmanship often turned lunchtime chit chat into a guerilla war over the principal currencies for peer esteem. Chatter at faculty get togethers was quite unlike the focus on football, sports and movies that dominated bar talk among the assistant US attorneys and FBI agents he hung with in his former life. The main coin of the realm in the School Lunch Program seemed to be travel, with invocations of exotic locations others had not visited. Estonia, Helsinki, Sardinia, the Belle Epoque in Baden Baden, the Roman Ruins in Croatia.

He walked by as Cathcart was pontificating, "You've got to go to Aarhus. None of you have been there? Jesus! The Vadestedet, the cafés, shops, art. Really puts Prague in its place." Cities with umlauts, food with cidellas, hotels with bidets seemed to be important items to name drop. McNeely usually found himself nodding sagely but fooling no one. He had committed an early rookie mistake at one of his first lunches with colleagues, confessing that his international travel consisted of a one-week tour to London and Paris on his hurry-up honeymoon to beat the birth of their daughter. Not hard to read colleagues' reaction.

Beyond the myriad personality, religious, gender, and age differences that separated them, there were intellectual divides on the faculty as well. Several younger faculty could be classified as "Crits"—Critical Legal Scholars, adherents of one or another version of Critical Legal Theory. This camp contended that legal principles were easily manipulated and judges were the creatures of their own political, class, and psychological biases. Beyond that, the Crits had a definitive leftist tilt. The main goal of teaching law, argued Duncan Kennedy, one of McNeely's professors at Harvard, was to "promote a more humane, egalitarian, and democratic society." This stood in stark contrast to traditional, doctrinal legal analysis scholars who saw the law as ineluctably evolving through a process of reasoned elaboration to produce a just result, whatever that might mean. Yet another school of thought viewed law through an economic lens. The law and economics school, birthed and housed at the University of Chicago, contended that neoclassical economic principles could both explain and justify legal principles. The market would set things right, provided the legal system didn't screw things up. Some L&E scholars actually voted for Trump, though few admitted it. Unlike many other law school faculties, St. Sebastian housed a good assortment of all these competing camps. It was left to the Deans to put on their blue helmets, and try to prevent civil wars.

Nevertheless, pervasive political, intellectual, and social divides inevitably provoked unrest. To say, as CLS thinkers did, that law was "indeterminate" was to say that the positions staked out by their mainstream colleagues were essentially gratuitous. When they went further and asserted that law was "incoherent" or "contradictory" they edged toward closer to the cliff of those who once contended that law was not really an academic discipline fit for a university. But even their more modest claim—that law was thinly disguised politics—proved to be the most cutting claim of all. It was essentially calling their mainstream colleagues' self-abnegation before the altar of an objective truth a transparently dishonest ruse, and that their teaching was a ridiculous enterprise. So as disappointing as it was, it was not surprising that the School Lunch Program's quest for faculty concord was doomed from the start. It did however keep everyone well fed.

Passing the Y&R table, he observed several of the youngsters yucking it up with Cathcart and heard the punchline to a story delivered by the faculty's lone gay member, Abe Block. "*That's so gay*, I told him!!" followed by a scream of laughter and a fist bump across the table from Cathcart. Block had achieved some notoriety testifying before the New Jersey Senate on gay rights legislation and writing extensively on the subject. McNeely wondered if he was even aware of how St. Sebastian had become so welcoming and made a mental note to pass along the legend of Barney Schatz, the Rosa Parks of gay faculty at the law school.

Schatz was hired as an Assistant Professor in the 1980s at a time Ronald Reagan's team was laughingly referring to AIDs "the gay plague," the Catholic Church was condemning the use of condoms (even though gay males were obviously not using them for birth control), and the country was embarking on a new-found culture war. Understandably, Schatz took the only option available if he hoped to gain tenure from the predominantly conservative Catholic faculty at St. Sebastian. Following the advice of several liberal tenured colleagues, he remained closeted for six years, kept silent on gay rights issues, and even acquiesced to being accompanied to faculty events by "beards"—women who served as his pretend dates. The strategy worked: Schatz was unanimously voted tenure.

His Rosa Parks moment came at the faculty Christmas Party just days after his tenured status become official. Schatz arrived fashionably late to the cocktail party in the St. Sebastian Church reception area. His entrance was carefully orchestrated as he walked into the crowded room with his date. *A male! Holding hands!! A former student!!!!* They raised their joined hands in air like two bobsledders who had won an Olympic Gold Medal and exchanged a kiss. Then they moved on to chat up each of the three faculty members who had married their former students. Over the following two decades, Schatz's presence at faculty meetings silenced the Senior Doctrinal Catholics and no anti-gay issues ever surfaced. And in 2016, Block, who was openly gay and writing extensively on discrimination issues, was hired without a peep. Nor did any faculty object to student clinic cases challenging discrimination against gays or to faculty testimony, articles, and amicus briefs on gender-related issues. Tenure has some underappreciated benefits, McNeely mused.

Surveying the room, he saw two prototype Lotus Eaters seated together. Neither had ever missed a free lunch, cocktail party, or alumni reception and were thoroughly invested in devouring their food, clearly uninterested in exchanging thoughts about evolving trends in the law or anything else for that matter. Bill Donnelly, a morose, uni-browed 58-year-old professor had made it clear in their first meeting after McNeely became Associate Dean that he was not one who thought it necessary to make concessions for the good of the team. When asked to teach his Civil Procedure class on a Tuesday-Thursday afternoon schedule, he explained that Tuesday afternoon classes were out of the question because he did his grocery shopping then.

Not knowing him well, McNeely assumed he was kidding, "O.K. Well, I'm hoping then that Wednesdays aren't your laundry day?"

Donnelly's surly response made it abundantly clear he was not kidding, adding with an elevated unibrow evidencing pique that there was an unspecified problem with Wednesday afternoons as well. Following an exchange of a half dozen emails, Donnelly agreed to a compromise: a Tuesday afternoon class provided that it start at 1 p.m. and end at 3:30. The cut-man's grandson had stitched up another bleed for the law school. But he had also picked up another reminder that tenure is a double-edged sword.

Next to Donnelly was Amon Evers, a 50-year-old tax law professor who had gained almost legendary status for a series of unfortunate events. Thanks to Jewel Henderson's close rapport with students, McNeely had a pipeline to the gossip and intrigues of the student body. The story she passed along, elaborated in graphic detail, and punctuated by loud guffaws, involved Evers appearing in class not once, not twice, but three times with a large wet stain on his khaki pants just below the zipper. Evers' last-minute visits to the men's room before his class had obviously been rushed. After the stain appeared for a second time, an enterprising student began a lottery to guess the next appearance which he dubbed the "Evers Visitation Contest." McNeely never wore khaki pants to class again.

He had some favorites, though he often did an internal audit trying to unwrap the mystery of his genuine affection for them. Maybe it was a soft spot for offbeat characters. The courageous eccentric, the quietly intense loner, the unambiguously decent religious. Was he drawn to them because they had attributes he lacked, aspired to, or simply couldn't fathom?

Case in point: Phill ("Double L") Abelman, a 45-year-old unabashed hipster, shoulder length hair, teaching and preaching environmental justice, and performing monthly as lead guitar at the Badlands of Bayonne with his Gen X pick up band. He did his job, taught competently with predictably enthusiastic student evaluations, and even wrote the occasional noteworthy law review article. However, two years ago he had put McNeely in a rather dicey box. Following the annual faculty-student softball game (which ended as a mercy finish with the student team up 30 runs after three innings), Double L had joined several students in the woods adjoining the ball field to smoke weed. Word spread instantly on social media, not only on SSLS sites, but also on two prominent law school blogs, as well as Instagram and Reditt.

What was an Associate Dean to do? Especially an Associate Dean who him-self had gotten wasted several times with the internet's now-notorious "Half-Baked Professor." McNeely had a robust internal debate: *Why the fuck not? It's off campus. He's a grown up and so are the students. They're just playing softball in a public park. No coercion. No pressure on anyone. Give me a fucking break. I should have the balls to just go out and do some carousing without always sweating the consequences. What's the point of tenure after all?*

Much as he was intrigued with the possibility that the incident might increase applications for admission to St. Sebastian, McNeely knew something had to be done. The academic cut man reached into his dopp kit and applied a home brew of anti-infection ointments: One month of unpaid administrative leave for Double L, a press release announcing the law school's prompt handling of the matter, a memo to the President and University General Counsel advising them of the law school's new zero tolerance policy—albeit addressing only on-campus consumption of con-trolled substances—and a carefully-worded memo reminding faculty to "observe appropriate boundaries when engaging in social events with students."

But there were also colleagues whom he admired for their quiet courage. Ame-lia Abdelnour, the only Muslim on the faculty, had lost two husbands, one to cancer and the other to a waitress in Brooklyn, and was raising three young sons as a single mom. She had written courageous articles about the history of slavery in Islam, examining the issue from pre-Islamic times through to the nineteenth century and analyzing the impact of Western abolitionism on the conceptions and practice of slavery in the Muslim world. Her scholarship decrying the enslaving ideologies of ISIS and Boko Haram and arguing that Muslims had an urgent imperative and responsibility to foster abolition under the aegis of Islamic law drew widespread attention and more than a few death threats. Despite the turmoil in her life, she taught large classes, worked diligently on faculty committees, and had never asked for—or complained about—anything. More than once, McNeely had to fight the temptation to tell a whining colleague to try to "be like Amelia."

His geo-mapping of the lounge almost complete, McNeely spotted Father Fitzgibbon sitting by himself, as calm as a Hindu cow as his grandfather used to say.

"May I join you?" he asked.

"By all means, Dean. Please."

Seeing the paperback copy of Christopher Hitchens book, *The Crimes of Henry Kissinger* on the table, McNeely asked, "First Orwell, now Hitchens? Methinks you're becoming one of those lefty Jesuits our Bishop doesn't approve of."

Bishop John Michaels, archbishop of Newark, a notoriously conservative—if not partisan Republican—cleric, had unabashedly lined up with the political right. Years ago he'd publicly announced he would not give communion to presidential candidate John Kerry and refused to permit the law school to allow former Attorney General Janet Reno to speak at the law school's academic forum because of their positions on abortion. And now he was showing up as a regular at President Trump's bimonthly assembly of religious leaders. He also did not hesitate to make it clear he had little use for his Jesuit brothers, whom he regarded as socialist, soft, scholastic, and not quite authentically Catholic.

Choosing his words carefullly, Father Fitzgibbon responded, "Well, the Bishop and I apparently worship at different churches. In any event, I've had a longstanding interest in politics and the story of Kissinger's role in the Vietnam war is, let's say . . . worth revisiting these days."

"Yeah, I had an uncle who fought in Nam. Didn't talk much about it though," McNeely said.

"Lot of memories you don't want to remember . . ." Father Fitzgibbon paused and fingered his book.

McNeely noticed a faraway look coming into the old priest's eyes. "You weren't over there were you?" he asked, astonished.

"Oh yeah. Took out eleven souls," then added with a tight smile, "Not counting my own."

"My God. Where were you?"

"All over the place. I was army . . . Was in Huế during the Tet Offensive. You know what that was don't you?"

"Sort of . . . that was the attack during a holiday, right?"

"Yep. Lunar New Year, 1968. The day the music died. Supposed to be a holiday, South Viet regulars on leave, caught everyone with their pants down. Literally for some of my buddies who hung out at the brothels. Cong took over the American embassy for a while. I was with the 12th Calvary in Hué. The VC ransacked the town, mortared our bases, and destroyed most of our choppers. We fought for four weeks to retake the city. Was all rubble by the time we won."

The priest giving the classic double fingered wave designating air quotes. "Won! Nonsense! The deception, the lies! The brass claimed victory. And the fucking sainted Vietcong! What did they do? Slaughtered thousands of their own people. Civilians, women, children."

Father Fitz displayed an apologetic palm. "Sorry. Been fighting this battle for 50 years. Kissinger and Nixon cut a deal with the corrupt South Vietnamese government to ditch Lyndon Johnson's peace agreement with the North. Promised the corrupt South Viet stoolies they'd get a better deal. All so Nixon could win the election. Then he dragged the war out for five years. Another 20,000 dead American boys. Man, Hitchens got it right. If that's not treason . . . Absolute power corrupts absolutely."

Sensing Father Fitz's mounting distress, McNeely switched gears. "So, what about your return? How'd you manage to adjust so well?"

"Well, it turned out that's how I became a Man of God. Got home, decided I could drink myself to death or find something else to do. Ran over to Fordham. Signed onto the Jesuit's *cura personalis*—care for the whole person. Helped me big time. And so, I've spent the last 40 years making amends."

He paused and looked at McNeely with a gentle smile. "You know what Hegel wrote, don't you? '*The owl of Minerva spreads its wings only with the falling of dusk.*'"

McNeely nodded sagely, making a mental note to look up the meaning of Father Fitz's enigmatic epigram when he got back to his office.

24

Hopping off the PATH train at 7 a.m., McNeely was greeted by a loudspeaker spewing out a report of the day's outages.

Service Change and Routing Announcement. Elevators at Hoboken and Journal Square are not in operation. Passengers unable to ascend stairs should reroute through Newark Penn Station and consult Jersey Transit Bus schedule for alternative services.

Service Change and Routing Announcement. Elevators at Hoboken and Journal Square are not in operation . . .

Eager to escape three more repetitions of the announcement, McNeely not only two-timed, but sprinted the 40-step stairway that led to the open but cadaverous gray skies of Baytown. It was the closest he'd get to an aerobic workout this week and doubly rewarding as it halved the minutes inhaling the mixed aromas of urine, tobacco, and sweat that filled the Baytown terminal. His nine-pound backpack, loaded with laptop and law books, made the rapid ascent a challenge, but one he was sure would someday help get him back down to his fighting weight of 235 pounds.

Greeted by relatively fresh air and a cacophony of police and fire engine sirens on Commerce Avenue, McNeely strode briskly toward the law school. Though thoroughly familiar, the signage along the way of his 10-minute walk always felt like time travel. Vinnie's Rent a Flick (now mostly porn); 4500 Sq. Feet Office Space For Rent (elegant graffiti courtesy of YONI); Sonny's Donuts & Gormet (sic) Coffee; Loyal Order of Moose Lodge 223; vacant lot; Handy Hardware (closed); Pipes, Papers and Vapes; Midtown Chiropractic; Store for Rent (YONI signing in again); Glazed and Confused Donuts; Psychic Chakras Healing; vacant lot; Sammy's Halal; and his favorite, an abandoned liquor store adorned with two elegant graffiti: *Post-*

pone Entropy and *Carpe Noctem,* and one angry scrawl: *Yankees Suck.*

All words to live by, he felt.

Properties near the law school were largely student housing, including many nominally "single family" brick homes that actually housed a half-dozen enterprising law students who heated their garages and basements with code-violating space heaters. Also in abundance in Western Baytown were dilapidated—and therefore affordable—apartment buildings owned by investors willing to ignore occupancy laws in exchange for low expectations on upkeep.

As he turned the corner onto the newly renamed Derek Jeter Street, McNeely glanced up at the massive seven-story block of cement bearing the designation St. Sebastian School of Law, though when illuminated at night, the malfunctioning sign read *St. Sebastian School o Law*, giving it a Celtic flavor that he much enjoyed. A visiting professor from Poland had once remarked nostalgically that the Brutalist design of the building reminded him of the architecture of Lodz, ruefully adding that most such monstrosities had long since disappeared, along with totalitarian rule and undrinkable wine. Father Balducci had promised a new building for the law school. Just added one hitch: Dean Eckstein had to come up with the first five million dollars, just as the St. Sebastian Business School had done.

In truth, the business school precedent was not one that Father Balducci wanted to replicate. Back in 2006, during the go-go years on Wall Street, a graduate of St. Sebastian's MBA program, Dennis Butakowski, had donated $20 million to the university to erect a new building for his alma mater. Which naturally would bear his name, as would the business school itself. Every logo, item of stationary, bumper sticker, and the marble edifice of the spectacular new building bore the imprint "Dennis J. Butakowski School of Business." All of which made the process of excising the Butakowski imprint on St. Sebastian pretty taxing after his convictions for insider trading, money laundering, price fixing, and violations of the Foreign Corrupt Practices Act. Not to mention the negative branding generated by videos of Butakowski's 60th birthday toga party in Mykonos which appeared on every news and late-night talk show for months.

Whenever he needed to boost his spirits, McNeely would play the viral video of workmen in rigging high atop of the business school building removing the Butakowski signage. He ranked schadenfreude as his favorite deadly sin, even if it hadn't cracked the top seven.

Guessing that fewer than half of the law school's five elevators were likely to be in operation, McNeely decided to continue his aerobic workout by sprinting the six floors up to the Deanplex. Stairs creaking in protest announced his arrival and Jewel greeted him with a smirk, "You decided to jog from the train again?"

"No. Not really. What do you mean?"

"You're sweating like LeBron in the fourth quarter. I bet your shirt is pitted out," Henderson said, wrinkling her nose to suggest that he probably also smelled.

"Don't worry about it. I'll be OK," McNeely said, edging toward his office.

Henderson blocked his exit and extended an upraised palm like a parent making her son hand over the candy he had taken from his sister, "Give it to me and put on one of your old ones in the closet. I'll take it to the cleaners. Johnny will get it back by noon."

Horrified, McNeely thought of repercussions if anyone found out he had his assistant take his laundry to the dry cleaners. It would be worse than any affront, sexual, financial, or otherwise, that could be attributed to him.

She saw his petrified look. "Relax Neels. I'll be discreet. You can't be going to a meeting with the President and the Sanus people looking like a sweaty undergraduate. If anyone asks, I'll tell them you sent me on an urgent mission to buy you a bottle of Jameson for lunch. Also, lose that tie."

Recalling with a start the crucial sit-down that Father Balducci had arranged regarding the proposed Sanus Institute, McNeely relented. Fumbling for his wallet, he handed Jewel a ten-dollar bill. "OK thanks. Get lunch for yourself."

Doing the math in her head, Henderson smiled. "Wow. Thanks Mr. Buffet. Let me call Ruth's Chris to get a reservation."

Dropping into his chair, unpacking his laptop, and signing in on the second try to his email account, McNeely undertook his customary triage. Worst comes first.

An email from Professor Lanyard, chair of the Faculty Appointments Committee, labeled "URGENT: Faculty Appointments Discussion"

Neels: As you know, we're looking at some stellar résumés for the open slot. I don't have to remind you that with the accreditation inspection coming up, we need to show we're in the big leagues. So, I'm trying to persuade some of our colleagues you put on this committee that there are graduates of five law schools whom we will interview at the meet market, and not waste our time—or theirs—on pointless sessions just to make us feel welcoming and satisfy the AALS. Unfortunately, it has come to a stalemate. I've relented on interviewing two minority candidates (one Asian) and quite a few women, but I refuse to assent to throwing the process open to all comers. And

The memo concerned an annual event in Washington D.C. sponsored by the Association of American Law Schools at which virtually every law school in the country conducted interviews with applicants for faculty positions. Typically, the law school would cram some 25 half-hour interviews with committee members into the three-day session, and then select a handful to invite back to campus for meetings with the entire faculty and get-to-know-you dinners. When it came to hiring new faculty, McNeely knew one lasting truth. Every law professor wanted the same thing: Someone just like them.

All of which made determining the composition of the Faculty Appointments Committee a tricky business. Deans Eckstein and McNeely spent hours strategizing on how to balance the committee based on the usual factors—age, gender, race, politics—but to do so in a way that would come out with candidates that met the school's burning needs, improve diversity, and uncover a candidate with a genuine desire to teach who had something to say in his or her scholarship. They had decided to let Professor Lanyard continue to chair the committee, as he had for 12 years, but placed on the committee several professors they felt shared their hiring priorities. The impending shit storm signaled in the email meant that one of them would have to shake Professor Lanyard's tree. Or possibly uproot it. McNeely had a pretty good idea who that would be.

McNeely had become acquainted early on with his new profession's unspoken biases. The subtler ones reached beyond gender and race. This insight came home to him while attending his first major conference of law professors soon after he joined the St. Sebastian faculty. Based on the reception to his first published article on insider trading, he had been invited to speak on a panel comprised of faculty far above his station discussing "Constitutional Law and The Role of the Corporation in the Caldron of *Revanchisme*." The session had gone well, with most of the audience questions directed to his co-panelists from Big Five law schools. The only one addressed to him seemed to confuse his talk with that of the other white male professor on the panel. Still, he felt great. Swimming with the big fish.

After the session ended the chair of his panel proposed getting a drink at a nearby bar she knew. Piling into a cab, McNeely found himself in the middle seat flanked by two of the more renowned names in corporate law, Edith McPherson, Boston University, who was famous for a leading article on sex discrimination and corporate governance, and Elias Propter, Yale, author of a 12-volume treatise on securities law.

It immediately became apparent that Edith and Elias would be talking exclusively to each other during the ride, so McNeely politely swiveled his head to show proper attentiveness to both. After exchanging a few disparaging words about the decline of the Harvard faculty over the last decade, Edith ventured some thoughts on working "in an environment of abject cultural and social cluelessness."

"You know, I've been trying to coach my assistant, Leon, about making a good impression. He's gay, but really doesn't have the panache I'd been hoping for. I'm really trying to help him climb up the ladder, but it's a tough slog." She offered a conspiratorial smile and lowered her voice.

"For one thing, *he smokes*. Cigarettes, for God's sakes. Takes a walk every two hours and smokes in the courtyard. *That's so lower class*, I told him."

McNeely shot a glance at the rear-view mirror where he could see the cabbie's face and dour expression. He was looking directly back at him.

Don't compromise yourself. You're all you got.

—Janis Joplin

Maggie took a long disapproving look at herself in the mirror affixed to the inside of her locker, slammed the door shut, and braced herself against the door. What a sorry fool I am, she thought. How could I ever stand up in court and defend someone on trial for her life when I can't summon up a plan to defend myself? Who was I kidding, thinking I was going to climb out of the swamps of Rahway and become Michelle Obama?

She shuddered as she recalled her calamitous, comically inept plot to entrap her accuser. The plan—which had made eminent sense over five tequilas with her pal Jenna—was to visit Professor Gleason, somehow lure him into a compromising position, record the encounter, and presto, like a clever trial lawyer in a Grisham novel, she'd pass the evidence of his nefarious behavior to the Dean and the complaint against her would be dismissed.

It hadn't quite worked out that way. She had managed to dress provocatively and practiced in the mirror some suggestive forays like "Isn't there anything I can do to make this go away?" "You must know that I'm willing to atone for my bad behavior." She knew it sounded like low-end porn, but Jenna had convinced her that all she needed was to evoke just a hint of impropriety and—this being the era of Harvey Weinstein, et al—Gleason would fold and she just might walk.

No sooner had she sat down in his office however, Gleason unleashed a barrage of homilies, religious scripture, and jurisprudential pontification. When he got through invoking Jesus, St. Augustine, and the Pope, Maggie had heard enough. She didn't recall the entire flow of her rebuttal argument, but was pretty sure the words sanctimonious, bloated, and pompous fucking hypocrite came into play.

But even with her imminent pre-sentencing meeting with the Associate Dean looming, she felt a sudden rush of exhilaration. She had stood up for herself and called out a sanctimonious, bloated, pompous hypocrite. And he did display a nice shade of purple as she looked over her shoulder on exiting. I might not have a career in law, she thought, but maybe mom's Neapolitan DNA might get me somewhere in politics.

Maggie took an elevator to the top floor and cautiously entered the Dean-plex, which was empty. After spending a few minutes examining the portraits of deceased white male deans, she sat down and worked her cellphone. No news from the Term which meant her father hadn't arrived yet and couldn't be asking for reminders about how to tap kegs. Suddenly the door sprang open with a crash and a tall woman walked in carrying a shirt on a hanger.

"Hi, I'm Jewel Henderson, Professor McNeely's laundress. Just kidding, I'm his Administrative Assistant. But he needed a clean shirt, and it's all in a day's work. Don't tell him I told you. He's a prince, but some things have to be kept confidential in big-time law school administration."

Looking at her appointment book she asked, "You're Ms. Holloran?"

"Yes, I have a 10:30 appointment with Dean McNeely."

"Right. Let me see if he's done with his Pilates," Henderson said without looking up.

"Pilates?"

"I'm still kidding. Does he look like a Pilates kind of guy? He is a prince, though. Go easy on him." Henderson walked to the door, knocked, and showed Maggie in.

Looking up and standing awkwardly, McNeely gestured to the table at the end of his office. "Ah, Ms. Holloran, sit down, sit down."

Maggie had seen the Associate Dean at some law school functions but had not taken any of his classes. Her first reaction, looking at his bulging waist and ill-fitting wrinkled shirt was that he's definitely not a Pilates kind of guy. Looking around, she noticed that his was different than other professors' offices she had visited. No framed degrees, plaques, or photographs with important people. Instead, there was a large three-colored flag of a country she couldn't identify, a collection of photographs of baseball players, and a picture of an actor whose name she couldn't remember but recalled was the star of her mother's favorite movie, *Casablanca.*

McNeely hoisted an enormous three-ring binder which he dropped on the table and with a grunt, plopped down into the chair across from Maggie.

"All right. I've been through all the documents, transcripts, and appeal memos regarding your case. What this meeting is about is your opportunity to tell me in your own words your side of the story which will help me decide what to do with this matter. Do you have anyone representing you?"

"Well, the school assigned Professor Wagner, but he's been busy with . . ."

Knowing that having Fred Wagner as your counsel meant you were effectively a *pro se* defendant, McNeely interrupted "Enough said. I'm actually not a prosecutor or judge in these matters. Just someone who has to find a way to resolve this kind of thing. So, let's do this. Just tell me what happened."

Maggie was not about to take McNeely's question and relaxed façade at face value. She ran some possibilities through her mind. Was he being coy, playing good cop? Did his experience as a lawyer train him to ask open-ended questions to get the witness talking? Maybe talking too much? Was he just an inept bureaucrat who didn't know how to get to the point? Had he already made up his mind and just wants to make a show of conducting a fair hearing? She had sized up a lot of middle-aged guys at the bar, usually accurately predicting when and how they would hit on her. But this was trickier. Was he genuinely interested in hearing an honest telling of her story? And more important, could it possibly make a difference?

She decided to test the water. "Well, Dean, I certainly will go through all the details. But first, could you tell me what are the standards you apply in determining the appropriate punishment? What I mean is: exactly what factors would count in mitigation of my sentence?"

McNeely shifted in his chair and Maggie could see she'd lined a single to left field. That word, "exactly," was exactly the right word.

"Well, there's a variety of issues. Certainly, your understanding of the rules of plagiarism, extenuating circumstances, prejudicial treatment, the overall context, and so on."

Good, she thought. In fact, maybe it was a triple. There's no real standard here. It's all a black box left up to the discretion of this chubby Associate Dean. No surprise. Law schools don't need to abide by rules. *'Badges? We don't need no stinkin' badges'* she thought, suppressing a smile. Recalling that the guy in the photo on the wall was in that movie too.

"I understand. OK here's what happened." Maggie proceeded to give a detailed account of her research, subtly revealing the enormous number of hours spent reading cases and obtaining trial transcripts of hearings involving contested abortion legislation. She could see the Associate Dean's surprise when she recounted the interviews she had conducted with state legislators and litigants in the cases. When he interrupted her to ask how many interviews she had done, she pulled out her laptop and positioned it at an angle so he would catch a glimpse of the three dozen file folders containing documents. Maggie had never presented a case to a jury but based on McNeely's facial expressions she knew she had made her case pretty effectively.

After five minutes of summarizing her paper's findings and analysis, she realized it was time for her closing argument. "Dean McNeely, I'm not going to give you a sob story. There's a lot of law students working long hours to pay their tuition and support their families. I was pretty tied up with stuff at home and was rushing out this first draft of my paper. And yes, I did know I shouldn't cut and paste material from another source. But I only did it with respect to these footnotes. I'm sorry, but I promise you, I am an honest woman, and I am going to be an honest, hard-working lawyer for people who need help."

"OK, OK. Ms. Holloran, you've made a good argument. I have to examine the record carefully and consult with the Dean and the Ethics Committee members. I'll be back to you in a couple of days."

Seeing disappointment in her face as he walked her to the door, McNeely recalled his own fury when he first read her remarkable paper. "You just keep on working. We'll see what we can do."

Jewel Henderson looked closely at McNeely after Maggie left. "Neels, I accidentally read that girl's file on your desk. You need to fix that shit! You know why they're going after her! By the way, you got a call from the Provost while you were in your meeting. Said it was pretty important."

Pretty important could only mean bad news. And coming from Griff, the Provost—with her wireless connection to Sheehan Hall—it meant another message from an unhappy President.

He picked up the phone and steadied himself for the next assault on his digestive system. "Hi Griff. Hit me with your best shot."

"OK. Got an edict from Sheehan Hall this morning. He wants me to—and I quote—'find out about that pro-abortion paper some damn law student is writing.' No idea what he's talking about, but as you know, when I'm not cleaning up someone's shit I'm tasked with depositing shit on some other poor soul. Put on a raincoat Tommy, looks like it's your turn."

McNeely quickly surmised what happened. Professor Gleason had leaked—more likely bragged—to the President about how he had single-handedly stopped a godless FemiNazi from writing a law school paper that extolled the virtues of killing the unborn. But he had probably also cautioned that it was not a done deal until the Associate Dean made a final ruling. Hence, the follow-up assigned to his beleaguered Provost.

"Griff, as per usual, we have intrigues worthy of the Vatican circa 1400. It involves one of my more pious faculty colleagues trying to mistreat a fine young woman and simultaneously curry favor with the Pope . . . I mean with the President. Let me spare you the details for the moment as I'm just now reviewing the file and trying to find a way to resolve the matter without resorting to physical violence."

"That sounds like a very measured, mature approach," Griff responded. "If it comes to the latter, please hire a discreet intermediary. And kindly have it done it off campus."

This was why McNeely loved the Provost. And why in stressful situations he liked to remind himself that she was next in the line of succession should some misfortune befall the President.

History is much more the product of chaos than of conspiracy.

—Zbigniew Brzezinski

Deans Eckstein and McNeely met every Thursday morning for their "State of the Union" breakfast at the Miss America Diner, an opportunity to review upcoming events and tasks and to share their hopes, fears and ambitions for the law school. And of course, to dish some dirt. They had become something of a mutual admiration society. McNeely genuinely believed the Dean might someday make it to the Supreme Court. She had all the necessary academic credentials, Yale and Stanford; clerkships on the Second Circuit and for Justice Breyer on the Supreme Court; a boatload of important publications and books; and perhaps most important, regular appearances on MSNBC and pithy quotations in the *New York Times* and *Washington Post* on important Supreme Court cases. She'd been trekking to Washington for several years to testify at Congressional hearings and chat up Senate staffers. If a Democrat ever made it to the White House again, she'd be at the top of the list for a US Court of Appeals slot. And after that, McNeely mused, who knows? There are five Catholics and only three Jews on the Supreme Court. Time to balance things out. McNeely felt he was put there to help make that happen. Michael Jordan, GOAT of the NBA, needed Scottie Pippen, a rugged rebounder and defender who couldn't shoot a lick, to win all those championships.

Eckstein, in turn, admired McNeely for being and doing everything she couldn't. Or wouldn't. Managing the faculty—"herding cats"—pounding out memos to professors, students, and Sheehan Hall bureaucrats, and placating unruly student organizations. Just last week he had issued his magnum opus, a fifty-page memo on St. Sebastian's Title IX Sexual Misconduct Policy which contained two pages of "Tips for Healthy Sexual Relationships." It covered the full spectrum of troublesome faculty behavior, along with helpful reminders such as don't bring up explicit sexual matters or try out lewd jokes in class. Out of consideration for his three colleagues who married former students, McNeely chose to tread lightly on faculty-student sexual relationships.

While this week's agenda for the two deans consisted of the usual array of administrative assignments, faculty crises, and impending calamities, McNeely wanted to begin with the Dean's sit-down with the President. "So how did your meeting with Father B go?" he asked

"Not great. He's supremely pissed off about our admission numbers. Seems to think it's a secular plot to undermine him. Wants more students, preferably Catholic and paying full tuition." Deepening her voice and making the President's church steeple with her hands, she did her Father B impersonation: "*I know a lot of Presidents of Catholic colleges who would send us boatloads of good, deserving kids.*"

"Bravo," said a genuinely impressed McNeely. "If there's ever an opening on *Saturday Night Live*, you've got a shot."

"Flabbergasting! Those exact words. Sounded like he was channeling boat people escaping Sudan. Anyway, I promised him we'd reach out to any college he wanted. But if they send us a bunch of double majors in rugby and Gregorian Chants and a 2.4 GPA, fuck 'em."

McNeely chuckling, "OK, we'll boost our Catholic applicant pool. I'll have the Admissions Committee schedule a recruiting visit to the College of Our Lady of Immaculate Scrums. Anything else?"

Giving a disconsolate sigh, Eckstein held up four fingers. "He's got a four-part agenda for what he's now calling 'The Turnaround.' And, get ready: he's received some help from the B School."

An incredulous McNeely sat upright. "Say what?"

"He's asked Bill Novick, who he pointedly reminded me is the Rufus T. Firestone Distinguished Chair in Business Management at St. Sebastian's Business School, to review the law school's performance in view of its laggard showing in the *US News* Law School rankings."

McNeely was thunderstruck. "Unfuckingbelievable!"

Eckstein continued in the somber voice of someone describing a plane crash, "Novick has studied our *US News* ranking criteria, run some regression analyses, talked to some consultants, and . . ."

McNeely now unable to contain himself, "and climbed up the President's ass."

A tight smile from the Dean. "Yes, undoubtedly. He's produced a four-point plan to *get us back in the game* . . . Father B's words. He even waved around what looked like an Excel spreadsheet. Just to show me this was all science-based."

"OK, I'm ready." McNeely switching to a slightly higher pitch denoting impending sarcasm, "I assume it involves giving us a new building and money to support faculty research, scholarships, and technical assistance for students?"

"Yeah, right. No, as you might guess it involves cutting costs."

McNeely slapping a hand on the table. "This is positively Trumpian. The best way to help the poor is cut taxes for the one percenters and eliminate food stamps."

"Sort of. He wants to eliminate our Summer Institute and make all scholarships merit based."

Another church steeple, the Dean resuming her Father B persona, " *'No more money for second raters who become ambulance chasers and don't give us a dime after they graduate.'* Those were his words. Also, all scholarships are to be cut off if the student doesn't make it into the top half of the class after her first year."

The Summer Institute was a program the law school had begun fifteen years earlier to bring in disadvantaged students to take preparatory law classes the summer before they started at St. Sebastian. It helped increase the number of minority students at the law school and provided a jump start for those with marginal academic credentials. While only half of the Institute students successfully completed the program and became eligible to start law school, it had produced some remarkable success stories, including a state senator and two judges on the New Jersey Superior Court. It did however result in somewhat lower average test scores for St. Sebastian, something they knew Professor Novick's spread sheet would reveal had lowered the school's *US News* ranking. McNeely resignedly slumped back in his chair. "I'm dying here. Cut me, Mick. Give me the needle. Put me out of my misery. What did he say about this Sanus Institute?"

"Oh, quite a lot. He's pretty clueless about what they stand for or why they've singled us out. All he knows is they're waving around $30 million and want to promote business. I've got a bad feeling he's already signed on to something."

"Without consulting us? We're supposed to welcome these Visigoth invaders not knowing what they expect from us? Jesus, Mary and Joseph! Did he offer up into bondage any of our nubile students?"

"No details, but Father B did flash a binder as thick as the Third Restatement of Torts. If he's already signed on, we may be in for a bumpy ride. He does seem to think though that *you* are the man to pull this thing together."

A distraught look appeared on McNeely's face, "Me? Why me?"

"Let's see. You're white, male, Catholic, teach corporate law, arguably heterosexual, and possibly the next Dean of this law school."

"Deb, we've talked about this. I'll be cleaning the men's room in the New York Port Authority before I would agree to become dean. That's my word of honor. If you leave, I'm on the Jersey Central to 42nd Street the next day. No shit."

"I know. And thank you for your willingness to change careers. We just need to finesse this thing."

McNeely let out an exasperated and exaggerated sigh. "OK. I meant to tell you, I've got a contact who can . . . well, let's say, find out about these Sanus people. Turn over a few rocks and see what's crawling underneath."

"Is this the *National Enquirer*?"

"Better. This guy has guns."

27

Politeness, n. The most acceptable hypocrisy.

—Ambrose Bierce, *The Devil's Dictionary*

In spite of himself, McNeely couldn't help staring at the man's suit. It was a perfectly tailored subtle grey pinstripe, with a slight tuck at the waist making a perfect flow from shoulder to hips when Sanus' attorney Trey Anderson moved. It brought back a memory years back when he stopped at Barneys on 7th Avenue. Casually pawing the suits, he heard a soft, purring voice behind him.

"Forty-four large?"

Pivoting, he confronted an elegantly dressed salesman who could have passed as a Barney's mannequin if called upon during the Christmas rush. A gentle smile and quick movement to a rack ten yards from where McNeely was standing, he stabbed a suit from the rack, effortlessly flipping and suspending it from an invisible hook. "A windowpane woolen here that goes well with your coloring. Canali. They're really making inroads on Armani these days. Maybe let out the waist a tad."

McNeely assayed a series of transparent excuses for not trying on the jacket, but was desperate to know the price. No price tags at Barneys. He put the coat on, sucking in his stomach to button it. Taking a quick look at the imposter in the mirror, he finally waved the white flag, "what's it run?"

"1995."

"That was a good year," McNeely offering a lame joke. Exposed as a charlatan, he fled to the subway. Remarkable, he thought. A two-thousand dollar off-the-rack suit. What a time this is, but maybe not that unique. Thinking back to his undergraduate Introduction to Economic Theory course and good old Thorstein Veblen's classic 1899 opus, *The Theory of Conspicuous Consumption*. Rich people buy a boatload of shit just to show off their economic superiority. But it's only conspicuous to those who know what's being displayed. You must have pressed your nose against Barney's display window to recognize what is being conspicuously consumed.

McNeely knew the suit, undoubtedly custom made, not only fit but suited Bradford K. Anderson III perfectly. One of the youngest partners at the mega Wall Street law firm Wolfson, Grey & Fugasi, "Trey" Anderson had begun to make a name for himself among litigators at white shoe Manhattan law firms. He'd led Wolfson's pitched battle defending Execon against Justice Department charges of violating the Foreign Corrupt Practices Act by exchanging blood diamonds as secret payments in order to gain market access in the Congo. A jury fell victim to Trey's charm and bought his argument that the diamonds were meant to provide relief for Ebola victims.

Trey's mission today was far from adversarial. Indeed, it called for serving up a charm offensive. Maybe with a side dish of pandering.

"I'm well aware I don't have to help with translating Latin at a Jesuit institution but let me remind everyone that the word Sanus means 'healthy.' I admit I had to look into the etymology, but the word also can mean 'sane,' or 'sensible.' Or even 'correct.' And in a nutshell, Father Balducci, that's what the Sanus Foundation is all about: health. Channeling the nation's resources to improve the health of our fellow citizens while also putting our institutions on a sane and sensible path to get there. The donors for this charitable enterprise aren't asking for anything in return. Like St. Sebastian University, Sanus is a charitable institution, recognized as such by the IRS, and committed to furthering a mission. And again, like your fine institution, Father Balducci, we are trying to marshal the energy and resources of a community to serve the public good."

McNeely surveyed the room. Edward McNaughton, a retired hedge fund manager and Chairman of St. Sebastian's Board of Trustees, was listening carefully and nodding appreciatively each time the word "resources" was uttered.

"And to be sure, we've done our homework on St. Sebastian. We know the deep commitment you have to the welfare of your community and to preparing your students for the rough and tumble of the marketplace. And we know you've accomplished these goals with only a fraction of the resources that your rival universities have. So at bottom, what we're offering is a partnership. Sanus can bring to the table a national footprint, a wealth of expertise, and the earnest commitment to making St. Sebastian the nation's preeminent law school in the battle for effective health care reform." Pausing to scan his audience, Trey was rewarded with a slight, but approving nod from McNaughton.

"Now, Father Balducci, we know we can't iron out all the details today. But I'm hoping we can come to a specific agreement along the lines of the Memorandum of Understanding we've agreed to with you. And of course, I'd certainly be happy to answer any questions you may have."

Careful not to betray his discomfort about the reference to a MOU that neither he nor the Dean had seen, McNeely tapped his own knee with his middle finger. Eckstein responded by clearing her throat, signaling their tacit agreement that trouble was afoot. She raised her hand and displayed the biggest smile McNeely had ever seen on her. "Mr. Anderson, I was wondering . . ."

Trey matching the Dean tooth for tooth, "Dean, please, call me "Trey.""

"Oh, thank you, Trey. I want you to know we are very excited about expanding the law school's community and our network of outside friends to reach the broadest array of talent and ideas. As I'm sure you're aware, these are tremendously challenging times for law schools and especially for students burdened with enormous debt. Now, we're about to undergo our seven-year accreditation review by the Association of American Law Schools and the American Bar Association. Here's something those reviewers often ask: 'what is the core mission of your law school and what steps are you taking to achieve it?' I'm wondering if you think that—in addition to helping us add to our *resources*—do you also think we need to adjust our *mission* in some way?"

Recalling his own cowardice in dealing with Father Balducci, McNeely felt a rush of pure admiration for his Dean. Here she was, having been all but threatened with losing her job by the President a few days ago, standing up for her law school and dropping the clear message that she was not about to be pushed around.

Accustomed to law firm hierarchies in which subordinate associates do not jump in to call the shots, Trey was caught off guard. "Oh, certainly not, Dean Eckstein. Our hope is to work as your helpmate, er . . . partner . . . that is, colleague . . . in achieving your mission. We see synergy and cooperation as the key to . . ."

"How terrific!" Eckstein interrupted, smiling even more broadly. "Let's put our calendars together to work out a game plan next week."

The meeting drifted off to a series of pleasantries about St. Sebastian's basketball prospects and speculation as to whether the new storm forming off the coast of North Carolina could become another Hurricane Sandy. It seemed to McNeely that the law school had dodged a catastrophic shit storm of its own. Dean Eckstein had subtly reminded everyone that the accreditation inspectors would not look kindly on a hostile corporate takeover of the law school and that such confrontations would not be overlooked by the media. Or the Vatican.

Sanus would have to brace itself for the arrival of Hurricane Deborah.

Late Thursday afternoon, faculty offices deserted, McNeely hustled back to his office to pack his things and make a quick stop at the Black Law Students Association reception. Quickening his stride as he passed the only illuminated office, he heard the excited voice from within. "Neels, how opportune! Was just going to pop by your office."

McNeely knew there was no avoiding what was to come. Professor Alicia Pendleton, one of the first women to gain tenure at St. Sebastian Law School, had summoned him for a detailed exposition of her accomplishments. Unlike some senior colleagues who had long abandoned producing scholarship, Pendleton had written two books and had achieved recognition in her field of property law. Her article on implied covenants in the sale of haunted houses had gained some notoriety, mostly among property law professors trying to infuse something fun into their classes. And most important for McNeely, she taught a full load of large classes that students rarely complained about. All an Associate Dean could hope for.

But as with almost every member of the faculty, there were some quirks. Pendleton's office was a trash heap. Papers, books, and files cluttered the floor, empty yoghurt containers and half eaten power bars lined her bookshelves and her desk was awash with unread articles that she intended to get to someday. On one legendary occasion, a mouse was seen running out of her office. Quick to take charge, Jewel Henderson had found yellow masking tape, sealed off the office door in crime scene fashion, and refused to let Professor Pendleton reenter until the maintenance staff had installed mouse traps and removed all open food containers.

The other characteristic that bothered McNeely was her neediness. Pendleton was like a puppy constantly searching for attention, and a pat on the back. On her agenda for today was filling him in on the progress of her latest article.

"Neels, just a quick question. I've just gotten an acceptance on my "Indefatigable Indefeasibility" piece. You remember it don't you? I presented it at our faculty workshop last year."

McNeely had no recollection of the article but was not without experience bluffing when cornered. "Oh, of course. I knew you were on to something path-breaking. Who's the lucky journal?"

"Ah well, that's the issue. I've got an acceptance from the *Cincinnati Law Review*, but of course I'm hoping to move up the ladder and see who else bites."

Unlike many academic fields, law school publications are controlled by student editors, and it is permissible to send articles to multiple journals. The name of the game is to try to move up the ladder to the journals of higher ranked law schools once you have an acceptance.

"Now Neels, I know you've published at Harvard and Columbia, so my efforts to move up here may seem pedestrian to you, but . . ."

"Oh, no, no. This is the business we have chosen, ha, ha." Looking for acknowl-edgement, but it was clear Professor Pendleton had not seen *Godfather I* or *II*, so McNeely decided to forego further references to pop culture. "How many schools have you sent the article to?"

"One hundred and twenty-three." Seeing McNeely's astonishment, she added sheepishly, " Just wanted to see what kind of response I'd get. So, here's my dilemma, Cincinnati's editors will only hold the offer open for seven days. What should I do?"

"Well, of course you can call some of the . . . did you say one hundred twenty three schools? . . . and see whether they can expedite their review. I'd suggest you triage the ones you think you have a good shot at. But in any event, bravo! Will be a great and lasting contribution to the literature, I'm sure. We'll salute you at the Faculty Happy Hour next week."

McNeely knew that *she* knew exactly what to do, but simply wanted a firm pat on the back. Figurative pat, of course. His skill in conveying boisterous, faux enthu-siasm and support was what made him the man for this part of the job of Associate Dean. And seeing her obvious joy in getting some positive feedback in their lonely calling wasn't so bad for him either.

There were other personality quirks that were downright infuriating. He had concluded that his faculty was well represented in most of the American Psychiatric Association's commonly diagnosed personality disorders: Narcissistic, Dependent,

Histrionic, Anti-social, Neurotic, Avoidant, and of course, Paranoid. Would that he could divert the time he wasted attending to his faculty's kvetching to helping those with real-world troubles—St. Sebastian's students, which would be a better use of his skills and maybe an antidote for his digestive issues.

The last stop of his day, the Black Law Student Association reception, seemed a promising chance to connect with St. Sebastian's real customers. Tonight was the annual BLSA Casino Night fund raiser, and he had agreed to deal blackjack for half an hour. Students were given tokens to bet and which they could trade in for donated prizes at the end of the night. The crowd was large, festive, and comprised of many of the law school's African American alums. Loud music was playing, a few people were dancing, women students were dressed for night clubbing, and men wore glittering vests and the occasional fedora. Not many law school events this lively, he thought. Only a couple of the faculty were in attendance, so he felt it important to move around and fly the Caucasian flag. He circulated quickly from group to group, laughingly threatening each that he would clean them out if they had the courage to come to his blackjack table.

Well-versed in the nuances of blackjack, he dealt quickly and handled the tokens smoothly, all the while dispensing the wisdom of his years toiling at the tables in Atlantic City. Where necessary, he gently guided students away from hitting on 18 and persuaded a few to double down on an 11. He liked to believe that some came away thinking that the stiffs they were subjected to in law school classrooms might have a spark of life in them after all.

Before leaving, McNeely stopped by the bar and entered a circle of students who were talking and laughing loudly. As he joined the group they quieted down and seemed reluctant to continue their conversation. "OK, whatever it was you were talking about, I can take it. So long as it doesn't require me to fire one of my colleagues, ha ha," McNeely said.

To his surprise his comment broke the ice and the students proceeded to explain that they were sharing their most memorable encounters with the police. Every one, six men and two women, had been pulled over multiple times driving through white neighborhoods, all the males had been stopped for no reason walking on the street, and two had been cuffed and detained when they questioned why they'd been stopped. Out of deference, or perhaps concern about seeming too radical, several tried to put a humorous spin on their stories or allude to how much worse it was in their parents' era. However, one student who had taken McNeely's large Business Associations class and whose name he didn't remember, became animated.

"For me, professor, those things that happened in high school, you know, they're why I'm here. Not gonna be rousted like that again. And neither is my family. We've watched Eric Garner, Michael Brown, and that kid, Tamir Rice get shot. And that's the tip of the iceberg. You know what I think? The day is coming, and I don't want this to sound like some kind of threat, but that day is coming when they're going to shoot one too many kids and someone's gonna get it all on his cell phone, and the country is gonna erupt."

McNeely couldn't shake those words as he surveyed the dark faces on the train back to Manhattan. Which of these guys might take to the streets? Was there a silent minority ready to explode? He'd just been to hear Terence Blanchard at the Vanguard and noticed his music had become louder and harsher. Reading an interview on the web, he learned that Blanchard said he'd become angry and that made him move away from the softer, melodic stuff he'd produced in the past. He'd composed the sound for a Spike Lee documentary and wrote "A Requiem for Katrina" after seeing the devastation on his mother's block in New Orleans. Neglect, callous disregard, government-sanctioned racism. Then came Eric Garner, and he composed a piece called "Breathless." Duke said it all, McNeely thought. "Dissonance is our way of life in America."

Anger all around. McNeely reminded of his naive, insulated world at Saint Sebastian. And how little he knew about his students. The faceless group of 85 he looked down on from his podium in class have some life experiences that would make what he thought was his hardscrabble history look tame. And the roots of it all—inequality, racism, apartheid, housing discrimination—have got to come home to roost someday. Especially if Trump sticks around. But, he asked himself for the two hundredth time, is it my job to tell them all this?

I always think of the real father what did he [Father Corrigan]
want to know when I already confessed to God.
—Molly Bloom on going to confession

—James Joyce, *Ulysses*

Father Fitzgibbon knocked gently and leaned his head around the half open door. "Am I disturbing? Just had a quick question."

Shit, McNeely said to himself, 7 p.m. and I thought I had a prayer of catching the second half of the Mets game. "By all means, come in, come in. Just catching up on the drudgery of administrative paperwork."

Father Fitz still standing at the doorway. "I don't want to take up your time, but just hoped to check in on something."

"Please, please. Sit down. Can I offer you some coffee? Tea? Jameson? 15-year-old Green Spot, ha ha."

To McNeely's surprise, Fitzgibbon broke into a broad grin and dropped onto the couch. "You know, just a taste would be grand."

Pouring more than a taste for both of them, McNeely asked "what can I do for you?"

"Just my Jesuit nosiness. How's Ms. Holloran's case coming?"

When caught off guard, McNeely always tried not to sound evasive while dodging a question. "You know it's a tricky business. Pretty tough stuff. Committee findings and all."

"Oh yes?" Father Fitz lobbing the ball back into McNeely's court, a small wrinkle of disapproval appeared on the Jesuit forehead.

"Father, you seemed pretty ticked off at the hearing," McNeely venturing a passing shot.

"You know, Tommy, I'm all for individuals bringing the spirit of the Lord into their work and living a life that follows Jesus' teachings. But when someone distorts those teachings and uses it to subjugate others, that's where I draw the line. Hypocrites like Gleason really fry my ass. So, here's my all-time number one for you: You know Generalissimo Franco?"

McNeely sensing another history lesson in the offing. "Not personally, ha ha . . . but of course I know he was the autocrat who ruled Spain in the Fifties."

"Fifties? He hung on till 1975. Autocrat? That's being polite. He was a horrible tyrant. Mass murderer, ran concentration camps, supported Hitler. Always made a big show of being a religious Catholic. So, he gets his thugs to steal the mummified hand of Saint Teresa from a convent that held it as a relic, and sleeps with it under his pillow every night for thirty years. He's dying in Madrid, winter of '75. Probably knows he's in for it when he gets to the other side. So what does he do? Takes out the hand and dies clutching it to his heart. Think that helped him? I personally doubt it. Guys like Gleason are cut from the same cloth. They roll out the religious stuff when it suits them. Anyway, I'm just hoping Ms. Holloran gets a fair hearing."

"Well, you know, there's a process and an evidentiary record that must be taken into consideration. And one must always give full effect to the underlying principles of the school's traditions." Pausing, then a sheepish follow on, "And, not to forget, of course, our Jesuit teachings." Which of course he had forgotten to mention.

As he spoke McNeely noted with some alarm Father's deepening forehead wrinkles, now accompanied by a raised eyebrow and tightened mouth.

Father Fitz sipping his Irish and flashing an ingratiating smile, "I'm sure there are legal nuances beyond my lay understanding."

Waving a friendly palm and hoping for an escape route, McNeely tried on an unctuous tone. "Oh please Father! You know better than me the trials of trying to carve out a just path for others to follow."

Father Fitz lobbed back his own helping of unctuosity: "Well Tommy, you are among the most learned . . . and trusted . . . law professors here at St. Sebastian. So, there is one legal aspect I hoped you might educate me about."

Relieved that Fitz seemed to be moving on, McNeely gave an understanding nod, "Oh, of course. Happy to help."

"Well as you know, I testified at Ms. Holloran's hearing."

"I do indeed. And might I say, you made a very compelling and compassionate case for her, one that I fully appreciate and . . ."

Father Fitz now conducting cross examination, "And I think you know that I talked at some length about her principles and devotion to justice."

"Yes you did. And you made a very compelling . . ."

"I hope it was," he interrupted. Father Fitz had not gone to law school thought McNeely, but he sure knew how to cut off a wandering nonresponse from an evasive witness. "But you may also recall that I testified that I have had many opportunities to hear from Ms. Holloran about her experiences and beliefs."

Now worried that Father Fitz might instruct him to just answer yes or no, as would any good prosecutor, McNeely answered meekly, "Yes you did, Father."

"And I think you know that besides providing secular counselling to students, I also offer religious counselling for those who seek it."

McNeely now reduced to nodding his assent.

"And of course, for Catholic students that sometimes involves Confession. With a capital C. The sacrament of Confession."

McNeely now nodding more slowly, as he began to absorb the thrust of the good Father's interrogation.

"And by the way, did you know Ms. Holloran was Catholic? Regularly attends my Sunday mass. Takes communion. Goes to Confession."

Holy shit, thought McNeely. Not what Joyce called a jejune Jesuit after all.

"Now the legal question that is beyond my area of expertise is this: Would the presentation of evidence that breached the priest-penitent privilege so corrupt a hearing as to render it . . . how to put it? Improper? Reversible error? A hideous embarrassment for a Jesuit law school?"

McNeely sat stunned for several seconds. The old coot had skillfully injected into his testimony the possibility that his words betrayed information Maggie had conveyed to him in confession! And now he had all but spelled out the implications so even a dim-witted legal administrator could grasp the impossibility of continuing the case against her.

An exuberant McNeely leapt out of his chair, fairly shrieking, "Father Fitz, you have made my day! My month! My year!" Grabbing the bottle of Irish and pounding the equally jubilant joyful Jesuit on his back, "A toast to the Jesuit Order. Sláinte!"

Never interrupt your enemy when he is making a mistake.

—Napoleon Bonaparte

A single loud knock with the door flying open simultaneously. In stormed a red-faced Professor Gleason, trailed by Jewel Henderson silently displaying her WTF face and waiving a hand signaling that she'd tried to stop the onrushing senior professor.

A surprised McNeely half rose out of his chair. "Francis! What can I do for you?"

"Your girl called me an hour ago and said it was urgent I come by to talk to you."

Standing behind Gleason, Henderson silently offered up double middle fingers to his back and closed the door loudly.

"You really need to do an attitude adjustment with some of the help…er secretarial staff. She got quite testy with me on the phone when I explained the appointments I had scheduled for today."

McNeely silently congratulated himself again for hiring Henderson. "Well, there is something I wanted to give you a heads up about before it went public. Sit down, sit down."

He had asked Henderson that morning to track down Gleason. "He's not here yet" she said, pointing out the door to the men's room. Her attendance check for senior male faculty was unfailingly accurate. If she hadn't spotted one visiting the men's room by 11 a.m., he wasn't in the building. She had privately diagnosed prostate problems for at least two professors before they had seen their urologist.

"Well, text or phone him to get him in here," McNeely had told her. "Tell him it's urgent. Be persuasive."

As Gleason arranged himself on the office couch, McNeely pulled out a file and shuffled some papers on his desk.

Gleason was not done venting about being summoned. "You know, I spend my Wednesdays at the Archbishop's retreat center. I lead a group of seniors in bible study and meditation. We call it 'Iron Sharpens Iron.' Proverbs 27:17. *As iron sharpens iron so one person sharpens another.* Have the group talk about their experiences, their relationship with the Lord, whatever moves them. I've witnessed some real breakthroughs. And the Archbishop loves it. Turns out he's gotten a couple of tidy bequests. The group's mostly in their 80s. Ready to start thinking about the big stuff."

He's making this easier for me, McNeely thought. "Most admirable work, Francis. I really admire your effort to reach out a hand to others. Not enough of that in these crazy times."

"Well, if you're alluding to President Trump, I really believe this open the borders bullshit the left is pushing on him . . ."

"No, no, no. Was just speaking in generalities." McNeely resisting the temptation to engage in debate about what was the Christian thing to do for children fleeing murder and oppression in Central America, a lot of them Catholic too. "Look, the reason I needed to see you today is to give you the first notice of my decision in the Margaret Holloran matter."

Gleason, leaning forward, sensing this was not going to be the verdict he was expecting.

McNeely also leaned forward. "I've done a very thorough review of the record, talked to Ms. Holloran and others, and I have decided to dismiss the charges against her."

Gleason emitting a noise that probably contained a word, but to McNeely sounded more like a growl.

"It appears that some of the testimony received by the Ethics Committee was tainted by Father Fitzgibbon inadvertently disclosing the contents of Ms. Holloran's Confession to him. As you know, the priest-penitent conversation is closely protected in the law, and certainly here at St. Sebastian we can brook no violations of the sacraments of Confession and Absolution. Now I know there was an error in judgment on her part, but . . ."

Gleason now standing. "Wait just a minute young man. You're telling me you're letting her off? We're sending an admitted plagiarist out into the practice of law? She's low rent, I can tell you that. Tattoos on both her legs for God's sake."

McNeely blinked. He hadn't noticed any tattoos, but apparently Professor Gleason was well practiced in scanning the territory.

Gleason now raising his voice, "Whatever that senile old priest said or knew is irrelevant. Harmless error. She admitted to lifting text."

"I've had a long conversation with her and am convinced there were extenuating circumstances, the violation was trivial, and punishment unwarranted. I am issuing an informal letter of reprimand but imposing no other sanction. You may not like it, but our faculty manual and rules of procedure vest final authority on these matters in my office."

A glowering Gleason now pointing a finger at McNeely. "The President may see things differently."

McNeely issued a practiced sigh of disappointment. "Ah yes, yes. I understand you've chosen to violate our rules of confidentiality and discuss the case with President Balducci while it's still proceeding. That's why you're going to send him an email saying there were extenuating circumstance that have come to your attention, and you agree with my decision to move on."

Now a foot stamp. "Pigs might fly!"

McNeely exuding confidence, "Well, they just might. I've seen a miracle or two in my time. You know, I have to keep an eye on things around here. There's been petty theft all over the place, ranging from the faculty lounge and kitchen to colleagues' offices. And don't get me started on some of the stuff going down in the private student study rooms. Some actual sexcapades going on there. Changing world for sure."

Now switching to a world-weary sigh, McNeely went on. "I've had to have some surveillance cameras installed. Have a couple in the lounge and faculty library. You know, those paintings the Oglivy law firm donated that hang in the lounge are pretty valuable."

Gleason, eyes bulging, collapsed back on to the couch.

"As you may realize, you've got a starring role in a couple of the videos focused on the computer terminal in the faculty library alcove. Saw one recorded late last Wednesday night in fact. Must have been a long day at your retreat. On the video, it looks like you were sharpening your own iron right there at the faculty computer. Looks like we caught you red-handed. Or maybe I should say, left-handed."

On a roll, McNeely couldn't contain himself, "As a Biblical scholar, I'm sure you know the warning of Genesis 38-8? Poor Onan got the death penalty. The surveillance system has audio, by the way. Be a shame if this leaked out on the internet.

And just as a precaution, I've asked IT to give me a confidential report on the web searches done on some faculty computers."

Gleason now glassy-eyed.

"So, on your way out, please tell my . . ." McNeely opening the door and raising his voice for emphasis, "my *Administrative Assistant, Ms. Jewel Henderson . . .* Kindly tell her what time tomorrow you'll be sending her a copy of your email to Father Balducci."

The Fall, 2018 semester was going to end on a high note. He'd spanked a hypocrite, saved a student's career, and was only a few days away from a badly needed Christmas break. For now he'd transfer the overflowing Father Balducci file to a separate file folder in his mental hard drive and try not to open it until next semester.

31

America is built on a tilt and everything loose slides to California.

—Mark Twain

"Man, this Orange asshole is totally crazy insane! Now he's locking up babies in Mexico. Turning the government into a police state. I know he's gonna try to take away the weed law we passed out here. Let him try. We're growing our own now anyway. And he doesn't think there's any global warming! Just go outside for fuck's sake. Or go on the internet. Hot as shit, tornados, melting icebergs. You know where I fish, the salmon are coming in a month late. You said you're a lawyer? I'm going to work for Bernie Sanders when he runs."

"Law professor. Used to be a lawyer." McNeely careful not to say "prosecutor."

"Oh. OK. But what's up with this douchebag they put on the Supreme Court? He sounds like some kind of frat boy who drinks beer and thinks he's hot shit."

One of the things McNeely loved about Santa Cruz, California was the amalgam of poets, crackpots, revolutionaries, hipsters, and occasional savants one encountered when you sat down at a bar. Johnny's Harborside usually drew a good assortment of the town's characters. Commercial fishermen, stoners, tattooists, and lost souls mingled at the bar. The crowd on January 5 was thin but vocal and opinionated. His neighbor on the adjacent stool, a rail-thin part time fisherman and full-time coffee server named Arlo, sported a weathered Oakland Raiders shirt, ponytail, and leather necklace. If Bernie Sanders needs volunteers, Santa Cruz was a pretty solid place to recruit.

McNeely's pilgrimages to Santa Cruz were stressful to say the least. He'd visited every Christmas and summer vacation for six years to spend a few weeks with his ex-wife and daughter. This year he stayed on to see in 2019 with them and spend a week in the sun before slouching back to New Jersey. His marriage had lasted only three years, at least as measured chronologically, the separation driven by the tragic events following the birth of their daughter Jackie. He'd married his high school girl friend Elizabeth during the summer of his sophomore year at Rutgers. They were among the last of an almost extinct breed: middle class college kids who felt they had to get married because of a pregnancy. Just doesn't happen any more with ready access to abortion and the stigma of "out of wedlock" childbearing disappearing he now realized. Both of them were raised under the same code: *don't ruin your parents' lives.* Jackie's birth had delivered the kind of emotional, physical, and psychic blow that few couples recovered from. And they didn't.

Jackie's diagnosis was Wolf-Hirschhorn syndrome, a rare genetic disorder caused by the deletion of genetic material. The clinical effects of the deletion of the "short arm" of Chromosome 4, which McNeely studied relentlessly, resulted in a wide variety of disabilities including heart defects, seizures, and mental impairments. Jackie got them all and the outcome was catastrophic. For years, she hardly moved or uttered sounds and certainly didn't recognize McNeely. They hadn't known of the risks before her birth. Neither had raised the possibility of an abortion, with McNeely feeling that if Elizabeth didn't mention it, her position was clear. He often speculated about what would have happened—how markedly his life would have changed—had he summoned the courage to raise the possibility. His ongoing torment was to curse himself for both cowardice and lack of compassion. Liz had made her way West in search of a cure for Jackie and a healing culture for herself. She lived in a comfortable group home and seemed to be sleeping with at least one of her five housemates. Neither she nor McNeely had any energy left for animosity. He doled out over half of his take-home pay, she waitressed, and disability payments kept them afloat.

He visited Jackie daily on his trips to Santa Cruz at the institute that housed her, quietly stroking her hair, talking, sometimes singing to her, even though it seemed she didn't know who he was. From the beginning, the doctors had prepared them for the worst. Her heart was badly compromised and her specialists said she might not live past three years old. She was now almost ten and her heart issues were steadily worsening. McNeely knew the hole in his heart wasn't going to heal either. In his long walks around New York, he studiously avoided school playgrounds. The sight of young girls laughing and playing would haunt him for hours afterwards.

One afternoon, he decided to explain himself to Jackie. He knew she didn't understand anything he was saying and probably wasn't even aware of who he was. Somehow though, he felt he owed her an explanation. More accurately, he felt he owed himself an explanation, or even more accurately, a rationalization. He went on for sixty-five minutes describing his own de facto orphan status, his brief and loveless marriage, his solitary life, his frustrating legal career, and his abject sorrow about how things had turned out for her. He then offered a litany of the cowardly and selfish behaviors that he blamed himself for. At some point it dawned on him that he was conducting a psychoanalysis session on himself without a license. Maybe there's something to this, he thought. He left Jackie's facility that day with a feeling of absolution he hadn't experienced since going to confession at age thirteen. He'd conronted his dark side straight up and didn't need to fill a prescription, listen to a priest's scolding, or say a hundred Hail Marys.

Exiting Johnny's, McNeely returned to his ocean-view B&B near the famed Santa Cruz boardwalk and undertook his well-practiced compartmentalization drill. Don't think about Jackie, Wolf-Hirschhorn, Trump, the fucked-up state of the Union, or Father Balducci. More of his grandfather's folk wisdom: *Life's a bitch, then you die.* Then there was Bill Belichick's wisdom, *Do your job.* Hate the damn cheater, but he had a point. Off to find a quiet workplace.

Squeezing into a narrow table at CCC, Cruz Caffeinated Coffee on the Santa Cruz pier, McNeely hoped a double espresso would crank up enough dopamine and glutamine to get him through the backlog of emails in the "action needed" folder on his laptop. The "Proposed Courses" subfolder showed an email from Professor Carter.

Neels: I'm thinking of proposing a variant of a course that my old prof at Yale has been teaching for the last few years. My approach of course would be to put my own stamp on the topic by minimizing the obvious cultural dissonance that multi-disciplinary investigations elicit and frame the dialogue as a dialectic between my own work and that of George Marcus' work on Tonga. Since this is a new prep for me, and one that potentially carves out a new path of ethno-aware scholarship for the law school, I would hope to be relieved of teaching first year torts for the next two academic years. Here's Professor Hathaway's course description (which of course I will fine tune):

>*This course examines the role that both law and language, as mutually constitutive mediating systems, occupy in constructing ethnoracial identity in the United States. We approach the law from a critical anthropological perspective, as a signifying and significant sociocultural system rather than as an abstract collection of rules, norms, and procedures, to examine how legal processes and discourses contribute to processes of cultural production and reproduction that contribute to the creation and maintenance of differential power relations. Course material draws*

on anthropological, linguistic, and critical race theory as well as ethnographic and legal material to guide and document our analyses.
Let me know what you think.

Alistair Carter
Professor of Law
acarter@ssulaw.edu
Saint Sebastian School of Law
Saint Sebastian University occupies the unceded homeland of the Nanticoke Lenni-Lenape Tribal Nation

Responses like "you're not in New Haven anymore" and "are there many New Jersey law firms specializing in Tongan law?" ran through McNeely's mind. He settled for a promise to take up the proposal with the Curriculum Committee, adding a gentle reminder that "under the law school's organizational manual, Section IV A (2)(ii), teaching releases have to be justified by 'extraordinary scholarly productivity or exigent and documented personal need.'" *Pigs might fly*, he muttered to himself.

The email was a reminder that when he got back to Baytown he would have to tackle any number of mind-numbing administrative tasks to prepare for the school's upcoming accreditation inspection. For example, the ABA was concerned that legal education had become too abstract and recently issued a rule requiring that every syllabus for every course contain specific "learning objectives" that evidenced the courses' contribution to making graduates "practice ready." The faculty instinctively balked at what they considered yet another bureaucratic incursion on their academic freedom. Several drafted snarky statements of objectives like "*teaching students not just 'think like a lawyer' but just think*" or "*pass the bar so they can pay us back their student loans.*" It fell to McNeely to point out to them that, as emotionally satisfying their trenchant satire might be, pissing off the accreditation inspectors was not in anyone's best interest. As with many issues that found their way to his desk, including student requests for accommodations due to disability or family crises, McNeely observed a yawning gap between faculty members' politics and empathy for the plight of individual students. No small irony, he felt, hearing his liberal colleagues adopting the same rationale for inflicting hard-ass treatment offered by Marine boot camp drill instructors: *Toughen 'em up so they won't wilt when they go to battle in court. We all went through it and survived.*

The quiet of the coffee shop was broken by Miles Davis' "So What," McNeely's ringtone signaling a call from Jewel Henderson. "Hey! how are things in sunny Baytown?" he offered.

"Oh, couldn't be better. No heat on the west side of the building. Professor Posey wants one of the reserved parking spaces because of his hip replacement, internet was out for three hours yesterday."

McNeely recalling his grandfather singing the theme song of his favorite TV show.

There's a holdup in the Bronx
Brooklyn's broken out in fights
There's a traffic jam in Harlem that's backed up to Jackson Heights
There's a scout troop short a child
Krushchev's due at Idlewild
Car 54, Where are You?

Returning from his reverie, McNeely said, "Sorry, we must have a bad connection. What were you saying?"

"Did you catch the part about Professor Slossberg?"

"No, what does he want?"

"Well, it's more what he needs than wants. He slipped on the ice in front of the school yesterday. I was just coming in, and the emergency techs were rolling him into the back of the ambulance."

"Oh my god! Is he OK?" an agitated McNeely screamed.

"Don't know, they put one of those metal halo rings around his head. You know, the kind they put on football players when they've been knocked out and may be paralyzed? Looked like something out of Star Wars. But he was cursing and yelling about the idiot janitors, so his brain seemed to be as full of racist crap as it always is."

McNeely now perspiring, "Very comforting. Thanks."

"You did get a call from a guy who said he's Professor Slossberg's lawyer . . ."

McNeely let out a yelp that silenced the other customers at the CCC. "Christ almighty!! . . . what's his name?"

"Neels, relax. I'm just fucking with you." He could hear Jewel's sputtering laughter.

McNeely trying to preserve a modicum of dignity, "I'm getting even. Someday, a live rodent in your desk. Straight from Professor Pendleton's office. Anything else?"

"Oh yeah. A big box arrived for you today. From someone named Luther."

McNeely now on his feet, rushing outside to the edge of the Santa Cruz pier. For some reason he spoke in a hushed tone. "What's in it?"

"A bunch of huge three-ring notebooks. And a letter."

"OK, open it and read it to me."

Without a moment's hesitation, Henderson began, "Dear Professor McNeely . . ."

"Wait, that was quick."

"I opened it a while ago. Knew you'd want to know what it said . . .

Dear Professor McNeely. The enclosed documents should provide ample evidence for you to draw up your own 95 Theses. Like my namesake, I find the sale of indulgences abhorrent. Looking forward to the Reformation. Yours in Christ. Luther Martin."

Henderson provided some commentary, "That's some crazy shit. Level with me, Neels. You joining some kind of cult? I'm moving on if you're doing exorcisms . . ." A pause and more suppressed laughter. "I'm still messing with you. It'll be awright."

God save me, he thought, looking out at an orange sunset over Monterey Bay. I've got a 5:40 out of SFO tomorrow morning to Newark with connections in L.A. and Pittsburg. All to get back to 16-degree temperatures, blackened snow drifts on the street, incessant faculty whining, and Father Balducci's raging discontents. Pray for engine trouble, maybe an emergency landing in the Baja.

32

How a Trump Tax Break for Poor Communities Became a Windfall for the Rich

—New York *Times*, August 31, 2019

Father Fitzgibbon had a hobby. He liked to think that a man with a vocation also deserved an avocation. Playing under the *nom de jeu* of Oliver Gogarty—a hat tip to Joyce's inspiration for his rowdy, boisterous character Buck Mulligan—he was a regular participant in a high stakes poker game. The game, which took place in various elegant suites in Hoboken or Jersey City, was hosted by a gambling entrepreneur who furnished a top-shelf bar, gourmet food, and stunning blonde servers while also taking a generous rake out of every pot. Though never openly discussed, the players all understood that the game was immune from interference from the local police or anyone prowling the neighborhood. The entrepreneur, "Fat Sal" Giordano, knew people. And people knew about him.

The good Father's ability to endure the precipitous ups and downs of big time poker stemmed from a sizable inheritance he had received from a great aunt as well as some considerable skills honed in his days in Vietnam and long hours at the tables in Atlantic City. Not to say he didn't suffer the occasional setback, but on balance he was able to generate an ample cash flow, all of which he secretly donated to local causes ranging from Baytown's homeless to AIDs clinics to needy students at St. Sebastian.

Besides filling his empty celibate hours, the game introduced Father Fitzgibbon to all manner of New Jersey's rich and infamous. Loosely modeled on Tony Soprano's "executive game," Fat Sal supplied a steady stream of affluent hedge fund honchos, professional athletes, and even the occasional movie star. Many came once and went home $40,000 lighter, while a few regulars, like the enigmatic Oliver Gogarty, feasted on a regular menu of corpulent, just-landed fish.

Unlike many of the players, Gogarty/Fitzgibbon remained closed-mouthed about his background, describing himself as a "happily retired investor." To maintain his credibility as a regular guy, he occasionally joined in banter about the stupidity of Obama voters and flirted with the hostesses but was generally happy to be viewed as an amiable senior citizen without a lot to say but a lot of money stashed away somewhere.

One of the more talkative regulars was Bucky, who was not shy about discussing his triumphs in the New Jersey real estate market or his conquests of young women who somehow fell for his charms—or perhaps for his Grand Banks 60 Skylounge named *BitchCraft,* which he moored in Kammerman's Marina in Atlantic City. Despite his claims of having access to unlimited capital, it became apparent that Bucky was eager to line up co-investors. Father Fitz was happy to shore up the legend of Oliver Gogarty as a successful player in the real estate game by allowing Bucky to pitch him the occasional sure thing, though always politely bowing out by saying the proposal sounded grand but demurring that "it's a young man's game." One evening however the target property got his full attention.

"Looking to score a big project in an Opportunity Zone just over here in Baytown. Got a deal cooking with the Catholic college there that should supply the perfect cover and help grease the wheels," Bucky announced late into the game one night.

A surprised Father Fitzgibbon dialed up his best Gogarty-the-Senior-Financier persona. "Really? I've always thought these Zone deals were manna from heaven. Never done one myself but always eager to learn new things. Let's grab a drink after the game and talk about it."

With Bucky well-lubricated by a half dozen of Fat Sal's Negronis, it wasn't hard to get the entire scheme out of him. He recounted how he had charmed the priest who runs St. Sebastian University and who was in his words "as eager as a Jew banker to cash in" on the land near his school. What the university president apparently didn't know, and Bucky was not about to tell him, was that the surrounding properties could be had for cheap, as they were mostly small single-family, vinyl-sided "Bayonne Box" houses and rundown apartment buildings occupied by students or retirees ready to move or check into a nursing home. Lots of property they could get for a song and sell to developers or hold for themselves once the gold rush started. Perfect conditions, Bucky explained, for one of Meadowlands Construction's corporate subsidiaries to deploy its alchemy and turn the Bayonne Boxes into gold.

"The beauty of this baby—and God bless those guys who call the shots in Washington who wrote the Opportunity Zone law—is that the area qualifies as depressed because, guess what, there's low-income people living in them. Who are these destitute folks? Students! Are they the starving poor of New Jersey? No, but they have no income. So, all those shacks and apartments they occupy are fair game. And all kinds of tax breaks flow to investors who pay squat for these properties and turn them into the high-class shops, restaurants, and condos like the ones you see all over Hoboken and Jersey City. The stores get to charge half the sales tax, investors can erase their capital gains. It goes on and on. It's a fucking piñata full of gold."

Pausing for a minute to swing an imaginary bat, Bucky chirped with delight, "And I got a Louisville Slugger." He was slurring his words a bit but the Negronis were working like truth serum. Leaning forward and speaking with a conspiratorial whisper, he went on, "By the way, the guy who greased the wheels to get this area declared an Opportunity Zone is . . . Guess who? The guy with two thumbs." Thumbs pointing to Bucky's chest solved the mystery. "It was me. You know, when I forked over $50 grand to support the President's Inaugural Committee, I wasn't sure if it was a good investment. My wife said I was nuts. Best investment I ever made. I've got this thing wired now with Secretary of the Treasury. Just to make sure, I also took care of the local aldermen. So, now I just need some partners. Are you in?"

In his role as Gogarty, the careful, seasoned investor, Father Fitz needed to appear cautious. "Sounds promising. But what's the deal with this priest?"

"Thinks he's a big shot. You should see his office. Looks like Brando's home in *The Godfather*. Doesn't seem to know anything about real estate but gives the impression of someone not to be scared off by some nervous general counsel. Wants to build a basketball stadium, dorms, God knows what else. But mainly he wants to be the Catholic Donald Trump. Probably will put his name on every building."

Father Fitz assured Bucky that he'd given him a lot to think about, poured him into an Uber, and wondered if his pal McNeely needed another helping hand.

33

Laws are like sausages. It is better not to see them being made.

—Otto Von Bismarck

Coming back from the holiday break in January, McNeely was responsible for preparing staff, students and especially faculty to focus on the quotidian tasks of getting on with a new semester of legal education. This entailed attending to countless mind-numbing administrative tasks that fell to the unlucky individual holding the title of Associate Dean. Most pressing at the moment was sending his faculty colleagues a friendly reminder of what exactly their job entails. Having learned the hard way that there was no detail too small or too obvious that could be overlooked, his "Class Readiness Checklist" memo grew with every passing semester.

- *assign on-line reading assignments for your first class no later than January 7;*
- *provide students a detailed syllabus on the first day of classes; but best practice is to post on-line by January 1;*
- *record classes on request by students with disabilities (but only for those so certified on Form Dis/12 and signed by the Assistant Dean for Student Affairs);*
- *confirm that the campus bookstore has all your required textbooks in stock and encourage your students to buy their books there rather than online;*
- *notify the library of books to be put on reserve; do <u>not</u> put a colleague's book on reserve if it is available at the campus bookstore;*
- *end classes promptly so students can navigate our functioning elevators to get to their next class on time;*
- *distribute name cards requesting students to identify the gender preference they desire to be addressed by along with a checklist of specific preferred pronouns (e.g. "she/her/hers/other"; "they, their, theirs, other");*
- *request the correct pronunciation of students' names; if you are not sure, please consult the international pronunciation guide available on the faculty website;*
- *ask students to designate all religious holidays they plan to observe but note*

- *provide full and complete disclosure of timing, length, and weighting for final grade of all exams, quizzes and writing assignments;*
- *require students to sign a Statement of Compliance with The Student Honor Code (Form 32A on Student Website) on all exams and final seminar papers;*
- *specify the maximum number of unexcused absences from class (not to exceed three, per AALS regulations); and*
- *direct all questions and requests for waivers to Associate Dean McNeely.*

All of which sent McNeely swirling down a black hole of existential questions. What are we trying to accomplish in "teaching law"? Is this about stamping a ticket like the New Jersey licensing board that certifies plumbers? Are we somehow supposed to "teach" lawyers to serve the public interest? Why bother talking about justice and equity in the age of Trump, Barr, and court-packing? A U.S. President denigrating the Department of Justice, FBI, the courts and the legal system. God help us if these kids see all this as normal.

In his adopted profession as an academic, McNeely had come to realize that law did not come close to the tidy narrative put forward at every level from junior high school civics class to law school. Lawmaking was more a Turkish bazaar than an Athenian forum. Ever since the Reagan Administration, Washington and state governments had been hard at work privatizing the job of running the country. Congress and state governments had effectively delegated responsibility for governing to corporate-funded think tanks, lobbying organizations, tax exempt foundations, and freelancing plutocrats. These private organizations were charged with generating ideas and policies, and most important, devising plausible rationalizations for them. They next went about processing their sausages thru the legislative meat grinder by deploying vast expenditures on lobbying, political campaign funding, and media outreach. Whenever possible, the lobbyists actually wrote the laws themselves, so they were able to cut out that pesky, inefficient middleman, the legislature.

All of which should have come as no surprise, he realized. It was carefully orchestrated and well-financed. On August 23, 1971, less than two months before he was nominated to serve as an Associate Justice of the Supreme Court of the United States, Lewis F. Powell, Jr. mailed a confidential memorandum to a friend who happened to be Chair of the Education Committee of the U.S. Chamber of

Commerce. In his paper, entitled "Attack On American Free Enterprise System," the future Supreme Court Justice issued a call to arms against what he described as a "broad attack" from "disquieting voices." It proposed first that corporate leaders unite and "confront this problem as a primary responsibility of corporate management." The memo urged the Chamber to exert political power and use it "aggressively and with determination — without embarrassment and without reluctance." As to the legal system, Powell proposed a strategy to counter the "activist-minded Supreme Court," specifically urging the corporate community to initiate its own activist agenda: participation in cases of financial consequence to the business community by filing precedent-setting lawsuits and amicus briefs.

But what struck closest to home for McNeely was Powell's explicit call to infiltrate the nation's academic institutions. The Chamber of Commerce, he suggested, should fund a "staff of highly qualified scholars in the social sciences who do believe in the system" to review textbooks, form a speakers' bureau to give talks on college campuses, and publish a "a fairly steady flow of scholarly articles" in academic and popular journals and magazines. Finally—no surprise here—the corporate community should establish a particularly strong rapport with the increasingly influential graduate schools of business. Mr. Soon-To-Be-Justice Powell concluded with a rhetorical question: "Should not the Chamber also request specific courses in such schools dealing with the entire scope of the problem addressed by this memorandum?"

What became an indispensable tool in implementing Powell's proposed enterprise was the right wing think tank. The growth of these organizations coincided—not coincidentally—with the birth of the Reagan era in the 1980s. Indeed, McNeely learned that the thoroughly regressive policies proposed by Barry Goldwater that his grandfather derided as "crackpot conservative crap" had become dogma under the avuncular actor/salesman/President. The nation's political transformation, it seemed, could be traced in part to the gravitas supplied by the high-minded principles that the business-friendly think tanks and their endowed academic puppets promoted.

All of which was eye-opening for McNeely. Having become an amateur anthropologist as well as a teacher of business law, he eagerly plunged into the arcana surrounding the institutions providing intellectual fig leaves for the right. Frank Luntz, genius of political propaganda, whom one pundit called "Goebbels on the Potomac," put it concisely in his book title: "Words that Work: It's Not What You

Say, It's What People Hear." The big lie. Talismanic phrases like *Free Markets, American Values, Economic Growth, Private Enterprise, Free Trade, Personal Responsibility,* abounded on the webpages of think tanks. Wordsmithing in service of thought control, he grumbled. They must teach a course in it at Harvard Business School.

Think tanks, he learned, were funded by large collectives of corporate money such as the Business Roundtable as well as the rogues' gallery of politically astute business barons like the Koch Brothers, Rupert Murdoch, and Richard Mellon Scaife. In turn, the think tanks hired armies of in-house researchers and funded professors and university research institutes dedicated to producing sympathetic policy papers and Congressional testimony. Distinguished and well-funded academic institutions such as Stanford, Harvard and Penn housed institutes that served as platforms for right wing ideologues. Even more striking for McNeely was how the law had facilitated the proliferation of these organizations. Early on, conservative zealots were provided a way to avoid the adverse publicity associated with advocacy that might tarnish their businesses. Tax lawyers concocted a scheme under federal charitable tax law to empower an organization called Donors Trust to launder the identities of its donors when they funded other organizations. The goal: making sure the public wouldn't know the real backers of the often-radical policies the think tanks were pushing. Among the recipients of the Donor Trust's $1.1 billion in donations over the years was an organization known as the Federalist Society which endowed lectures and programs at three hundred colleges and universities and furnished some $100 million per year to support academic proselytizing.

Not wanting to be outdone by business schools, many law schools took up courting the business community and the Federalist Society became a leading sponsor of law school programs and established chapters at almost every law school. The investment paid off just as Justice Powell's road map predicted, as the linkage between legal academia and the courts was executed with uncanny success. One of the society's founders, Michael Horowitz, made a bold claim exactly 20 years before Donald Trump's election: "Twenty years from now, we will see our federal justices coming from the Federalist Society." McNeely discovered to his astonishment how accurate that prediction proved to be: 80 percent of Trump's appointees were Federalist Society members, including young Mr. Kavanaugh, who –fittingly enough— would take the seat on the Supreme Court once occupied by Justice Powell.

The poster boy for well-spent corporate money was a little-known law school in Northern Virginia, George Mason University. In the 1980's the Koch brothers funded the Mercatus Center which promotes itself as "the world's premier university source for market-oriented ideas—bridging the gap between academic ideas and real-world problems." Donations from Koch, Heritage and others enabled GMU to put together numerous pro-business programs and sponsor economic education camps for law professors and judges. In 2019, GMU's law school was renamed the Antonin Scalia School of Law, courtesy of a $20 million anonymous donation likely laundered through the Federalist Society.

Hyper-rational allocation of scarce resources, thought McNeely. The law and economics crowd are practicing what they preach. If you want to influence legal education in the *most efficient* way, why not buy a couple of law schools? Cut out the middleman.

McNeely's online research was interrupted by Dylan's *Tangled Up in Blue*, the designated ringtone for his pal Jenks. "At last," he mumbled to himself as he struggled to dislodge his phone from his ill-fitting pants.

"Jinx, how the hell are you? I've been trying to reach you for a week. I'm badly in need of an update on my project."

"Tommy, Tommy, Tommy. This is a very complicated case. Lotta ins, lotta outs, lotta what-have-yous. Lotta strands to keep in my head."

"OK Dude, very funny. I get it. Like your hero Lebowski, you gotta follow your investigative instincts. But you know, I'm up against it. These Sanus guys are threatening a hostile takeover of the law school."

"Nice analogy. Look, I just took on a new client, but I'm homing in on your friends. Promise to have something in a week or two. Top priority. So, listen, my man. My friends downtown on Federal Plaza tell me half the agents are ready to revolt. Other half planning to bolt. Fucking Barr claims there's a deep state? Is one now. He's declared war on the Bureau and they're ready to bend him over. Anyway, I'll keep working on your problem."

McNeely had been hoping Jenks would take care of his Sanus problem. Hide the pistol behind the toilet like Clemenza did for Michael Corleone. Now he feared that he would walk into the sit down with Sanus next week with only his dick in his hand.

34

Man's memory shapes its own Eden within.

—Jorge Luis Borges

Maggie surveyed the Term with fresh eyes. Only a few months ago, it seemed a dark, depressing harbinger of the rest of her life. Noisy, privileged twenty-some-things crowding the booths, sotted old-timers draped over the bar, commuters looking to delay their return to the suburbs. A microcosm of America's decline. And a snapshot of her future, with her dreams of becoming a crusading lawyer crushed. But today, the same scene filled her with nostalgia and joy. Warm memories of her mother's cooking, her dad's proud presence behind the bar, and the stream of cops and locals who were her guardians and now her pals.

Maggie's emotional 180 reflected her reversal of fortunes at St. Sebastian. Just before the end of the semester, she received word that the Ethics Committee charges against her had been dismissed and that she was given permission to withdraw from Professor Gleason's seminar. She'd also been allowed to submit her paper for academic credit under the supervision of Professor Louise Auchincloss at NYU who taught a course on gender discrimination, and presumably was no fan of anti-abortion laws. Topping off the Christmas miracle, she had been rewarded for her determination not to go down without a fight, receiving the highest grades in her Advanced Civil Procedure and Evidence classes.

Cause for a celebratory bottle of Patron in her private booth with her pal Jen.

"Jen, did you have something to do with all this? Did you plead my case to Professor McNeely? Oh for God's sake, tell me you didn't sleep with him!"

"You're at it again, bitch. Trying to convince your sorry-little-Catholic-girl self you don't deserve to be treated well. Look, you were getting totally hosed by that fat bastard Geekson. And I'm sure McNeely figured that out. In fact, he was mighty impressed with you."

"Oh, sure."

"No, really. He told me your seminar paper is one of the best he's ever read. He sent it to some hot shit professor at UCLA. Seems to think she can help you get it published."

"Jesus, this is too much."

"Wait, there's more . . ."

"Now you're sounding like an infomercial."

"Just trying to make a sale to you. A sale to you *on* you. You've got to realize your potential."

"OK, now you've morphed into a self-help shill."

"And self-help it is!" Jen getting wound up and pouring two generous shots of Patron,

"You can put yourself in a position to get any kind of law job you want. Here's the first step. I told McNeely I can't be his research assistant this semester because I'm loaded down doing the legal aid housing law clinic and editing the law journal. So, I suggested that you take my place."

"Oh, yeah. I got nothing but leisure time." Maggie sweeping her arm gesturing an arc from the bar to the rest rooms, "Look around this place. Looks like it's humming along like a well-oiled machine? No, I've got my hands full keeping the bar tenders from stealing us blind and the drunks from pissing in the parking lot."

"OK, but it doesn't take that much time. Plus having McNeely on your side can be a big help. He knows a lot of people. Tried to talk me into applying for a judicial clerkship with the judge he clerked for. But I told him I'm committed to the Worsted law firm. For you, a clerkship with a big-time judge would be a ticket to anything you want to do . . . public interest law firms, the mayor's staff, you name it. All that do-good, save-the-homeless-whales stuff you've been preaching at me for two years."

Maggie knew she was right. It was helpful to have good grades and a couple of professors who could help you find the kind of job you want. But having a judge vouch for you could open a lot of doors even if you didn't go to Harvard or Yale.

Looking over to see her father staring glassy eyed at the Mets game, she knew there were some mountains to climb before she could stroll down Jen's yellow brick road to do-gooding. The amusing early warning signs she'd seen just a few months ago had now grown to textbook evidence of dementia. Forgetting names of his favorite cops, leaving the refrigerator door open and the toilet unflushed, and worst of all, calling her Norma. He came home one day with part of his Chevy's front bumper missing but his only explanation was that "someone must have stolen it."

His buddies at the bar knew what was going on, so they played along. Watching a Mets game, he started complaining about how Kranepool couldn't hit a curve ball and Swoboda strikes out too much. Bill Kelly, a retired detective as old as her father and who knew by heart the starting lineup of the '69 Mets, immediately launched into a discussion of whether Koosman or Seaver should pitch the first game of the World Series, if somehow, they made it that far. Maggie knew she'd never forget seeing her father's eyes twinkling and his body suddenly energized. At least for a few minutes.

Maggie did her research on WebMD and made an appointment with a favorably reviewed gerontologist at Rutgers Medical School in Newark. Convincing her father to go to he appointment however took some doing. She couldn't remember him ever going to a doctor other than the time he sliced off the tip of his finger slicing limes at the bar. And the misery of his wife's countless doctors' visits, chemo clinics, and her excruciating last week in the hospital ICU made it a difficult selling job. Maggie settled on telling a white—or more accurately, orange—lie. She told her father that he would lose his Medicare benefits if he didn't have a newly required "Senior Wellness Check-Up" mandated by the Trump Administration. Mickey said he couldn't believe President Kennedy would allow this kind of meddling, but when Maggie patiently explained that it was another scheme by Trump to force seniors off Medicare, he relented. "Not gonna let that asshole repeal the New Deal," he told her. "And you better put a stop to all this Republican crap when you're a lawyer."

Words Maggie knew she would someday repeat at his memorial service.

35

If you believe in unlimited quality and act in all your business dealings with total integrity, the rest will take care of itself."

—Frank Perdue

Perdue Met Mafia Boss, Sought Help Against Union

—*Washington Post* headline, March 7, 1986

"Good morning everybody. Hope you all had a good weekend. With my Knicks going nowhere this year and our miserable cold spell, I spent too much time reading and watching the news about what's going on in Washington. So, before we dive into today's readings, I thought I'd share a few thoughts with you. Some of what went on with the testimony—which I hope you all followed—by Michael Cohen, the President's former lawyer, and how it can teach us something about the themes of this course. I named this course "Topics in Corporate Governance" so it would reach the wide range of things that go into the decision-making of corporations, large and small. And I think what you heard from Mr. Cohen can give you some insights into how some CEOs may be insulated from any oversight whatsoever."

McNeely noticed with some surprise that he seemed to have the attention of almost everyone in the class. They're probably thinking I'm going to go upside Trump's head again, he thought. Much as he'd like to, he decided to disguise his assault with some academic nuance.

"What you should think about as this story develops—and as you know the Mueller Report is expected out soon—is a topic that is a big part of our course: how is it that a corporation, or more pointedly, a corporate titan, is able to skirt the law? Who serves as a check on the CEO? The Board of Directors? The Shareholders? The General Counsel? Spoiler Alert: In some corporations, the answer is: 'None of the Above.'"

Some stirring among the backbenchers sensing the possibility of fireworks.

OK, just a scosh, McNeely decided, his amygdala and medial prefrontal cortex firing in perfect harmony to call up a healthy shot of adrenalin.

"What did Mr. Cohen teach us? Well, he said that President Trump systematically defrauded banks, insurers, and lenders in his property dealings. Cohen also testified that as Trump's lawyer, he did his boss' bidding on corporate financial matters. He knew that much of what he was doing was immoral and illegal. Yet he became his willing accomplice. *Trump viewed Michael Cohen as his Roy Cohn.* Those of you who don't know who that is, Google him. After class, that is. Mr. Trump made it clear the kind of lawyer he wanted. 'Where's my Roy Cohn' he said. C-O-H-N. He was talking about Roy Cohn, one of the most corrupt lawyers in the nation's history. He led the McCarthy era's witch hunt of alleged communists in America and was ultimately convicted and disbarred for perjury, obstruction of justice and bribery. Our President left no doubt he wanted a lawyer just like Roy Cohn."

Tempting as it was, McNeely decided not to mention Cardinal Spellman, archbishop of New York who palled around with Cohn and he also elected to skip over the Catholic Church's complicity in the misdeeds of the McCarthy era. Stay focused on delivering the news on Trump, he told himself—keep it fair and balanced.

"In his testimony before the House of Representatives last week, *our* Mr. Cohen, that is, Michael, accused the President of committing insurance fraud, saying Mr. Trump inflated estimates of his assets to insurance companies and turned over private financial statements the President gave to Deutsche Bank AG in 2013 to get a loan to buy the Buffalo Bills football team. A pretty sorry football franchise, I'll add parenthetically. And under their business model, the Trump organization rountinely *deflated* their property values to avoid paying state property taxes while they'd also *inflate* the value of the very same properties in order to defraud banks into lending them money."

Some students were actually taking notes. It was clear that for some, this was the first they had heard of these things, Cohen's testimony apparently not trending on Instagram, TikTok, or Tinder.

"The issue for this class is the one we talked about when we studied the Enron fraud. Where were the watchdogs? That is, where were the board of directors, the corporation's lawyers, their bankers, the bankers' lawyers, and last but certainly not least, the government."

A familiar pink hand. God bless Mr. Oswald. Coming back to take another class from me, McNeely thought, secretly flattered that someone he gave a hard time to for a whole semester felt the give-and-take was worth it.

"But Professor McNeely, Cohen was the President's lawyer and has been indicted for his lawbreaking. First, how can we believe someone willing to violate the attorney-client privilege and on top of that, someone who wants to sanitize his record by making it seem like he was just doing what he was ordered to do? You were a prosecutor once, Professor. Would you put this guy on the stand?"

McNeely starting to genuinely admire Oswald. He wanted to tell him how wrong he was but at the same time would have to admit nothing would probably come of all this for a long, long time. He felt Cohen was credible precisely because he was such a sleazebag. His testimony could be reinforced with documents, depositions from Deutsche Bank officials, real estate appraisals, tax records and so on. All of which would take two years at a minimum. But impeachment couldn't wait that long, and Mueller, who now looked a bit mummified, didn't seem to have the energy, and half the voters didn't give a shit. McNeely decided to play dodgeball with a vague answer and an offer to take the Cohen testimony up with anyone who wanted to stay after class.

"We need to turn to today's reading assignments. Let's start with the basics we covered in the introductory corporate law course. What is the *theoretical role* of the Board of Directors in the modern corporation? And after you answer that, what is the real-world story of what they *actually* do?"

This being a course for high achievers, several hands shot up. "Ms. Suarez?"

"Theoretical is easy. The board is supposed to have final authority to make all decisions. They can and do, of course delegate most of that authority to management, the CEO and other guys. And of course, I do mean guys, since there aren't many women CEOs. Not yet at least."

Ms. Suarez has gumption. And McNeely liked gumption. In moderation.

Pausing to acknowledge supportive snickers, Suarez plowed on. "Now what really happens is the CEO usually gets to pick his own board members. They're just like him. Former CEOs, golfing buddies, investors who bought into his company. Not to mention a few who do business with his corporation and want to curry favor to get more business."

Remembering that his job description requires the occasional foray into Socratic dialogue, McNeely tossed out a riposte, "But what's bad about putting the CEO in charge? Are corporations supposed to be little democracies, with everyone having a vote on whether the iPhone should have five or ten color choices? Isn't it more efficient for the CEO to surround herself . . . ”

McNeely ignoring the intentionally loud snickering, "surround *herself or himself* with people with expertise, and experience in running a 50-billion-dollar operation? Who's to say what's the best way to make business decisions?"

"Well, the studies cited by Professor Mitchell in his article suggests that cozy relations between the board and the CEO are a breeding ground for the problems of the modern corporation. Too little innovation, neglect of their shareholders, and, finally, ridiculous compensation for guess who?"

This is what happens thought McNeely. They're forced to hear their professors' Socratic dialogue for three years and instinctively start doing it themselves.

On a roll, Ms. Suarez pressed on, "The CEO! Big corporations pay their CEOs 139 times what the average worker gets. You know what? That difference is six times what it was just a couple of decades ago."

An apoplectic Mr. Oswald furiously pumping his hand in the air. "Wait, wait. Professor Romano's article shows there are scads of studies proving that putting workers on corporate boards or allowing customers, or whoever Ms. Suarez wants to nominate, to sit on a corporate board doesn't make a bit of difference."

Ms. Suarez, loaded for bear, interrupted, "Difference? Measured by what? Stock market prices pumped up by short-term motives that don't help consumers get better new products? And what about having a board that at least gives a shit about its workers and . . ."

Now outright laughter from the class. Suarez undeterred, continued, "What about having a board that *cares* about its workers, like Henry Ford did, and cares about its community?"

Every now and then, thought McNeely, even in corporate law, you could be witness to that wonderful admixture of idealism, energy, and hope.

If only it would last.

Even the genius asks his questions.
—Tupac

He devoted his day off to his hobby. Walking. Walking Manhattan, north, south, east, and west, with occasional forays into the Bronx and Brooklyn. Cheaper and far more interesting than paying $2.75 to take a packed, odorous B train uptown. McNeely saw an old movie years ago that inspired him, *1000 Clowns,* in which Jason Robarts played an unemployed writer who lived a bohemian life, wandering the city shouting funny instructions to neighboring buildings ("I want to see a better class of garbage next week"), joining a crowd seeing off cruise ships, and observing the movements of the working stiffs in Manhattan. On his free day, McNeely did the same. He loaded his laptop in his backpack and trekked off, stopping at regular intervals at coffee shops, parks or bars to tackle some law school drudgery.

He began his brisk morning walk by passing through Sheridan Square and the site of the city's first integrated nightclub, Café Society—even the Cotton Club originally had separate sections for Negroes. Billy Holliday sang *Strange Fruit* for the first time there, a song McNeely firmly believed should be mandatory listening for every high school civics class. They may not remember anything about Jim Crow laws, or residential segregation, or Brown v. Board, but they'll remember *the bulging eyes and the twisted mouth* for the rest of their lives. Lots to teach about too, he thought. The song's origins offered a micro-portrait of some of New York City's history. It was written by a white guy, a Jewish high school teacher, member of the Communist party who had taught James Baldwin *as a student* at DeWitt Clinton, and, most incredible of all, had adopted Julius and Ethel Rosenberg's kids after their parents were executed in 1953 for espionage. Lots of history to be uncovered walking around the Naked City, all there just for the taking.

En route to Nolita Espresso Bar for his morning infusion, he passed by Old St. Patrick's on Mulberry St. The original Cathedral of the Archdiocese in the city and predecessor to the 5th Avenue landmark, it offered another teachable history lesson. Built in the early 1800's, it was attacked and nearly sacked by a gang of nativists, called the "Know-Nothings," who adhered to a virulent and violent anti-Catholic, anti-Irish, anti-immigrant ideology—a reminder that his peeps, the Irish Catholics, were the Muslims of 19th Century New York. But would that history lesson change the minds of today's third-generation Irish nativists? Would it defuse support for Trump's crusade to seal the borders? Pigs might fly, he regretfully concluded.

Moving on, he passed by 181 Mercer, NYU's latest building extravaganza and paused to conduct an angry real estate appraisal. Still under construction, the University promised the structure would contribute to Greenwich Village—or more accurately, to NYU's well-endowed students—some 750,000 square feet of theatres, swimming pools, classrooms, performing arts venues, four basketball courts, and, for Christ's sake, heavily subsidized housing for the University's overpaid faculty. Neighborhood and historic preservation groups fought it vigorously, but Mayor Bloomberg thought it just the upscale glass phallus the Village lacked. Jesus, McNeely grumbled outloud, NYU owns half of the Village, Columbia has bought up most of West Harlem, and the Catholic and Episcopal Churches own the rest. All allegedly in service of their nonprofit charitable and religious missions. Maybe another teachable moment for his corporate law class.

McNeely was especially alert to the subtle signs that the melting pot had not completely assimilated all of its ingredients. Pointed metal crowns atop city fireplugs, separators on benches, spikes on low level brick walls, all designed to keep street people from sitting, reclining, or gathering. The New York Times had a name for it: "Hostile Architecture." Then there were the city's POPS, "privately owned public spaces"—parks and alcoves that builders had agreed to furnish in exchange for lucrative zoning variances—all replete with barriers to any form of relaxation in their quarters. Further evidence of the ongoing battle to keep the homeless and transients at bay, while neglecting the social and mental health services that might have a lasting impact.

Many parts of the city had undergone a radical transformation from the landscape McNeely had explored as a teenager twenty years ago. It seemed like a sci-fi flick: vendors of cigars, liquor, hardware, secondhand clothing, and used furniture had disappeared overnight and been replaced by posh hair salons, gyms, eateries, and boutique clothing shops, all catering to an alien population transported from another planet. Or from Connecticut.

He especially enjoyed watching Manhattan waking up. For him, the city came alive when the natives were on the move like their ancestors, hunting for some carrion to drag home: early mornings when the shop keepers were unlocking and pulling up the protective metal gates in front of their stores and hosing away the needles and detritus on their sidewalks; swarms of fast-walking, well-appointed office workers sprinting to their workstations in midtown; feverish commuters navigating Fifth Avenue while juggling a to-go cappuccino and a rugelach; parades of yellow-vested construction workers toting lunch boxes, off to be suspended 80 floors up in the sky, looking, he thought, like his granddad probably did trooping off to the Brooklyn Navy Yard; an elegantly dressed octogenarian struggling to pick up her shiatzu's dog shit; busboys grabbing a last-minute smoke in the late afternoon while waiters folded napkins and fastidiously arranged outdoor seating; gaggles of upscale teenagers released from Stuy, Regis, Dalton, and other express ramps to the Ivies; doormen jumping to swing open a door or sprint to hail a cab; and the occasional stunningly beautiful girl to follow for a couple of blocks.

Other walks were a fresh slap in McNeely's conspicuously Caucasian face. In Bed Stuy, Jamaica, and Brownsville he saw posted signs welcoming him to another world.

This Store under 24-Hour Video Surveillance

Naxalone Available Here

Checks Cashed. Payday Loans

24 Hour Bail Bonds

 Safe Horizon: Moving victims of violence from crisis to confidence.

Drug and Weapon Free School Zone

Pediatric Trauma Center

Pawn Shop: We Buy Gold. You Get Cash Any Time

INJURED? Call 1-888-HURT-911

Student Entrance: Metal Detectors in Use.

Strolling by the grim façade of Ardmore Major High School in Queens, he found it curiously quiet. The curiosity was resolved when his Googling that evening explained that New York's open enrollment policy had produced some conspicuous losers. AMHS had a graduation rate of 39% which understandably caused parents to send their kids . . . anywhere else. But some were not so fortunate. Stuck in a school with no science program, rampant violence outside and inside the building, and a beleaguered faculty, those left behind were like prisoners in a bad zombie film. For them, the land of opportunity is just a pipe dream. Without admitting it to himself, McNeely felt like a latter-day Margaret Mead, observing his Samoans as they went about their quotidian rituals, while making mental notes about their struggles. Like a colonial anthropologist, he rationalized that he would draw from his travels to enrich his teaching and writing.

Returning from his eight-hour jaunt which took him as far north as the Metropolitan Museum and involved pitstops to do some work at three coffee lounges and one bar, he found himself at a store front that he had not noticed before. *Pet Portraits by Leeza.* The display window had several large paintings, each of an individual dog or cat and a collection of hand-painted post cards. Some were playful, like an animal driving a car or catching a football. Others were serious, one placing a plump Persian cat on a four-poster bed with elaborately colored bedspreads and pillows, another depicting a standard poodle cutting a swath through the grassland of an African savanna at sunset.

McNeely hoped he might be able to look at the paintings without having to concoct a story about a pet he wanted immortalized. But an attractive woman with long blond hair, dressed in overalls and waiving a paint brush emerged from a back room and extended her hand.

"Hi, I'm Leeza, owner, operator and . . ." smiling brightly, "and resident *artiste.*"

Before he could respond, she looked him up and down and continued. "You're just curious about what the hell this is, right? Don't be embarrassed, I get a lot of gawkers stopping in."

Her smile lit up the room and was doing some work on McNeely too. She had sized him up in fifteen seconds and avoided uncomfortable bullshitting, cheerfully setting the record straight—exactly the kind of attributes he imagined he'd someday come across. And the blond hair down to her butt didn't hurt either.

"Well, you got me. Just trying to get to know my neighbors." Letting her know he wasn't as down and out as his jeans and backpack might signal. And that he had an apartment nearby.

"I'm guessing you have some interesting clients? I'm a law professor, so I know a little about dealing with clients. And unruly customers, that is, students." Clumsy, he realized, but important to establish street cred with the law prof thing in case that might help.

They chatted for twenty minutes, with Leeza freely volunteering stories about her customers, some hilarious, some poignant: a deathbed visit to a lonely widow who wanted a portrait of her darling Siberian Forest cat to be interred with her; a gay couple who wanted a wedding invitation that captured them walking their Tibetan Mastiff under the Washington Square Arch where they first met; a pet piranha owned by a creepy guy in a sparsely furnished East Village studio apartment.

Sensing some common ground in their fascination with the quirky corners of their city, McNeely proposed a drink at a nearby pub. Leeza put on a serious look and said "Well, I'll have to forego the usual 6 p.m. rush of seniors who come by following afternoon memorial services, but OK."

His first authentic date in over a year. He had sworn off dating after enduring a run of a half dozen misguided fixups. For reasons he never understood, many faculty spouses had taken it upon themselves to pass along someone he "ought to meet." Most were divorced, the majority were overweight, and all were anxious to get serious real soon. He realized they had been forewarned about his weight, divorce, and disabled daughter because all studiously avoided mentions of children and declined dessert. One encounter had been going extremely well, and he thought the law of large numbers was finally working in his favor. At the end of a laugh-filled dinner and stop over at a local bar, she casually mentioned she had an uncle in the Boston area. McNeely confirmed he did too and that his lived in Quincy. Amazed, she said her uncle Phil worked in Quincy. He gave a surprised chuckle, "Wow, Phil? My uncle is named Phil!!!" They stared at each other for a moment, and simultaneously shouted the same question: "Phil Hanratty???" After a quick Google search of genetics counselling websites on their cell phones, the second cousins insincerely agreed to stay in touch and tell their uncle about their new-found relation.

McNeely spent twenty minutes pondering his wardrobe options for his dinner with Leeza. Shooting for something reasonably sporty, but still definitively West Village, New York, he settled for the safest: all black—shirt, sports coat, and shoes. He considered the blue socks with gold saxophones as a sign of his hidden hipster side but lost his nerve. Packing two condoms in his wallet, he hoped he remembered the fundamentals. The first hour went perfectly. They exchanged stories about their neighbors, laughed about the pretensions of her clients, talked seriously about the sad stories they saw on the streets every day. Both had cocktails and ordered mussels and cheese appetizers. She introduced him to her favorite aperitif, B&B, and conversation flowed easily.

Reviewing the evening's events later that night, he searched for the clues that signaled something was amiss. Leeza had displayed a few tells that, in retrospect, he realized should have put him on alert. Her response to one of his favorite stories about a female colleague—a law professor for God's sakes—who had somehow failed to pay her taxes for three years—was to suggest that the tax system was fundamentally unfair to "successful women." When he asked whether she was the sole owner of the business, she responded with a long tirade about the city's rules for small business owners, especially women who were "not the norm." His mention of his ex did not elicit the obligatory sympathetic questions, but instead led her to express concerns about the lack of discipline she sees among young parents marching their children to school. When asked about her reading interests, she said she avoids the "trendy, downbeat *New Yorker* magazine stuff" and preferred books that recounted "America's better eras."

The capper came after their waitress, a young redhead with a distinct Irish brogue, moved a portable umbrella to keep them in the shade at their outdoor table. Shaking her flowing red hair she cheerfully said, "Have to do this all the time. That sun just keeps moving." Leeza gave her a stiff, forced smile. "Actually, it's the Earth that's moving, dear. Rotating, spinning on its axis, you know?" Once the waitress had left, Leeza shook her head. "Our public school system in operation. And did you hear how she pronounced crème brûlée ?"

It was all there in plain sight. Not sure why it had taken so long to dawn on him. She was on the other team. A total mismatch.

She was a Republican.

The Trojans would go back in the refrigerator.

37

Out of the crooked tree of humanity, no straight thing can ever be made.

—Immanuel Kant

A knock accompanied by his door opening simultaneously. "Dean McNeely, your one o'clock meeting. The Sanus storm troopers have arrived."

The Deans had arranged to have the term contract negotiation session on their turf. The meeting was designed to allow the principals from the law school and Sanus to discuss and iron out the financial and governance arrangements that would link their organizations. For the Deans it was an opportunity to get a handle on exactly what they were up against.

"OK, Jewel. Please let the Dean know. Could you come by and offer them some coffee?"

"You bet. Shall I rush out to buy one of those new Nespresso machines to make them their pumpkin maculatas? Or just give them our sludge?"

"Sludge it is. Let them see how the other half drinks. And make sure they get paper cups."

Walking into the Dean's conference room, McNeely stopped in his tracks and stared in disbelief. Standing in the middle of a crew of five plain-vanilla corporate executives was an elegantly dressed, muscular African American right out of central casting. Returning McNeely's gaze, he directed an almost imperceptible nod across the room.

"Please, gentlemen, sit down," Dean Eckstein said. Recognizing the significance of the large gentleman's silent signal, McNeely averted his eyes and quickly sat down next to the Dean.

The apparent leader of the Sanus entourage spoke first. "Dean Eckstein, Dean McNeely, it is a genuine pleasure to finally meet you and a privilege to initiate this collaboration between our institutions. Let me first introduce my colleagues. First, from my left is John "Jake" Treehorn, Sanus Board member and former CEO of

Allegial Pharmaceuticals ; Allen Weinberger, Sanus Director of Program Management, former legislative assistant to Senator McConnell; Bill Francis, Sanus Director of Program Outreach; Dr. Sander "Skip" Jordan, Sanus Educational Programs Director; and our newest colleague, Alonzo Jenks, Consultant on Program Logistics and Security."

McNeely shot a glance at his friend, mentor, fellow white collar crime fighter, and now apparently, corporate spy. Jinks returned a modest smile and momentary eye contact. This confirms what I always knew, thought McNeely, Jinks is one unique piece of work. Back in the day at the FBI, he was known for his ability to read people and take command in dicey situations. All of which made him the Bureau's best urban chameleon. He could blend in and secure the confidence of anyone from Hell's Kitchen to Wall Street.

Sanus' silver-haired team captain continued on with an ingratiating smile. "And as some of you know, I'm Frederick Douglas . . . ha, ha, no relation of course…I'm Executive Director of Sanus. In my past lives, I've served as CEO of Questmat Pharmaceuticals, COO of Nexilabs, and in my misspent youth, ha, ha, I was Deputy Commissioner for Policy, Legislation, and International Affairs at the Food and Drug Administration. Now, I'm just a happy purveyor of concepts and distributor of funding in support of worthy causes."

Polite smiles all around, followed by some throat clearing from the happy purveyor. "If I may, Dean, I thought we might begin by learning a bit more about each other. If you were to list the three most pressing needs of St. Sebastian School of Law, what would they be?"

As McNeely knew she would, Eckstein, a serious chess player, was able to parry the amateur's Danish Gambit opening. After offering up a few vague generalities about the law school's needs for infrastructure and administrative simplification, she set her Monticelli trap. "As you may know, the law school is accountable to a number of what you might call higher authorities. One is the Bishop, who—and this is just between us—watches us like a hawk. He wants to make sure our programs and financial arrangements serve the Church's mission. And then there's the American Bar Association, which accredits every law school and monitors their income and expenditures to make sure they are serving the goal of educating the next generation of attorneys to serve the public."

Realizing he was not going to get away with returning vague generalities touting Sanus' mission to promote healthy choices and behaviors, Douglas had no choice but to lay out the financial architecture of Sanus' undertaking. It reminded McNeely of a classic encounter between a start-up and a venture capitalist. St. Sebastian was in the role of an eager, hardworking entrepreneur who walks into the lion's den of the VC seeking funding, only to be saddled with a series of nonnegotiable commitments, oversight, second-guessing, and thinly veiled threats. The ancient Golden Rule of Business, applied: "He who has the gold, rules."

Stripped to their essentials, Sanus' deal points were straightforward and predictably one-sided. It would indeed pledge $30 million to St. Sebastian School of Law with most of that sum to be paid in annual installments over a ten-year period. The new institute, to be named the Sanus Institute on Pharmaceutical and Health Law and Policy would conduct research, issue white papers, and contribute to policy formulation through advocacy before administrative agencies and legislatures. Sanus would fund half the salary of an "eminent law professor with expertise in pharmaceutical law and policy" who would be Director of the Institute. The Director, who would be chosen by the institute's board, would be authorized to hire a research staff of four professionals whose salary would be 50% funded by Sanus with the law school providing all necessary administrative and logistical support. Finally, Sanus would sponsor annual seminars in Rome, Geneva, or China which would charge tuition to participants, with all surplus revenues to be retained by Sanus. One St. Sebastian faculty member and two students would receive free tuition to one seminar, but no travel expenses would be provided. Critically, a simple formula on governance that made it clear who was going to sit in the pilot's seat: Sanus would appoint two members to the Board of Directors and St. Sebastian one.

McNeely immediately recognized that St. Sebastian would serve as Sanus' Potemkin village: Knock over the cardboard façade and you'd expose a well-lubricated corporate propaganda machine.

Flipping to the "Financial Appendix" at the end of the slick binder that Douglas handed out at the beginning of his presentation, a terse footnote caught McNeely's eye.

Annual contributions by the granting party may be suspended or terminated at the discretion of the grantor upon thirty-days' notice to the grantee.

He casually circled the provision and slid it over to Dean Eckstein with a note.

This is interesting. Perhaps they're taking a lien on our real estate too? Should I point out that SIPHLP sounds a bit like syphilis? Easy to contract, but hard to shake.

Still smiling, Dean Eckstein decied to put off for another day what would undoubtedly be a contentious discussion. "Gentlemen, you've given us a lot to chew on here. Let us do some drafting of bylaws and contractual commitments and meet again soon."

Now confident that peace would come to the Middle East before an agreement with Sanus was reached, McNeely breathed a sigh of relief.

38

*The man that hath no music in himself, nor is not moved with
concord of sweet sounds, is fit for treasons, stratagems, and spoils.*

—William Shakespeare, *The Merchant of Venice*

The St. Sebastian Law School Critical Drinking Society met every Thursday at 5 p.m. Society membership consisted of two tranches. The founding members were four of the cabal McNeely called The Young and the Restless—professors hired within the last five years, none yet tenured, and all from top five law schools. The second tier included two older tenured faculty members, also from top five law schools and still restless after all these years. What both tranches shared was a disdain for their colleagues and the abiding sense that someday soon a top tier law school would be recruiting them. Occasionally guest privileges were extended, usually to visiting or adjunct professors, or to friends of the Y&R who met the age and dour personality requirements. Locations varied, but fashionable cocktail lounges were favored. All of the Y&R lived in Manhattan or Brooklyn and were generally disposed to spend as little time as possible in the Garden State.

Thursday was the preferred time for meeting because it was the end of an exhausting week that may have involved as many as six hours of classroom teaching, one hour of "office hours" for brief encounters with students, and a one- or possibly two-hour committee meeting. Thursday afternoon also marked the beginning of everyone's three-day weekend since nobody wanted to teach on Fridays, and St. Sebastian had abandoned scheduling classes for tenured or tenure-track professors after 3 p.m. on Thursdays.

The Y&R contingent had much in common: all were single white men, products of upper-class families, graduates of top tier law schools, and had served as judicial law clerks and briefly practiced at white-shoe Manhattan law firms. Abraham Block (Berkeley, Stanford Law, district court clerkship), who was gay and wore an earring, supplied the diversity. The group's meetings were organized by Professor Raymond Williams (Dartmouth, Columbia, Second Circuit Court of Appeals clerkship) who fancied himself an expert mixologist, packing some 60 bottles of spirits into his 500 square foot Brooklyn co-op. He dutifully scouted bars and provided previews analyzing the bars' demographics, cocktail selection, prices, and "ambience," a code word all understood to signal hook-up possibilities. But when it came to setting the agenda and cheerless tone, Professor Julian Cathcart firmly ruled the roost. Deference from his untenured colleagues was the inevitable product of his status as a senior professor, previous role of Associate Dean of the law school, and future voter on the others' tenure status.

Professor Williams had scored a large leather booth near the fireplace in the back room of the Clover Club in Brooklyn. He had pre-ordered duck fat-fried chips and had highly recommended (four stars on the CDS scale of 1-5) the Aviation and Sazerac cocktails. The early chatter focused on the Attorney General's misleading summary of the Mueller Report and the President's declaration of "exoneration." All were suitably aghast that the Attorney General had taken it on himself to preempt the text of the report, provide what was apparently a false summary of the 400-page report, and top it off with his own conclusion that the President had not committed obstruction of justice. It was not clear when or how the full report would be released.

"These guys are geniuses," groused Professor Gangloff (Columbia, NYU Law, NJ Supreme Court clerkship). "They get the word out that all is copacetic and the President tweets out his message, *Exonerated. Witch hunt. Hoax.*"

Professor Anderson joining the frustration chorus, "And Fox News and the *NY Post* eat it up." Googling the Post headline, he exclaimed, "Look what it says: *'Trump Clean. No Crimes Committed. Dem Hoax Destroyed.'* What a joke. He calls the President of Ukraine and asks for a "favor"—please find me some dirt on Joe Biden. Then he fires Comey, tries to fire Mueller. If that's not obstruction of justice, what the fuck is?"

"Impeachment for sure," said Professor Gangloff surveying the Y&R and finding unanimity. None of them actually knew a single person who voted for Trump, but all were nonetheless confident those voters would see the error of their ways. "Where's Cathcart? Is he coming?"

"Never missed one yet. Maybe he's getting another divorce." Professor Block willing to disrespect the elder in his absence, alluding to Cathcart's three unhappy marriages.

On cue, a breathless Professor Cathcart rushed into the room and squeezed into the last spot in the booth. His scowling, asymmetrical face emitted a growl, "Fucking Brooklyn! Next week let's go somewhere that doesn't take three transfers and a two-mile walk."

The slim and fit Y&Rs suppressed smirks at their out-of-shape senior mentor, thinking "this is not going to be me in twenty years."

"OK gentlemen. Got some breaking news for you." Pausing dramatically to convey the gravity of his announcement and lowering his voice to a whisper, "Methinks the Dean wants us to jump into bed with Big Pharma."

Pleased with the hoped-for array of surprised, attentive faces, Cathcart continued. "Some of you may have noticed an army of suits came in for some kind of meeting yesterday morning. So, I happened to be walking through the Dean's conference room afterwards and noticed a brochure in the garbage can. The gist of it, as far as I can make out, is that this right-wing lobby group called Sanus is offering St. Sebastian big money to fund some kind of institute at the law school."

Another pregnant pause and sip of his Aviator, "Not bad, what is this? In any event, I Googled Sanus, and found out it's a 501(c)(4) that funds think tanks and research. Their website says it's dedicated to the usual Heritage, Cato, Manhattan Institute bullshit: free markets, deregulation, the whole Trump playbook. And who funds it? Dark Money!"

Professor Howard interrupting, "So what's Big Pharma got to do with it?"

A bit taken aback, Cathcart worried that Howard, whose specialty was administrative law, might not be appropriately appalled at a possible corporate incursion. The naïve kid might think that having some of Big Pharma's surplus profits trickle down on St. Sebastian is a good thing. "Well, their CEO seems to have a background in pharmaceutical companies, as do one or two of their board members. The web site is pretty vague on details. But you can be sure of one thing. Whatever they're cooking up will wind up fattening their wallets, while we are expected to do their dirty work."

Need to put a little fear of God into them, Cathcart thought. Offering a slightly exasperated sigh, he deployed his class lecture voice. "First, just a little caveat emptor here. Trojan horses, my friends, Trojan horses. Based on what I've seen happen over the years at other law schools, we may be at an inflection point."

Scanning his acolytes' faces for signs of acceptance, he continued, "This is precisely the kind of thing that requires full transparency. And most important, close faculty oversight. We don't want to be setting sail on some fraught excursion the Dean is pushing in order to embellish her resume. And I certainly don't want to become the George Mason of New Jersey." As he knew it would, the mere mention of the name George Mason, now Antonin Scalia School of Law, drew a round of knowing nods.

Thinking it time to remind the youngsters that someone's got their back, Cathcart went on, "I still have some pretty good contacts over in Sheehan Hall from my days as Associate Dean. I think they can get me the scuttlebutt about what our Dean is up to—before she springs a *fait accompli* on us. Trojan horses. We must be vigilant about Trojan horses, my friends."

*Managing university finances is very tricky business. We're nonprofits.
We're not supposed to accumulate large surpluses.*

—Richard Levin, President, Yale University

During Levin's tenure, Yale's endowment grew from
$3.2 billion to over $20 billion.

—Wikipedia

McNeely felt like he had a worn-out shock absorber. He woke up to Nina Totenberg of NPR on his clock radio, followed by outraged tweets on the legal blogs he scanned on his phone over breakfast, culminating with blistering commentary in the *New York Times* which he read on his train ride to the law school. All condemning his alma mater, the U.S. Department of Justice. He knew it was the aberrant conduct of that shill, the Attorney General, who was the target of their furor, but he still felt a pang in the pit of his stomach at the desecration of the institution he held dear. If the Justice Department came to be viewed as just another political organ, and its leader just another duplicitous spinmeister, he feared for the legitimacy of the institution and indeed for the entire legal system—the same legal system he was scheduled to profess about in 45 minutes.

He was tempted to ignore the controversy because, after all, his was a class on corporate law. He could easily dive into the topic of the day, nonprofit corporations. No one would expect anything different. But the job did involve teaching, and yes, professing. He settled on framing a quick editorial comment. Kind of an oral tweet, but with feeling. Like when the Challenger blew up when he was in second grade and Mrs. Robinski felt she had to say something.

"You've undoubtedly read about the Mueller Report and the Justice Department's summary of it. These are momentous times. We don't have all the facts yet, and the full Report may not be released for a while. But what we do know is that the

President may have committed obstruction of justice, although the report makes no firm conclusion on that. There was not enough evidence to reach a legal conclusion as to whether there was technical collusion with the Russians. But we also know that the Attorney General issued a *highly misleading* summary of the Mueller Report. And as to that, I just want you all to know, as one who proudly served as an Assistant U.S. Attorney in the Department of Justice . . ." McNeely paused as the words caught in his throat.

"As a proud former Justice Department attorney, that *really pisses me off.*"

He chose not to make eye contact with the students, mostly out of fear they might look disinterested. He just didn't want to know. Activating his PowerPoint slides, he went on. "OK, had to get that off my chest. Let's discuss this creature, the nonprofit corporation. Ms. Suarez, what's different about these entities? What distinguishes them, according to state statutory law from the for-profit corporations we've been studying?"

McNeely knew which students could be counted on to carry the ball today. With his nerves frayed, he needed a reliable halfback and Ms. Suarez had never disappointed. "Well to begin with the obvious, they don't have shareholders," she responded quickly. "And most important, they are supposed to be engaged in something the law finds useful to society, like being educational, religious, or charitable."

Ms. Suarez clearly ready to take the ball for a few more carries, McNeely handed off again, "So, what's the effect of not having shareholders? In studying for-profit corporations, we learned that their board members were supposed to do what? Do you remember their duty?"

He knew she would speed past this tackler. "Maximize shareholder wealth," she responded with just the slightest touch of sarcasm.

"Exactly. And, by contrast, what are nonprofit directors supposed to do given that they have no shareholders?"

"Their duty is to make sure the nonprofit is following its mission. That it's doing the charitable, or educational stuff it was incorporated to do. Do you want me to go on?"

Content to watch her high step her way into the end zone, McNeely suppressed a smile and nodded silently.

"So, they have to keep an eye on the CEO and those running the nonprofit to make sure they're pursuing the charitable or other goals, and not keeping the profits for themselves."

McNeely now teeing up the extra point, "Profits? I thought these were nonprofit corporations. For example, St. Sebastian University: it's a nonprofit corporation."

Ms. Suarez not taking the bait. "Every nonprofit that runs a business, like hospitals or colleges, has to make some money or it will disappear. Somewhere in the book someone said, no margin, no mission. Should I keep going?"

McNeely happy to keep her cruising on autopilot. "Please. And explain briefly: what are the risks you found from the cases we read?"

Ms. Suarez went on to detail the examples of nonprofit executives and board members of nonprofit corporations who had directed funds to their own use or had ignored the nonprofit's mission in favor of building their own empires, padding their salaries, or hiring their friends. "I guess we really need board members of these nonprofits to take their duties seriously, but many don't," she added.

"So, without shareholders to bring the derivative lawsuits we studied last week, who is going to protect us from these nonprofit CEOs and directors who are lazy or up to no good?"

"The state attorney general. She's got standing to do all sorts of things, including suing the directors and CEOs for breaches of their duties, like in the hospital case we read."

"Thanks Ms. Suarez. By the way, remember we're talking about nonprofit hospitals and universities here, including our beloved St. Sebastian University. Before we move on to the cases discussing the tax status of these organizations, let me plant an idea for you all to think about. If, as Ms. Suarez says, we must rely on the state attorney general to police these nonprofits, how do we assure that the AG finds out what's going on? Does the law have a way of rewarding those who expose the bad guys?"

"Whistleblowers?" Mr. Abramson answering a question with a question but getting it right.

"You bet, Mr. Abramson. And what impels the whistleblower to come forward? After a few moments of awkward silence, McNeely decided to drop a less than subtle hint, "What makes the world go 'round?"

"Money?" Another question/question dialogue, but McNeely just grateful the student didn't say gravity. "You got it. We reward these whistleblowers with a piece of whatever the government lawsuit recovers. They're called Qui Tam lawsuits, a law that goes back to the Civil War, when corrupt companies were selling defective rifles and diseased donkeys to the Union army. So, where someone has cheated the government, and the whistleblowers can expose it, the whistleblower law slides them a piece of the action."

The video gamers in the crowd seemed to be on board.

Pleased that he had touched all the important bases in class, McNeely composed a question for the final exam in his mind as he walked back to his office. Make sure they get the fundamental point that those in charge of nonprofits can't feed at the trough.

Anthony Aardvark, Chief Financial Officer of ABC University is given an all-expenses paid trip to attend a conference in Geneva by Bob Blueblood, who is CEO of Blueblood Industries and a member of the ABC University Board of Trustees. On his return from the conference Aardvark awards a large no-bid contract to Blueblood Industries that is significantly more costly than prevailing rates in the market. With no prior briefing, the Board of ABCU retroactively approves the Blueblood contract by telephonic meeting. Analyze all possible legal liabilities of Aardvark, ABC University, and the members of the University Board and indicate what facts will be relevant to determining liability.

Entering the corridor leading to the Deanplex, McNeely overheard his assistant Jewel Henderson engaged in a spirited conversation with Astrid, one of the cleaning crew. This was nothing unusual since she had become the trusted confidant of every staff member in the building, but when he heard Jewel utter an array of surprised utterances with a common theme ranging from "no shit?" to "you gotta be shitting me!" to "girl, this is some solid shit!" he surmised that some interesting shit was afoot. If it involved anything scandalous about his colleagues, he'd hear about it pretty quickly. But first, he had a pleasant surprise waiting for him outside his office: his new research assistant.

"Maggie, thank you for coming by. Come on in and grab a chair by the table."

Dropping a banker's box full of notebooks on the table with a groan that gave away that this was the first heavy lifting he had done in several weeks, McNeely dropped into a chair facing his new helper. "It's really great to have you agree to work with me. Jen couldn't have given you a higher recommendation, and I am, as you know, very familiar with your work."

"Yes, Professor. I want to thank you for your decision and just want to let you know that I am so sorry about what happened with my paper and Professor . . ."

Feeling he was not ordained by the Church to hear confession, McNeely interrupted, "Listen, if there's going to be any apologizing, someone should be apologizing to you. This whole episode was a travesty. And now it's over, done, fini. End of

Story. Ever see *Fargo*? Anyway, no need to ever mention it again. Agreed?"

A slight smile and nod, which McNeely sensed reflected her relief that they had entered into a binding contract to move on.

"So, the contents of this box: your first assignment. You'll find three big notebooks with the minutes of the meetings of Board of Directors and of some Board Committees of St. Sebastian University. SSU being a nonprofit, its board members like to call themselves 'Trustees.' Next, three more large notebooks filled with contracts and invoices. Then, another notebook with the names and affiliations of the members of the Board of Trustees. Now what I want you to do is create a few Excel spreadsheets. One listing the dates and amounts of each contract or invoice. Another has the dates and board votes, with names of the Trustees voting for, against, or abstaining from approving each contract or invoice. I want you to analyze patterns in the Trustees' voting and anything else that will clarify who is voting for what." Looking across the table, McNeely saw a face that was not lighting up at her first exposure to the exciting world of nonprofit corporate law.

"Believe me. This is going to be interesting. Eventually. But for now, just dig in and plow through these documents. By the way, I notice you didn't take Business Associations with me. I trust you took the course?

"Oh yes, I had . . ." a pause that McNeely interpreted as Maggie fighting off a temptation to editorialize, "Professor Warren."

McNeely was thoroughly familiar with the strengths and shortcomings of his colleagues from the student evaluations he had to read every semester. Professor Julia Warren, who taught the same introductory Business Associations course as McNeely, received comments ranging from "low energy," and "stupifyingly dull" to "everything I was afraid corporate law would turn out to be." But because she taught her classes by reading out loud from long PowerPoint slides and never challenging students with annoying hypotheticals, she generally received passable ratings in student evaluations, and hence had been permitted to continue to anesthetize students for thirteen years. Truth be told, McNeely took secret delight having the only "rival" faculty member teaching the same course referred to as "The Queen of Power Points" in student reviews. He also realized that Maggie might need a refresher on some of the fine points of corporate law that may have been omitted in his sleep-inducing colleague's PowerPoint slides.

"We'll track down later the legal significance of all the information you assemble. In the meantime, you might brush up on the legal obligations of the board of directors of nonprofit corporations. Also take a look at the RICO statute. You never know where things may wind up when you start an investigation."

"By the way, as I suggested in my email, please consider applying for a judicial clerkship. You've cracked the top five percent of the class, and I didn't tell you, but I sent your abortion legislation paper around, and it's getting good reviews. One person I know wants to push it onto a big-time law journal."

To McNeely's disappointment, her response was somewhat muted. "Oh. Thanks so much. It's such a great thing for you to do. But what I want to do is become a legal aid lawyer. Help people who don't have anyone to turn to. I know it sounds pretty lame, and you've probably heard it a million times, but how do I get there from here?" Maggie leaning forward, looking intently at McNeely.

Jesus. he thought, in a revelatory moment of self-awareness. This is the daughter I never had. And never will. Better cover with deflection or you'll reveal yourself as one sad puppy. "I understand. There's a lot of ways to get there. But a judicial clerkship is like pulling into the parking lot in a Ferrari. Everyone will say "who the hell is that? You'll get to call your shots. Don't miss your shot . . . Did you see *Hamilton*?"

McNeely turned beet red, acutely aware of how lame he sounded. But Maggie's faint smile and nodding acceptance gave the chubby professor a warm glow.

Arriving home to prepare dinner for her father, Maggie heard him muttering and cursing in his bedroom. Rushing upstairs, she found him in a state of high agitation, rifling through his navy chest in which he stored everything: old tax returns, his kids' report cards, photos, his army reserve uniform, and God knows what else.

She had been told to expect moments of lucidity as her dad's dementia progressed, with memories sometimes flooding back and recounted with clarity and emotion. But her dad's gerontologist also cautioned not to think he had turned a corner. "The brain is our most mysterious organ. We're not sure how or why it calls up memories or emotions. And for patients with dementia, the linkages are more opaque than anyone's. We simply don't know how or why they recall things or are suddenly able to speak Spanish which they haven't done in thirty years."

"Dad, what are you looking for?" she asked.

"Something important. Maybe the cleaning lady threw it away. I had a conversation today at the Term, and a guy says to me what's wrong with your Mets? So, I tells him: It's that damn Jewish banker. Whadaya mean? he says. I tell him it's that guy Barney Maddox. He didn't understand, and laughed at me. So, I'm looking for the article from the Star Ledger I put in my trunk here."

"Barney Maddox? Do you mean the pitcher for the Braves? Greg Maddux?" asked Maggie.

Mickey getting agitated, "No, No, No! The Jewish banker. The guy who stole all that money."

Well accustomed to dealing with her father's confusions, Maggie was some-what relieved. "Oh, OK, OK. You mean Bernie Madoff! Right, but dad, he's not got anything to do with the Mets. He was a Wall Street crook, but he wasn't responsible for the Mets problems."

Mickey nodding vigorously, "Oh yes he was!!! He fucked over the Wilburs, the family that owns the Mets. So they couldn't buy a couple of hitters to help out poor old deGrom. And now another rich Wall Street crook is going to buy the team."

Maggie patting her dad's arm and extending a soothing voice, "OK, OK, dad. Lots of people are responsible for the Mets' problems."

Fighting off boredom during an excruciating Wills and Trusts Law class the next day, Maggie Googled "*Bernie Madoff and Mets.*" To her astonishment, a dozen articles appeared detailing how Madoff had become a financial advisor for Mets owner Fred Wilpon and had siphoned off millions from him, essentially forcing the Mets to cut their payroll from $125 million to $80 million and lose any chance of being a contender in the National League for years. And now another Wall Street crook, Steven Cohen, was maneuvering to buy the team.

Dementia, Maggie realized, plays tricks on everyone.

*The reason that university politics are especially vicious is
precisely because the stakes are so small.*

—Henry Kissinger

The law school's March, 2019 faculty meeting was an event that even the Lotus Eaters took seriously. Hiring a new tenure-track faculty member aroused passions, preconceptions, and prejudices that lay dormant for most of the year. For McNeely, the underlying dynamics of faculty appointments were captured in an old episode of "The Twilight Zone" he'd seen on Nick at Nite. The episode opened in an old-time men's club, with two senior members sitting in wing chairs sipping their brandy when a loud, boisterous young member comes by, brags about himself, and insults the elders. Their contempt grows and one of the old guys finally snaps. He offers the young colleague one million dollars if he can go an entire year without uttering a word. In classic *Twilight Zone* framing, the young member is placed in a glass booth in the basement of the club and is continuously monitored. Cut ahead 364 days, and the old member, obviously worried about losing his bet, visits the basement, and tries to bait the young guy into talking by fabricating a story that his wife is cheating on him. The episode concludes with one of Rod Sterling's customary dark messages. Unbeknownst to the older member, the young guy had his vocal cords cut in order to win the bet. And unbeknownst to him, the old guy was a fraud and had no money. An apt metaphor for faculty recruitment. Avoid hiring a bloviating fool whom you might wind up listening to for forty years. And trust no one.

The Appointments Committee had conducted initial interviews with 35 candidates at the AALS "meet market" in Washington D.C. Seven had been invited back to Baytown for interviews and to give a "job talk" to the faculty. The choice had come down to two candidates who were undeterred by the prospect of joining the faculty of the 97th ranked school in the nation. In the intervening weeks since the prospects' on-campus visits, the faculty was abuzz with closed-door meetings, emails, and texts about the choices. Proponents of each candidate kept a running count of committed and uncommitted votes and assigned colleagues who were friendly with the undecideds to have a heart-to-heart about their candidate. If it were possible to put a yard sign in front of their offices, they probably would, McNeely concluded.

The two remaining candidates couldn't have presented a starker—or more polarizing—choice. Thadeus Kerabatsos: Catholic, white, male, Notre Dame B.A., NYU J.D., clerkship with a federal district court judge in Indiana, one year at a Manhattan white shoe law firm. Make that very Catholic. Alexandra Powers: Not Catholic, African American, female, Connecticut College B.A., Temple University J.D., clerkship with a federal district court judge in New Jersey, and five years as a litigator with the Civil Division of the U.S. Department of Justice in Washington.

Although professing neutrality, there wasn't much question where the two deans stood. St. Sebastian had a terrible record when it came to hiring African Americans, with only one tenured professor, three clinical law teachers, and one writing instructor being persons of color. The school had also somehow managed to miss the demographic gender shift among law schools, having not hired a female candidate in five years, and showing an East Coast law school low (7%) of tenured women professors. But Ms. Powers also possessed most of the key indicia of a promising academic career: she had somehow found time and energy to publish three notable articles on labor law and regulation and one on gender discrimination in hiring—all while being lead lawyer or second chair on seven major cases for the Department of Justice. Not that it mattered to most of the faculty, but Powers had also wowed the students who interviewed her, with several indicating that they would take any class she offered. One student-interviewer commented, "Would be nice to have a woman as a mentor, for a change. Not to mention someone who's actually been inside a courtroom."

Dean Eckstein came away from her individual meeting with the candidate thoroughly impressed. "Let's make it clear to the faculty. She's not a minority hire. Not a gender hire. The sharpest candidate I've come across in seven years and undoubtedly the most personable," she gushed to McNeely.

McNeely, hired six years ago, did the math but nodded in complete agreement. "We're going to have to do some heavy lifting. You-know-who will be all over this one."

His grapevine had tipped off McNeely that there was some serious lobbying going on and that the leader of the Kerabatsos Political Action Committee was none other than the Dean's nemesis, Professor Cathcart. The scuttlebutt also suggested that he had stitched together an unholy alliance among the Y&R, the old timer Catholics, and a handful of Lotus Eaters. Most disturbing was information that McNeely's source, Julia Hemmings, an untenured junior faculty member, had provided about the tactics employed. In closed-door sessions with the untenured professors, Cathcart was advising that it was critically important for them to maintain good relationships with all their faculty colleagues because "one never knows" what may influence their votes on the junior members' tenure application years from now. For McNeely, the final straw was what sounded like a mixture of sedition and solicitation of conspiracy. "You know what Cathcart told me?" said the incredulous Hemmings, "Everyone needs someone to captain their cause come the vote on their tenure. And I'm going to be around here for a long time. No telling how long the Dean is going to hold on."

This guy's worse than Trump, thought McNeely. And about as subtle.

The day before the faculty vote on the candidates, McNeely had been visited by Professor Roth-Himmelfarb. ERH was not shy about using the influence that came with her preeminent position among St. Sebastian faculty. Compared to her colleagues, her social media and network news appearances stood out like a tarantula on angel food cake, as Raymond Chandler once put it. The law school's web page ran a monthly "In the News" feature that listed the public appearances and media hits of the faculty, along with a head shot of the faculty member. Scrolling down each month, one saw as many as fifteen entries for ERH, quotes in the *New York Times* and *Wall Street Journal*, and regular appearances on Rachel Madow's show. Sandwiched among ERH's media hits on the law school web site were a smattering of sadly prosaic entries for other faculty: Professor Gleason addressing the Westfield CYO, Professor Jordan in the West Orange Shopper, Professor Anderson cited in a subReddit. When it came to opining on scholarly potential, ERH had her some genuine street cred.

ERH had come to give McNeely some unambiguous marching orders. She and Dean Eckstein had established a close bond over the years, and although ERH rarely involved herself in the prosaic matters of faculty governance, she used her capital whenever the Dean really needed help. McNeely's cynically speculated that the symbiosis between the two went beyond their shared political and social beliefs. The Dean undoubtedly knew that ERH's political network would be of enormous help should she ever get a judicial nomination and ERH knew that helping someone to become a "mentionable" for the Supreme Court wouldn't hurt her career either. Nothing wrong with that, McNeely told himself as a way of excusing a somewhat jaundiced appraisal of his friends' motives.

ERH's message was clear. She would be called on first when the discussion of the candidates began and would announce that she had read all the articles written by both candidates and had found Ms. Powers' work to be among the most promising scholarship by a junior candidate she had seen in 25 years. That, McNeely felt, would put an end to questions about the academic chops of this graduate of humble Temple Law School, as no one would dare to challenge ERH's analysis. She also instructed McNeely to round up the three tenured women on the faculty to make sure they coordinated their remarks. With a sly smile she laughed, "It would be nice if this turned out to be a better version of the Clarence Thomas confirmation hearing. Anyone questioning this woman candidate would be guilty of a sexist lynching."

Nevertheless, the faculty meeting proved to be as rancorous and divisive as the Deans had feared. Despite ERH's strong endorsement, the Y&R/Catholic alliance did not hold back. The Kerabatsos partisans suggested that hiring a candidate outside the Big Five law schools would entrench St. Sebastian in its low/middle spot in the *US News* Rankings. Some expressed doubts that anyone who had practiced law for an extended period—in Powers' case, six years—was probably not serious about becoming an academic and only eager to escape the drudgery and long hours of law practice.

When it came time for final comments, Cathcart rose to deliver a closing statement. His lower lip protruding—a look intended to project an aggressive mien—he scanned his audience and began in a piercing adenoidal voice, "I want to lend my strong support to Mr. Kerabatsos. We've talked about his credentials, his agenda for future writing projects, his plans to become active in prestigious legal blogs, and his continuing correspondence with his well-known professors at NYU. I just want to add a note about how important it is for us if we want to finally begin to see the upward movement we've been promised over the years. We've got to dive into the arenas that the academy takes seriously. Mr. Kerabatsos plans to engage with scholars at the cutting edge of crypto currency law. His scholarship will cut a path through the maze of regulation and securities law that apply to this disruptor of all disruptors. And his work will get some notice across the river from a financial world that, quite frankly, doesn't know we exist."

Sipping his lemon Pellegrino, Cathcart adopted a softer tone. "Now I'm not going to say anything negative about Alex. I'm sure she's a fine practitioner who has worked hard to get where she is today. And I am second to none in advocating that we redouble our efforts to recruit minority candidates who will give St. Sebastian the footprint in the urban community that it needs. But while she seems to satisfy some of those objectives, her academic interests are focused on labor law and her personal background is not one of the urban experience that has given rise to the leaders of the Critical Race Studies movement. So, going forward, I think we should focus on finding a minority candidate who . . ."

"Excuse me Professor Cathcart." Standing up behind his table was Andrew Grayson, St. Sebastian's only tenured African American professor. "I'd like to interpose a thought or two."

Cathcart's face darkened. Thoroughly shocked that Grayson, a quiet, somewhat diffident middle-aged tax professor who rarely engaged in faculty meeting discussions would have the temerity to interrupt, he stammered, "Yes, of course Lamar, I'm just wrapping up and will be done in a . . ."

There was a stunned silence in the room, Cathcart turning beet red. A couple of nervous coughs from members of the faculty and all eyes trained on their visibly shaken colleague. Lamar was the first name of the African American security guard stationed at the front entrance of the law school. He was six inches taller than Professor Grayson and had a full beard.

Voice quivering, Cathcart tried to recover. "Sorry, sorry, Professor Grayson. My point being that when we prioritize, as we must . . ."

Grayson gesturing with a sharp downward palm motion, an unmistakable signal to sit the fuck down. "No, I think we've heard quite enough. Let me respond to the several theses you have advanced. One, Ms. Powers apparently is not quite Black enough for you. True, she comes from an upper middle-class family, grew up in suburban Philadelphia rather than the projects, and plans to teach mainstream courses. Simply put, she does not fit your vision of the contemporary Black law professor. Second, you seem to assume that this might be our one and only minority hire for some time, and that we won't have to be doing much of that in the future, so let's make this one plug all the holes you think we have in our *minority bucket*. Finally, you seem to conflate some shiny academic credentials with the potential to produce scholarship and teach effectively. I'd submit her articles in the Michigan and Columbia Law Reviews and her fluid, insightful job talk should quell your fears. The things we should be taking note of are . . ."

Displaying a slight tremor in his hand holding note cards, Cathcart was now pleading, "Please, please, Andy, you misunderstand my . . ."

"Oh perhaps, perhaps." A studied contrast to Cathcart, Grayson calmly cleaned the lenses of his gold wire-frame glasses as he spoke, "But let me just mention something that speaks to the deeper issue of who we are as a community. In chatting with Ms. Powers, she mentioned that in her one-on-one chats with some of you, the question was raised as to why she chose labor law as a focus of her academic research. She didn't quite put it this way, but I will, since I've had some similar dialogues over the years, given that my chosen area of study is, as you all know, that most mundane of all mundane fields—tax law. For some, apparently it is a source of confusion—indeed one might say disappointment—that an African American professor might toil in these areas. So, it turns out, my good friends, racial profiling isn't just for traffic cops."

McNeely stole a glance at the Dean, who winked at him. The tenor of the discussion changed, and only a few faculty members had anything more to say. He sensed that the many in the faculty's silent majority—the Lotus Eaters, the progressive Catholics, the quiet worker bees—and maybe even a couple of the Y&R would come around. Cathcart's protruding lip now made him look pouty and resigned while the Y&R contingent at his table were intently studying their cell phones.

Because he was charged with administering the voting process, McNeely stood to wrap up the meeting with an explanation of the voting process. And perhaps take the opportunity to right a few wrongs.

"For those of you who haven't had the pleasure of participating in the selection process before, a few words. First, as provided in the faculty manual, the voting will be done by secret ballot and your vote will be entirely anonymous. I will hand each of you a ballot at the end of this meeting. You simply check the name of the person you choose to vote for or select "abstain," and deposit the ballot in this secure ballot box. You may vote now if you choose to do so, or any time before 8 p.m. tomorrow evening. The box will be in the Deanplex under the watchful eye of my administrative assistant, Ms. Henderson. As you know, nothing gets past her."

A few scattered chuckles, which he hoped would relax the audience before executing his plan to drop the hammer. "Finally, let me direct a few words to my colleagues who are not yet tenured and who have not participated before in a faculty hiring. This is an important decision. This decision is probably the most significant responsibility you have. It's a responsibility you owe to St. Sebastian, to your colleagues, and to your students. I know most of you have attended the job talks and I hope you all take the time to read the candidates' files, especially their published works and letters of recommendation. What's equally important is that you cast your vote with an eye to doing what's best for St. Sebastian. I ardently hope that no one has been given reason to believe they need to vote a certain way to curry someone's favor. Or harbors any fear of retribution for voting their conscience. And I fervently hope this school never devolves into a state of warring factions or one in which tenure evaluations are in any way compromised."

Then, casting a steely stare at Cathcart, he went on, "And if anyone has any such concerns, I want to know about it."

McNeely found himself smiling and even chuckling out loud several times during the rest of the day. He never nailed Stevie Cohen, but rousting Cathcart was a pretty satisfying day's work.

At 9 p.m. the following evening, Dean Eckstein, McNeely, and Jewel Henderson gathered to open the ballot box and count the votes. As Henderson read out each name, the three became increasingly giddy. The final tally: Powers 24, Kerabatsos 5, Abstentions 3.

Henderson produced a bottle of champagne and delivered the toast. "Bout damn time!"

41

Priests are not men of the world; it is not intended that they should be;
and a University training is the one best adapted to prevent their becoming so.

—Samuel Butler

Rodney strode purposefully into Father Balducci's office and placed the Intrecciato leather portfolio on the large conference table. Reaching in, he displayed and shook an envelope producing a gentle rattle. "Your medicine."

Digging in again, he produced a box labeled *Nokia C3 Prepaid*. "Your burner. Calls are not traceable. You can toss it off the Ingram Bridge on your way home."

Next came two sets of keys and a file folder. "I've called the Meadowlands Construction Properties agent. You've got the bungalow through Monday noon. Car is gassed up. Wine, pasta, groceries are loaded in the back, and I got your half pound of Soppressata at Carmines. I set the Google map directions to Avalon. Looks like two hours and ten minutes, no traffic on the Parkway. EZ Pass is activated for the tolls. Early Spring this year, great weather all weekend."

"Great. I'm going to just make a light dinner tonight. Did you make the reservation for tomorrow?" Father Balducci asked.

Rodney vigorously nodding confirmation, though not expecting any signs of appreciation, "Yes sir. You have a primo table at Bobby Flay's at the Borgata in AC. 7:30. Using the same name, Frank D'Angelo, OK?"

"Yeah, that's' fine." Father B said somewhat wistfully. Frankie D'Angelo was the name of the bully who picked on him in sixth grade at St. Cecilia's grammar school in Gary, Indiana. "And the cash?"

"It's in the case. I got $3500, mostly hundreds." Rodney betraying a sly smile, "The receipt for the cash in the Discretionary Fund is labeled *Development and Outreach*."

Father B returned an unsmiling nod, pocketed the keys, snapped the portfolio shut and moved to the door. Stopping suddenly just as he reached the door, "Oh, did you pick up the other item at the drug store?"

"Oh, yeah, they're in your case too. Plain brown bag. Same brand as last month."

With that, the well-equipped President walked quickly out of his office and climbed into the Escalade parked in front of Sheehan Hall. He knew that his choice six years earlier of Rodney Leporello, a newly arrived brother at St. Sebastian, as his personal aide de camp was an inspired move. He had loyally performed, with utmost discretion, a variety of personal services that Father B needed to be handled with utmost discretion. Packing his portfolio with Viagra, condoms, and a phone that would leave no trace of his affiliations during his *vacanza* were the kind of tasks that could only be delegated to a trusted—and amply rewarded—subordinate. With Rodney's new administrative authority as Chief of Staff came access to a life-style and rewards that few Jesuit Brothers enjoyed. His willing participation in the President's financial misconduct, not to mention his own sexual indiscretions (well documented in video recordings in Father B's possession) made him an eminently reliable partner.

The Escalade had been the gift to the University from Amex Services, the food and beverage supplier to the University's five restaurants and cafeterias. Father Balducci had not asked for an SUV, let alone a luxury brand, but Alan Chase, Amex's CEO had consulted with Rodney, who had casually mentioned the need for reliable transport for the many pilgrimages to religious events the University arranged for visiting clerics and alumni. Owing to Father B's sensitivity to bright sunlight he also strongly suggested that the SUV should have tinted windows, .

The vehicle was well supplied with CDs of Italian operas, with Verdi and Rossini the particular favorites of the President. Aida was his favorite, but he had learned the hard way that an opera involving the pursuit of an Ethiopian slave was not the best choice for background music when having the Faculty Women's Empower-ment Committee to his house for dinner. Today's musical accompaniment en route to the Jersey shore was a radical departure. Blaring away, with enhanced bass, was the Rolling Stones, a choice inspired by Father's dinner companion this weekend. *Sympathy for the Devil* had been playing when they first locked eyes.

Father Balducci considered himself, first and foremost, a worldly priest. Not one of those local parish lap dogs, sucking up to widows and performing endless weddings and baptisms to keep the local church afloat. He was a mover and shaker. He had earned a Ph.D. in philosophy and tenure at a Jesuit university and eventually became a University President. He dealt regularly with Jersey's top corporate executives and threw his weight around in local politics when necessary. His two years in graduate studies in the 1980s at Casa Santa Mari School, part of the Pontifical North America College of Rome, had opened his eyes to what it meant to be an Italian Jesuit in the modern era. Rome was alive, revolution was in the air, and many in the church were experimenting in the rapidly changing world of modern Catholicism.

To be sure, sexual freedom was not new to the Catholic clerics and contrary to popular beliefs, heterosexuality was not unknown among the clergy. Many popes and cardinals had had mistresses and fathered children over the years. Fluent in Italian, Father Balducci had befriended many Italian priests in his years in Rome, attending their late evening get-togethers and assimilating the culture of the Italian priesthood. Mistresses, liaisons, and opportunistic encounters were commonplace. For some, the vow of celibacy was an aspiration, not a fixed rule and the ethos of the Italian clerics was clear: self-abnegation was not part of the deal. Many of his most seriously committed brothers seemed to lead fulfilling lives without sacrificing food, laughter, and love. Their motto, *Mangia bene, ridi spesso, ama multo*, was firmly imprinted on Father B when he returned to the States.

On arriving at the Jersey Shore he decided to luxuriate on the beach house deck, soaking in the early Spring sun as he surveyed the rolling sand dunes and crashing waves not 50 yards from his perch. The advantages of having ready access to a spectacular secluded getaway on the Jersey Shore courtesy of the Meadowlands Construction Public Interest Trust was not lost on Father Balducci. In the early 1990s, Cardinal McCarrick's beach house in Sea Girt figured prominently in tabloid accounts of his seduction of young seminarians. A private beach house, acquired with church resources, serving as a crash pad for sex: stuff that the National Enquirer would have to invent if it wasn't totally true. The man was such a fool in Father B's view, not so much for his shameful exploits, but for the pure crassness of his methods. Inviting four young men to spend a weekend of prayerful reflection, and then announcing there were only three beds available, so, guess what? The lesson was clear: owning a beach house was out of the question. And the Cardinal's downfall was a reminder that it was prudent to take multiple precautions to protect one's privacy.

Although still early in the day, he thought a start on one of the half dozen Brunellos Rodney had stocked for him would quell his anxiety about the evening ahead. Checking his watch, he ran through calculations about when to start making his red sauce and when to drop his first blue pill. Dinner at seven, some music and chit chat, and then onward and upward. Better check Google to estimate the absorption time for Viagra after prosciutto salad, linguini, and a bottle of the Ciacci Piccolomini d'Aragona.

Pouring a tall glass, he found himself quietly humming, *Please allow me to introduce myself, I'm a man of wealth and taste.*

They had met six months ago the old-fashioned way. At a strip club. Father B had had a rocky night at the blackjack tables at Caesars and chose to take a walk to clear his head. He decided to stop into A Touch of Venus, just a few blocks from the Boardwalk, a location he had saved on his cellphone after performing extensive internet research. On stage gyrating to "Sympathy for the Devil" when he entered, she returned his stare with a big smile. For Father B, this was something totally different. The women he encountered at the bordello he frequented during his summers in Rome were raven-haired, olive-skinned, voluptuous, and more than a little slutty. She was slim, blond, athletic, and basically, a Philly girl. And no pubic hair. When had that happened he wondered. Her "o's" were fully rounded, the beachscape was "beau-tee-ful" and she talked more about football and hockey than things erotic. She had given Father B a lap dance, and to his surprise, hung around to chat. She talked about the weather, the Flyers, and made jokes about the contingent of "childish college boys" making noise at a nearby booth. Within a couple of hours she had one smitten Jesuit under her butt.

Unsure how to approach making The Ask, Father B, a.k.a. Frank D'Angelo, decided to play it old school. He proposed dinner the following night, and let it be known that he didn't usually visit strip clubs, let alone hit on the dancers. Her answer floored him. "Sure, would be delighted. But just to be clear, Frank, if you want to enter into a business arrangement, I'm open. I've got a mother with diabetes I'm supporting and college tuition to pay, so let me know if you're up for more than dinner." Reading nervous middle-aged guys wearing expensive clothes was her specialty. She knew he'd be good for $800 and would be done in half an hour. She told him her real name was Elle, not Misty. Frank did not share his real name but did confide that he was a real estate investor in Hoboken.

The rest is history. He saw her every three or four weeks at the Meadowlands Construction retreat for six months. In Father B's mind, Elle was not a hooker. Far from it. She was his *mistress.* For God sakes, he ruminated, Pope Alexander VI had mistresses, fathered children, and what is his legacy? Bringing in Michelangelo and Raphael to beautify the Vatican. As would any good *patrono,* Father B felt he was just helping his great and good friend with some of her living expenses. Presents really, not payments. He tucked the envelope with $2500 between two bottles of the Ciacci in the cute wicker basket Rodney had thoughtfully procured. He would help her discover the black cherry and licorice notes tonight.

If you want to know who controls you,
look at who you are not allowed to criticize.

—Voltaire

Stopping at Glazed and Confused on his walk from the PATH train to school, McNeely decided to splurge for two dozen. Picking an assortment of donuts that would please the diverse palates of his constituency in the St. Sebastian administrative offices involved some delicate calculations. Someone was bound to require gluten free, there would be a fight over the jellies if there weren't enough, pink glazes were in surprisingly high demand, and so on. It is indeed lonely at the top, he mused. But the faculty vote the evening before was clearly cause for celebration, and he promised himself that he would offset the sugar calories by two timing the stairs in his climb to the sixth floor once again.

He was greeted on arrival by a whispered warning from Henderson. "She's pissed at something. Threw a book, cursing, and looking for you. You wearing your protective gear?" she said pointing to his crotch.

It didn't sound like donuts were going to help, so he left them on Henderson's desk and knocked softly on the Dean's door. McNeely interpreted her annoyed "What??" as an invitation to come in. One look at her told the story. "What did he do now?" he asked. It had to be Father B.

"Sit down, you're not going to believe it. He's outdone himself, the pompous shit. I get in at 8:30, and there's a voice mail that came in at 7:10 a.m. He says *'Where are you? Call me immediately.'* So I do. And I get this outpouring of venom, sounding like he wants to go full intifada on me. *'What do you think you're doing? You're fucking with the University's endowment here. Do you arrogant lawyers think you can make decisions that contradict mine?'* Tommy, I didn't know which of his holy orders I'd violated but he was clearly on a warpath."

McNeely thought it not the best time to explain to his Jewish Dean that the sacrament of Holy Orders was the rite by which someone becomes a priest, not some kind of papal edict as she apparently thought.

"It finally became clear that he's pissed that we didn't get down and kiss the collective asses of those Sanus stiffs. They must have gone whining to him that we didn't seem sufficiently grateful or willing to grovel for their money."

Seeing McNeely about to lend support, she waved him off. "Wait, it gets worse. Seems like our President has just signed some new Memorandum of Understanding that Sanus handed him. In fact, the stupid shit called it a *contract*. I didn't have time to explain to him what a contract is, but *he thinks* it's a done deal. I asked—*politely*, believe me I know better than to get into it with him—I say, 'Father, what are the terms of this contract'? I told him we had met with Sanus just a week ago and had begun to work out the details of our arrangement. But he says 'I don't want to wait for you lawyers to get your heads out of your collective butts.'"

"To which I respond, 'Maybe the general counsel should look at the document you signed. And we at the law school may be able to offer a few suggestions.'"

McNeely trying to lighten the tone a bit. "Let me guess. The GC's office has already sprinkled holy water on it. And Father B refused your offer of help?"

"Exactamundo!!! Oh, and by the way, after a few more probing—but *very polite*—questions from me, it became apparent that the Good Father has no clue as to what he signed. May have sold us like chattel property. We may now be a corporate subsidiary of Sanus. I knew that fuckface Trey was a slimeball!"

Worried that the Dean's version of asking polite questions might have struck Father B as more like a gestapo shakedown, McNeely tried to find a ray of sunlight, "Well, I hope you parted on good terms?"

"It came down to him reminding me who I worked for and how easy it would be to replace me. And also reminding me that the law school's on shaky financial grounds and how at some point he would have to cut salaries, raise tuition, disapprove new faculty hires, stop cleaning the rest rooms, etc, etc."

McNeely fearing the worst, "And you politely reminded him . . . ?"

"Don't sweat it, Tommy. I told him we'd work it out. You would be in charge of straightening out any misunderstandings, and . . ."

McNeely gulped, feeling a BP spike in his temple, but trying to play it cool. "OK, OK I got it covered. Just need to make a phone call." Jumping out of his chair, he sprinted to his office, pausing only momentarily to grab the last jelly donut.

"Godspeed." Eckstein said as the door slammed shut. God, he seems cool, calm, and collected, she thought. Wish I could stay on an even keel. This is one of those moral turning points. Do I go along and preserve the financial viability of the law school for the sake of the students and faculty? Or preserve my dignity and self-esteem and quit? Guess for now, I'll ride it out and hope Tommy can use his training as a federal hit man to take out our nemesis. Or at least castrate him.

McNeely dialed Jenks six times, leaving three messages with ascending degrees of desperation. The last one ended with a plaintive cry, "I'm dying here, Jinx."

His self-pity party was interrupted by a knock on the door and Henderson's head bobbing around the side of the door. "There's some nun here to see you."

McNeely smiled. *Some nun*, like it's a Jehovah's Witness selling prayer cards. Jewel didn't bother getting a name. Probably felt the word "nun" was warning enough.

"Hello Dean McNeely, I'm Sister Amelia Francisco. Provost Griffin suggested I talk to you. Do you have a minute?"

It dawned on him that this was THE Sister Francisco, the first woman Dean of a School of Public Health in the nation, founding Dean of St. Sebastian's School of Nursing, recipient of every honor the St. Sebastian has to convey. Even has a fucking building named after her.

"Please have a seat. It's really a pleasure to meet you." McNeely thinking of pulling the chair out for the sister but realized that would make his unease even more obvious, thirty years of anxiety in the presence of nuns flooding back.

"Provost Griffin suggested you could help me. As you may know, I'm on the Board of Trustees of the University . . . have been for fifteen years in fact . . . and despite my many years as a member, I'm still pretty uninformed about the complexities of nonprofit corporate governance. My doctorate is in genetics, so I'm a novice when it comes to the mysteries of the law. The Provost said you were the expert here on campus and I could ask you a few questions. And please forgive me if I am not grasping some pretty rudimentary legal concepts. "

Oh sure, thought McNeely. This woman has cut her way through the jungles of academia, the Catholic Church, and hard science, so she's not been able pick up the law of charitable corporations? Not exactly a convenient time, but Griff sent her his way, so something must be up besides her needing a primer on the law.

"As you know, St. Sebastian has a large board of trustees. In fact, there are 48 members, 50 if you include Father Balducci and his General Counsel. As a result, the meetings are pretty pro forma. *Staged*, actually would more accurately describe it. He has committees that deal with the major issues. Theoretically, at least. And an Executive Committee that makes the final recommendations to the full board. And the full board is . . . well, I'm going to be frank here."

Resisting the temptation to offer an analogy to the secrecy of the confessional, McNeely said, "Please, speak freely. I will keep this conversation confidential,"

"Well the truth is, the Board of Trustees is a rubber stamp. No debates. Hasn't been a dissenting vote or even a word of criticism in my fifteen years. Father Balducci sets the agenda. If the magic word for you lawyers is that the board is responsible for "oversight," that's exactly the right *word*. But with the opposite *meaning*. Total oversight of what's really going on. Forty-eight souls having a nice lunch with Father Balducci four times a year."

McNeely was eager to find out what exactly was bothering her and what she wanted to do, but Sister Francisco was not tipping her hand. Her questions all pertained to procedural issues, the rights of individual board members, processes required to make formal board resolutions, and their ability to bind the President to follow the board's instructions. McNeely noted one slip of the tongue, however. Sister Francisco had said at one point, "we have several issues." We? Plural. All not copacetic in the board room, he wondered. Insurrection looming? Given the good sister's guarded approach to their meeting, he decided not to press and instead await further discussions. He explained that he needed to examine the board's bylaws to give her more complete answers and promised to be in touch soon. At which time, he hoped to hear some juicy tales that might foreshadow a palace coup.

Getting ready for his 2 p.m. class, McNeely was annoyed to hear a knock on his door. Jewel must be out working the crowd, he groused to himself, but brightened immediately on seeing that his visitor was someone who invariably brightened his day.

"Maggie, good to see you. Grab a seat. What's up? Slipping into a coma plowing through all those meeting minutes and invoices?"

"No, it's pretty interesting actually. Even though I don't know what you're looking for."

Ah, the complaint of every junior associate in law firms, he thought. High pressure, short deadlines, assignments chasing down rat holes with no indication why. Just do the partner's bidding. "Well, we're going to have a meeting once you assemble all the data, and I can decide whether we've got something. It's sort of a sensitive topic, so I'm being cautious."

"Oh, I understand Professor. Just wanted to run a question by you. What's a discretionary fund? Here's why I'm asking. As I was entering the information you requested on my spread sheets, I noticed that some of the invoices were designated as "PDF." At first, I thought there was some PDF document that hadn't been reproduced in hard copy. But then, and I'm sorry to be so curious, so I won't bill the law school for the time I spent doing this, but I decided to search through all the duplicate copies of documents that we were given. I promise I won't charge the school for the time I spend on this . . ."

"Maggie, if you ever go into private law practice there's an iron rule that all associates must follow. It's called the BFEM Rule. *Bill For Every Minute.* Sometimes there's an extra F in it.'"

"OK, thanks. Another reason to be a public defender. In any event, I'm flipping through these documents, and I see someone has written some words that are hard to read, but finally I realize it says "Pres Disc Fnd." That's what PDF stands for. I realize there's some accounting mumbo jumbo going on here and Professor Warren really didn't teach us much about corporate finance, so I was wondering if this was something I should be paying attention to. I assume PDF means President's Discretionary Fund. There's a lot of these PDFs in the pile."

McNeely musing on whether he could adopt Maggie. "Wow. That could be important. Could you create a separate designation for each document to show whether it's PDF or not? I hope that doesn't mean you have to dive back into the piles of documents you've already been through?"

Maggie gave a rueful smile which indicated that it sure did, but immediately said, "No prob. I'm on the clock and this is more interesting than serving boilermakers to the late afternoon crowd at my dad's bar."

"Great. We'll meet next week and try to figure out our game plan for all this data. By the way, where's your dad's bar?"

43

In itself, the practice of deception is not particularly exacting;
it is a matter of experience, of professional expertise,
it is a facility most of us can acquire.

—John Le Carre, *The Spy Who Came in From the Cold*

The text from Jinx came late in the day. To McNeely it sounded like he thought he was being tracked by Russian spies.

Let's grab a drink and talk over old times and new friends. Best to keep a low profile. I'll call at 5:10. Pick a rustic spot. AJ.

Much as he wanted to believe the deep cover had something to do with Sanus, McNeely assumed Jinx was just being cute. But as a precaution, he chose a place he wanted to scout out anyway.

Walking into the Terminal Bar in Rahway, McNeely felt it was exactly the kind of place where his grandfather probably hung out. Old photos of New York Mets and Joe Namath, vintage beer signs of now-defunct brews like Ballantine and Rheingold, and a mixed crowd of old-timers, hipsters, and commuters. He was greeted by an older gent behind the bar who looked a lot like Maggie.

"Hi, I'm gonna have a Jameson, neat. But first let me introduce myself, I'm Tommy McNeely. Are you Mr. Holloran?"

"Mr. Holloran's my dad. Passed thirty years ago. I'm Micky," Extending his hand for the traditional bartender handshake. "You're not from a collection agency I hope" he said chuckling.

"Not at all. I am in fact your daughter's employer and a professor at St. Sebastian. And I'm here to give you a report card."

"Uh oh. Is she playing well with others? Cutting phys ed?"

McNeely realized he had a professional bartender on his hands. "Nope. Just wanted to pass along the news that she's one of the smartest, most personable students I've had, and you should be a proud dad."

He could see a slight watering of the old man's eyes, heard a muffled cough, and realized he'd struck home. The sentimental Irish, we cry at commercials, he thought.

"Well, her mom raised her right. We're mighty proud. She's not here tonight, she's working her butt off at your factory."

The two talked for a while, McNeely noticing a little hesitation in the senior Holloran's speech, which he attributed to the workplace hazards of being surrounded by alcohol and drunkards for years. When Jenks arrived, McNeely settled up and threw another handshake across the bar. He decided to take another shot at making the old guy cry, "Maggie's going places, I promise you."

McNeely directed Jenks to a booth in the back of the bar. Sliding into the seat across from him, the anxious Associate Dean wasted no time. "What the fuck, Jinx? How the hell did you wind up at Sanus?"

Jenks gave a sly smile. "They needed security. My business is selling security. And my résumé is pretty impressive. I'll email you a copy. I was a pretty good fit. Just consulting, but I've gotten to know my colleagues pretty well."

Jenks went on to describe the Sanus officers' and board members' affinity for high-end steak houses, toney gyms, and strip clubs. He also explained that the high degree of male bonding occurring at these locales provided him the opportunity to suss out the mission of Sanus and its strategic plans. The bottom line, he suggested, was that Sanus needed a fig leaf in academia to promote the interests of the pharmaceutical industry.

"You know what? They call their strategy *Think Tank 2.0*. They know the success the Heritages and Manhattan Institutes have had, but so far, it's all been directed at advancing old-timey right-wing causes. Deregulation, free markets, conservative judges, stuff you know better than me, Tommy. Their new wrinkle is to create a think tank that can focus like a laser on their product: Drugs. They want to have a platform to advance the cause of pharmaceutical sales, without interference from the government, doctors, patients, or anybody else."

"What exactly do they want from St. Sebastian? We're a pretty low-profile target, to tell you the truth." McNeely confessed.

"They talk a lot about this law school in Virginia, George something?"

"George Mason?"

"Yeah, that's the one. They say a law school can become some kind of breeding ground—that's their words I think—a kind of breeding ground for future lawyers and judges, and especially for placing people at the FDA, HHS and CDC. And, with all due respect to your fine profession Tommy, they think they can buy law professors on the cheap."

"Sad, but true," McNeely confessed.

"Well, you may not find this funny, but I did, to be honest. One night we're all at Scores, the strip club over on 28th Street, and they start looking around and guessing the profession of the guys getting lap dances. Doctors, lawyers, accountants, etc. Then they start in and talk about how much it costs to buy a doctor."

"What do you mean?"

"They were quoting the cost of getting doctors to prescribe their medicines, or to give talks at conferences. Pretty pricey, $50K, $100K and more. But man, it pays off. Not only on what that doctor prescribes, but each doc they buy becomes what they call an 'influencer.' Like those kids on the internet, but a lot more costly."

McNeely nodding in agreement, "Yeah, there's a lot of legal cases. Our alma maters, DOJ and FBI, have gone after those guys. Kickbacks, false claims, some criminal cases. A few docs getting some serious jail time."

A brief snort from Jinx, "Lotta good it's done. Like with everything else, your Justice Department has been asleep at the wheel for the last few years. Anyway, what I thought was funny—and you probably won't—was the way they analyzed how Sanus could go after law professors, compared to what they have to pay their doctors. They laugh and say they can buy you guys for nothing. Some unflattering comparisons of you guys to the hard-working young ladies grinding on laps at Scores."

McNeely feeling pressed to get back to begging for a lifeline, "So, Doctor Jinx, can you help me find a way to cut off their balls?"

"The tricky part of surgery is getting a good MRI of the targeted organ. I need to find out where the money comes from, who's buttering their bread. Not easy, as you know. Your wonderful legal system protects the privacy of investors in this kind of think tank." Jinx raised his glass in a toast, "Dark Money! You guys invented it."

"Yeah, I know. But it sure would be helpful to get a peek at the family jewels."

"Pretty clever. No wonder your students manage to stay awake in those god-awful classes you teach. Well, I do have access to some high-tech devices, and my new buddies at Sanus get talkative around 3 a.m., so I'll see what I can come up with."

McNeely displaying a wide smile of gratitude, "Thanks, you're a credit to the FBI alumni *cloob*."

"Speaking of that, I've heard some rumblings from the club. Don't count on Mueller saving our bacon. Word is he's over the hill, constipated with a serious blockage of legal niceties up his butt that are keeping his team from going anywhere. They won't subpoena the President, for God's sake. Or his deadbeat kids. Just a couple weeks ago that Cohen clown laid out a half dozen indictable offenses Trump committed. And Mueller totally screwed up on Russia. There's not a doubt in the mind of anyone in the agency that Trump was working hand in hand with Putin on the leaks. So, now the fat douchebag is dumping on the Bureau, calling it corrupt, while it's really the lawyers— both Team Mueller and your buddies at Team Barr—that fucked the pooch, as you guys from New Jersey like to say."

McNeely raised his glass in a return toast, "Wow. Colorful speech, Dr. J! May have you in as a guest lecturer in my class. OK, so please get me something if you can." McNeely couldn't dispute Jinx's analysis. The lawyers enabling the deranged conduct regularly emanating from the White House deserved to be held to account. He chose not to remind himself about the array of legal doctrines shielding his profession from being named as co-conspirators. All created by his profession.

On the long, pricey Uber ride back to the West Village, McNeely reviewed the evening's lessons and made a firm resolution to scrupulously avoid any pooch-fucking on the Sanus affair.

44

*One rare and exceptional deed is worth far more than
a thousand commonplace ones.*

—Saint Ignatius Loyola

Building empty, 8 p.m., McNeely happy to be alone with his thoughts. No such luck. "Knock, knock. Am I disturbing?" Father Fitzgibbon peeking around the door jam.

Mustering as much sincerity as he could on an empty stomach, McNeely invited the priest in, "No certainly not. Come in and take a load off, Father."

Father Fitzgibbon jogged around the door and waived a brown paper bag. "Tommy, you were kind enough to share a taste of Green Spot with me a while ago, and I wanted to return the favor." Looking a bit like the winos on the southeast corner of the law school, he reached into his brown paper bag and produced a bottle with a label portraying a sketch of a monk with his arms fully outstretched horizontally and holding a bird in the palm of one hand.

Father Fitz held the bottle up for McNeely's inspection. "So, this is Glendalough Whiskey, a fine smooth Irish, double casked in bourbon barrels. The guy with his arms ourstretched on the label with a bird in his hand is Saint Kevin of Glendalough, born in 498 and a certified saint of the Catholic Church. But the more important point is the story of Kevin's sainthood. He was living in a small hut in the wilderness when, on the first day of Lent a blackbird landed in his palm and proceeded to construct a nest. Kevin remained perfectly still, so as not to disturb the bird for the whole of Lent and was fed by the blackbird with berries and nuts. By the end of Lent, the last blackbird hatchlings had flown from the nest, which now lay empty in his hand, and Kevin returned to his monastery. It took three miracles to get sainthood back in the day. Now you can get one with a couple of card tricks. Can you get us a couple of glasses?"

McNeely realized he was in for a long evening but obliged. It did look like a good bottle.

Drinks poured, *sláintes* exchanged, Father Fitz opened the conversation, "Well, I understand Ms. Holloran is working for you. So glad things have worked out for her."

"It's all your doing, Father. She is a superstar, and a wonderful person. I'm trying to help her land a judicial clerkship."

"Bless you, Tommy. I think there's payback for these kinds of things, not to get too priestly on you. So, listen. I have a few things on my mind if you've got a couple of minutes."

McNeely putting the over/under at an hour and a half, "Oh sure, just working through some student papers, my book manuscript, and a few administrative crises. What's up?"

"If you'll forgive a brief detour, let me say something about the Jesuit Order. When a Jesuit novice is about to be inducted into the higher levels of the Order, he kneels on a cross before the Superior of the Order. Before him are two flags, the familiar yellow and white flag of the papacy, and the black flag with a dagger and red cross above skull and crossbones, the flag of the Jesuit Order. On the Jesuit flag is written the words, IUSTUM, NECAR, REGES, IMPIOS. Now I'll come back to those words in a few minutes. The Superior of the Order hands the novice a small black crucifix which he presses to his heart, and the Superior then presents a dagger to the novice. The novice grasps the bare blade and presses the point to his heart."

McNeely feigning interest and trying not to shift in his chair, but aware that the good Father was just warming up in the bullpen. Fitzgibbon had saved his bacon in the Maggie Holloran matter, so he felt he owed him a respectful audience.

"Now I'm sure you learned back in grammar school, what the letters INRI stands for . . . , it's on crosses and crucifixes, needlework and religious art, even on a tattoo here and there, but don't get me started on that. It represents the Latin words "Iesus Nazarenus Rex Iudeum" or "Jesus of Nazareth, King of the Jews," the Latin words that Pontius Pilate had written on a placard and nailed above Jesus' head at the crucifixion."

Nodding vigorously to indicate that he had taken the introductory course twenty-eight years earlier with Sister Magdalene at St. Casmir's in Newark, McNeely searched for a polite way to move things along. "Oh, for sure, Father. One doesn't forget that."

A regretful shake of the Jesuit head. "Yes. That's what you were taught and what every good Catholic boy knows, or thinks he knows. But you may be interested to know, and here I'm giving you a DaVinci Code secret."

Father Fitz paused, stared into McNeely's eyes for 10 seconds and then broke into a loud guffaw, "Just kidding. The DaVinci Code was pure Hollywood bullshit. But we Jesuits have understood the true historical Jesus for 500 years."

"First of all, you probably were taught that "INRI, Jesus King of the Jews was meant to be scornful or ironic, which assumes irony existed during the Bronze era. Well, no. What the inscription was talking about here is the *lestai*, the closest translation of which we have is "bandit," but that doesn't capture it. The *lestai* were roving bands of Jews who were intent on resisting Roman rule. For sure, they were thieves, but the real threat they posed was rebellion against Rome's taxation and oppression."

Father Fitz paused to sip his Irish, "Sorry to be so pedantic."

"No, no, Frank. I'm all ears. My knowledge of theological debates is embarrassingly shallow."

"Well, you're not alone on that score. What they surely ignored in your CYO classes was that Jesus was *not* the gentle, peace-loving soul the nuns swoon over. Nope. Not close. He was a rabble-rouser, a rebel, a revolutionary. The *only crime* that the Romans were crucifying people for in those days was . . . *sedition!* And every criminal they crucified had a *titulus*—a plaque placed on his cross. But INRI was indicating he was guilty of . . . *sedition!* For Jesus, as was true of almost all the souls who were crucified, it meant he was a *political enemy* to Rome. Jesus was a threat, the emperor believed, because he was striving for *kingly power*. He was talking about imposing a Kingdom of God. He was killed for being *a rebel!*"

Feigning interest, McNeely rocked back in his chair. "Wow. Hard to believe I've achieved the ripe old age of 37 and don't know any of this stuff. So where are you Jebbies on all of this?"

"Good question. We Jesuits are not without our clever disguises. We've come up with and use a far different set of words using that infamous *titulus*. For us, INRI stands for IUSTUM, NECAR, REGES, IMPIOS."

McNeely, pointing to his forehead, "Sorry, my four years of high school Latin are not retrievable. My hard disc is full . . . I'm good with *Arma virumque cano . . .* but that's about it."

"For us Jesuits, our adopted motto, IUSTUM, NECAR, REGES, IMPIOS means *It is just to exterminate or annihilate impious or heretical kings, governments, or rulers.* It's right there on the Jesuit flag. We are pledged to be rebels, spies, and insurgents, all in service of a higher order." Reaching into the pocket of his cassock, Father Fitz produced a wrinkled document, "You think I'm making this up? Here's the text that Jesuits used to swear allegiance to:

You have been taught your duty as a spy, to gather all statistics, facts and information in your power from every source; to ingratiate yourself into the confidence of the family circle of Protestants and heretics of every class and character, as well as that of the merchant, the banker, the lawyer, among the schools and universities, in parliaments and legislatures, and in the judiciaries councils of state, and to "be all things to all men," for the Pope's sake, whose servants we are unto death."

Father Fitz gave a triumphant tap on the table. "So, there you are. When necessary, we are spies, moles, *the Jesuit underground!*" He flashed a broad smile, with twinkling eyes that McNeely couldn't distinguish as playful or serious. "There are lots of what we call *mysteries*—things that go unexplained—in our religion." Pausing for a beat, then saying, "Mysteries, like what does the "H" in "Jesus H. Christ" stand for," which he followed with a loud sputtering roar of laughter at his own joke.

He wasn't done yet. "But you know Tommy, there's an old joke we Jesuits tell on ourselves. Representatives of three Catholic orders, Jesuit, Franciscan, and Holy Ghost, gather together to discuss the relative merits of their orders. The Jesuit says, 'We are Princes of the Church, the intellectual leaders of the faith." The Holy Ghost priest says "That's fine, but we bring the light of faith and word of God to the most remote corners of the world. We are the missionaries who spread the faith.' They turn to the poor Franciscan, dressed in a simple brown robe with bare footed sandals, and ask, "Your order, Father, what's it famous for?" And he responds, "Well, actually, we're tops in humility.'"

The old guy is just playing around, McNeely concluded. Closing his laptop, standing, pretending to stretch and looking to escape, "Well a thousand thanks Father, so very interesting. A lot to think about. In fact, I may pick up some historical texts if you have any." Looking at his watch, "Oh my goodness! 8:45. I need to catch the train and grab some dinner . . ."

"Hold on just a moment. I'm so very sorry Tommy, didn't mean to tie you up. But I had a reason for all that ancient history. I've come across some information about Father Balducci's plans for the University that I think deserve your attention. It's a bit delicate how I uncovered this intelligence . . . Look at me! Intelligence! Talking like a spy! Sometimes this kind of thing reminds me of the way Nixon and Kissinger acted during the Vietnam War. The kind of deception that . . ."

McNeely now moving toward the door, "I'm so sorry Father, but I need to run. I have an early morning meeting tomorrow and need to do some extensive prep work tonight. I'm circulating a petition to all former Assistant US Attorneys about signing a letter condemning Trump and Barr. May have to pull an all-nighter." Picking up his briefcase, McNeely felt bad about disrespecting the kindly old guy, but for once, was not going to let his good nature trap him into listening to an hour of rants about Vietnam. "How about we grab lunch on . . . uh . . . later this week?"

Father Fitzgibbon followed McNeely to the door, "Yes indeed. Please reserve an hour for me. Some interesting tidbits to relate. Not unlike Caesar moving to conquer Gaul, our President wants to plant his flag and expand his territory right up to the Rhine. *Omnia Gallia in tres partes divisa est.* Ruthless autocrats are all of the same stripe!"

Looking out at the desolate Jersey Meadows landscape as he rode the Jersey Central back to get a late dinner uptown, McNeely suddenly realized that he had misunderstood Father Fitz's parting history lesson. The president he was talking about was not Nixon or Trump, but Balducci! And his tidbits had something to do with his ruthless conquest of some territory. It will probably take a couple hours with him to unpack his metaphor, he thought to himself, but it was worth putting lunch with Father B on the calendar.

45

I have made the tough decisions, always with an eye toward the bottom line. Perhaps it's time America was run like a business.

—Donald Trump

He woke up tired and crapulous—the byproduct of a late night at the Vanguard drinking and talking with a bass player long after closing. The old timer had sat in with Grover Washington twenty years ago and was a font of anecdotes and gossip about the legends of jazz. Lots of stories about traveling the country, making his way without a care while watching music legends self-destruct on H and booze. All of which left McNeely regretting that he'd have no stories of a misspent youth to pass along when he was 70. He promised himself to keep an eye out for a cause that in his declining years could support a good night of storytelling to some youngsters at the Vanguard.

As seemed to happen every morning, the NPR news waking him up served to activate his bile ducts. Looking at the glowering, self-pitying face staring back at him in the bathroom mirror, he mulled over each news item. Trump had overruled the White House Counsel and ordered his chief of staff to give that pompous twerp Kushner his security clearance. Homeland Security was still separating families at the border despite pledges to stop. Nina Totenberg provided a sobering recital of the lowlights of Trump's first two years in office: a recap of Michael Cohen's testimony, rumors about Trump's prior knowledge of the Russian hacks and email leaks, his payments to porn stars, numerous acts in furtherance of a conspiracy to violate campaign finance law, and details of bank fraud in securing loans and misrepresenting the value of property for tax assessments. All having no discernable effect on his approval ratings or support from his Gentlemen's Club in the US Senate, McNeely grumbled to himself. William Barr, a guy who had sent the President an unsolicited memo last summer that was really a job application questioning the basis for the Mueller investigation, was now the Attorney General of the United States.

Rule of Law? McNeely was beginning to think it's a wet dream that law professors refuse to awake from.

Scowling again at the reflection of his Jackie Gleason jowls in the harsh morning light, he sensed he was in for more intestinal discomfort. Against his better judgment, he took a peek at his cellphone and saw to his dismay that Dean Eckstein had sent him a text. A bad sign, as she only texted when signals were blinking Code Red.

Tommy. I've spent a sleepless night thinking this thing through. Father B has given us a Hobson's choice. If we challenge him, he'll screw over the law school. You saw the email, he'll demand salary cuts, block us from hiring Ms. Powers, mess with us on our building maintenance needs. You name it. But if I resign, he will appoint some clown he hangs out with at his country club who will do whatever he wants. Now I didn't tell you yesterday that Father B's twisted the knife in my back at the end of our meeting. He told me that in order to demonstrate my fealty to his project, he wants ME to present the Sanus proposal to the Board of Trustees at their next meeting. Apparently, he expects me to make it clear that we are totally down with this project and downright excited about the deal. Said he expects me to carefully explain to the Board how his project will "resurrect" the law school. His word, honest to God. I'll be honest with you. I gave some serious thought to resigning, but it's clear to me that would leave the law school in a worse position. So, to borrow one of your favorite expressions, I will eat shit and smile. We'll find a way to get this under control. Let's chat tomorrow.

Deb.

This was Friday. The day he had no classes. No meetings either. A day he didn't have to schlepp under the river to Baytown. He'd call the Dean later, take her temperature, and try to devise a strategy for dealing with Sanus. Maybe the appointment uptown would give him an angle.

He opened his closet and considered his options. The array of vintage sport jackets was the first fork in the road. He chose a six-year-old herringbone tweed he'd picked up at Goodwill. The strategy was to go full academic. Faded jeans were next, paired with a black sweater. Hiking boots to deal with the slush and complete the image. He had some second thoughts about his initial decision not to shave, fearing overkill on the academic message, but finally decided to go with the full West Village Professor theme. Will be entertaining to see how it resonates in a sea of pin-striped suits, he thought, and it would give him a read on what cards Sanus is holding.

The invitation for brunch was a surprise. Frederick Douglas had said it didn't so much involve his Sanus Institute proposal but rather he wanted to explore some other issues that pertained only to McNeely. Implying *just us guys*, no need to bring along Dean Eckstein. Breakfast at the Empire Hotel rooftop restaurant at Lincoln Center was a big step up from McNeely's customary donut and OJ at Glazed and Confused. And of course, it was on Sanus' dime.

They met in the hotel lobby, and as anticipated, McNeely looked like a visitor from another planet among the bustling crowd of well-appointed uptowners and international hotel guests. Douglas' up and down inspection which lingered on his hiking boots left McNeely gratified that his academic wardrobe message had been received.

"Any problems wading through the slush?" Douglas said, still focusing on the boots.

"Not at all. The Number 2 train is almost door to door from my home in the Village," McNeely adding to the legend of a guy willing to brave the New York subway system and in nasty weather to boot.

Douglas had reserved the primo window table overlooking Columbus Square with a spectacular view of Central Park. They exchanged small talk about the weather, global warming, and the hopeless plight of the Knicks. Douglas mentioned his reluctance to sell the courtside season tickets he's had for fifteen years and invited McNeely to pick any game he was interested in seeing.

McNeely knew he had to make a good will overture regarding their upcoming negotiations about the Institute. "As you probably have surmised, we will need to maneuver through a hornet's nest of academic bureaucracy and faculty politics to get things going. But we are certainly excited about the venture. Health care law and policy is at the top of the agenda for academics these days, just as it is for government and business. The timing of all this couldn't be more fortuitous."

True to his eat shit and smile mantra, McNeely knew he was having a heaping side dish to go with his eggs benedict.

Douglas offered the avuncular smile of a man who could make life easier for his young companion, "Oh, I am completely confident that we'll have a wonderful partnership. But let me get to the reason I wanted to talk to you today. Do you have discretionary time that you can devote to outside endeavors? I know you are carrying a lot of weight with your teaching and administrative duties, but I was wondering if you are open to doing some outside consulting work?"

McNeely silently kicking himself. Should have seen this coming. Smooth as silk. Probably as easy for Douglas as palming a twenty to the maître d' to get this table. Thoughts of the costs of Jackie's care needs in Santa Cruz and his own squalid living conditions flashed by but were instantly relegated to an unused storage folder in his mental hard disc. Deploy some poker strategy, he thought. Best to play him along, let him think he's controlling the betting, just call his raise for now. Get him after the flop.

Offering up a sly, conspiratorial smile, McNeely said "I am pretty overloaded right now, but my philosophy has always been, keep an eye out for new horizons."

McNeely pinched his own thigh in anger. Jesus Christ, he thought to himself, "new horizons?" I must sound like a rube. But Douglas, smiling broadly, took the response as an unequivocal *Proceed to Go and Hand Out $200* signal, and went on to describe in broad terms various legislative policy issues that could adversely affect his former company Questmat and the businesses of several of Sanus' key investors.

"On top of all these possible legislative challenges, our group also faces some potentially serious legal entanglements. In fact, your former employer, the Department of Justice along with those bureaucrats at the Federal Trade Commission have several ongoing investigations. And of course, the state Attorneys General want to feed at the trough too. Kicking the pharmaceutical industry in the nuts is the flavor of the month these days. Anyway, we'd like to get some fresh eyes on a lot of what's going on."

McNeely successfully feigned interest and Douglas was apparently content with mutual assurances to "keep the dialogue going." Looking over Central Park as he walked to the elevator, McNeely could see new horizons stretching all the way to Baytown. Then he remembered the name of a Scorsese movie entitled *The Last Temptation of Christ*. Would have to rent it for inspiration, he thought.

The attraction between them was immediate, and Nora, who had to be back at Finn's by 11:30, wasted no time. To Joyce's grateful astonishment, she unbuttoned his trousers and (according to his later account) "made me a man."

—Brenda Maddox, *Joyce, Nora, and the Word Known to All Men,*
N.Y. Times Book Review (May15, 1988)

Out for his Friday sojourn, McNeely found himself passing by the Wilde Thyme Bistro, the site of his disastrous date with Leeza. Looking through the window he recognized the red headed waitress who had served them setting tables for the dinner crowd. An opportunity to make things right, he thought. Entering the restaurant, he walked hesitantly into the dining room.

"Excuse me, my name is Tommy, and you served me and my date a couple of weeks ago and I . . ."

Not looking up, she interrupted, "Oh yeah, I remember. You were with that arrogant blonde cunt with the cheap hair extensions."

A flummoxed McNeely sputtered, "Well yes, yes, she was not exactly . . ."

She threw him a tolerant smile, "Hey, don't sweat it. Cunts, dworks, and pricks, they breed around here. My name is Nora. And I could see you took her bullshit worse than I did."

McNeely still sputtering, "Well I certainly didn't approve . . . that is, I don't tolerate that kind of . . ." Trying to gain some footing on the slippery path he'd embarked on, he succumbed to an irresistible impulse to find out why he'd been so easy to read. Feigning an academic interest in a truly puzzling situation, he asked with a raised eyebrow, "So what made you think that?"

"Well, let's see. You turned a bright shade of pink, couldn't look me in the eye, and overtipped by 200 percent. It was kind of cute, actually. Don't see many guys actually get embarrassed these days." She was herself making eye contact and flashing a pretty inviting smile.

The moment had come. McNeely furiously running through in his mind approaches to smoothly seize the opportunity to ask her out but coming up empty. Fortunately, Nora, who was nothing if not to the point, took the initiative. "Ok. Assuming you are well rid of the blonde—and if you're not, I will withdraw this offer—I'll let you make amends by buying me a drink after the last seating tonight. Ten o'clock. That work for you? By the way, I'm writing about Nora Barnacle. I was named after her. Know who she was?"

Thank God I took that Irish Lit course, thought McNeely. "Sure. Joyce's wife."

"Well, yeah, eventually. You might want to check out how their first date went," she said with a mysterious smile.

Walking out of the restaurant, McNeely tried to understand what had just transpired. Did he just win the lottery? *You were with that arrogant blonde cunt.* Hair extensions? Who knew? Words he thought he might be carrying around for a long time. Better Google that thing about Joyce's first date.

47

Every life is in many days, day after day. We walk through ourselves, meeting robbers, ghosts, giants, old men, young men, wives, widows, brothers-in-love, but always meeting ourselves.

—James Joyce, *Ulysses*

Maggie couldn't believe the speed at which things were happening. It felt like her entire future was going to be locked in by the events of the next few weeks. Here she was, only a year away from becoming an actual, card-carrying lawyer, while also shouldering responsibility for keeping the Term afloat and dealing with her father's dementia. She'd had an interview for a great job, a clerkship with a federal trial judge, and was knee deep in assembling documents for a presentation to the Dean on a matter she didn't fully understand but knew was of critical importance to the future of St. Sebastian Law School.

Sorting through these life-changing events, Maggie discovered to her surprise that she came to the fight equipped with some useful talents. She found herself making lists and spreadsheets to prioritize, evaluate, and tackle each challenge. Priority Number One was her father. On this, she had acquired enough information to map out a strategy. The Hoboken Memory Care Clinic had provided her a timeline that illustrated the range of likely changes in Mickey's cognitive and physical status. He would need pretty constant monitoring soon and would have to discontinue working at the Term. Maggie's strategy was straightforward and clear-eyed: sell the bar and restaurant and put the cash into full time home care. She enlisted the help of one of the Term's long-time regulars who worked as a commercial real estate and business broker. The potential bottom line from the sale, she calculated, would cover care for her father and upkeep of the house for many years. She attached one condition to the sale: the buyer must agree to retain all employees for at least one year. But one ominous cloud loomed: "How to persuade Dad?"

Maggie's second critical turning point—getting a job—was now in the hands of a federal judge in Newark. Competition for federal court clerkships is intense, with the selection process beginning in students' second year of law school. She had discovered that having a shot was helped immeasurably by (1) who you know and (2) who he or she knows. For her, Professor McNeely's close relationship with Judge Louis Escriva in the federal district court in Newark opened the door. Getting the job was another matter. The judge had begun her interview by telling her that she would be the first clerk he had hired in fifteen years who had not gone to Harvard, Yale, or Penn. The second question involved a hypothetical about a complex procedural issue with which she was totally unfamiliar. She addressed the first issue by joking that she didn't think there was anything special in the drinking waters of New Haven or Cambridge, and because she worked 18 hours a day, she'd never been to Philly, but she'd take a drive down there if she ever got a few hours off. On the second question, she immediately confessed she had no idea whatever what the answer was but mapped out a clear research path by which she could track down a solution. She added that's why she wanted to start out as a judicial law clerk, so she could answer hard questions on her own, since her career goals would probably not involve having a lot of helpers at her disposal.

When she ran her answers past Professor McNeely in a post-mortem, he told her that both were absolutely perfect answers. The first question was a test to see if she could stand up to pestering lawyers who would try to bully her. "Outside of the Fifth Amendment, humor is the best defensive remedy. Remember that," McNeely said. He explained that the second question was designed to see if she would try to blow smoke. "Judges want clerks they can trust. You aced another exam, Maggie," McNeely assured her. So, she had a shot.

The third challenge was the wrap up of her six weeks of mind-numbing research. It involved assembling hundreds of documents, quantifying data on spread sheets, and performing various statistical charts illustrating the contents of the documents. All she knew about the purpose of this exercise was that it was a big deal for Deans McNeely and Eckstein. They had posted a large "NO ACCESS" sign on the entrance to the Dean's conference room and asked her and Jen—whom they had enlisted a few weeks ago—to work nonstop over the weekend. She was only told that the project was important to the Deans and her research needed to be flawless.

Jewel had laughed about the weekend "War Room" preparations, "Should be pretty interesting. The Deans are goin' all gangsta on this one. Watch yourself, girl."

Returning home, she heard her father's snores before she opened the door. "Hey Dad, how you feeling?" Maggie gently shaking her father's arm, not sure if he was sleeping. The Mets postgame show was flickering on the TV, and analysts were busy diagnosing the 3-0 loss in extra innings.

Her father straightening himself in his La-Z-Boy recliner, "Just resting my eyes. Feeling grand. Damn Mets suck, but after 50 years I'm used to it. How's by you? Did the Bud truck show up?"

Good, she thought, checking off a couple of positive cognitive signals. Sense of humor intact. He remembered that the delivery of Budweiser kegs was expected today and showed fatherly concern about her. Not so good: concerns about the Term front and center on his mind.

"So listen, Dad. I'm just a year away from graduating. Then next summer I've got to really hump it studying for the bar exam. And I'm still waiting to hear about the judicial clerkship. I've got a lot on my plate."

"If that dumb ass judge doesn't hire you, he'll have me to answer to," Mickey announced gruffly.

A dementia warning signal flashing: *intermittent anger*. Maggie looked carefully at her dad and tried to recall her internet research. Is this Stage 3 on the Alzheimer's chart? Then she saw his eyes sparkling, him breaking out in a grin. He was kidding, I think. I hope, she said to herself.

"No worries about me getting a job. I've got a lot of irons in the fire," she lied. "Listen, I'm just thinking that it's going to be hard for me to watch over the Term as much. You know, passing the bar exam is a big deal. Any job offer I may get is cancelled if I fail the bar, and my career is kaput." Maggie had decided to lay it on thick. "And you know I promised mom I'd be the kind of lawyer who'd be helping people. So, I've got to really burrow down next summer and study my ass off."

Her father looking pensive, "You know, honey. I'm getting tired of nursing those drunks and yuppies. Maybe we should think about selling. I had that guy a couple of years ago offer me a million dollars for the Term. You remember that?"

She remembered. It was actually fifteen years ago and became a legend in the Holloran household. She and her mom laughed about it for years. The guy was either drunk or mobbed up, they thought. Never heard from him again.

"Well let me look into it. I took some advanced courses in law school specializing in real estate and business sales," Maggie lying again, but felt it was for a good cause. "We get that million bucks and we'll buy primo season tickets for the Mets."

"Let's wait 'til they find a couple of hitters," the old man's eyes sparkling with the hopeful glow of a true fan.

Do not wait to strike till the iron is hot but make it hot by striking.

—W.B. Yeats

Team Eckstein assembled in the War Room, gathered their boxes and displays, and marched off to battle. They'd been working nonstop on their project for ten days, and each had carefully assigned roles for the items they would be transporting to Sheehan Hall. McNeely carried the large poster boards while also toting files and flash drives in his overstuffed backpack. Jewel and Maggie carried boxes and a large easel while the Dean strode confidently ahead bearing only her slim briefcase. Everyone was dressed to the nines, albeit in dark outfits equally suitable for a wake as a wedding. On arriving at Shannon Hall, they climbed three flights up to the President's conference room. Decamping in an adjacent anteroom, the team unloaded their boxes and assembled the posters.

McNeely opened the door to the conference room a few inches and peeked in. Seated or standing around the enormous four-sided adjoining tables were at least thirty SSU board members, all talking loudly, seemingly in high spirits. Father Balducci was seated at the head table browsing a large notebook.

McNeely turned to look at Dean Eckstein. "Looks like the break is almost over. You should be on in a few minutes." Checking for signs of anxiety, he saw none. "Ready?"

She smiled back. "Born ready. Just keep the door ajar and be ready to jump when I ask for permission to bring in the posters."

"Quicker than I look." McNeely patting his belly, smiling, and pumped.

Father Balducci's voice could be heard clearly in the annex. "The next topic on our agenda is Item 12 in your binder. The item is a motion to approve a proposal to create a new Institute of Pharmaceutical Law and Policy at the Law School. I've invited the Dean of the Law School, Deborah Eckstein, to describe this wonderful opportunity and what it will mean for our law school and how it will advance the mission of St. Sebastian."

Eckstein walked briskly to the front table, plucked a hand-held mike off the table next to Father Balducci, and proceeded to walk up and down the front aisle as she spoke. The team had agreed that making her presentation as a lawyer would deliver an opening statement to a jury would have the greatest impact.

"Thanks, Father. Ladies and Gentlemen of the Board: I've met many, but not all of you. It's a pleasure and honor to be here today, and I hope to open a line of communication between you and the School of Law. I want to invite each and every one of you to stay in touch. I'd be delighted to take you on a tour of our venerable building and discuss what we at the law school can do to advance the mission of St. Sebastian.

"Let me begin by thanking Father Balducci for his support for the law school. He has recognized that we serve St. Sebastian's mission of education, charity, and service to the community in various ways. We train students to advance social justice and charitable causes in their practice of law *and* in their lives. Father has understood that we need resources and administrative support to advance these goals." Eckstein shot a smile over her shoulder at the President, which he acknowledged with a modest nod of appreciation.

"And today, we have been offered support for that mission through the significant grant offered by the Sanus Institute. In brief, the grant would support research and the study of health care law and policy, with a focus on the special role of pharmaceuticals in improving the health of the nation. The law school would receive a generous endowment to fund academic research and student scholarship."

"Let me take a minute to describe how this Institute, called the Sanus Institute on Pharmaceutical and Health Law and Policy—that's a mouthful, I'll call it '*SIPH-LIP*' —would interact with the University. The law school will appoint one member of a three-member board that will set the academic agenda for the Institute. Sanus would appoint the other two members. That board will also choose the director of *SIPHLIP* and oversee his or her performance. The funds supplied by Sanus will also support researchers and policy advocates. Again, all research topics and personnel are to be selected by the three-member board. As you can see, Sanus will be calling the shots, but as one of my colleagues likes to say, it's the Golden Rule of Business: *He who has the gold, rules*," Eckstein chuckling lightly to signal an ostensibly friendly joke.

"So, we at the law school will be embarking on a new joint undertaking. Let me introduce you members of the board to our new partners. Now Sanus is a 501(c)(4) organization, which means it is a nonprofit, charitable corporation under the law. Don't want to bore you non-lawyers on the board with the legal nuances, but these organizations don't disclose their supporters. That is, their donors remain completely anonymous. My colleagues at the law school did some research so you could know a little more about who comprises the group that controls Sanus and who, going forward, will control an important part of St. Sebastian Law School. We wanted to answer the question that's probably on your minds: who exactly are our generous benefactors and new partners?" Eckstein paused and signaled to the door of the annex.

"With your permission, I've asked one of our outstanding law students, Ms. Margaret Holloran, to track down just what the Sanus Institute is, and how they go about dispensing large amounts of money to humble institutions like ours. Our team gathered some interesting information about our new friends and we have a few charts showing who our new partners are."

Not mentioned was the valuable assistance provided by one Alonzo Jenks who had furnished a dozen flash drives containing documents that set forth the money trail supporting Sanus. Also found on the drives were some colorful recordings and photographs of the off-hour's activities of some of Sanus' contributors and executives. Feeling like the military aide who carries the nuclear football for the President of the United States, McNeely was closely guarding the flash drives and CDs in his backpack.

Maggie and Jewel entered the conference room and quickly assembled an easel on which they placed a stack of enormous charts.

Armed with a laser light pointer, Dean Eckstein began her guided tour. "So this chart shows the numerous corporations, LLCs, and partnerships that contribute to Sanus. As you can see, there are a lot of boxes shown on the easel. Twenty-three, in fact. That's because many of the contributions to Sanus flow through a series of intermediate entities, which are popularly called "shell" organizations. This serves to make it hard to identify who ultimately made the donation. But Ms, Holloran and our team managed to unpack most of the shell corps. The full history of Sanus' funding is shown in the boxes on the bottom of the chart. But let me just give you a few highlights. Maggie, next chart please."

Maggie hoisted another large chart onto the easel. "Here's one example. This corporation—which sent at least $1.5 million to Sanus over the last few years—is Androsync Pharmaceuticals, a producer of several brand name drugs. The next seven lines describe the federal civil and criminal charges filed against Andro. You'll see five resulted in settlements or fines exceeding $50 million. Charges included fixing prices and agreeing with rivals to limit competition in ways that raised prices dramatically to consumers. Now let's turn to Sihon Corporation, an Israeli corporation that is the parent of Ammon Pharma. As you can see, they were accused a few years ago of distributing vaccines to children that contained . . ."

"Now just hold on a moment Dean Eckstein," a beet-red Father Balducci interrupted. "I'm sure the board does not want to hear an apparently biased critique of these companies' performance. They have provided lifesaving . . ."

"Excuse me father," a woman's mild voice could be heard. Heads swiveling to locate the brave soul who would presume to interrupt the President, the board members were shocked to discover tiny Sister Francisco, holding the microphone Dean Eckstein had conveniently made available to her. "I'd certainly be interested in hearing . . ."

"Ah, of course, of course, Sister Francisco, we'll certainly get you whatever information you want. But now I have to invoke as a point of order . . . " Father B scanning the board for support and finding thirty male heads looking at the Sister, many smiling.

Sister Francisco reclaiming the floor, "Well, as a technical matter of procedure, if we actually need to go there, Father, as I understand Roberts Rules of Order, I think it's certainly in order for any board member to ask a question during a discussion of a pending motion. Especially on the pivotal issue of whether this organization is compatible with the mission of St. Sebastian. And so, I *shall* ask a question. Dean Eckstein, could you please tell us more about Sanus and its contributors, specifically whether they've served the public interest over the years."

Scouring his board again for support, Father Balducci saw thirty heads staring down at their notebooks and studiously avoiding eye contact.

Handed back the microphone, Dean Eckstein resumed her walk up and down in front of Father B's table. "Certainly, Sister Francisco. Rather than take us through the activities of all the pharmaceutical companies, lobbying firms, and trade associations that have funded and control Sanus, let me jump to a summary exhibit we've prepared. Maggie, can you bring up chart number 11?" Now here we have a list of the number of federal and civil cases pending against the fifteen Sanus sponsors we've been able to identify so far. That last one, a class action brought by 49 of the nation's 50 attorneys general is said to be the largest antitrust class action in history. The claim is that the leading generic drug companies have been fixing prices . . . that is *gouging patients* and their employers on those very *"lifesaving"* advances Father Balducci mentioned a few minutes ago. Finally, we can make available to you some disturbing documents and videos in which Sanus personnel use words that I won't repeat here that make it clear they planned to use St. Sebastian School of Law as an unwitting smokescreen to advance their political ends."

Eckstein shot a quick look at the President, who was returning a stare which she guessed replicated that of Tomas de Torquemada during the Spanish Inquisition.

"Let me make absolutely clear that I am sure Father Balducci had no knowledge of all this information we've gathered until today," she said, offering a deferential nod to the President. "We've been scrambling to put this presentation together and felt it incumbent on us to fill in you board members about our discoveries before arrangements with Sanus were finalized. And of course, before the press could get hold of these rather troubling details."

Recognizing that his board was about to declare a TKO, Father Balducci threw in the white towel. "In light of all this new-found controversy, I'm going to withdraw Item 12 from consideration *for now*. Let's move on to Item 13."

Team Eckstein scrambled to gather their posters, exited quickly, and ran back to the law school. No one said a word until they reached the Deanplex.

"Remember, don't answer any tweets, texts, phone calls, or emails. And there will be plenty. World War III starts tomorrow," Eckstein said.

McNeely offered a full military salute. "Yes Ma'am. Tail gunner McNeely reporting for duty."

You can shear a sheep a hundred times, but you can skin it only once.
—Amarillo Slim Preston

Jewel Henderson arrived at the Deanplex early the next morning, ready to greet, or more accurately, berate, McNeely when he arrived. "Who the hell do they think they are? And do they know who the fuck they're dealing with? *10:46 p.m.!!* That little punk ass kid calls me *at my home! At my home!* 10:46! I wrote it down."

McNeely was pretty sure of the given name of the little punk ass kid, as he too had received, but didn't answer, some late evening phone calls. "Who are we talking about Jewel?"

"That little punk Rodney whatever his name is. Father Balducci's poodle. And how does he have my home telephone number?"

"It's in the University system for emergency contacts." McNeely knew this was not going to calm things down.

"Emergency? There's going to be an emergency all right, when I get that twerp alone in the back of Sheehan Hall. Anyway, as I'm sure you know from the 30 emails and texts, he says there is a top priority meeting the Dean has to attend in his office in Sheehan at 10 a.m. this morning. I told Mr. Rodney to call me at 9 a.m. *On my St. Sebastian office phone,* thank you very much, and I will review the Dean's busy schedule and get back to him." Henderson tapping her calendar and adding with emphasis. "We will get back to him *at that time.*"

"OK, when he calls in . . ." McNeely checking his watch, "in fifteen minutes, you tell him that the Dean is at a breakfast meeting, and you're not sure when she's due back, but you will forward the message."

Seeing her grimace, he added, "Politely. Patiently. We need to convey that this is just another ordinary scheduling matter, on an ordinary day, by a very *relaxed* assistant, just taking an ordinary message. Not the time to unload. *Capisce?*"

Henderson biting her lip, "I'll hold off till I get him in that dark alley."

McNeely signaling a vertical wrist roll to Maggie, "Great. Maggie, you come on with me to Sheehan Hall."

Maggie, dressed in her civilian attire, St. Sebastian jersey, sweatpants, and sneakers, was taken aback. "To the President's office? Look at how I'm dressed . . ."

"No worries. I'll explain on the way. You need to carry a few things for me."

Arriving at Shannon Hall, Maggie, as instructed, went into the lady's room outside the President's suite of offices and McNeely rushed in to the reception desk. He greeted the woman at the front desk with an alarmed shout, "Please, could you go into the rest room and check on my student assistant? She seems to be quite ill and has been in there for a while."

As soon as the receptionist cleared the door, McNeely headed for the President's office. Getting no answer to his knock, he opened the door briskly, prepared to announce himself, only to find the office empty. Hearing some voices down the hall, he trotted down to the President's conference room, and again threw the door open dramatically and announced in a loud voice, "Gentlemen, good morning."

Huddling over a seated President Balducci were Gilbert Morris, the University General Counsel, and two young men, who McNeely assumed were the GC's junior associates. Arrayed in front of them were three neatly stacked piles of documents, several pens, and an open laptop. McNeely guessed they were intended for the Dean's signature at the ten o'clock meeting. One undoubtedly was a letter of resignation, the second a nondisclosure form, and the third . . . who knows? Maybe a confession to stealing a silver chalice and patens from the cathedral.

McNeely had decided to employ the tough guy, surprise gambit Jenks had taught him for interviewing suspects. Motioning to the General Counsel and his two associates he issued a stentorian announcement, "Ladies, I'm going to need a few minutes with the President. So, if you'll please leave us alone, we are going to have a man-to-man chat about a number of things that don't have anything to do with the GC's legal advice to the University." McNeely holding the door open and staring down at Father B, "Mr. President?"

Balducci doing a quick mental recap of the sins, venial and mortal, that he might be accused of, nodded to his lawyers. "I'll come to get you if I need anything."

Seating himself across from Father Balducci, McNeely dialed up his prosecutorial persona. "To begin with, you can discard your little collection of legal papers there. Dean Eckstein won't be resigning. Nor will she be intimidated by any kind of threats your law team may have cooked up. You and I have some things to talk about concerning *your* performance rating."

Seeing Father B flushed and silent, *this is working*, McNeely thought. Exactly what he had fantasized for years he would have done with Stevie Cohen had he the opportunity. Read him the riot act, explain to him that he was going down, and watch him crumble. No New York Mets for you, buddy.

"Father, let's start with the easy stuff, that Sanus crowd. You and I both know it's a takeover. They're planning to control hiring and set the research agenda for an Institute that will bear the St. Sebastian name. We've been able to talk to someone who can confirm that the Sanus guys you met think of you as a *mark*. You know what a mark is, don't you Father? They plan to use St. Sebastian as their credible academic mouthpiece. Their proprietary think tank, if you want to call it that—I look at it as more like Pravda West—the Institute will be spewing out propaganda."

Pulling a manila folder out of his backpack, McNeely went on. "Here's the short version scenario, taken from PowerPoint documents the Sanus PR department wants to use to describe to its donors what our newfound mission at St. Sebastian will entail. All stuff we decided NOT to disclose to the board yesterday:

The pharmaceutical industry is under attack.

Big Brother wants to deny you life-saving cures.

President Sanders, Warren, whoever the next president is, wants to play doctor.

Research by the Sanus Institute at St. Sebastian University Law School shows how socialism will destroy the innovation and cures that the pharmaceutical companies offer. "

Father B, stonily florid, stared steadily into McNeely's eyes. Summoning up his best Robert DeNiro imitation, McNeely offered a concise summary of his team's research.

"So what do we know about these guys? Well, you heard just the tip of the iceberg yesterday. You've got a rogues' gallery of thieves and corporate criminals on your hands. Here's one, Elliot Reed, who is now on the board of Sanus, but before that was head of marketing for Galaxy Pharmaceuticals. You know them? Fortune 500 company, 38.5 billion dollars in annual revenues? Under our new friend Mr. Elliot's watch, Galaxy engaged in a laundry list of criminal and civil law violations. Father, you seem to like spending time with lawyers, so let me give you just a few details of what the Justice Department found out about the drug marketing he directed during his days at Galaxy. They marketed anti-depressant drugs to children. Drugs that were known to cause suicidal thoughts and behaviors. They failed to disclose heart risks they knew about in other drugs. One was approved by the FDA *only* for severe depression: and what did Galaxy do? It bribed doctors with trips to Europe and Jamaica, elaborate pheasant-hunting excursions, and some visits to Thailand, of which I'll spare you the sordid details. All to get them to prescribe their new blockbuster drug for a broader clientele: for weight loss, for sexual dysfunction, and for attention deficit hyperactivity disorder. All uses *not approved* by the FDA. You want to know what their salesmen called it? Their *happy, horny, skinny pill.*"

Still no reaction. Only a silent, steady glare from the President.

"So that's who you're jumping into bed with. Be a shame if this got leaked to the *Newark Star Ledger*. Or the *National Enquirer*. But the Dean and I earnestly want to avoid all that. What we need to do now is open a dialogue about what the *University* is going to do to help the *law school*. We want to reach an accord as to financial support, maintenance, and upkeep of the physical plant, and scholarships to help us recruit students and compete with our many local rival law schools."

Father Balducci finally stirred. Shuffling a few papers on his desk, he pulled out his MontBlanc pen and, with a flourish, scrawled a brief note. Looking up at McNeely, he hissed softly through gritted teeth, "*Bastardo pazzo!* Amateur hour. You're out of your element. You think you can blackmail me? No wonder you couldn't make it as a big city prosecutor. You've just cost your law school $30 million. Maybe a lot more."

Sealing his note in an envelope, he thrust it at McNeely with a waspish sneer, "See that she gets this. *Immediatamente!*"

50

If you can meet with triumph and disaster
And treat those two impostors just the same . . .

Yours is the Earth and everything that's in it,
And—which is more—you'll be a Man, my son!

—Rudyard Kipling, *If . . .*

Dejected and chastened, McNeely slumped into a chair in the War Room and tried to gather his thoughts about what to tell the Dean concerning his failed attempt to play Eliot Ness. And how to handle the inevitable news contained in Father Balducci's note to her. He was confident the message was that she was fired, would never get another deanship, judgeship, or any other respectable job, and God knows what else. He couldn't excommunicate a Jew. At least she had that going for her.

But the gnawing in the pit of his stomach was as much out of self-pity as sympathy for the Dean. What stuck in his mind was the calm way the President had appraised him and pierced his tough guy façade. He'd fooled no one and been exposed as an *amateur. Amateur.* That word indelibly seared into his memory. *Out of your element?* Had Father B seen *The Big Lebowski*? On top of that, he was right. What had he accomplished? The Sanus deal was dead. Great. But all that meant was the law school was out $30 million, and now it was worse off, facing a furious President who would probably starve its faculty and students out of spite. And who would he install as the new Dean? Maybe one of those right-wing legal *poseurs* from Fox News? All too horrible to contemplate.

When Dean Eckstein arrived, McNeely explained briefly that the President did not take their proposal well and gave him a note to deliver. The Dean tore open the thick cream envelope embossed with the multi-colored St. Sebastian seal. She glanced at the message, and immediately let out a loud guffaw. "Unbelievable! This is perfect! I'm having it framed." She handed the note to McNeely. It was short, to the point, and written in the President's a bold ornate hand. Only two words:

"*Your fired.*"

They agreed they would defer leaking the President's illiteracy to social media until the most opportune moment. As they began to discuss what was needed to plan for the imminent transition, Maggie arrived toting a large banker's box.

"Professor McNeely, Dean! So glad I found you here! I've finished sorting through those documents you gave me. I took the liberty of doing some regression analyses and have prepared some Excel spread sheets showing some interesting patterns." Maggie opened the box and handed a binder to the deans.

Eckstein looked at McNeely. "What's all this?"

McNeely striking his forehead, "Oh, Deb, I should have mentioned to you that we received several boxes of documents a month ago. Sent anonymously from someone calling himself "Luther Martin." Lots of University invoices, donation records and, interestingly, some of the minutes of Board of Trustees' meetings. I thought it was from some crackpot, but the documents looked authentic. It was all pretty confusing, so I asked Maggie to put the data in some accessible form so we could analyze it." As McNeely spoke, Maggie connected her laptop to the display apparatus in the War Room and called up a file folder entitled "University Contracts, 2008-2018" on the large conference room screen.

To McNeely's surprise, Maggie took command of the room. "Why don't you both sit down and let me show you what I've found. I'm going to cut to the chase at the beginning for you because I know you're both busy. The bottom line of the first slide shows that some University Board members are getting favored treatment on contracts for their businesses—the ones they own, or for corporations on which they are an officer or director. I examined all the contracts let by the University that went to companies that had a University Board member as an executive or board member. Of those *connected* companies that were awarded contracts, 94.6% were awarded *without* a competitive bid."

Two bar charts appeared on the next slide, with St. Sebastian Board members' column printed in the University magenta, dwarfing the one next to it.

"That's a lot higher than the rest of the University's contracts, of which only 35% were let without a competitive bid. I did some regression analyses by size of contract, duration, and several other factors. I won't bore you with the statistical details, but the important thing is this: those factors _do not_ explain the high correlation. You guys still with me?"

A somewhat startled Dean Eckstein laughed and said, "You bet. Carry on, professor."

"OK. Here's where it gets really interesting. This slide shows the donations to the University from board members or their companies. You'll see first, that 89% of the companies receiving the no-bid contracts made charitable gifts to the University within two months of being awarded the contract. And, *get this*, the amount of those donations all ranged between 15-20% of the amount of the contract awarded. A pretty tight statistical grouping IMHO," Maggie allowing herself a little self-congratulatory chuckle. "Oh, and by the way, almost all the donations coming from board members' companies go into an account labeled 'President's Discretionary Fund,' which Professor McNeely explained to me was a special fund that Father Balducci controls without needing board approvals."

"Again, I've done some analysis on potential complicating factors, using what the statheads call difference in difference analysis, comparing the giving patterns of non-board member companies to board member companies. And guess what?"

McNeely raised his hand. "Only firms with connections to St. Sebastian board members follow that two-month giving pattern, Professor?"

Maggie's eyes twinkling as she suppressed a smile. "Yes indeed. It looks like . . . if you'll pardon the expression . . . *It pays to be a board member. And board members pay for their privileges.*"

McNeely showing an upraised palm. "Well, Maggie, as I've told you, everything we're doing here must remain strictly confidential. But we do need to know what you've found that reflects on . . . well, let's call it 'University governance.' This is stuff we need to explore fully."

Maggie paused for a moment and went on, "OK, one more thing . . . well, this comes out of something I heard from Jewel Henderson. We were having a glass of wine at the Secaucus Meadows Yacht Club, and she mentioned . . . "

Before he could realize how impolitic the comment was, McNeely blurted out, "What? You and Jewel were . . ."

"Oh yeah. She's really cool and funny. Takes a couple of us out now and then. She really knows what's going on at the law school. Please don't let this get her into any trouble. I shouldn't have said where it came from."

"That's OK. Jewel is the person I trust the most around here," said McNeely. Then, glancing at the Dean and reddening, he realized that he'd just put his foot in it again.

"Well, she mentioned that one of the university's cleaning crew had been sent down to the town of Avalon in Cape May County to clean up a house, which surprised me, since it's so far away and no one knew of any St. Sebastian property way down there. Right on the beach too." Maggie pausing for a reaction, got it. McNeely and Eckstein looking at each other wide-eyed.

"Anyway, I remembered seeing some invoices in our boxes that I had paid no attention to because they didn't appear to be connected to any University board member. But they involved some construction work in Avalon, which seemed like a pretty big coincidence, it being a tiny resort town, so I decided to do a little snooping. I checked out the property address on the invoices, did a quick title search, and looked through the Cape May County tax records, and found out the property was owned by a subsidiary of Meadowlands Construction Corporation. As you may know, Mr. Buckner, who is one of our board members, is CEO of Meadowlands Construction."

Feeling the pride of a parent whose kid had just won an Olympic Gold Medal, McNeely wanted to shout, but felt he should play it cool. "My oh my," he said, but with obvious enthusiasm.

Maggie nodded and decided to venture a little editorializing. "I don't know what it means, Dean, but IMHO, it seems a bit peculiar that the University would be picking up construction costs and cleaning for a beach house it didn't own. Some of the costs incidentally were for laying down a cement pad for a hot tub. And for what it's worth, I did some checking and noticed that the payments for that seemed to come from the President's Discretionary Fund."

The meeting ended with Dean Eckstein thanking Maggie and praising her work and initiative and explaining that she and Associate Dean McNeely needed to confer over next steps. As soon as the door closed, the two Deans looked at each other, shaking their heads in disbelief for a minute.

Eckstein broke the silence. "Holy shit!! What do we have here? Let me count the crimes. Bid rigging? Tax fraud? Kickbacks disguised as charitable donations? RICO, for God's sake? The Church used to call this "simony"! And he's getting 20% back from each contract? For shit's sake, he's demanding a *double tithe*!"

McNeely still shaking his head. "It's beyond belief. A cynic might say he's running the University as a criminal enterprise. In any event, this is the Attorney General's bailiwick. He's charged with supervising charitable institutions in New Jersey."

"Shall we invoke the Archer Protocol?" McNeely asked, his eyes twinkling.

"This may be the moment our counter-intelligence unit had in mind," replied the Dean.

The Archer Protocol was the product of a late evening dinner two years earlier at an Ecuadorian restaurant in Baytown. Lubricated by several shots of mezcal and demoralized by President Balducci's proposed budget cuts for the law school, the two Deans were commiserating about their plight. Eckstein was uncharacteristically exercised, "Takes a piece out of every department in the University for himself. He's like a feudal lord claiming his *droit de seigneur.* And it's the students he's screwing . . . Figuratively . . . I assume."

McNeely perked up, "Well, what if we uncovered . . ."

Eckstein's eyes lit up, "Oh yes, yes! What if we came across some juicy bit of information. We could post some rumors on social media, feed a story or two to the papers or maybe to the bishop, get a friendly Trustee or two on board. A scandal might be the answer to all our problems."

The Deans resolved to be fully prepared for that happy, inevitable day when a piece of toxic, incriminating information came to their attention. Stimulated by the mezcal, they concocted a detailed scenario as to how they would deploy their resources to force Balducci out. Dean Eckstein, a devoted reader of John LeCarre's espionage novels, came up with the name. "Let's call it the Archer Protocol. When the right opportunity comes up, we'll aim our crossbows and . . ." The image of a forlorn Father Balducci riddled with arrows seemed to them a fitting metaphor for how his tenure at St. Sebastian should be terminated.

Eckstein now smiling mischievously over her upraised espresso cup. "You know, I think I can put the Protocol in motion. I'm the Chair of the Governor's Court Reform Task Force and have pretty regular contact with the Attorney General, who's also on the panel. In fact, I know him quite well. Don't repeat this, but we dated back in the day, *way back* in the day, when we were undergrads at Yale."

McNeely couldn't resist. "Well, Boola Boola. Good to know those old-school Ivy League ties are good for more than getting your kids admitted."

51

God is a comedian playing to an audience too afraid to laugh.

—Voltaire

Viewed under Baytown's leaden morning light, things did not seem quite so cut and dried as they had the night before. As they did every couple of weeks, they went to the Miss America Diner to review their strategic options. If one didn't know what was on the menu, a quick survey of the clientele told all you needed to know. This was not a crowd that was after avocado toast. McNeely was drowning his sorrows with the All American (eggs, sausage, home fries and a stack of pancakes), while Dean Eckstein, invoking her personal religious/dietary exceptions whenever stressed, went for a bacon and cheddar omelet.

Exposing the rampant conflicts of interest they had uncovered was not as simple as it first seemed and the two could find no workable way to launch their guerilla attack. It would certainly take a long time to get the Attorney General moving, even for an old flame, and any investigation would drag on for months. By then, the summary dismissal of the two deans would be old news and even a front-page scandal was not likely to salvage their careers. Newspapers might run a leaked story or two, but the facts seemed unlikely to produce public outrage. After all, there was no sex or overt plundering of the University till to get the *New York Post* interested. Finally, the organization responsible for serving as watchdog, Saint Sebastian's Board of Trustees, was not likely to be disposed to investigate itself.

"He's like Trump. He can withstand anything. I told you about those cockroaches the size of a Buick in my apartment? They've survived 10,000 years! Remember when impeachment seemed inevitable? Remember the pornstars? Remember the allegations of sexual assault? Conspiring with the Russians?" McNeely knew the Dean didn't need to be reminded but venting the frustration they shared about their two Presidents seemed about all they could do at this point.

"Look Tommy. If I go public with all this dirt, I'll be OK. I can find a landing place at a dozen law schools. And I promise, I'll make sure you're protected. You know Alicia Benjamin-Holtzapple? She's the new Dean at Nebraska. She's a good friend, and I can give her a call."

They decided to talk later in the day. Eckstein hailed an Uber, saying she needed to pick up a dead fish to leave on the President's doorstep before she packed up her office later in the day. "Not going to give the asshole the satisfaction of a meeting. Any recommendation on what fish pairs well with a decanal firing?" she asked as they departed.

Thoroughly depressed and trying to erase any thought of moving to Nebraska, McNeely walked back to the law school. Where exactly is Nebraska, he wondered. Will Google it when I get back. He was relieved to find Jewel was not around when he arrived at the Deanplex. He didn't know how he would break the news of his likely firing to her and harbored a fear that she would not take it lying down. In fact, he ran through several short speeches to deter her from physically assaulting President Balducci, finally deciding he could mollify her by telling the story about a former girlfriend who had been groped by her dentist while she was under gas. Rather than report the guy, she took direct action. Called him at home every night at 3 a.m. for a week, and blew a police whistle into the phone. McNeely hoped he could persuade Jewel to take the high road just like his friend.

Feet up on his desk and smiling contentedly, McNeely dreamily ran through a series of scenarios involving Jewel's possible reactions to his firing. His reverie was interrupted by a sharp tapping sound followed by the familiar face of Father Fitzgibbon poking around the door once again. "Knock, Knock. Hope I'm not interrupting . . ."

"Oh no, Father. Just going over alternative theories of punishment. Retribution, deterrence, corrective justice, and so on," said McNeely chuckling at his own private joke.

"Yes, Yes. *Nullum crimen sine lege* and *nulla poena sine lege* . . . right?" A smiling Father Fitz making himself comfortable on the Associate Dean's couch.

Catching McNeely's blank look, Father Fitz continued. "I forgot. Your Latin is a bit rusty. It means *no crime without law, no punishment without law.* We need to temper punishment with justice."

McNeely stacking the folders on his desk. "For sure, for sure. Hard to argue with that. Wish I had time to explore this with you, but I've got a load of administrative headaches that I need to . . ."

Father Fitz settling in on the couch, "So I've heard. You know, over at Jesuit Hall where we all live, we've got a pretty active social media."

"What? You guys are on Twitter? Facebook?" McNeely almost added Grinder, but for once, his internal editor was on the job.

Father Fitzgibbon stretching his legs out on the sofa, "No, No. Those childish internet toys are not for us. What I meant is the Jesuit *grapevine.* Quite literally, a grapevine. A number of us share a glass or two of wine, or port, maybe Green Spot, after dinner and review the events of the day. Or as the kids say, we dish. Get a lot of interesting information that way. And unlike Facebook, *our* grapevine leaves no footprints, ha, ha."

McNeely wondering if Father Fitz was angling for a drink. At 11:30 for God's sake?

"I've heard about your confrontation. Not the details, but I know Father Balducci is on your case and is intent on firing Dean Eckstein. He's not one to keep his triumphs to himself. He's like Caesar. You've studied the history of Rome? Caesar leads his army off to conquer Gaul. Has no authority from the Senate. But is enormously successful. Goes on to launch an attack on Britain. Writes some self-aggrandizing propaganda about his triumphs and becomes immensely popular with everyone back in Rome. Except the Senate. Caesar keeps moving and switching allegiances, betrays his mentor Pompey, becomes all-powerful dictator when he gets back to Rome. He was not shy about pressing his advantage and letting everyone know about it."

McNeely getting restless, trying to make a gracious escape. "Well, it worked for a while, I guess, but . . ."

"Yes, it worked. Until he was deposed. Deposed the old-fashioned way." Father Fitz thrusting an imaginary shiv into Caesar's chest.

Shifting from his relaxed position on the couch and leaning forward, the Jesuit continued, "Well, pardon my historical digressions, but I'm here to give some reinforcements to help you and Dean Eckstein in your little Punic War. Now as I'm sure you know, those were the wars fought by Carthage trying to shake the iron fist of Rome . . . kind of analogous to what you and the Dean are up to, no?"

Assuming the same bearing he adopted weeks ago when he cross-examined McNeely about Maggie, Father Fitz went on, "I've gathered some information. Remember what I told you about us Jesuit spies? Well, I've enlisted. Rather, re-upped. Had an opportunity to gather some intel that should be of use to you guys. Might prove as effective as the twenty-three hacks they gave Caesar."

Without disclosing how he came across his information, Father Fitzgibbon proceeded to describe Meadowlands Construction's maneuvers in securing federal "Qualified Opportunity Zone" status for the parcels abutting the University and its business plan for developing the area and securing additional investors. The first thing that caught McNeely's attention was Father Fitz's use of the phrase "grease the wheels." It didn't take a trained prosecutor to unravel the story, though the father's proclivity to lapse into anecdotes about Roman history and Irish saints slowed the process. What became apparent was that he had reason to believe that the 19-block sector adjacent to the law school had been designated as a federal QOZ shortly after Bucky had made campaign donations to the mayor, three city council members, and the Republican Inaugural Committee. The fact that the area was almost entirely middle class was not unusual according to Father Fitzgibbon, who to McNeely's surprise seemed to have become an expert on federal subsidies and urban development. His "source" had told him that it wasn't clear whether the palm-greased local politicians had prevailed upon the governor to make the designation or whether the U.S. Secretary of the Treasury had unilaterally made the call. What was clear was that Bucky had supplied the lubricant.

Making matters worse was the strategy Fitzgibbon said the developer was pursuing: a blitz of local homeowners to force quick sales by spreading rumors of a state-sponsored, massive development of Section 8 housing, i.e., inexpensive apartments for low income (read Black and immigrant) residents. All of which would crush local property values and quicken Meadowlands Construction's capture of properties in the zone. St. Sebastian's investment would get it co-ownership of some of the acquired property. Father Fitz explained that President Balducci hoped this scheme would provide funds enabling him to construct his basketball stadium and dorms. And even better, he could sell some of the land at a premium to developers of luxury condos.

"They're promising Balducci the area will become New Jersey's equivalent of Brooklyn Heights. Awash in 3BR, 2-Bath $900K condos," Fitgibbon explained.

McNeely played out several other consequences in his mind. Soaring property values that will inure to St. Sebastian's benefit. Not so much for students' needing affordable housing. Or for the duped homeowners who got taken on their only asset for pennies on the dollar and lose a chance to cash in on their one great asset, the one they're not making any more: real estate.

Shocked by the magnitude and genius of the duplicity, but even more amazed that his gentle Jesuit pal had come into possession of such incriminating information, he asked, "Don't tell me your Jesuit grapevine is dabbling in real estate?"

Father Fitzgibbon not flustered. "Oh, no, no. I have other sources. Have to protect them though."

Time for some lawyering, McNeely felt. "All this is not another tidbit you picked up hearing confessions, I hope?"

"Heavens no. Let's just say a little fish told me. But I haven't given you the real scoop yet. This is what puts Father Balducci in a box. Gives you a full house to play against him. Do you play any poker?"

McNeely angling for some sympathy, "A little. But I know when to fold them. The President is dealing from the bottom of the deck and can beat any hand I'm dealt."

"Maybe, maybe not. Here's what he doesn't know. Meadowlands Construction is playing *him.* They're holding on to the primo properties and he will get the dregs. And when he tries to build his stadium or dorms, Meadowlands Construction's properties will block him. Can't build a stadium on a few scattered 50 by 50 lots. He'll wind up selling back to Meadowlands Construction's shell corporations at a loss. Or they'll insist on other covenants that give Meadowlands Construction the rights to some of the proceeds from any sale he makes. If you'll forgive the crudeness, they've got him by the short hairs," Father Fitzgibbon beaming with the look of missionary who had just converted a native village.

McNeely offering two raised eyebrows, "I've got to hand it to you Father. You travel in interesting circles. Hope the archbishop doesn't catch up with you."

Giving the conspiratorial wink of a Jesuit spy, he responded, "Don't worry. We spies know how to cover our tracks."

52

Every saint has a past and every sinner has a future.

—Oscar Wilde

It had already been a very long day. She had stopped by her mother's house in South Philly, cooked her breakfast, ran to CVS to pick up her mom's Metformin, and drove to ACME for groceries. Then the two-hour drive to AC to sign in for the late shift at The Touch. Elle set her date with Frank in Avalon for 6:30, apologizing that she had to get back to Philadelphia by midnight because her mother was not feeling well. He would of course put on one of those Italian dinner extravaganzas he was so proud of and plead with her to stay the night. But she was multi-tasking tonight. She would finish him off by 10 and hustle up to the club to go after the late night, big money crowd. Working only two nights a week meant making use of the whole workday.

Frank had been unusually forthcoming about his work. He had told her he had encountered some problems with subordinates who were looking to screw him over financially. She had tried to cheer him up with elaborate praise of his pasta, wine, and performance in the sack. He was still uncomfortable with anything other than straight up, missionary position, didn't particularly like her to talk dirty, and rarely good for round two. She knew he dropped Viagra before she arrived but was always nervous when they started. Unlike most Johns she encountered, he was nice enough afterwards, once even had them dance to a romantic Frank Sinatra CD. She smiled remembering the look on his face when they first met, and she told him she was "open for business." Took him a minute to sink in, but he had the look of a grateful puppy who's just had his ears scratched. But she sensed he didn't really mind her wanting to bug out after the main event.

Elle knew Frank clearly had money to burn, but she wasn't buying his real estate tycoon story. When she asked about his properties in Hoboken, he was evasive and didn't seem to know anything about rental properties in Philadelphia either. He was decent enough to avoid the usual questions about her background, though she knew that, like every other guy, he wanted to know: why this? She had come to understand that they all needed an explanation that made them feel like they were paying to help right some wrong that had been done to her. She had settled long ago on a story about an abusive boyfriend. He'd beaten her, left her without a dime, and she had to turn to stripping to make ends meet. The hooking was a kind of side deal. If she liked the guy, and he showed some evidence of caring about her, she'd work a contract. Guys like Frank liked that. He felt he was a missionary of a kind. That was his favorite position too.

Elle had managed to leave Frank's house in Avalon by 11:30 and sped up to Atlantic City. Spring in AC was unpredictable, but on weekends after midnight the money usually started rolling into the club. Only a five-minute walk from the main casinos on the Boardwalk, the Touch got a good helping of guys who had been playing at the $50 blackjack tables for hours. Dropping a couple hundred for a private dance was just one bad shoe at the tables.

She quickly assembled herself in the prep room. Eyeliner, thong, stripper heels, spangles, and blown-out hair. She declined a bump of cocaine from Tiffany, shared a joint with Epiphany, and was ready to go. "Good crowd tonight, Misty" said Josh, the late-night MC as Elle made her way to the stage. Like this douchebag would know, she thought. *You* sit down on top of a drunken, smelly asshole and listen to his words of wisdom, and then *you* tell me about the quality of the crowd, she thought. Onward and upward.

She went through the obligatory stage dance, stripping down to the minimal panties and pasties allowable under New Jersey law, collected a handful of singles strewn on the floor, and went in search of a deep-pocketed customer in need of a lap dance.

As she descended from the stage, she saw a hand waving her to his table: a large, well-built African American in a business suit. Looks promising, she thought.

He greeted her with a big accommodating smile. "Hi, my name is Alonzo. Good to meet you, Elle."

53

An exultant Maggie greeted her best bud from behind the Term bar. "Can you believe it? Our second year of law school almost in the book! You and I, girl, down to the shore every weekend this summer! Then, two more semesters and we're free!"

"Yeah, but then there's that bar exam thing," Jen Battaglini responded sullenly. "People tell me it's the worst three months of their lives. Studying round the clock, scared shitless, realizing you didn't learn squat in law school."

Maggie attributed Jen's *disastrophe-is-coming* philosophy to her privileged, drama-free background. Down deep, Jen felt it made no sense to have been so fortunate. So sooner or later a lot of shit was going to hit her fan.

Maggie's run of good luck had her lurching in the other direction. "Now it's time for me to set *you* straight, sister. There's no way you flunk the bar. Top of the class, working harder than anyone I know, and born on third base. You have as much chance of failing as Trump getting the Nobel Prize." Maggie grabbed the Patron and gestured to her booth.

Jen, not going to be out-negged, "Actually, someone already nominated him. The creep is going to get away with everything. If only Melania would get some pruning scissors and . . ."

Maggie having none of this. "Listen, I've been talking to Professor McNeely about this. Man, is he tripping! Sometimes when I'm working outside his office, I hear him muttering curses and talking to himself. He says it's just a matter of time, Trump will self-destruct. The House is about to impeach him, and it will only take a couple of Republicans in the Senate to send him off. Just like they did to Nixon. You know, the only person that my father actually hated was Nixon. Course, he loved Kennedy and look how that turned out."

Jen had a double major in feminist history and philosophy at Wesleyan. "You know it. In fact, there's a lesson with those two. JFK fucked everything in sight, even a Mafia moll, and was a total prick to Jackie. Nixon was devoted to his sad-sack wife, and never got a smell outside as far as I know. But which one showed some humanity when it came to helping people?"

Maggie laughing, "OK, so you're saying we should start prowling the Federalist Society for hook-ups?"

"No, but if you find someone you think you're going to marry, he's got to pass the Jen Battaglini bar exam." Pointing one finger to her shot glass. "Pour me another, Little Miss Candide."

"OK, but I'm convinced Tommy has it right, Trump can't . . ."

Jen let out a shriek. "Tommy? Tommy? You are on a first name basis with Professor McNeely? Your new BFF, Tommy! Don't tell me you're . . ."

"No, no. It's just that I'm working there twenty or thirty hours a week and it's no different than being an associate at your tight-ass law firm, Worsted and Wasted. It's a real professional relationship. Anyway, he's been circulating a letter to every former Assistant U.S. Attorney getting them to condemn that asshole Barr and call for his resignation. Pretty amazing. A thousand of them had the guts to speak out. How many of your Worsted buddies have opened their mouths?"

"OK, OK, there are trade-offs to be made. But what does he think will happen?"

"Look, once Trump is impeached there'll be a trial! And the Senate is over half lawyers. They know what counts as evidence. They took ethics courses in law school. They took the bar exam. You meet with Russians, you ask them to help you, you tell the world you want someone to take down Hillary, and it happens. *And* you have people inside the White House who knew that was the deal. *And* then you instruct everyone who works for you to lie. *And* you tell them you'll hand out pardons like candy on Halloween. Just wear your costume. Fired Comey, tried to fire Mueller. *And* his former butt-boy Cohen laid out the tax evasion crimes and porn star payoffs. No way the Senate lets him walk."

Battaglini waving a stop sign. "OK, OK, just calm down. I'm with you. Let's hope for the best. What is it you're working on with *Tommy*?"

"Well, it's a pretty long and hush-hush story, but the Dean and Tom . . . that is Professor McNeely, have put together a bunch of material that seems to make it look like President Balducci is a snake. Not quite sure where it's all going, but they've been working with some big shots on this project. You ever hear of Oren Gilliam?"

"The Supreme Court Judge? St. Sebastian alum? Basketball star? Incredible stud?"

Maggie laughing, and not disagreeing, "Yeah, yeah. And maybe future governor. Anyway, I've been prepping him on some of this stuff, working with his law firm associates at Cosgrove, Simpson & Blanchard. OG is pretty amazing . . . "

Another shriek. "Oh no, no!! 'OG'? OG? Maggie, please don't tell me you're . . . "

"Jen, you got to stop watching soap operas or porn or whatever it is that's left you so twisted. I've just come to see that Big Law has some decent people who are working to do the right thing."

"Aha! You give me shit about working for Worsted, but you've bent over for Cosgrove, the biggest, most corporate firm in New Jersey!" Battaglini triumphantly slamming her shot glass to the table.

Maggie finishing her last shot and crawling out of the booth, "OK, but I'm learning a lot. If OG does run for governor, maybe I can find a job that doesn't involve kissing corporate butt. At least not full time. Anyway, thanks for coming by. See you in class tomorrow."

Battaglini was not leaving without the last word, "Remember Monica Lewinsky. Hope your Mr. OG doesn't like cigars."

54

*Most college presidents are running something
between a faltering corporation and a hotel.*

—Leon Botstein, President of Bard College

The Executive Committee of the St. Sebastian University Board of Trustees did the heavy lifting for the rest of the board, handling all matters that have significant economic or political ramifications. Accordingly, Father Balducci had carefully stacked the membership of Exec Com with loyalists who also had credentials in business, politics, or law. Owing to the need to display fealty to University's mission, he was required to also include representatives of the Jesuit Order and the local community. The Committee's recommendations were consistently rubberstamped by the full 48-member board who were provided with enormous explanatory binders forty-eight hours before their meetings—which, as planned, largely went unread except for matters dealing with the University's basketball team. Discussions at the full board meeting rarely consumed more than a few minutes, and decisions always were unanimous. It was a very collegial board.

Consideration of the proposed affiliation with Meadowlands Construction's Opportunity Zone project was the main item on the agenda for the May Exec Com meeting. The project, the largest financial undertaking in Father Balducci's tenure, had consumed his attention for weeks. Given what he regarded as a public humiliation before the full board over the law school fiasco just a few weeks earlier, he was in need of a quick infusion of credibility. He was confident that rolling out his master plan for expanding St. Sebastian's footprint and producing an ingenious way to pay for it would silence any rumblings from the discontented.

Pushing the matter forward at the ExecCom meeting was nevertheless a herculean task, one that required Father Balducci to crack the whip on his staff. But it had been worth it, he felt, as he surveyed the stacks of binders containing a massive collection of spreadsheets, appraisals, legal memoranda, and regulatory materials piled next to each committee member's seat. The materials had been provided to the committee by internet transmittals and flash drives had been had been delivered to the Board members just a day earlier. Confident that few had strayed beyond the executive summaries of a few of these memos, Father Balducci had arranged for a detailed PowerPoint presentation by his Chief Financial Officer, and a briefing from Mitchell ("Bucky") Buckner, President of Meadowlands Construction and Chair of the Baytown Opportunity Zone Commission. Their talks dragged on for almost two hours, but to Father B's relief, only a few technical questions were raised during the detailed, indecipherable slide presentations. An outside observer would hardly suspect that St. Sebastian was entering into a complex financial arrangement that would entail borrowing a huge sum of money while also pledging over half of its endowment as collateral for a rather speculative real estate deal. Or that it was doing so with a partner whose background and credentials—had anyone thought to examine them—more closely resembled North Jersey's shadier enterprises rather than seasoned real estate developers.

With a sumptuous lunch at the Metropolitan Club awaiting the Exec Com members after the meeting, Father Balducci was optimistic he could get a quick call of the question. The smiling and confident President dramatically snapped shut his binder and addressed the committee. "Well, we've heard in exquisite detail how this project can lift St. Sebastian's profile and enable us to join the ranks of elite universities in the Northeast. Now before I entertain a motion that the Executive Committee recommend to the full board approval of the University's participation in the Baytown Renewal Project . . . " —he had carefully arranged for William Stinson, retired senior executive with Morgan Trust in Manhattan to make the motion, and for it to be seconded by Albert Breckenridge, Chief Financial Officer of Somerset Investments, Cherry Hill New Jersey— ". . . let me make sure there aren't any final questions."

What Father Balducci had viewed as a rhetorical courtesy was greeted by a slim, boney hand at the corner of the table of the seated committee members. The head peeking around the large corporate lawyer seated next to her was, to Father B's dismay, Sister Francisco.

Forcing a taut smile, Father Balducci acknowledged the sister, "Ah yes, Sister Francisco. You have a question?"

"Well, several as it turns out, Father. As you know, I'm trained in genetics and bioscience, and we scientists know it is always best to defer to experts in their field when tackling complex questions. So, with your permission, Father, I'd like to turn the floor over to one of our esteemed board members, and of course, a member of St. Sebastian's Class of 1991, Oren Gilliam. Although he's not a member of this committee, he is a longstanding member of our board, and given his remarkable legal and business credentials, he's better equipped than me to address this proposal. And if I may brag for just one moment, Oren is also my former student. OG, if you will?"

Cold eyes betraying his forced smile, Father Balducci gave a brisk nod. Whatever this was, there was no way to stop it, he realized. Rising to his feet, the six-foot three alumnus cut a striking figure. His designer suit was tailored to an athletic frame that had not changed since he led the St. Sebastian Archers to their first MAC basketball championship thirty-five years earlier. His series of firsts continued after graduation: First SSU graduate to attend Stanford Law School, first African American partner at Cosgrove, Simpson & Blanchard, New Jersey's leading corporate law firm, first African American on the New Jersey Supreme Court. After serving one term, he returned as managing partner at Cosgrove to spend his time preparing to become New Jersey's first African American governor.

An experienced litigator, Gilliam knew it was essential to get right to the point, "Fellow Trustees, let me get right to the painful point. This Opportunity Zone project is *not* something we want to be involved with. I have three serious concerns. First, it will tarnish St. Sebastian's name, betray our Baytown community, and cast a cloud of suspicion over those who participate in it. Friends, this Opportunity Zone is a thinly veiled urban renewal project, aimed at pushing out our hard-working neighbors and designed to replace a blue-collar neighborhood with upscale development that neither our students or our employees can afford."

Pausing, he turned to address an unsmiling Father Balducci. "Second, and Father, it distresses me to say this, but you've been *played*. I've had some associates at my law firm help me research the land grab that shell companies controlled by Meadowlands Construction have been undertaking. They've snarfed up some of the prime properties and made it impossible for you to go forward with your dream of building a basketball arena or student center. Whatever parcels St. Sebastian winds up with will be worthless if they are encircled by Meadowlands Construction's properties or properties owned by its shell subsidiaries. On top of that, my team has come across evidence that high pressure, scare tactics—which I'm sad to report, were racially tinged—were used to prompt homeowners and small business owners to sell their properties."

"That brings me to my final point. And ladies and gentlemen of the board, this is serious business. It appears to me that the approval of this Opportunity Zone may have involved some highly questionable tactics and payments, including campaign donations. Now I don't claim to have done a full investigation, but thanks to the assistance of a highly reputable source who was approached by Mr. Buckner to become an investor, I've gained access to some of the plans and tactics that have been employed. As a practicing lawyer—we like to call ourselves "officers of the court"—I had a duty to pass along this information to the New Jersey Attorney General. While I can't reveal any of the details, I'm sure the project will be closely examined by the authorities."

Turning to look directly at Father Balducci, Gilliam shook his head slightly and added "According to my source, Meadowlands Construction has played pretty fast and loose with handing out favors to those it wants to ingratiate itself with. My sincere hope—my prayer if you will—is that the investigation does not uncover any improper gratuities flowing to St. Sebastian personnel."

McNeely had stationed himself outside the conference room to listen in. As Gilliam completed his talk, he cracked the door to peek in. Father Balducci abruptly tabled the proposal and quickly ended the meeting. Recalling that moment years later, he mentally accompanied the frozen look on Father Balducci's face with Tony's look in the final episode of The Sopranos, with "Don't Stop Believin'" playing before the scene faded to black.

As the meeting adjourned, Bucky rushed up to Father Balducci and grabbed his elbow to escort him out of the conference room. McNeely positioned himself in a spot where he could observe the two as they walked down a hallway toward the President's office. Father B and Bucky stopped abruptly as they saw four individuals seated on a bench near the elevator bank.

Bucky was the first to react. "Oliver???" Obviously confused to see his poker companion and erstwhile co-investor wearing a priest's cossack and collar, he sputtered the name again in disbelief and said, "Is that really you?"

Father B simply stared, mouth agape, as he surveyed the other occupants of the bench. First he noticed a large African American wearing an FBI sweatshirt whom he remembered from his meeting with the Sanus representatives. Next to him was Father's trusted assistant Rodney who was studiously avoiding eye contact, and . . .

No, it can't be, he thought. This is a bad dream. A lovely, conservatively dressed young lady was silently mouthing the word "sorry" while extending a palms-up a "what could I do" shrug. Elle (AKA Misty) Kozinski had somehow been delivered to her *patrono's* place of business.

McNeely flashed the big, shit-eating smile he had hoped to display to Steven Cohen years earlier. In his brief career as a prosecutor, he'd learned a couple of things. First, it is important to keep your surprise witnesses at the ready. Second, nothing beats seeing that look of anguish on the bad guys when they realized they're cooked.

Epilogue

55

*It's one person coming in from China, and we have it
under control. It's going to be just fine.*

—Donald Trump, Jan. 27, 2020

McNeely had spent the warm January day luxuriating on the 26th Avenue beach in Santa Cruz. Surfers sprinting to the water, dogs running amuck, and a diverse population savoring the weather. A bald sixty-year-old surfer clad in a full-body black wetsuit jogged by who he thought looked identical to Father Balducci in his religious garb but for the collar. I wonder if Father B has found his own beach, he mused.

He had a sheaf of administrative tedium and seminar papers to tackle, but was totally chill, as they say on the Left Coast, enjoying a comforting sense of accomplishment. He'd be heading back to New Jersey tomorrow for the start of the Spring 2020 semester, having spent the afternoon reflecting on the tumultuous events of the past six months. The Archer Protocol had worked its magic and things couldn't have turned out better. Father Balducci's resignation—"retirement" according to the University's press release—in the wake of the New Jersey Attorney General's investigations of the Baytown Opportunity Zone scandal was all but inevitable. However, a host of other factors accelerated his departure: revelations regarding his secret "discretionary fund," the corporate beach house on the Jersey shore, and gifts from Meadowlands Construction and other companies associated with board members. The SSU hierarchy experienced a thorough housecleaning as several members of the University Board who were forced to resign under the cloud that the *New York Post* headlined as "Balducci-gate."

Best of all, Griff had assumed the position of Interim University President and had a plausible chance of becoming the first woman and first non-Jesuit President of St. Sebastian University. He chuckled aloud as he recalled her visit to his office after the crucial Exec Com meeting, when she slyly mentioned how much she respected the courage of Father Fitzgibbon, comparing him to historical figures who spoke out against injustice. And then, stunningly, she looked McNeely in the eye and included Martin Luther among her examples of principled heroes. Still staring at him, she laughed and said, "We should all be as courageous as Luther comma Martin."

It was their little secret. Annie Griffin, AKA Luther Martin: Provost, Mole, and now Interim University President. She had learned a thing or two from studying both Machiavelli and Balducci.

Griff had taken over just in time to save the University from falling victim to an enormous scandal. She severed the University's relationship with Meadowlands Construction and withdrew from the Opportunity Zone Investment Partnership. The timing of her scrubbing St. Sebastian's involvement with the project was opportune, as Meadowlands Construction's catastrophic rollout of the project had gathered national attention. Just hours after the Vice President of the United States and the Secretary of the Treasury had posed, shovels in hand, to dedicate the first development in the new Opportunity Zone, the Newark Star Ledger had posted an exclusive investigative report detailing a series of political contributions whose donors had achieved fast-track status for the project's OZ status. The article featured interviews with several homeowners who described encounters with developers who told them that the coming socialist Democratic administration would devastate their property values and usher in a wave of immigrants. The article concluded with a link to a report quoting the U.S. President's tweet: "Suburban housewives: . . . you will no longer be bothered or financially hurt by having low-income housing built in your neighborhood."

Not much question what that was all about, thought McNeely. The imagery didn't get better when the President's surrogates took center stage. The New York Daily News had run a frontpage headline, "No Flies on Veep?" displaying a photo showing the Vice President struggling to plant his shovel in the dirt at the Baytown Opportunity Zone ground-breaking as a swarm of Hackensack Bay gnats circled his bright grey head of hair. The article speculated that the VP may have used a scented hair spray that attracted the insects. It went on to explain that the Governor of New Jersey had declined to attend the ceremonial groundbreaking because of claims that the approval of the Baytown Opportunity Zone had been influenced by political donations to the local politicians and to the 2016 Presidential Inaugural Committee.

Also working a shovel in the photo was the Secretary of the Treasury, who had been the President's top fundraiser during the 2016 Presidential campaign and was instrumental in establishing the Inaugural Committee Project which created an enormous slush fund whose ultimate destination remained a mystery. The Daily News story reported that several prominent donors to the fund were also investors in Baytown Opportunity Zone properties and noted their connections to Republican fundraising events.

The stars had aligned on a host of other matters. The law school had avoided the corporate takeover by Sanus. Maggie had been hired as a law clerk by a prominent federal district court judge. Father Fitz had found a family of undocumented Guatemalan refugees to provide day care and cooking for Maggie's father in exchange for sharing his large house. Dean Eckstein had unearthed money from donors to start a new Center on Law and Urban Development. The faculty had come together to support her initiative to expand recruitment of minority students and increase diversity among staff and faculty.

With more than a little tutoring from his friend the law professor, Jenks had tapped into his treasure chest of dirt on several of Sanus' sponsors and become a Qui Tam law whistleblower. He was promising to give a nice endowment to his favorite law school whenever his multi-million dollar bounty comes in. Even the dark clouds hovering over national politics were lifting, or so it seemed to McNeely. Trump had thoroughly discredited himself and was sure to lose to Sanders or Warren in the upcoming election. Impeached and almost removed from office, a laundry list of indictable crimes, and an approval rating hovering around the political Mendoza line of 40% for his whole term: he's toast for sure. Once he's gone in a landslide—in just eleven more months!—the Rule of Law will start to mean something again, McNeely assured himself.

All seemed right with the world, with McNeely venturing into that uncharted territory of having a "social life." His seduction by Nora at the Wilde Thyme Bistro had progressed from weekly dating, to frequent dinners, to the point that co-habitation now seemed the next step. She turned out to be the perfect complement to his cloistered academic world. Writing her doctoral dissertation on Molly Bloom as the precursor of the modern woman, she broadened his horizons and stimulated him in other ways. Late at night she'd read to him a page or two of Joyce's eroticism, close her book and say, "Give us a touch, Poldy. I'm dying for it." She took charge, which was just fine with him.

The constant running through all these events, McNeely realized, was that he had been bailed out again and again by others who pulled the arrows out of him just as St. Irene did for St. Sebastian. He'd have some sure-fire plan and, sure enough, things would blow up in his face. But then, mirabile dictu, one after another, Father Fitz, Griff, Maggie, Jinx, Eckstein, Sister Francisco, Jewel, and now, Nora, had intervened to save his bacon. Takes a village. To save my sorry ass, he muttered to himself.

Sliding onto a stool at the bar at Johnny's Harborside, he shook hands with the bartender and to his surprise, found Arlo sitting in the exact same seat he had occupied twelve months earlier. Same Oakland Raiders shirt and same enthusiastic rant. But this time it was all about epidemiology.

"I'm tellin' you man. This new flu's gonna blow up. From someplace called Wahoo or something in China. It's gonna be bigger than global warming. Will kill a lot of people, and not just Chinese either. It moves through the air for God's sake. You can catch it by just talking to someone. Or touching them! It's a fucking plague like the one that wiped out half of Europe a couple hundred years ago."

Arlo evidently had been combing the internet during his down time at Cruz Coffee Cartel and apparently believed he had discovered fire. Having become accustomed to receiving conspiracy theories and spectacular fantasies delivered from adjacent bar stools around town, McNeely attributed this one to the joint, now legal in Santa Cruz, tucked above Arlo's right ear. His rant would make a good story to pass along when he got back to the West Village.

Mistaking McNeely's signal to the bartender for a refill as an expression of interest in his update, Arlo went on. "There was a movie about this years ago. Brad Pitt. Zombies spreading a virus that came from China. Pitt is trapped in Newark, New Jersey. Thought it was pretty lame at the time, but now I see it can happen. If Bernie doesn't win, that asshole Trump will let this flu thing ruin the country. That happens and I'm gonna lease a boat and sail away. Been crewing for this Samoan dude for years. I'm off to New Zealand soon as this flu hits California."

That's fine. Nice to have an escape plan, thought McNeely. But I don't need one. I'm returning to the real world tomorrow.

END

Acknowledgements

First and foremost, my wonderful wife Nancy's support and enthusiasm made me believe this project was worth undertaking. She read and commented on multiple drafts and convinced me that it might entertain at least a few people. Thanks to my several friends who gave me helpful comments and (almost unanimous) encouragement. I owe a special debt of gratitude to Barbara Jones who tirelessly and patiently entered about three thousand text edits, designed the layout for the book, and created the cover. She's a real pro, and anyone writing a book should hire her.

Father Fitz's rants on Catholicism and the Jesuit Order are drawn from *ZEALOT: THE LIFE AND TIMES OF JESUS OF NAZARETH,* by Reza Aslan. The history of the investigation of Steven Cohen's conduct is comprehensively reported by Sheelah Kolhatkar in *BLACK EDGE: INSIDE INFORMATION, DIRTY MONEY, AND THE QUEST TO BRING DOWN THE MOST WANTED MAN ON WALL STREET.* Jane Mayer's outstanding book, *DARK MONEY: THE HIDDEN HISTORY OF BILLIONAIRES BEHIND THE RISE OF THE RADICAL RIGHT* traces the corrupting influence of money on academic institutions and contemporary politics.

Finally, a reminder that this is a work of fiction, which means it is the product of an author's febrile imagination. It should not be taken to reflect on the many fine academic colleagues and educational institutions I have had the privilege to encounter during my careers as a prosecutor and academic. That said, I'll add one final quotation from the greatest satirist of all, Voltaire:

> *I have never made but one prayer to God, a very short one:*
> *Oh Lord, make my enemies ridiculous. And God granted it.*

Tim Greaney is Chester A. Myers Professor Emeritus at Saint Louis University School of Law and Research Professor at UC Law SF. Before entering academia, he served as a trial lawyer and Assistant Chief in the Antitrust Division of the U.S. Department of Justice in Washington, D.C.